"Hold!" Owen cried as roars and growls came from all sides. "If you drive away the humans, you will die imprisoned in these hills forever! The Dark One is at work here."

Pran'del broke past Mar'ador before the old bear could stop him.

"Liar! Traitor! You come to weaken our resolve, and keep us in this exile! You are the Dark One! I say no to your kind forever! We helped you once, when the flying death burned and killed all alike, animal and man. We helped overthrow them, and look what rewards we got for our trouble." The huge bear's rage was terrible to behold; his fangs were bared and near Owen. "At least if we die now, we die in the struggle! Let your two clans kill each other! So much the better for us. Every human dead is one less enemy of mine!"

The younger bears in the gathering were worked into a frenzy by Pran'del's impassioned speech. More than a few of them had begun their terrible war cry...

THE BRIDGE OF DAWN

Also by Niel Hancock

Dragon Winter

THE BRIDGE OF DAWN

BY NIEL HANCOCK

POPULAR LIBRARY

An Imprint of Warner Books, Inc

A Time Warner Company

A friend showed me the Bridge once, just at dawn, off Virgin Gorda. It was the first I'd heard of it, but it was good news to know it was really there. Bruce Cobb and "I'll Do" are gone now, but the Bridge is waiting still.

Thanks, amigo.

Safe Havens.

POPULAR LIBRARY EDITION

Popular Library®, the fanciful P design, and Questar® are registered trademarks of Warner Books, Inc.

Cover design by Don Puckey
Cover illustration by Tim Hildebrandt

Popular Library books are published by
Warner Books, Inc.
666 Fifth Avenue
New York, N.Y. 10103

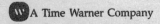A Time Warner Company

Printed in the United States of America

First Printing: January, 1991

10 9 8 7 6 5 4 3 2 1

Prologue

✳

Owen stared at the brightness of the sea far beyond the rim of the green land, and soon the water began to churn itself into a fierce storm, with howling winds and white-capped waves that rose higher and higher until he was once more in the heart of the gale that had swept him from the Thistle Cloud. Then he saw a tranquil winter sea lapping softly at the pillars of the quays of a city dressed in white, with a long strand of salt flats that ran behind. There were people gathered on the stone landings, and as his vision grew clearer, he began to recognize faces there, and his heart grew glad. There were his old friends Kegin Thornby and Chellin Duchin, talking with the minstrel Emerald. Elita was with him, and just beside her, his mother and father were locked in earnest conversation with a stranger who seemed to be an Elder.

A cloud descended then, with fire and ash, and the white settlement was gone, replaced with a sea full of ships of all sizes and kinds sailing toward a crimson sunrise. Owen cried out then to Colvages Domel, for he did not wish to see farther, but one of the ships in the vision loomed larger, as though he were falling upon it from a great height. He closed his eyes to shut out the sight, but he still saw what was there; it was the Thistle Cloud under full sail, making for an island straight ahead, where seabirds whirled and circled in the sky above. Soon he saw that they weren't birds at all, but many dragons, scorching the land with their fiery breath and crushing ships with their powerful talons and deadly tails.

At the rail of the familiar ship, he saw Deros next to Ulen Scarlett, who stood rigidly gazing away at the carnage, his ringed hand calmly grasping the young woman's shoulder. Owen cried out desperately, calling for the terrible dream to end. "I knew he would have been better left! He will betray us all!"

Colvages Domel appeared before him again, and the window of the Walengaad grew dark, as though its mind were asleep. "You have seen what you need to know to help your friends. The Walengaad does not give answers, but asks questions. Did you find what you sought?"

Owen shook his head, suddenly very weary. "I saw more than I wanted. Most I already knew."

"Then we must go now. There is little time. The others await us." Colvages Domel drew a hand across his face, and the air about them seemed to split into thousands of moonbeams, each glimmering and reflecting the others until the very floor of the mountain was lighter than a breath. They rose through the roof of Roshagel, straight up into the cloak of night, deep and silent, except for the tiny bright echoes of stars, spread away in a thick carpet toward the south, where Owen heard the small, high voice of his heart calling to him.

In the great hall of the High Dragon that night, there were many old friends gathered to meet him. Owen rested in the soft grace of wisdom and love there, and waited for his dream to come again, so that he might ride the wings of the Master's breath back to Eirn Bol, where the forces of the Dark One were gathered to strike a fatal blow to the followers of Windameir.

Times
Boundaries

The Halls of the High Dragon

❋

Above the broad, heavily laden table sat Ephinias and Gillerman, joined by Beran and Politar. Golden tapestries edged with silver thread seemed to blow gently in an unseen wind, making the sewn figures appear alive, and even after Owen stared at them for a time, they took on more life than those at table, and stepped down to take their place in the banquet hall.

Owen's clothes were purple and blue, and he was dazzled by the reflections the many gems cast from the subdued light. He felt a crown on his head and, removing it, found a simple mithra band, set with five small pearls.

"Welcome to Corum Mont," said a voice, although no one had spoken openly. Owen turned to Ephinias and tried to take his hand, but it seemed as though there was nothing but empty air behind the finely arrayed figure of his friend.

Gillerman was the same.

"What manner of place is this?" cried Owen. He plucked at his own arm to see if he was real. The cloth was fine to his touch, and the stones in the crown were cool against his skin.

"This is Corum Mont," repeated the same voice that had spoken before. "You see before you the Ministers of this initiation, Lord Gillerman, Lord Ephinias, Lord Beran, and Lord Politar. I am Lord Minister. You may remember me as someone else." For a brief instant, Owen's mind was filled with the terror of the dragon in his fiery lair.

"Colvages Domel? Is that you?"

"I am. You will find your strength here for a time. These Ministers will ask you things that you must answer, and you will be given knowledge to help you in your journey."

"Where are you? Show yourself to me."

"I can't, my young friend. Now you shall have to undergo the rites, but you must do it alone."

The voice faded, and Owen found himself looking at a plain table, which seemed strangely like his mother's table when he was young. The spoon and bowl were his, he knew, when he was young. The handle of the spoon was wrought in the likeness of a dancing fish, and there was a drawing on the side of the bowl of a pair of rams beneath a tree with silver leaves. His mother always said they came from the Middle Islands, but he had not paid much attention then, and was more interested in watching Kegin Thornby try to train all the new recruits for the squadrons of The Line.

"When you find the story of the rams beneath the silver tree, you will know one of the rhymes that opens the Tentogel."

But Kegin did not know the story nor the rhyme, and chastised him for his slow footwork. Chellin Duchin once gave him a hint, merely saying the word smacked of something elfish.

And now here he sat in the very room that might have been his own kitchen in Sweet Rock, looking at the bowl and spoon as though for the first time.

He examined them carefully, one after the other, and did not find it strange that upon looking closer, the spoon began a dance, and the two rams beneath the silver tree transformed themselves into two old men, who sat across from him, tugging at their beards and whispering loudly to each other about something he could not understand.

They seemed to anger then, and became the rams again, and battered their heads together with such force it shattered the bowl into a hundred pieces. Owen's heart sank when he saw the broken bowl, but as he knelt to try to pick up the shards and splinters, one of them nicked his finger badly, causing it to bleed.

"Now you see a part of that secret," came a voice, neutral-sounding and unfamiliar.

"What? That sharp objects cut?" Owen asked curtly.

"That things are not what they seem. Now you see the rest."

As the voice trailed off, the broken bowl resumed its old shape, and the two rams were once again standing beneath the silver tree. "This was with you since your youngest days. You should be able to recite it all by memory."

"Recite what?" groaned Owen. "There is nothing to recite."

"The chant of the Twin Rams."

"That was a bedside tale my mother used to sing to me when I couldn't sleep," protested Owen. "How could I remember that?"

"You shall have to start. It is one of the oldest rhymes of power there is."

Owen thought about that, trying to recall his childhood song. He held his head, repeating aloud his thoughts as they came, then started anew again.

> "Something, something olden day,
>   Something, rainbow and something
>   fade away,
> da dam dum reel beneath the tree
>   where two fine archers wait
>   for me."

He started over again, beginning to pace excitedly about the table.

> "The Cauldron's Eye of the Olden Day
>   is shone upon Tirhan's Rainbow
>   as it fades away,
>   and dance the Widow's Reel
>   against the pale blue sky
>   beneath the alder tree
> where two fine Archers
>   wait for me."

He repeated the verse again, changing a word here and there, but growing more sure he had remembered the bulk of it.

"I have it, but what does it mean? I've said it aloud, and nothing happens."

He was startled by the reply, which came in the guise of Stearborn's voice. "You haven't delivered it where it is to be spoken, my fine young buck!"

"How will I know that?"

"When you see the bowl and spoon!''

"But that was a long time ago in Sweet Rock!''

"It will come again. You will know when you see it.''

Owen tried to focus on the voice, but it died away, leaving a long silence in its place, and the next breath brought another figure to the table. Turning to see who it was, he was surprised to find his old friend Kegin Thornby.

A New Face to an Old Friend

"Kegin! Is that you? I can hardly believe it!''

His longtime companion smiled slightly. "It's a wonder you've been so long in discovering all this, lad. It was done long before you were old enough to crawl about, and it seems the secret just went on unanswered.''

"Are there others in this that I don't know of yet?'' asked Owen, half angry at his own blindness to the truth.

"We could list almost everyone, but it wouldn't be to our purpose here. You have a need to hear our information, and to begin the journey to help keep the Alberion Novas from the grasp of the Dark One.''

"At least we agree on that,'' shot Owen. "Everyone else has been putting me off and filling my ears with all that has to be done before we leave for Eirn Bol.''

His old friend laughed. "The same as always, my impetuous pup! Well, you won't be denied too long now. These halls have brought everyone together, and we know the direction the enemy will come at us from. There is not much left to do now, but stand and deliver.''

"Good old Kegin! I'm sorry about all I used to say to you when I was trying to learn your weaponry.''

"Just remember not to hesitate in that little left-hand feint with the sword stroke. It will let your opponent come in over the top of your guard, and I still don't want a student of mine to be chopped in two to spite me!''

The fire in the great fireplace was burning cheerfully, and

two mithra goblets sat on the board in front of them. From the far right-hand ceiling of the room, a soft, lilting melody began, played on the reed pipe of Beran, slowly growing louder, until it was all they heard. As the music stopped, the gray muzzle of the curious otter peered over the tabletop, and a small paw reached out to drag down a fork to play with.

"You can sit here with us without the horseplay," scolded Kegin. "What news do you bring us?"

"No news for grumps," shot the otter. "You'd think you would have found something to take to heart after all this time you've been with us, Thornby. I knew you would be a hard-shelled oaf right from the first time I ever laid eyes on you!" Beran darted beneath the table, and ran between Kegin's legs with a whoop, and made a complete circle of the room before returning to his chair.

"I wish you'd show a bit of restraint," grumbled Kegin good-naturedly. "It doesn't seem fitting here." He indicated the grand hall with a sweep of his arm.

"The Hall of Dragons?" The otter laughed. "Why, of anywhere you could be, this is the most precise place you could come off your lump and take a noser through the platters, or tear down a tapestry from a wall. Bumblerot and stuffy to boot!" He made a feint at ripping down one of the living blue and gold tapestries off the high wall, but another voice came from someone behind him, scolding him soundly.

"Leave it to you, you squirming weasel, to be at some mischief in my home! For shame, Beran! You should stay in your human form when you are visiting shrines of the likes of this!"

"You make yourself so I can find you, and I'll give you something to regret me by," shot the otter, leaping onto the table, small ears laid back and tiny fangs bared. Owen was standing, ready to intercede in what looked to be a bloody confrontation, when the speaker appeared at the head of the long table, dressed in ordinary riding clothes, with a deep blue cloak slung over his shoulder.

With his war cry piercing their ears, the small animal leapt directly for the newcomer, aiming right for the man's throat. In a flash, the blue cloak was over Beran, and man and animal disappeared below the table, thrashing around in a dreadful clamor of falling goblets and broken plates. Owen was grabbing for the newcomer's neck, to pull him away, but Kegin stopped him.

"They're at play. You don't need to trouble."

"Play! You call this play?" shot Owen, his eyes wide. The long bench that ran along the right side of the long table was overturned, and the combatants rolled clear and into the center of the room. They were on a deep rust-colored carpet, which had many strange animals and birds done in gold and silver thread, and as he watched in amazement, the two struggling figures disappeared into the warp and weave of the rug.

"What's happened to them?" gasped Owen.

Kegin laughed lightly. "This is not my idea of maintaining discipline, but this camp is out of my jurisdiction. They have done this every time I've seen them meet."

"Who is the other one?" asked Owen, still staring at the carpet where they had disappeared.

"Colvages Domel's brother, Iochan. His friends call him Io."

"A dragon."

"Hard to believe one could be so silly, isn't it? I've had to change my way of thinking where all this comes in."

Owen looked about him at the vast, high chamber, and the glittering white stones that lit the room, and reflected off the single rich woods of the furniture, and the gleaming cups and plates. The fire blazed higher behind him, drawing his attention back to the great hearth. Sitting on the low stool at the hob, lighting a long-stemmed pipe with a coal, was Gillerman.

Old Friendships Renewed

A blazing ember popped from the fire, landing at Owen's feet, and began to take shape, whirling and slowly coming to be a small globe, which lifted slowly upward, growing as it did so. Owen watched it, fascinated, still too surprised to speak to his old friend.

The glowing ball cooled, and he could see there was something inside it, so he peered closer, stepping nearer the hearth. He was shocked then, for what he saw was the three of them, Kegin, Gillerman, and himself, standing before a hearth exactly like the one he was standing beside. Owen turned to question the old man, and was shaken again, finding the two of them alone in his mother's old kitchen in Sweet Rock.

"Now we have a chance to take a long look at it, my boy, you and I. Do you recognize this place?"

"It's my mother's old kitchen! How could I forget?"

"People do, Owen. It's not unusual to let all the important things slip away as we get older."

"What are we doing here?"

"It's a safe place to meet for now. It is the past, and we know all there is to know of it, and what happened, and what we did."

"Are Seravan and Gitel with you?"

His old mentor nodded. "They are never very far away. This was the very night that you met them for the first time."

Owen walked to the low outside door of the kitchen and threw it open. What he saw made him gasp. "It is that night! There goes two of my father's friends on their way to the gathering hall where I met you."

"If you left here and went with them now, you could see it is the truth."

"Could I do that?" he asked, thinking in his mind of all the unpleasantness and death he could erase.

"You could. Would you want to do it all over again, knowing what you know?"

"You mean it would all be the same again?"

"It can't be any other way, lad. You can't put a bird into water and expect him to swim. He's made for the air, and flying. Our little lessons are much the same."

"It would stay the same if we did it again?"

Gillerman nodded his head, his eyes full of unspoken thoughts. "On the face of it, that would seem to be a grand thing. But no, it couldn't be any way else except the same. If you walk through that door now, and go to where I'm waiting, we should have to stumble through all those same events again, just as they've already happened, only now you would know of it all, and remember."

Owen's brow knitted into a frown. "I wouldn't want it, if it had to be like that."

His companion smiled. "I doubt any of us would ever progress, if we could keep going back to the safe times. A human frailty, I'm afraid, and one that's hard to overcome."

"There's nothing wrong with wanting to be safe," protested Owen, although he knew the old man was right. But for a moment, he thought, it would be good to have a warm hearth before him, and none of the things that had happened would have begun yet.

Then maybe he could be ready.

"Nothing wrong with it, but a folly we can't afford for long. As we speak here, our friends are at their work for us, preparing the way." As they sat watching the fire, Owen saw the two horses, Seravan and Gitel.

"Will I have them back?" he asked wistfully.

"Sooner than you think. We must move swiftly once we leave here."

"Will I go with Politar?"

"Much more quickly than he can go. Colvages Domel will take you."

"And Beran?"

"All of us will be with you, in one manner or another."

"Where is Wallach now?"

Gillerman stopped to reload his pipe once more, tamping it carefully. As he lit it, the thin trail of curling smoke rose slowly above his head, and began to weave itself into a wreath of moving colors. It changed from soft peach to red, to blue, and then a rainbow appeared, beginning from a small part of the smoke cloud, and running all the way to the top of a great white cliff. There it burst into a bright flame, revealing a smiling Wallach, waving cheerfully from the vision, as though he could see all who were present.

"That doesn't help me much," complained Owen.

"It will, my boy, when you discover where it is."

"An answer Ephinias might give me."

"And one he will, you can count on it. He is next to see you."

With a slight popping sound, like that of a wood fire burning wet wood, Gillerman was gone, and there on the hearth of the fireplace a small red terrier was curled onto a rug.

Ephinias Once Again

"No!" snapped Owen, despite himself, realizing he was already changing, as was the habit of his old teacher.

"Now, now, my boy, we couldn't carry on our business without you in a suitable shape. You shall need to learn this, if you are to finally be seated as a full member of the Council."

Owen looked down to find himself in the shape of a large spaniel. "I don't want to do this again, Ephinias!"

"Then what shall you do about it? If you dislike it so much, you should take on your old form."

"I can't do that, and you know it. I don't know anything about your bindings."

Ephinias chuckled. "There is not much secret about concentrating on your form. Look inside and see what's there."

"What are you talking about? There's nothing at work here, but what you've done!"

"And all I did was think of what I wished to change to. All you have to remember is to center yourself. When you hold that part of your mind still, you can make these changes easily."

"That would take too long to learn how to do," complained Owen. "I don't have the time to spare."

"That's where you're mistaken, lad. We have more than enough time to settle this all here and now. Turn your thoughts inside, to where you see what form you're in."

To his surprise, Owen found that he was able to shift his vision from outside himself to a quiet place that appeared to be just behind what his eyes saw of his new spaniel body. When he was able to see what was there, it was his own body, which was unchanged.

"Now you have it, lad. That's very good. With a little practice, you shall have this down nicely."

Owen imagined himself back in the shape of the sturdy

spaniel, and when he looked at himself again, he was greeted with the vision of a black and white dog's form.

"This will no doubt come to be of some use when you leave here. I'm sorry we won't be able to be with you when you land on Eirn Bol."

"Where will you be?" asked Owen, feeling hurt that he would still be left alone once more.

"With your mother and father. They shall be in need of my help."

"Do you know where they are?" Owen forgot his anger and hurt for a moment. "Are you not telling me something?" He studied the old man carefully, suddenly full of a numb dread that hovered about the pit of his stomach.

Ephinias was once again in his old identity, and paced to the fire. He held out his hands to the flames as though he were warming himself, even though the room was not cold. "There are so many things we don't know until we're there," he offered vaguely, avoiding looking at the young man.

"Are they still in White Bird? Surely you know that!"

"They are in White Bird as we talk, lad, but they won't be there when you depart here for Eirn Bol."

"Will they come there, then? That's all I want to know."

"They shall make their way from where they are now. There is not much more I can tell you than that."

"Emerald and Elita? Chellin and the Brothers? Will I see them again?"

Ephinias raised a hand to stop the rattle of questions. "You shall know everything in due time. You need to look to your basics first.'

A low note of a horn had blown, and seemed to echo through the high room. Ripples of light and color began to whirl about Owen, spinning faster and faster, until the scene began to dissolve into a brilliant sunlit day, where he looked down from a great height onto a stretch of white beach, and the soft curve of a coastline that curved inward into a great bay. When he looked again, he was aware of some crude hut set back into the hills behind the sea, and it seemed to him that that was where he was bound, although he had more questions for Ephinias.

But the old teacher was nowhere to be found.

Alone in a Strange Land

✳

As Owen felt himself nearing the strange land, the daylight faded into a deep nightfall, and a low line of clouds skated in front of the setting moon, leaving a faint halo of stars out to light the deserted fields that surrounded the simple hut he had seen. He was confused and angry at Ephinias, but knew it was of no use to pout about that. Not knowing what else to do, he drew the sword from Skye, and placed it out before him.

"You've always given me answers before," he began, hoping to hear a voice in reply, or at least the familiar bright light that came from deep within the blade. The sword lay still and dark, so he tried again.

Before he could finish his plea, a faint popping noise from outside drew him to the door, where he saw what looked to be a fireworks display that Ephinias might put on, very low on the horizon. Dazzling rockets burst in bright colors against the shiny midnight blue dome of sky behind, and it went on for what seemed a long time, then ceased, leaving the blackness afterward even more complete.

Owen was still pondering what it could have meant when he saw the flaring of the fires, and solved the mystery by the sheer vastness of the flames. Someone had torched a settlement. Having no better plan than to simply start walking toward the fires, which lit a portion of the horizon in the distance, he started to slip the sword back into its sheath. A faint flickering of the blue-white light licked at the edges of the blade, and as he watched, a scene unfolded, very much like looking at something taking place in a mirror. A harbor full of ships was lit by the light of flames leaping high above burning buildings, and there was a fierce struggle going on in the open square of the town, with the bodies of the dead and dying strewn everywhere. Owen held the sword out before him, and he

15

suddenly understood that the fires he had seen in the distance were the fires he was seeing in the blade.

There was no way he could make out details more clearly, so he placed the blade into its sheath and set off at a run toward the distant settlement, hoping that by the time he reached there, Ephinias or some of the others from the Dragon Hall might again be with him. He was encouraged by the sight of the boats in the harbor, for that meant the coast, and the Wind Rhyme might well be there when he arrived.

Thoughts of Deros came to him then, as he dog-trotted along over the even fields that led downward at a slight incline toward the coastal plain below. If he were already on Eirn Bol, as he suspected, then she would be upon her way there as well! His memories of the faces and events that had taken place in the mysterious meeting he had just been taken to were still fresh in his mind, of the golden tapestries that hung upon the high walls, and which breathed life into all the figures upon it, and a voice came back to him, soft and melodic. It was a voice, but more, and ran through his veins like his own pulse, speaking of time before time, and reminding him of the last of the High Islands, where the seat of Windameir was said to be. There was only a half-empty water jug next to the chart on the crude table in the shepherd's hut, and nothing to eat, and he began to grow ravenous now, when he started to think of food. He felt for the old familiar leather pouch that held the small bottles Politar had given him, which contained the two strange worlds within the soft green light, but his belt was empty. He felt a knot of fear in his stomach for a moment, but then remembered that Colvages Domel had told him to use the words of the spell as he was taught, and that he would find it worked as always.

Slowing to a fast walk, Owen began going over in his head the words he had spoken to go into the bottle that held the stores and arms, and much to his amazement, the moment he had finished speaking the words, he found himself standing in the very hallway that led to the mysterious stairways, and was surrounded by the same weapons as before. In the large kitchen that was off the hall, he helped himself to a huge piece of sharp cheese and bread, and wolfed it down, followed by four sweet pears. He put another loaf in the pocket of his cloak, and went back to the arms room, where he took one of the tall, powerful bows and a quiver of arrows.

As the words of exit to the bottle died away, he was once more in the cold darkness of the plain, broken here and there by hedges that had been planted as fences to keep herds in or out, and as he went on, he came onto a clear track that ran beside a chest-high hedgerow, disappearing away into the night in the direction of the burning settlement. He had gotten close enough now to hear an occasional sound of battle, and could make out distant war horns, although not plainly enough to identify them clearly.

One note came through recognizable enough, and his heart hammered in his chest to recall the Hulin Vipre horn notes, which were etched in his memory as vividly as though the first attack of the charging riders in the streets of Sweet Rock had been only the day before. For a brief instant, he stood frozen in his tracks as he watched what appeared to be the grotesque form of a firesnake lifting away above the burning ruins, but it was only flames reflected off of the thick black smoke. Owen was close enough now to see the ships plainly in the harbor, and watch as the fire-arrows arched high above the already burning buildings, and were swallowed by the raging inferno.

He crouched by the side of the tall hedge watching for a time, until he saw the raiders' boats begin to slip their cables, and slowly pull away into the darkness. The night was cold but clear, except for the few patches of clouds that appeared now and then, and a slight wind blew offshore, soon filling the sails of the enemy vessels. Owen stood, and hurried toward the settlement where he now heard the cries and calls of the survivors, and saw the beginning of the battle to put out the flames.

At the very outskirts of the village, he was put to work handing a bucket to help douse the flames in a crumbling shelter. He worked alongside a dozen men and women until the fire devoured the dry wood and thatch, then they pressed on to the next, which was also hopelessly engulfed in flames.

"It's no use," he finally gasped, exhausted by their futile efforts. "These shelters are gone. Try to rest, and in the morning we'll see what we can save."

It was as though his command broke through the shock of their loss, and the inhabitants of the village all put down their buckets, staring blankly at him.

"We can't stop the fires, but tomorrow we'll salvage what we can. You can rebuild."

A tired woman's voice came from the knot of people gathered beside the burning shelter. "That's what we've been doing for my whole life here. We build, and the filthy Vipre burn. It's been this way since I was a little girl.''

"Burn and kill," echoed another woman, her haggard features lit by the flames.

Owen saw that most of the party fighting the fire were women. "Where are your men? Were they all killed tonight?"

"They left this morning to patrol the North Ride. There were only the old ones here, and the children."

"The North Ride?" repeated Owen, trying to gain information of where he had landed.

"There has been a threat of the Purge there these past days, and Alban Ram has sent out the Bellream Readers. Our men went with them as escort."

Owen nodded absently. "Will they help? These Bellream Readers?"

The woman who spoke first came and stood next to him, studying his face. "Where have you gotten from? I don't recall your gybe!" A small rustle of surprise ran through the group, as it took up the woman's question.

Raising his hands for silence, he waited until the chattering died away so he could be heard. "My name is Helwin, Owen Helwin. I hail from the Line, on the Roaring Sea. I am a friend of the Lady Deros."

"A spy!" spat a gaunt, middle-aged woman, brandishing a short stabbing sword. "No one has spoken that name aloud since the Passing!"

"No spy," shouted Owen, throwing back his cloak to free his sword. "The Lady Deros sought out my father for help. She and I have seen the Fords of Silver, and the underground paths of the Darien Mounds. Now they have burned my settlement as well, and we came aboard the Thistle Cloud, with the Lady Rewen!"

An awed hush fell over the ground before Owen, and the fire crackled and roared loudly behind them.

"I was lost overboard," he went on, "but I find myself here now, so the others must be close at hand."

The gaunt woman stepped forward, looking about anxiously. "You may have the tongue of truth, sir, but if you find pity in your heart for us, don't speak her name aloud here!"

"It was from here she sailed," explained another woman, her face and arms blackened from fighting the fires. "We have kept her passing secret among us for fear the Vipre would have word of her being alive."

Owen looked at the exhausted faces of those gathered around him, and felt the daily state of siege that the inhabitants of the coastal settlement faced. "You have been left uninformed, citizens. The Hulin Vipre knew she was gone, and sent an army to find her. They were partially responsible for the destruction of my own homelands."

"They can't know she excaped," insisted the gaunt-faced woman. "We went to great lengths to let the Vipre think she had been killed in a battle here!"

"I knew that would never carry weight, Anetha," cried a woman. "There was no official state of mourning at Cairn Weal, and the island wasn't decked in black for long enough. And no one saw the girl lying in state. I don't fool my good wits with the idea that they don't have spies among us to keep up on what we're planning." The woman paused a moment, then with narrowed eyes shot another question at Owen. "What I'd like to know, is how you happen to be here so quick like, right on the heels of these curs?"

Owen raised a hand to quiet the group again, pulling the sword of Skye from beneath his cloak. "Here is the proof of my intentions," he cried, holding it high above his head, letting all in the gathering see it. A thin tongue of pale blue flames licked at the edges of the sword and, as they watched, became lighter still, until the surface of the blade became the face of a flowing body of water that turned from a pale gray to silver. A ship leapt into view in that silent surface, then faces appeared, as though viewed from above in water, and there among them was Deros, her beauty darkened by sadness and fear. At her side was another familiar face to Owen, but it was gone before he could recall it. He had surprised himself with the display, and it seemed to him there was something different about the sword now, and that what his old teachers had taught him was true. Politar had chided him about not knowing the full use of his power with the sword, which had been true, for he was astounded when he had called for the weapon while he was aboard the Wind Rhyme. He only imagined where the weapon was, lying beside his bunk on the Thistle Cloud, but after that, it suddenly was strapped to his side, which put Politar into high spirits and bouts of laughter that puzzled Owen at the time.

Anetha, the leader of the settlement women, had turned to the others as the sword darkened again. "We must send word to the Corum of this man. It is news that will make his heart lighter."

Owen touched the woman's arm lightly. "No. We can't tell her father yet, or let him know I'm on Eirn Bol. I can't tell you why now, but you will understand soon. If we give away our presence, we'll have no hope."

Anetha looked sternly at the young man before her. "Then if you don't want to be known to Cairn Weal, you haven't much time to go back to wherever you got here from. The Readers will have seen the fires, and will be here soon." Owen's puzzled look caused the woman to continue. "The Bellreams are read to keep the Purge at bay. It was so in the last days of the fireworms, and it has been kept up. They will have word of Dahlrin afire, and be here to keep the beasts away."

"Have there been any firesnakes in these last turnings?" asked Owen.

"The Readers do their work well," answered the woman. "None. Now you must go! There is a place near here where you can keep out of sight, if you wish. I'll send Jalen to show you." She called a name, and a young boy appeared, his blue eyes shining behind a mask of soot. He was about the age Owen had been when he first met Deros, and his heart ached suddenly to remember those times, now long flown.

A Young Guide

❋

There were dark red clouds at sunrise that cast a pall over the smoldering ruins of Dahlrin, and as Owen looked back, he could see the procession of men called the Bellream Readers making their way along the coast road. His young guide, Jalen, pointed them out.

"They have come every time the raiders strike. My father always called them the birds of ill omen. Anytime we saw them, it meant there was a reason for sadness."

Owen watched the group, which was made up of about two

dozen figures dressed in light-colored robes, and led by two men at the front of the procession holding tall staffs decorated with blue and gold pennants. "These are the ones who keep the firesnakes away?" he asked.

"There have been no attacks on Eirn Bol by the Purge since the death of Gingus Pashon. It is said by some the Black Hood has called back the Lost Fire, but we have not seen them."

"They are back," replied Owen evenly, noticing the look the lad turned on him.

"How do you know that?"

"I have seen them. They have destroyed Fionten, on the Delos Sound. I saw one devour two sailors off a ship I was on in the Roaring Sea."

Jalen gasped, his eyes wide in awe. "How did you escape?"

"I was with Politar, who is a caliphan. He had powers that helped us get away."

"Was it as awful as they say?" asked Jalen, his features drawn.

"Worse," reported Owen. "Everything they tell you of them can't give you the feeling of horror you have when you see one. Your knees go to water, and your mind turns to mush. They have a way of getting inside your head, and can read your thoughts."

"I have seen a likeness of them. The Bookmaster has shown us the drawings that were made by the Loremen in the old wars."

"A drawing is a cozy cup of tea by the fire, compared to hearing their wings drumming the air, and feeling your head exploding with their terrible promises. They can find whatever it is you fear the most, and torment you with it."

"Do they really breathe fire?"

"Enough to fry you as quick as you'd blink an eye."

The youth's eyes grew even wider, but he asked nothing more. They spent the next half hour in silence, watching the day break, promising a storm. The clouds had thickened, and a chilly wind from the north picked up, bringing a reminder that the full blast of winter was not long in coming.

His guide had kept to a direction that led back to the shepherd's hut, but they turned before they got there, and began a slight climb toward the two high peaks that rose in the distance.

"Are we going there?" Owen asked after another long period of walking in silence.

The youth looked at him blankly for a moment, then laughed, which cleared his young face of tension. "I don't think so. That's where Cairn Weal is! Anetha told me to hide you from everyone."

"The Lady Deros never described much of her country. All I knew for certain was that it was under attack."

Owen looked again at the lad. "How old are you?"

"I have passed my crossing," he answered proudly. "I was able to swim the course and return from the Rock of Salt in under a day."

"Was that your quest? Do they do that here?"

"All of us who are to join the Sacred Thistle have to complete the ritual before we are fifteen turnings."

"Then you are familiar with the Thistle Cloud? And the Lady Rewen?"

Jalen lowered his eyes, blushing. "We have all sworn our lives to her. I thought it was just another empty reading of the old books," he admitted. "Like the Bellream Readers and their firesnakes."

"The Lady Rewen is flesh and blood," confirmed Owen. "And the beasts as well."

"You won't say anything," said Jalen shyly, looking away. "About my not believing, I mean?"

"No need, old fellow," soothed Owen, seeing the youth was truly disturbed. "You are sworn to her service. She will be very pleased."

"Do you think?" Jalen brightened.

"If you get me safely hidden, and serve me well, I will recommend you to her personally."

"Is that your word?" persisted Jalen. "Do you promise?"

"My word," returned Owen. "Do your work well, and you have my promise."

The youth broke into a gallop and raced ahead, turning cartwheels along the edge of a stone fence that began at the top of a gently rising hill. It continued on for some distance before ending in a large circular dome that looked out over the valley that stretched back below them. It was higher than a mounted rider's head, and had slits throughout where an archer or crossbowman could shoot from, and there were many strange runes across the face of it. One of them attracted Owen's attention. It was a large design, with a horse plainly showing, and a hooded rider standing next to its side. The colors were clean and looked freshly done, and Owen asked about it, pointing it out. He also asked about where the stones came from, for they seemed so out of place.

"It is one of the Culdin Bier," replied Jalen. "They are the burial grounds for the Order of the Thistle."

"It looks like a fortress," said Owen.

"It is. These are built throughout Eirn Bol. When the Black Hood invades in force, and the Last Day has come, these are where we shall make our last stand."

"And that design there?"

"It is the mark of the one who shall bring the Last Day upon us."

Owen studied the vast rock fortress, and the valley spread out below, the scene tranquil and picturesque in the crisp morning. Only the ominous thread of black smoke trailing up into the pale blue sky along the coast brought ugly rumors of war, and the threat from the north that hung over the island like a storm cloud.

There were also sails farther out to sea, but they were too distant to read, although Owen stood for a long time with his eyes shielded against the sun, trying to decipher their mystery. Jalen dashed his optimism with the simple announcement that they must be more Hulin Vipre raiders. Yet as he turned away, a ray of light seemed to catch fire in a colored sail, and it kept recurring with such semblance of order that he thought it might be a signal of some sort. It did raise his spirits somewhat, enough so that he pulled back his cloak and drew his sword, holding it aloft to catch the sun. A brilliant beam of reflected light burst into a golden white shaft of sunlight that suddenly lit up the entire hill and fortress, and traveled out over the valley and coast as well. It died away as Owen lowered the sword of Skye, and the morning seemed paler than before, but this time there was an unmistakable wink of a signal from the distant ship.

"Let's get on to where you must take me," said Owen at last, turning to the awestruck youth.

"We're here," Jalen replied after finding his voice. "This is where Anetha told me to take you. No one comes here."

The youth was further startled when Owen suddenly vanished into thin air, and returned a few moments later, putting out a cheese and loaf of bread on a cloak spread on the ground before him.

"Let's eat," he said simply. "We shall need our strength."

The Aldora

Following his young guide into the dim light of the outer keep, Owen tripped over a loose stone at the door.

"Watch out for the rats," warned Jalen. "They have this place to themselves for long periods of time. They will begin to sense us by now."

Owen's hand jerked back from examining the object on the floor. "Rats!"

"Huge beasts, with beady red eyes. I've seen some here as big as dogs."

"Can't you do something about them?"

"We bring food to keep them docile," replied the youth. "They make good watchmen for these places when we're away. No one wants to think of being here with a pack of the beasts at them in the dark."

Owen paused, still within leaping distance of the doorway. "Then why are we tempting them?"

"They won't attack us. I have the Dolride."

"What?"

"This!" Jalen held out a small object that was attached to a chain.

"How would that stop them? It doesn't look like much of a weapon."

"Oh, it's not a weapon like you think of them. It's more of a locket than something to use as a dagger."

Owen peered through the gloom at it, hesitating near the door. He had begun to have second thoughts about his young guide, and the good citizens who had troubled themselves to hide him away.

"It whistles," offered Jalen. "Listen." He began to rapidly twirl the small piece about his head, which sung in a faint, hardly recognizable tone, which strenghtened as it went on. Soon a thin, high hum made Owen's ears ring, and he held out a hand toward his new acquaintance to motion him to stop. His mind was slowly lulled into a pleasant trance, and he smiled.

"It affects everyone like that," Jalen explained. "Even the rats."

"Would it work on a dragon?" asked Owen, blinking his eyes and trying to stop the fanciful ringing in his ears.

"The Purge? No one ever said. I don't know. The Bellream Readers keep them from our shores. This is mostly for the rats."

"Is that what they told you?"

"No one had to tell me of the Dolride. It has been the secret key to the lower tunnels for as long as we've been on Eirn Bol."

Owen stepped farther into the outer chamber of the watchtower, still minding where he placed his feet. His eyes were slowly beginning to adjust to the gloom of the place, and he could make out objects plainly now.

"What are those? he asked, indicating the wooden wheels that bristled from the walls on three sides.

"They control the workings of the gates. A single one of us can man the keep, if we have to. You can lower the portal at any one of the outer walls, and once in, there's no way out, unless these wheels are used. You will see some of the places where the Vipre were caught in our snares. We've left the bones to be found by any of their brothers who may find it in their unlucky stars to come searching for their kinsmen."

"You sound like a hard nut, Jalen," said Owen. "It's a shame we live in times so harsh." He felt suddenly old, looking at the young man, who was hardly into his teens.

The boy shook his head. "We've had it easy here. You should hear the stories they tell of what's been happening on the Southern Ride."

A rustling sound distracted Owen, and he peered away into the shadows near the far wall.

"It's the light. That always brings them up from their basement." Jalen pointed to the entryway they had just come through. "We have snares laid here for anyone who might chance upon the place." The young man motioned toward his shadow across the floor. "It will break the spell of the Bellream. You can hear them below, now."

A slight burr in Owen's ear began to register, and he could begin to hear the distant commotion that rolled toward them, growing louder every second.

"If the intruder didn't know to do this, or didn't have a Dolride, it would be a gruesome end." His young guide shuddered.

Still not comprehending, Owen looked about, puzzled.

"Come! I'll show you."

Jalen went forward into the next portal, laid carefully with huge blocks of stone that Owen marveled at, wondering how the people of Eirn Bol had ever managed to move them about, much less set them in place to construct the walls of the keep. As they went through the tall doorway, a low rumbling noise came from deep within the center of the foundations, and before he could turn to see what had happened, a great stone slab rolled into place, sealing off the chamber with a dreadful sound that slowly faded into a dark silence.

And then the other noise was quite clear, the collected voice of the rats, thousands strong, coming up from beneath the stone floor.

"Look," said Jalen, lighting the edge of the walls with the small lantern he had taken from a hidden niche. "An intruder wouldn't have light, but he could hear the scrabbling feet, and know what was coming. In another minute or two, this hallway would be knee-deep in the Aldora."

"What?" gasped Owen.

"The Aldora! The guards we leave to protect us here, and below."

Owen shivered involuntarily, his mind blank with horror. Jalen continued.

"My great-great-great-grandfather Alric was with the good Chamberlain when he discovered the lava chambers that were left after our island came to the surface of the sea. There was a famous battle there in the days before Alban Ram became Lord Keeper."

"Will Deros take over from her father?" Owen's curiosity was aroused, even though he still listened carefully to the growing squeals and squeaking of the advancing sentinel army.

"There was another Lady Keeper once, after the last of the High Chamberlains died. Deros's mother would have been next in line, had she lived. But Deros has not been heard from, until you came.''

"Now you know she is safe, or at least was when I left her.''

Jalen nodded slightly. "I'm glad to hear the Lady Deros is safe.''

"Has no one ever mentioned the Dark One, or the role she plays here?''

"The Dark One? Those were stories my mother tried to use to keep me from misbehaving.'' Jalen tried to scowl to make himself appear older. "I gave up those things when I outgrew my childhood, and found out the real names for the dangers we face.''

"The Purge are her lapdogs. I'm sure you know of them.''

"They were called up by the Hulin Vipre. Everyone knows they come from the fire mountain.''

The squealing of the rats had grown so loud now, it was difficult to hear. Jalen pulled out the chain and locket, and whirled it about his head until the odd hum began, and the streaming army below them quieted and turned back to their underground haunts.

"Enough of that. You get the picture of what would happen to someone here without this.'' He held up the locket at his neck. "You'll need one, as well, if I'm to leave you here alone.''

"Am I to be left here?'' asked Owen, suddenly alarmed.

"Until Anetha feels it's safe. We don't dare try taking you to Alban Ram, for it's long been suspected that there are spies among us.''

Owen paced about in great agitation. "I wish Politar would show up! Or Ephinias!'' As he spoke, he had a brief flash of memory, and both of his friends passed before his eyes in a swirl of stars and deep blue night sky. Beran was also there for a moment, pointing toward a distant white mountain. He tried to focus and heard a tiny bell peal, and then the dragon was there, drawing back a veil of dark cloud, which revealed to him a huge, glittering golden room, lit by the blazing red stones. The light there was so dazzling he was forced to shield his eyes. As the intensity lessened, he was able to see an old man sitting by the fire, hunched over in complete concentration as though he were examining something in the flames. Owen stepped quietly closer, afraid of disturbing the man, for the scene seemed so real he could smell the wood smoke and heavy incense. Nearing close enough to peer over the old man's shoulder, Owen drew in his breath sharply, for there clearly outlined in the fire was Deros.

When he looked again, he was staring into the concerned face of Jalen.

"Are you all right? You're white as the Cairn Cliffs!"

There was something nagging at the back of Owen's mind, something that he needed to remember, but he was having a difficult time with what it was. Faces played before him, and a dozen voices seemed to be speaking at once. "I'll be all right," he managed, leaning against the cool wall of the chamber. It was then his mind went back to the rats.

"Come! Sit here," said Jalen, leading him to a table and chair near the door.

"Are those things gone?" Owen asked. "Have you sent them back?"

"They're gone," the young man assured him.

"Can I speak frankly, boy? I need to have a friend here. All my comrades are still at sea, and I have no one here to help me."

The young man studied Owen briefly. "I am a son of Eirn Bol. I am sworn to the Alberion Novas, and Alban Ram. If you are an honorable man, and seek to serve our order, then you can count me a friend."

A thin pain had found its way to a place just behind his eyes. Owen rubbed them, trying to force himself to think clearly. "I am sworn to the Lady Deros and her father. I shall help her in any way I can. That's what troubles me most now, for I don't know the lay of the land, or where our enemies will strike at us."

Jalen laughed a dry, humorless laugh. "You won't have to wait to see where they strike. As likely as not, they'll be back on another raid tonight. It has been that way for my whole life. And if not here, then somewhere along the coast."

"I must reach someone in Cairn Weal," said Owen, his features clouded. "If only I knew who to trust!"

A shore breeze had sprung up while the two companions talked, and a short series of notes was blown on a conch shell, which attracted Jalen's attention.

"There are those my mother can reach, but it will take time," replied the youth. "We have other things to concern us now. That is a signal announcing the sighting of sails."

"The Hulin Vipre again?"

Jalen shook his head. "These are flying banners of another color. They are asking permission to land at our jetties."

"Allies? Do you have other friends yet along these parts?"

"Good friends and true," replied the boy. "But they haven't been able to contain the Black Scourge any better than ourselves."

"Go and find out who they are, and bring me back news. I'll use you for my ears until I can make myself known." He clasped the young lad's shoulder. "Can you do that for me?"

"If you'll promise I can come with you when you go to Deros. My mother says I am too young to be fighting, but I'm practically grown now." Jalen's face set in a hardened scowl. "I have my father's sword to serve me."

"Then you shall certainly come with me to pledge yourself to the Lady Deros," assured Owen. "In the meanwhile, gather what you can of the news in your settlement, and bring me all the gossip you hear. Anything at all! And leave me that locket, in case any of your sentries come back."

"They are effective, are they not?"

"Yes. Go on now, lad, and don't let anything hold you up." Owen hardly dared hope that any of his old companions had made their way safely to Eirn Bol, but it was all he had to help him keep his spirits up. As he watched Jalen leave and walk quickly away into the outer courtyard of the keep, he thought of the horrible guardians below, and held tightly to the locket the boy called the Dolride.

Then his thoughts turned back to the strange old man and the fire, and he knew he must try to reach Deros's father in Cairn Weal, to let him know his daughter was on her way back to him, and what Jalen had said of the spies at court. He might also know the identity of the man in his vision. A fleeting thought ran through his mind, but only briefly, of wondering why he had been left here in this dangerous place. Were Jalen and his mother the spies he should steer clear of, who would betray him to the darkness? He had no time to think further, for the distinct sound of footsteps turned his attention to finding a safe hiding place among the huge stones of the ancient fastness.

Below the Culdin Bier

❋

The voices were hushed, but Owen could make them out plainly. It seemed as if they were only around the next corner, but he went up one corridor, then another, and had still not found who was speaking. After a long period of silence, another sound came from somewhere close by, and he crouched, dodging into the dark shadows along the dimly lit wall. The smell of a rushlamp reached his nose, and he crept slowly forward, his hand on his sword. As he reached the turning of one more corridor, a low voice could be heard, calling out a name. It came twice more, and then there was the sound of one of the great stones rolling back. Hardly daring to breathe, Owen knelt and cautiously brought himself to peek around the corner. A man dressed in the same manner as Jalen was standing there, facing the opposite wall, which was slowly opening to reveal a dark slit of a secret passage in the sheer face of the rock. Owen picked up a snatch of the conversation.

"You will have this crossing secured for our men when we move! There must be no danger that someone will discover us, I tell you! We have to bring our troops in quickly once the plan is set in motion. You have done well, so far, Efile. Those fools in Cairn Weal shall leave these passages open to us, if they did intend to drown us all by flooding them, or turning those rotten beasts lose on us!" A dark ripple of laughter came then. "They don't know we possess one of these little trinkets, my friend. Only the most trusted of the Culdin Bier Watch are issued them." The laughter came again. "They have misplaced their trust in the loyal Efile! Jatal Ra will reward you for this. Lacon Rie was a good man when he was younger, but he lost his juice."

"All the old order is finished. We must look to our future," said the man Efile.

"And our future is what we must talk of now. It is becoming too risky to meet again for a while," whispered the other man.

30

"I have heard others here today. Are we alone now?" asked the second low voice, heavy and cold, which sent shivers down Owen's back.

"It's all right now, we're alone," assured Efile. "There was the sprout Jalen playing about here earlier. I saw him as he was leaving. That's why I had to wait before I risked calling you."

"Good. Our plans are going well. Your work is to get the locals to relax their guard along this coast. We want everyone to think that our landings will be against the Northern Ride. No one will think to look for us along the roads we'll be using."

"Did that trinket work for you?" asked Efile.

"Well enough that you see me here. I don't want to think of what would happen if it failed."

"Have some copies made so that your troops coming through the old flows will have protection. And give me back mine! I don't want to be caught without it. There is already suspicion that there is a spy among us."

The figure in the darker shadows of the tunnel laughed a low, menacing laugh. "I shouldn't wonder."

At that moment, Owen was trying to find a position that would enable him to observe the faces of the two men, and touched a small pile of stones, which clattered softly to the floor, making a barely perceptible noise, but both figures in the other room froze.

"What was that?" hissed the man in the hidden passage.

"Rats, I expect," replied his companion, walking toward where Owen crouched. The young Steward's hand was on his sword, and he was ready to draw and fight for his life, but then a muffled sound came from the opposite direction, drawing the man back toward another corridor.

"Leave it! There's nothing there but the rats! Give us a bit of the Dolride!"

The same strange humming noise he had heard earlier began to fill his ears, making him feel secure enough to not want to hide from the two men in the other chamber. He struggled with the urge to simply walk in and speak, but there was an inner part of him that kept him hidden, and he clutched the sword tightly. He still had not seen the face of either man, although he was sure he could recognize the voice of the one. It was cold and hard, and for some reason he thought the man must be heavyset and dark-featured. It gave him chills when he heard the voice again.

"We shall have the same signal as before. Don't risk using it unless something important enough to alter our plans occurs. We don't want to compromise the new Emperor.''

"The cripple! Hah. It's a sad day we've fallen on, Agrate, when the leaders of the two most powerful clans on the Silent Sea should be a crippled boy and a senile old fool who sits upon the Alberion Novas without a clue as to the true power he could wield, if he but used them.''

"Keep your thoughts to yourself, my good Efile. You do your job well, but the last blow has not been struck. If we fail in even the smallest detail, all our work shall have gone for naught.'' Agrate paused, and Owen could hear the sound of his breathing for a moment. "That would displease my companions and I very much.''

There was no further threat, but none was needed. When Efile spoke, his voice was tight with fear.

"You have no cause for concern here, Agrate. You know I have done everything exactly as you wanted, and more.''

"Yes," agreed Agrate slowly. "We are not unaware of all the errands you have performed, my good fellow. You shall be rewarded generously for your work. Now off with you! The moment of victory draws nearer.''

The voices fell silent then, and Owen heard the sound of footsteps fading toward the outer keep. He remained frozen along the wall, waiting to hear movement from the remaining man. He breathed a silent sigh of relief when the shadow figure strode through the chamber, muttering aloud to himself. "We shall have our fun when this is done, and we're free of the foul stench of Alban Ram!'' Retreating footsteps accompanied the voice down the corridor that led into the rooms beyond, and Owen followed cautiously along, noticing for the first time in the semidarkness the flickering blue-white light that played along the edges of his sword.

Agrate had entered the room where Jalen had shown Owen the wooden wheels, and paused there, scanning the ramps and passages that led outside for a moment. "This shall be a perfect place to launch an attack on their rear,'' he growled half-aloud. "That fool Efile has done his work well.'' The man wheeled and returned to the inner hallways so quickly, Owen was almost caught out of hiding.

His mind raced, wondering what he should do, to confront the man or let him go. If he moved, he risked revealing his presence on Eirn Bol, and yet if he did nothing, there might be no further chance for him to thwart the treachery that grew in secrecy at the very heart of Alban Ram's realm. He was saved by any further decision by the touch of a spider on the wall he had brushed against with his hand, and the sudden start touched the sword gently along the stone, causing a dull clang that was clearly audible.

Agrate stopped short, drawing his weapons. "Who passes? Step out here where I can see you! Is it you, Efile?" He spoke reassuringly, but through the gloom Owen could see that the man had not lowered his weapons, and advanced toward him with cold, hard eyes and a grimace that stretched his lips into a thin line of hatred. Owen, seeing that he would be discovered by the man in another step, boldly stepped out of his hiding, the sword from Skye held lightly in his hand.

The man leapt backward at the sight of the stranger with the flickering lights dancing on the bared blade, but caught himself and prepared to fight.

"Who are you? What do you want in the Culdin Bier?" The man circled about Owen, looking for an opening to strike and hoping that this armed stranger would be lulled by his chatter.

"I am Owen," he replied, not wishing to give any other name, on the off chance the man should escape. "I have come to find why there are so many rats bred in these tunnels."

Agrate snorted a short, humorless laugh. "Another philosopher! We are brim full of you and your kind!" An ugly smile crossed the man's shadowed features. "I hope you fight as well as you philosophize, my friend! Otherwise, you shall soon find out that what keeps all these rats here well fed are the carcasses of young fools like you, who put their trim little noses in where they're not wanted."

As he finished speaking, Agrate lunged forward with his sword, striking at Owen's chest. The blow was deflected easily, and Owen now stood ready to receive any further attack.

"Aren't we the pretty one?" chided Agrate. "The boy has his basics, that's plain to see. And a trick blade that tries to blind me! What will they be sending next?"

"I find the information that I have might be of interest to those in Cairn Weal, my fat stoat! Someone will be shocked to learn that even in times like these, when there are enough enemies abroad for everyone, the most dangerous one of all is the man who stands nearest as a friend."

The man circled once more, forcing the point of his sword into Owen's defense, testing his skills as a fighter.

"No accusations, please! You'll offend my good friend Efile! Spare me the trouble of having to cut your tongue out. I can tell by your remarks that you have heard too much here. It will give me great pleasure to rip your stomach a bit. Nasty way to die, waiting to bleed to death looking at your entrails."

Owen repeated the words to enter the bottle that held the arms, leaving a badly distraugt Agrate to slash wildly about the room, his eyes wide in disbelief.

A single red apple appeared from the very air before him, and buried itself on his brandished sword. It was followed by a pear and a slab of cheese, and Owen's laughter. "You make a convenient place to keep my meal, Agrate! That's as good a use as you're going to get to put your sword to, as far as we're concerned."

Agrate flung the fruit from his blade and hacked away in the direction of the voice.

"And Alban Ram shall be highly distressed to find out that Efile has been conversing secretly with Agrate in one of the old watchtowers."

"You treacherous little snake, come out here where I can see you!" roared Agrate. "Don't hide behind your devilish tricks! That's for weirdochs, not men!"

"You'll have to come find me," replied Owen, reappearing at the outer door of the keep, standing on a tall stone wall, his sword resting at his side.

"I'll skewer you like a piece of meat," snarled the man, lunging out to meet his elusive enemy.

"I would be curious to know what you offered Efile to turn him against his fellows," said Owen evenly. "It must take something quite unusual to do that."

The man crouched, moving closer to Owen, exactly as Kegin had always shown him to do when closing with an enemy. "What would you know of Efile or his reasons?"

"I know it takes something worthy of a story to turn a man against his own. You spoke to him below, when he knows it will mean the death or capture of his countrymen. What could you have offered him to make him do that?"

"His heart's desire, you fool! Power and riches! Women! All the things the poor wretch thinks will make him happy!" Agrate launched a violent attack, suddenly springing with both sword and dagger slashing viciously, ripping Owen's cloak.

Whatever else the man was, Owen thought, he was a seasoned fighter. It was then that the faint light of a rushlamp caught a red glint on the man's right hand, and Owen saw the Rhion Stone there, in a ring identical to the one Ulen Scarlett wore.

Owen set to work in earnest then, countering the savage blows the man struck, and returning his own. The two combatants circled and parried for a time, until it seemed that neither would get an advantage. Turning and bowing, the man suddenly sprang for the entrance again, and disappeared into the gloom of the guardhouse. Owen was right on his heels, but Agrate had vanished into thin air.

Owen searched cautiously through each chamber, but had to concede the man had disappeared into one of the secret passages that were concealed somewhere in the maze of passages and chambers. He would ask Jalen about them when he saw him, and he knew that would have to be soon, for he had to find a way to warn the people of Eirn Bol of the traitor Efile, and of the dangers that were to come from below the Culdin Bier.

The Warling
Council

The Collandar of the Warling

✳

Owen was silently watching the Bellream Readers winding their way along the wagon track that led into the outer walls of the fortified keep Jalen called one of the Culdin Bier. He toyed with the idea of simply going out to the procession of the Readers and warning them of the traitor that was at work within their ranks, but as he watched the slow progress of the walkers, he suddenly began to think of how his information would be received. It was doubtful they would believe an outsider's report on one of their own, and he could easily see how he himself might be made out to be a spy.

That there was no time to lose, he knew, but as to the method he was to use to warn the citizens of Eirn Bol, he was at a loss. If he could reach Jalen again, he knew the lad would believe him, and that perhaps he would be able to send word to Cairn Weal in a rapid manner. Owen knew from the conversations he had overheard that no one suspected that they were so vulnerable to an attack from beneath their own island's depths.

The slow chant had grown louder and louder, until now the Bellream Readers were at the very gates of the keep, and Owen was forced to hide himself again, waiting for the hooded figures to go along on their way, and leave him to find his own path back to the village where Jalen and his mother lived. He also thought of trying to contact Beran or Politar, or perhaps Ephinias. The sword was in his hand then, and it surprised him

39

to find a flickering thin blue line of light playing at the edges of the blade. At first, he thought it surely must be a trick of the poor visibility in his shadowed hiding place, but the slow, steady hum that accompanied it began, and he felt the warm pulses of the living blade creep through the cool skin of his hand, setting his heartbeat racing beneath his cloak.

Owen stole a careful glance around the corner of the stone watchtower, to see where the Readers had gotten to, and was surpised to find the entire procession standing in a large circle not twenty paces from where he was hidden, and each of the members seemed to be going from pillar to pillar in the slow, methodical way of someone searching carefully for something.

Without another look at the now-shimmering blue light along the blade of the sword from Skye, he knew for certain that the Readers were searching for him. That thought sent a jolt of pure panic through him for a split second, then he calmed, remembering the Dolride and the hidden passages below. If the Bellream Readers or the others hadn't discovered that the enemy was using the old passages, then he would be safe from discovery on Eirn Bol, although he wasn't too sure if the comings and goings in those places weren't watched by Hulin Vipre troops.

And he wasn't sure himself that he would be able to open them. It had been simple to watch Jalen, and he had seen the one where Efile talked to the Black Hood, Agrate, but he was unsure exactly how to get back to that room, or what to do after he had managed.

One of the hooded figures suddenly spoke. The noise of a human voice sounded odd, after the almost silent scratching of boots over the stone floor. He could not understand the words, and another of the cloaked men replied, and then continued on with their search. It would now only be a matter of moments before he was discovered, if he did not move, but just as he was tensing his muscles to quietly slip away, he heard a familiar voice that chilled his blood, speaking in the common tongue.

"You may as well come out, Jalen! We know you're here. I've told my brothers there is a Hulin spy in our midst. They are a very exacting order. You know they are the descendants of the old holy order of the Monks of Corum Mont. They are dedicated to the preservation and safety of the Alberion Novas, and any enemy who is caught is treated to an exquisitely refined torment that will cleanse his mortal soul of any evil doing." Efile, for it was the very man Owen had heard only a short while earlier, laughed a dry laugh that sounded as deadly as a dagger being drawn from its sheath in the darkness.

The soft scratching of boots on the stone floor alerted Owen that the searchers were coming ever nearer, and he frantically looked about in the gloom for some hiding place, cursing himself for not thinking that the traitor would possibly come back.

There was something ominous about the cloaked figures, and even when Owen had first been told of them by Jalen and his mother, there was a certain menace to the way they walked, as he watched their procession winding its way along the coast road toward the town. It also occurred to Owen then that it would be the perfect cover for spies who had a need to move about freely to report changes in troop strength or weak points in the island's defenses. No one spoke to the hooded figures, and they had full run of Eirn Bol, running through their ceremonies that were supposed to keep the dragons away.

A hand as hard as iron suddenly fastened itself to his mouth, and he felt an arm encircle his own, pinning him helplessly against the wall. He had difficulty breathing, and his body struggled helplessly in a wild attempt to free himself, but the pressure of the crushing grip of his assailant soon exhausted him, and he fell into a black despair, captured by the enemy. It was too bitter a thing to contemplate, and his mind tried to blank out the overwhelming emotions with thoughts of death.

Owen went limp in his captor's grip, hoping it might momentarily cause the bone-crushing pressure to be loosened, but nothing happened, and Owen felt his chest being flattened beneath his cape, and he was growing faint from lack of breath.

A slight sound caught his attention, only a mere hint of a whisper at his ear, but in the roar of the blood rushing through his head, it sounded like a shout.

"You've squashed him," chided the voice. It didn't sound right, or not human, but Owen was on the verge of passing out, and he wasn't sure it might not be an illusion of the sort he'd had when he had been in a fever from a wound or under the dark, powerful spell of the Olgnite, which even now threatened to erupt again.

"No, I'm not. If I am, then it's his fault for folding up."

"Let him go a little!"

"No! We have to get out of here. We can't let them see us!"

"He's all black and blue!"

"That's the way they look. Just skin! Doesn't make any sense to me how the Great Brother would let them stay like this, naked to the world!"

Owen felt the pressure over his mouth and nose relax slightly, and he gasped in a lungful of air gratefully.

"Shhh!" hissed the first voice, but someone on the other side of the corridor had heard, and now made their way toward where Owen was held still locked in the vise-like arms of his captor. His mind was reeling, letting in bits of information that confused him and made him doubt his senses.

The arm that held him was fur-covered, as though cloaked in a heavy cape, and the smell was from some deep, soft cave, lined with fragant pine boughs. And as that thought floated gingerly through his consciousness, the other arm, with a great silver-gray paw attached at the end of it, swiftly clúbbed the hooded figure of one of the Bellream Readers, who had suddenly appeared around the corner, brandishing a wicked-looking stabbing blade on the end of a walking staff.

Bears, thought Owen. These were bears!

Efile called out to the unconscious figure on the floor of the guardroom, and spoke something else in the unfamiliar language. He started to speak to let the bear that held him know he could still fight, but before the words were out, the very stones in the wall behind him murmured a soft, silent ruffle of sound, and in the next breath, he was being hurried along a smooth stone tunnel, with round sides and ceiling, like the inside of a water reed, only big enough for him to walk upright, next to the two large figures of the lumbering bears at his side.

No matter what, he thought idly, bears running or walking on all fours waddle with that odd gait that makes them seem like such jolly fellows. When he was still a boy, he remembered going out into the woods with his father, or Stearborn, and watching the animals there. Bears were always some of his favorite animals to watch, and no one was ever allowed to kill them. Owen was suddenly grateful for that. And after his visit to the Halls of the High Dragon, it did not seem unusual that he should be able to understand these two huge animals, both a deep cinnamon-gray color, with patches of silver in their muzzle and on their paws.

"Well, chubblet, you have dipped your paw in a fine sauce pan here! It's lucky for you that two snout-rooters like us were off on patrol to keep the Bridge open!"

"If he had a tongue, he'd be thanking us now, I should think. I don't want to know what that pack of curs would have done to him, but I don't think they meant to take him back to the White Cliffs to tea and cake."

"Don't bring up cake, you old barkscratcher! I'm hungry and tired, and not in a mood to be tormented!"

"There he goes again," complained the other bear, grumbling, although Owen detected it was good-natured banter, much as it might be if he were listening to Stearborn and Chellin Duchin. "Thinks of nothing but his honeycake and naps, even when there's plenty of work to paw! It's a wonder the Warling clans have lasted as long as they have, no thanks to him!"

Owen started to question them, for the mention of the word *Warling* had jogged a memory of something that had been said when he was still with Ephinias and the others before the fire in the High Halls of the Dragon.

They had not slacked their speed, and although they had come a good distance, it seemed they still had not reached where they were bound. Owen could see no source of light, no lamps or torches, but a brilliant golden glow seemed to pervade throughout the shaft, the color of late autumn sunlight through shallow woods. There was a slight bend in the shaft then, and it opened out into a high-domed cavern, enormous in size, and as deep as the pit he had found at the Forge of Roshagel. The shape of the mountain was the same, but here there were no fiery blasts, no cauldron of intense white heat.

And then he became aware of the bears, all similar to his two companions, seated in a great circle, as if they had been awaiting him.

"Welcome to our Collandar, chubblet," said one of the two bears who had brought him. "Please be seated."

There seemed to be nothing else to do.

The Warling Stone

❋

A deep booming chant began then, reverberating through the great natural ampitheater in the very heart of the mountain. It sounded to Owen something like what the Stewards did when they saluted a courageous man, by clenching their hands and beating it against their mail; then the two bears who had brought Owen safely through the passages moved forward, and bowed low before a huge animal sitting alone in the very center of the gathering.

"You have been saluted, chubblet! Don't you learn manners as a man-cub?" The animal who had held him in such an iron grip spoke, his muzzle drawn into a disapproving frown.

"Leave him alone, Lach Lamal! You are turning more foul-tempered than a porcupine about your manners. What sort of animal have you become, insulting our guest this way?"

"I'm doing well enough to put up with your constant pawing and complaining about my general conduct, Pa'lage! You'd think a Warling wouldn't have to hear attacks from his own kind, but in these times, it fits that this is a just reward for faithful service."

Owen listened in great confusion, watching as the great silver-gray bear with the dark mottled patches rose onto his hindpaws and lifted himself fully erect, which made him stand a full arm's length taller than his own head. He recalled the huge, fierce red bear aboard the Thistle Cloud, and suddenly remembered his manners.

"All hail, Bruinthor," he muttered, touching his hand to his forehead and bowing twice in succession, which Ephinias had spent a great deal of time explaining to him.

"A great Light from the west be upon you, little brother. I am called Mar'ador. I am surprised to see you here!"

Owen bowed again, turning to the two bears who had brought him. "I was not expecting the journey, either. I was trying to reach Alban Ram to warn him of the Hulin Vipre using these tunnels to come upon them from behind. I would have been killed, if it hadn't been for these two." Owen remembered Ephinias telling him how fond the bear clans were of praise for their efforts.

"The strange ones in the red hoods were there," said Lach Lamal. "There are more than a few dark hearts who move about freely here, who have come from our sister island."

Mar'ador looked away, his thoughts seeming to wander, then he stretched lazily and sat back down. "We have watched them for a long time now. The Keeper of the Scrolls in the White Cliffs has trusted these red hoods always, yet we Warlings know another tale of them." The great bear turned to Owen, lowering his muzzle to be at eye level with the young man. "It's been this way since the last War of the Flying Death. The ones who sleep below Corum Mont are the true ones. But they won't rise until the holy Scrolls in the White Cliffs are taken from their hiding."

Owen began to feel more at ease among his newly found friends, and looked around more carefully. He lost count at over a hundred of the animals, ranging in size from those as large as Lach Lamal and Pa'lage and the leader, to yearling cubs, hardly bigger than himself. He tried remembering the binding that Ephinias had taught him, which would let him take the bear form, but one single, odd-sounding word escaped him for the moment. The bear called Mar'ador was still speaking.

"There is a way we have which you might use to reach the Old One at the White Cliffs. The island is full of the old fire holes, and some of them run right into the keep."

Owen's heart fell. "Do these red hoods know of those passages?"

"No one knows all the ways of the Warling. We have guarded our secrets with blood."

"Then you know about the rats, too?"

"They have been driven to the havens of these places just as the Warling. We help each other, when we can."

Owen took the small locket from beneath his cloak and blew

a short note on it. The bear's eyes softened, and the entire gathering gave out a short sigh, almost as one animal.

"They came from the Old Ones at Corum Mont, before they slept. Some have said that music will wake them one day."

Pa'lage spoke then. "Are we to get the chubblet to the White Cliffs, or shall we spend our time jawing here? The red hoods in the Culdin Bier will be looking to find where he went. One of them knows a little of some of these passages."

"His name is Efile. He has also given the enemy a Dolride, and they are to make copies of them!" reported Owen, suddenly remembering the fact that Agrate had one of the small lockets in his possession now.

Mar'ador snuffled a soft laugh, sitting back on his haunches. "Then they will do us a greater service than we could hope. I don't know what means they might try to use to make a Dolride, but I want to be present when they try it out in the old roads below the mountain." He emitted a deeper growl of laughter, and was joined by the others.

"Is something funny about being betrayed this way?" asked Owen, growing hot with indignation.

"Not laughing at betrayal," managed Lach Lamal. "Thinking of the Black Hoods trying to make a Dolride."

Mar'ador snorted and snuffled, and rearranged himself in his fur, then reached out a great paw to touch Owen's arm. "Those came from the silent Old Ones at Corum Mont. There is no way they could be made by the ones in the Barrens."

"They have caliphans there, too," argued Owen. "They have the Rhion Stones, just like the Lady Rewen wears."

"The weirdochs," repeated the old bear. "Yes, they have their fill of those. We have fought the best we can against them, and have lost many brave animals doing it."

"After the last War of the Flying Death, both our islands became as closed as a den in winter. Mistrust and fear were everywhere, and your clans began to shun us, to drive us farther away, because we were beasts, just like the vile creatures from the pits of the fire mountain."

"But that's not true," objected Owen.

"Not true, but look at us. Were you afraid when you felt the bear hug of Lach Lamal? If you were just a chubblet lost in the passages of the Culdin Bier, would you have felt fear?"

"You were trying to help!"

"No one saw that. The bitterness of the long war had turned

everyone's heart hard. The bitterness began to touch our former friends. Places where we had been welcome, they began to leave poisoned meat and water, settlements became more fortified, so that in the end, we were forced to find our own havens."

Pa'lage continued the tale. "Mar'ador had old friends on the Council at the White Cliffs. They remained true, and allowed us free run of these paths below."

Owen sat down heavily. "Sometimes I wonder at what it will take to wake them up. It doesn't seem any use to keep on going, when you're fighting even with your own kind."

Mar'ador nodded his huge head. "We have given up the practice of taking human form. We could do that at one time, when my great-great-great-grandsires were roaming these parts. Now none but the masters still have the skill, or the use of such a thing. But beneath our bearness, within these clans, there still burns the true fire." He snorted, moving a paw back and forth in front of him, rolling a small stone across the floor. "Now we are caught like this pebble, pushed to and fro, scorned, feared, and attacked by both sides of this fight."

Owen recalled the fierce form of the great red bear aboard the Thistle Cloud. "Your clans have a friend by the name of Coglan who will be here to help us. He may already be ashore. He'll be coming with the Lady Deros."

"Coglan?" echoed the bears around Owen. "It rings no bells."

"I hope not, if it's anything like the bells the Bellream Readers carry! But you'll recognize him as a master when you see him."

Pa'lage made his way through the circle of bears, and stood before a carving that was done on the living stone wall of the vast underground dome. "Here is a record of all our clans, starting from the time the fire mountain came to life, then died."

Owen could almost hear Ephinias at his side, whispering urgently for him to pay attention.

Pran'del

✳

"This is the Warling Stone," Mar'ador was explaining. "It was done by our clans when we still went about freely. All the clans were at peace then."

"This was before the first war of the dragon?" asked Owen.

The big animal nodded. "So long ago seems like walking in fog. Nothing real to touch. But yes, it was then I speak of. We watched the two sides of the fire mountain slowly split apart, until now you see what's left. The Black Hood has besieged the White Cliffs, and it has slowly drawn all the other clans down, too. Now we're hunted like common beasts, and the flying death is abroad again."

"Which is why I'm here," replied Owen.

"You, chubblet?" Pa'lage's laughter rumbled through his body, shaking the big animal.

Owen tried not to be offended, but he was hurt by the laughter, and he let his pride speak a little too loudly.

"My name is Owen Helwin, son of Famhart the Pure. I have been seated at the High Dragon's Hall, and carry the sword from Skye!" As he finished speaking, he drew the weapon from the scabbard and held it out before him, watching the slowly brightening blade come to life in his hand. He tried to remember all the words Ephinias had taught him, in order to make the blade do certain things, and he surprised himself to see the pearl-crystal bubble that was drawn on the very air, suddenly filled with the snow-capped mountains of the wilderness below the Boundaries.

Scenes of great armies clashing, and the fiery destruction of the dragons blazed forth into the domed cavern, spilling out over the gathering of animals in writhing white clouds that spun about, then disappeared into the shadows above. Mar'ador watched, never moving from Owen's side.

"So you have sat at the table with the Elders," he said at

48

last. "It has been a long time since we have been visited by any of the High Council."

Owen felt like blushing at being regarded so highly, and was secretly astounded at the things he had seen. It was difficult knowing exactly what his own powers were, but the bears obviously thought of him as someone special, for they were all raised onto their hindpaws, and had lifted their muzzles into the air, and now sang a low, whuffling song that seemed to go on as easily as breathing. Lach Lamal stepped forward into the center of them and began a dance.

The sword had quietened, and now had returned to a deep silver-blue color along the blade, which flickered weakly.

"There is still some danger for us somewhere near," said Owen, glad for a diversion.

"The red hoods above will be trying to find the passages," answered Pa'lage. "They will find many paths, but none that will lead them here."

"They may not give up so easily this time. Efile knows I'm here, and that I know his name. I am too dangerous to leave alive."

"Which makes you a great danger to us," observed Mar'ador. "We need to speed you on your way to the White Cliffs, out of simple self-defense."

"I can go to guide him," offered a younger bear, who had been standing next to the older bear who was the head of the clan.

"You, Lanidel? You are barely old enough to be in the patrols. This would be dangerous work, and you would be at great risk so close to the outer edges."

"I know the way," insisted the yearling. "Someone will have to try me sometime, either now or later. And we need every bear for the coming of the day when we shall have to come out from our hiding."

Mar'ador's low rumble of warning surprised Owen, and he barely escaped in time to avoid the cuffing the younger bear got. "You will mind your elders, and keep your saucy tongue to yourself! We have a guest among us, and it's not proper for such behavior!"

Lanidel, chastened, hung his head and shuffled his forepaws across the smooth stone floor in front of the old bear in apology.

"I'm sorry, Mar'ador. I just want to help."

The grizzled old leader softened, lowering himself from his fighting stance. "You shall have your chance, youngster. We shall all be called on to do our part."

"Then who shall it be?" asked another bear. "One of us will have to go."

Mar'ador's great muzzle turned from one to the next, going around the room. His gaze finally settled on a smaller, discolored animal sitting quietly near the far side of the Warling Stone. "You, Parnod, shall guide this chubblet to the holes beneath the White Cliffs."

A ripple of disagreement flowed through the gathering, but was quelled by the stern look that Mar'ador settled upon them. "Who among you questions me? If there is one who thinks he knows better than I, let him come forward!" The old bear's eyes were terrible in his rage, and Owen was glad he was not the object of his anger.

A stout bear with the same cinnamon-gray color of Pa'lage and Lach Lamal lumbered forward, turning to address the others.

"You all know me," he rumbled, raising onto his hindpaws. "My life has been spent fighting for the protection of the clan, and it has not been all fancy speech here in the sacred vault where the Stone is kept!"

Rumbling growls of agreement puncuated his speech, and the bear went on, warming to his task. "We have known trouble, brothers and sisters, and always it has come from the outsiders. This very stone that shows the heart of our clans tells the tale more clearly than I ever could." He held out a paw, pointing to the intricate carvings that ran across the wall of the dome.

"Come to your point, Pran'del," said Mar'ador shortly.

"My point is a simple one, Mar'ador! We are here because of the human clans on our sister islands, and we have been hounded and hunted all these turnings by them! Now, when we have the chance to strike a blow and be rid of them, you expect us to fold our paws and bow down again to them! We shall be going back to the way it was before, and we will not have freed a single Warling from the human chains that have bound us!"

A ripple of deep, unspoken anger stirred through the gathering, and more than a few of the animals there were on their hindpaws, raising themselves into the fighting stance of the bear. In the soft light, Owen saw the pale gleam of claws and fangs among them, and saw the terrible red eyes he had seen in Coglan, aboard the Thistle Cloud, when the snake-men had attacked.

The moment had turned ugly before Mar'ador could stop it, and Owen knew he must do something quickly.

"Hear me!" cried the old leader. "Warlings, heed me now!"

Roars and growls came from all sides, and the din was so great Owen couldn't hear distinctive voices anymore. Mar'ador was beside him one moment, then gone the next, making straight for Pran'del, bowling bears out of his way in his anger. The two were almost equal in size, and the younger animal rose up to his fighting stance to meet the old elder of the Warling clans, and was prepared to attack, when Owen finally remembered the bindings Ephinias had taught him.

"Hold!" he roared out, now in the unfamiliar-feeling body of a stout bear, dark brown in color, with reddish patches of fur at his head and shoulder. "Hold!" he called out again, beginning to feel the strength that filled this body.

A stunned moment of silence fell across the divided gathering, and the tempers that had flared cooled somewhat.

"You can see that the High Council has not forgotten their brothers," Owen called out, hoping he would know the right thing to say. He muttered a quick prayer to Ephinias and Beran and Colvages Domel under his breath, and went on as the others stood staring at him in disbelief.

"My master has taught me of the brave souls who have always fallen on the side of the Light. Windameir counts you all among His staunch defenders, and bearers of the Sacred Flame."

Pran'del had recovered, and was rising to challenge Owen, but was stopped by Mar'ador. "Let him be heard out! Common clan law dictates that!"

"A human weirdoch," snorted Pran'del. "Being able to take on a bear form does not make the chubblet a bear!"

"I take this form because I honor it, and I honor all who belong to the clan! I take this form because my master, and all the other Elders of the Circle, honor this clan, and all clans alike! You say you are ready to strike out and drive away the humans, the good and bad alike, and will be free! I say this, and heed me well! If you take that rash course, you will die imprisoned alone in these hills forever! The Dark One is at work here, and it is the Dark One who will replace the humans with something worse."

Pran'del broke past Mar'ador before the old bear could move to stop him.

"Liar! Traitor! You come to weaken our resolve, and to keep

us in this exile we've been forced into by your race! Look at you now! Standing before us, looking for all to see like one of us, asking us to follow you and fight your fight, and win your battles for you! You are from the Dark One! I say no to your kind, forever! We have done that before, gone down that path, when the flying death burned and killed all alike, animal and man. We helped overthrow them, and look at what rewards we got for our trouble.'' The huge bear's rage was terrible to behold, and his fangs were bared and near Owen as he spoke. ''It does not take the Dark One to put the evil touch upon our clans! It is already done by your cursed race!''

The domed chamber of the Warling Stone was a sea of rage and confusion now, the animals beginning to scuffle and spar among themselves. Parnod and Lach Lamal stood next to Owen, looking to Mar'ador for his instructions.

''That was then,'' cried Owen loudly, surprised at the deep roar of his bear voice. ''I have been sent to be with you! The Circle of Elders know of the troubles you speak of, and I am to be here with you. It is a sign of our good faith!''

''There is no good in the faith of a human,'' roared Pran'del. ''His faith changes like the wind blows! You need us now, so you swear blood loyalty to the Warling. The minute the Black Hoods are no more danger, then it's back to the old ways. We frighten the children! We need too much land! We don't belong! The settlements will grow again, when there is no wars or dragons, and we'll find ourselves pushed away again, then finally we'll be a danger to the humans. That's when the bounties will start, and we'll have no more freedom. At least if we die now, we shall die in the struggle! Let your two clans kill each other! So much the better for us. Every human dead is one less enemy of mine!''

The younger bears in the gathering were worked into a frenzy by Pran'del's impassioned speech, and their claws and fangs were bared dangerously, and more than a few of them had begun their terrible war cry, swaying about the chamber of the Warling Stone in a widening circle that threatened to ignite into violence at any moment.

The Messenger of Bruinthor

＊

The immense cavern was filled with enraged factions from both sides, and Owen saw that Pran'del was advancing toward him, raised into his fighting stance, his eyes blood-red. "Traitor! Betrayer of the Warling!"

Other savage voices caught up the cry, and the roaring of the throng deafened him. A slow refrain suddenly came into his mind, crystal clear, as though he were standing by the sea next to Politar, and he slowly began to recite the words aloud.

> "The Crown of Nine floats in time,
> Come from the ancient Warling,
> And once more the ancient door
> Will open to their calling."

He could not remember if it had been Politar, or Colvages Domel, or if they had been still aboard the Wind Rhyme, or in the High Halls of the Dragon. It took a moment for the words he had spoken to take effect, and Pran'del was still poised to join battle, his powerful jaws open and his paw raised to strike.

Owen repeated the couplet again, this time in a louder voice.

Lach Lamal made himself heard over the noisy confusion.

"Who but the truest heart could know those words?" he cried, raising himself on his hindlegs. "If you fear we have a traitor in our midst who would betray us to the Black Hoods, or the chubblets of the White Cliffs, then you can rest your concern now. This is a bear!"

A roar of approval swept the gathering, and Pran'del, seeing his moment slipping away, slunk back into the rear of the throng, and went to seek his own followers. He had posted them all through the others, and coached them on what to say, and when to rile their neighbors. No one noticed his absence for a few moments, until Crale called out his name.

53

"Come along, Pran'del! We have an answer for your accusations now. Let us hear the rest of what you had to say. It can't be said of the Warling that they don't allow a bear to have his day before the Council."

There were other cries for the troublemaker to show himself, but Pran'del had retreated to safety, planning for another day. He had waited a long time already, and knew there would be another chance to overthrow the old regime that followed Mar'ador and Crale.

"It's not that he is a bad one," Mar'ador was explaining to Owen. "It seems to be something that happens in any clan, as regular as seasons. The old grow closed and the young come along and feel they have discovered a better way to hunt, or to live in the forest." He chuckled to himself as he spoke. "And sometimes they do, at that."

"What will happen to him now?" asked Owen, wondering if he had seen the last of the stout red bear.

"Pran'del? Oh, he'll find something to carry him away from us for a while. Maybe a scouting patrol through the lower reaches, or perhaps some bold deed that will restore the luster to his coat."

"He won't be punished?"

Mar'ador shook his head. "He is punished by his behavior here. He has lost face among his companions, and bears have long memories. Those who were in his camp will be taking a second look at what the young fire-tongue was spouting. We are not against better ways, or ridding ourselves of the old, but we do not wish to replace something of proven value with a whisker of wind."

There was a tremor that rippled through the great cavern then, and fine dust from the domed ceiling fell like powdered snow over the gathering.

"It's the old fire mountain," cried Crale. "It was said that it would come back to life when the Black Hoods reach the White Cliffs."

Owen's heart skipped a beat. "What was that?"

"Warling lore. Part of it says that the fire mountain that split the two islands will come to life again when the Black Hood comes to the White Cliffs."

Thoughts of Deros arriving back on Eirn Bol only to be taken prisoner by the Hulin Vipre were too cruel to linger over. He tried to turn his mind to the business at hand. There was a deep rumbling noise that was constant now, and the solid stone beneath his feet rolled and shook, making it hard to stay upright. He returned to his human form, looking about for his guide. "I have to get to Cairn Weal as quickly as possible now. It's a matter of great urgency. Are these shafts still usable?"

Mar'ador nodded. "These little shakes have come now and then, but they have not been this bad. Crale will take you. You must hurry, though. I don't like the feel of this."

"And Efile is still somewhere above," remembered Owen. "Our going will be tricky."

"Not where there's a bear concerned," growled Crale. "I may have a little gray in my coat, but there's not enough of the red hoods in the tunnels to keep us from our path!"

"Can you bring your clans together on short notice?" Owen asked the older bear. "I think we're in for it now. If the Vipre spy has told them in Hulingaad they have been discovered, they will be moving in force before reinforcements can be brought."

Mar'ador walked to the great stone in the center of the immense cavern. "The Warling Stone can be heard by any bear, no matter where he is on these islands. It has been in the code from the beginning that there will come to pass a time when we shall all need to stand together. Even our hot paws like Pran'del will be called upon to deliver."

As Owen watched, the many animals assembled began to disappear down various tunnels, and soon the cavern was empty. Crale made a motion with his head. "If we are to get through the lower shafts to the White Cliffs, we'd best be going. Sometimes these shakes fill the tunnels with the sea, and it takes some time to find a way around."

"Thank you, Mar'ador. We'll meet again." Owen raised his hand in the ancient bear salute, and followed his guide into the dark gloom of the tunnels, now filled with dust and the sound of a distant rumble that for a moment reminded him of a dragon.

Running ahead of Crale was another dim figure that Owen could scarcely make out between the gloom and the dust, but it was clearly a bear, and going in the same direction, toward Cairn Weal.

Owen tried to think of what he would say to Deros's father, and how he would explain being there without her. That thought seemed more frightening to him at the moment than the distant thunder and rolling stone floors.

The Challenge

❋

The old lava flows beneath the two islands were still passable, although it was rough going in places. The steady tremors felt through the cool stone constantly threatened to let the sea in upon them, or block the tunnel altogether. Crale loped steadily along in front of him, and Owen could not help remembering those old memories of bears from his childhood, lumbering along through the woods around Sweet Rock. And from time to time, he caught sight of the other figure ahead of them, staying just out of hailing distance. Owen had asked Crale if he knew who it might be, but the old bear had made no answer, but merely growled over his shoulder to keep up. In the very deepest part of the cavern, there was the sound of rushing water and the smell of salt.

"There is a leak," shot Crale. "That's not good. If we can't get by, we may drown here!"

Owen noted that there was indeed water beginning to flood the floor of the shaft.

"It's not far. We are almost to the old Limanol Gate," went on the bear.

"Whoever's in front of us must have made it," said Owen. "He hasn't been forced back."

"Or he's drowned already," snapped the big animal.

"That's a cheerful thought," returned Owen. It was another few steps before he realized he might be capable of opening the passageway, or protecting them. He moved closer to Crale, and shouted for him to stay near him if the water was too deep, or they were in danger.

"I don't think it's too much for us yet, but it will be if we don't hurry. These shakes have never been this bad before now."

They had reached a portion of the tunnel now that was dimmed almost to blackness, for the inner lights of the walls had tumbled and fallen. Owen removed the sword, and held it

56

out before them. Water was over the tops of his boots, and steadily rising, but they forged ahead, and in another short time were on the other side of the worst of the break in the shaft. The rumble and roar of the sea cascading in was clearly growing louder, and Owen did not need Crale to remind him to hurry on.

The passage began to narrow and slowly climbed now, and the pale golden glow of the light was stronger. He also began to smell fresh air, which tickled his lungs and made him hurry forward.

"Wait," hissed Crale, "there is a sentry!"

"I have the sword," replied Owen, not slowing down.

"Not from the White Cliffs. From the mountain!"

"What?"

Crale slowed to a halt, and gazed ahead into the shadowy distance, where the tunnel bent to the left. "I hope that young sprout has remembered his lessons," grumbled the old bear, half under his breath.

Before Owen could ask him who he was speaking of, a warning cry reached their ears, followed by an even louder rumbling noise. The ground danced madly beneath them, then was quiet, and Crale drew him forward hurriedly.

"We must hurry! I think our shadow has been taken."

"Then you know someone is up there ahead!"

"All along. It is Lanidel. He's trying to rid himself of cubhood, and he thinks this will do it."

"The young guide who was supposed to bring me here?"

"The same."

"What's happened to him?"

"There are many things too old to understand, good chubblet. I think this sentry is one of them."

"But doesn't this sentry guard Cairn Weal from enemies? Why should we fear him?"

Crale slowed to a halt, his ears thrown forward, listening intently. "There are times you can't determine. And times when good is evil, and evil is good. You should have been around enough of your Elders to have begun to understand that by now."

"You sound like an echo of my old teacher," muttered Owen. "He was forever feeding me stories to that effect."

"Shut your eyes a moment and listen. You will begin to feel this sentry I speak of."

Owen looked sidelong at the big animal, then shut his eyes as he was instructed. It was difficult to sort out all the sounds from the outside, for the earth still moved beneath them, and there were noises ahead and behind them, but there was an eerie, ominous silence that lurked behind all the commotion, a stillness that was so deep it threatened to pull Owen into it and drown him beneath the heavy finality of it.

"They say it is one of the Old Ones of Corum Mont left here. I have seen it more than once myself, but I couldn't stay to argue with it."

"What if it has Lanidel?"

"The sentry puts his prisoners inside the walls. You will see. I'm afraid my poor youngster may have landed himself into something I can't help."

"And you were going to send him to guide me," accused Owen. "Then we'd both be finished. Was that your honey-tongued way of getting rid of the outsider?"

Crale studied him a moment, his ears still alert, and listening to sounds beyond the turning of the shaft. "You carry the sword, and say you have been in the Hall of Elders. If you could not save you and your guide from the sentry at the Limanol Gate, then you would be of no use at the White Cliffs. There are other riddles that have to be understood there, as well. When you told me you had been with the Elders, I confess, I believed you knew these things. I did not think to fear for Lanidel."

Stung by his words, Owen yet knew them to be the truth. And it came back to him that there would be no Ephinias or Beran or Gillerman to come to his rescue at the last moment. It would be up to him to remember his lessons, and do what was necessary to get through to warn Alban Ram. They had paced forward slowly as they talked, and he felt the stillness inside him growing ever deeper, and a strange face began to flirt with the edges of his consciousness, wavering into focus as an image of a face in dark, moving water might.

A thin, high humming noise began to make itself heard over the sounds of the earth and water, boring into their hearing with a dull intensity that was maddening. It sounded to Owen like the dragon-weld for a moment, but it was of a different texture, and did not probe his mind in quite the same way. After another few steps, he was challenged by a deep, resonant voice, calling out for their lives.

"Who are you to question me?" snapped Owen, brandishing the sword from Skye aloft. "I am come to help Alban Ram, and am sworn to serve the Lady Rewen and the Order of the Sacred Thistle!"

"Do you know the order of the cup and spoon? Where do they lie?" returned the voice, seemingly from the very bowels of the earth and stone.

Crale raised onto his hindpaws next to Owen, staring about, his ears laid down flat against his huge head. "I've never been called to spell out my heritage," he growled. "What new nonsense is this? And where is my young sprout? Have you harmed him?"

A numbing silence followed, and Owen felt the weight of a thousand arms clasping him tightly, binding him so that he almost dropped the sword. Crale grunted and struggled next to him, but it was of no use, and soon they were imprisoned in solid stone, with nothing but their heads showing clear.

"You have not satisfied me yet. I am the roots of earth, and the Keeper of the Limanol Gate. Only those with the answer to the riddle can find their way past me."

Owen felt the strong pulsing of the sword from Skye coursing through him, and the humming sound began as a pattern of brilliant lights, and soon a picture was spun on the very air in golden silver outlines, of a spreading tree, with two starched white rams beneath it. Owen shouted out his answer.

"The bowl and spoon are under the tree and between the rams. It was the same on my table in Sweet Rock, when Ephinias taught me.

> "Star and moon
>   are come and gone,
> and no one sees the dawn
>   is fading,
> two by two
>   the Old Ones go
> to find the Gates awaiting."

The unmovable pressure of the stone prison seemed to tighten even more, threatening to suffocate him, but then a blinding white explosion of light swallowed them, and Owen looked around to see the old bear sitting on his haunches beside him, his eyes full of wonder and awe.

"It was them," he mumbled beneath his breath.

"Who?" asked the lad.

"An Old One from the Corum Mont."

"That's what your lore told you, wasn't it?"

"But it really *was* one of them," went on Crale. "I never thought I would live to see the day when I would feel that presence myself."

A startled wuff and cough brought their attention to the other bear who had now joined them. Lanidel stood shocked and bewildered.

"Now you've done it," began Crale. "First we warn you about not being too bear-headed about your business, then you find a way to almost have us all clapped up in this stone wall here, just because you want to find your seat among the Warling warriors."

"It wasn't me," began the young bear, but was cut off by the sound of excited voices, and not too far away.

The Sacred Thistle

A Return Voyage

Farther away, far from where Owen Helwin was lost upon the broad back of the sea, Deros stood on deck, gazing at the dark sky. She had turned to go below when she saw the blazing pattern of stars that lit the east. "Stearborn! Rewen!" she cried, hardly daring to believe her eyes. The gruff old Steward was at her side instantly, followed by Rewen.

"I saw, my lady," he replied.

"If you wondered whether there is yet time to reach your father, then there's your sign," said Rewen softly. "If you doubted, then there is proof for your heart."

"The Great Dragon," breathed Deros. "It was said to have shone over Eirn Bol in all its trouble, and that it would forever keep her safe."

"It still shines, my lady," said Stearborn. "Look at how brightly it lights the eastern sky."

"But now we are fewer than we were," returned Deros. "And scattered to the winds."

"The sand that blows away flies but to another place, my lady, it does not disappear. And the oldest law there is states that what is broken apart shall be brought back together again. It is a simple thing that cannot be changed."

"It is not what I have seen," argued the young woman. "I have seen only death and destruction, and the falling away of anything good."

"You look at but a moment on the face of time, Deros. In order to see, you must look at all the players, and finish the play."

"Then we are looking at the finish of this play," she said flatly. "It does not matter so much, for we shall die at the end. What matters now is that we finish like warriors. It won't be written that we passed from the field without honor."

The gruff old soldier hugged her roughly. "Why, you jostle this old war horse with your speech, lass! That sounds as good a line as any Stearborn's ever given his troopers! You are truly fit to wear a Steward's cloak."

"You need not talk of dying yet," rejoined Rewen. "The sign of the dragon is an omen that speaks well for our cause."

As they stood gazing away at the dazzling display of stars, Ulen Scarlett joined them, his face darkened by shadows. "We have visitors, it seems," he said, drawing their attention toward the stern of the Thistle Cloud.

"Well, stuff my boots, we do," shot Stearborn, walking to the taffrail. "Plenty of them, too."

"Are they friendly?" asked Deros, growing anxious as she looked out at the floating shadows against the dark sea.

"It'll be dawn soon," said Rewen. "We'll see plainly enough then who we have as companions."

Ulen stood looking back at the ghostly sails, and did not see when his old hostlers came beside him.

"They is a powerful lot of blighters back there! I hopes for old Lofen's sake they ain't after aslittin' his skull." Lofen had been baffled and worried by Ulen's behavior since he had found the Hulin Vipre ring, and had made a promise to himself to try to break through the growing distance that separated them.

"You'd best look to yourself, my man," replied the young horseman coldly. "These ships may prove your undoing." He spun on his heel and left the rail.

"There ain't no talkin' to him!" said McKandles. "It ain't agoin' to do no good, Lofen. We mights just as well take up a boot and step off to the moon afore he's agoin' to come back to his old self."

"That wasn't no sweet 'tater walk, neither, but it was better than this!" Lofen turned to Deros. "Does you think he's got a slip of a chance, ma'am? Just to smooth old Lofen's ticker a bit?"

Deros tried to reassure the upset hostler, but without much conviction.

While they had been talking, the Thistle Cloud rounded up and returned the way she had come, gliding silently back toward the fleet behind. As they sailed among the many ships, Findlin and Lorimen were beside themselves in their excitement, and both kept clapping the young Enlid heartily upon the back.

"Flags from ewery port along the Sound," shouted Lorimen. "Look at that! We'we hit a load of gossip here, my lads! Our ears won't recower in time for Laching Day!"

Findlin danced a little jig, throwing the young lad wildly about with his mad gyrations.

Deros had gone to the rail, and stood studying the assembled fleet. "Aren't they afraid they may draw attention this way? The Purge can't be far away."

"The Thistle Cloud is beyond the sight of her enemies, but these ships risk being discovered when the morning comes. We should tell them of their danger." Rewen's face was drawn, as though from great fatigue. "They shall have a surprise in store when they're hailed from the empty sea."

"It won't be completely empty. We have land dead ahead," Coglan called. "It's Marlintop, in the Horinfal Straits! There's good ground for holding, and room enough to call in three or four of these other vessels to gam, if we like. We might find the latest news, and hear how things stand between here and Eirn Bol."

Findlin was pointing to one of the ships with a distinctive red and gray pennant flying from her main mast. "It's Shere Dal! I'd know that wessel in the bottom part of the night's heart! Look to it, Lorimen! Let's see if we can shout him up!"

His friend squinted in the dim starlight, trying to see the outline of the graceful craft in question. "She's from Fionten, right enough," Lorimen concluded. "There's some others, too!" He pointed at another cluster of ships farther behind.

"The firesnakes hawe grown lazy to let these prizes escape," growled Findlin. "It will spell the end of them, by the Conch's Windlass, or I'll take my time drinking down the Widow's Reel."

The wind had picked up as they neared the first island of the Straits, and Coglan had the sheets eased, and bore off on a course that would allow him to round the point. "It's called

The Pike,'' he said. ''We'll round here, and drop our hook in the cove on the north side. We can set signals at the top there, to call any of our friends who want to meet.''

Stearborn's expression was guarded, but he was obviously upset. ''I'd give a month's ration of ale to find enough horses to mount a troop of Stewards. I don't relish the idea of having to fight afoot.''

''Eirn Bol is known for her fine mounts,'' said Deros. ''We have some of the swiftest horses of all.''

''All the better,'' muttered Jeremy. ''The Gortlander seems to have a love of fast horses when it comes to finding himself near a fight.''

Ulen glared, but remained silent. His hands were hidden in his cloak, but Deros sensed the rage that burned in him.

Deros glared until Jeremy bowed apologetically. ''Forgive me, my lady. It won't happen again.''

''Ulen?'' demanded Deros.

He glared angrily about, then bent stiffly, but did not speak.

Rewen had Coglan anchor close in, a short distance from a white, sandy beach that formed a small cup between the rocks. ''This looks like a good place to set up a camp ashore,'' she said. ''Findlin, you and your men can set up the signals to the others, and watch for any signs of the Purge. We would be best served if we could give these other vessels the protection of the Thistle Cloud. It would not last as long, but it would give us a chance to reach Eirn Bol undetected.''

''Could you do that, my lady?'' asked Stearborn.

''I could do it easily, if we were along a coast I know, and could find the Old Ones. But for now, we shall take small pieces of the Thistle Cloud aboard the other ships, and unite them with the ordinary wood. That will carry them for a time as though their ships had been constructed as our own stout vessel.''

McKandles, who had been looking out over the bow railing, suddenly let out a yelp. ''Them other ships is acomin' in here with us! Hoof it up, Lofen, and get them pins arunnin' and bring us our arms!''

''Hold, hold,'' cried Coglan to the pair. ''We're looking to meet these vessels! It's all right!''

''You fellows seem honed a little fine at the edges,'' chided Stearborn. ''Took too long to sea, and kept spoiling for a fight, eh? Good lads! You'll ride with my bunch, if we ever get solid ground beneath us again, and proper mounts.''

Ulen Scarlett laughed aloud scornfully. ''You'd serve yourself better by finding other riding mates. If they don't kill you in your sleep, they'll desert you in the first hard scrape.''

''You is so high and mighty now, Ulen Scarlett, just a'cause you found that Hoolin ring you is awearin'! But you mark my say, you ain't agoin' to come to no good end a'cause of it, and that don't make old Kandles no happier for the thought.''

''I don't wonder,'' replied Ulen. ''You have both proven your loyalty is not to be trusted, even by one who took you in when you were starving on the Reed Plains. Our score will be settled one day.'' The young horseman's eyes were dark and unreadable.

McKandles looked confused and troubled, and turned away abruptly.

Rewen interrupted the argument with a stern look. ''They are putting the skiffs over now. You two can go with the Archaels,'' she said to the two friends.

''Lofen Tackman ain't atakin' no guff, Mister Up-snoot! You is abendin' that snout of yours all out of whack now that you is awearin' that Hoolin's ring, but it's amakin' you plumb barmy. You is a fine fool that you ain't after aseein' that!''

''Go on with you,'' ordered Stearborn gruffly. ''We need good eyes to watch. Today is to be an important day, if we are to meet with those others who will sail with us to Eirn Bol.''

The boats were lowered away, and the shore parties rowed the few yards to the beach, and were soon seen clambering the high ground that led to the top of the point facing the rest of the fleet. Ulen Scarlett watched darkly as the Archaels made up a signal fire, and waved and called to their companions at sea. His mind was clouded by the same faceless fear he felt when he wore the ring too long, but he had been unable to remove it of late. There were visions there as well, of a fortress high on a cliff, and faces peered into his mind, probing, but the promises were always there, and he had begun to see an image of himself, wrapped in a purple cloak with a great coat of arms across it, and beside him was his queen, bowing and pledging her service to him. He turned from his dream to the young woman next to him, and smiled coldly.

Meetings on the Straits

One of the first of the crews from the gathered fleet was an old friend of Findlin, named Culin, aboard a shapely craft called Boride Col. There were handshakes all around, and a good deal of backslapping by Lorimen, as the news was given and received of what had taken place since they had been separated by a fateful storm that had sunk two of their ships. The skipper of the Archael vessel grew serious as he talked to Rewen and Coglan, who moved about the deck, touching the wood with the small leather sack of sawdust they had brought from the Thistle Cloud. He told them of what ships he had seen, and how many sightings he had made of the firesnakes.

"They hawe been active, but I don't know what new trick they're up to. We hawen't seen a trace of them since we'we entered these waters."

"It does appear out of character for them," agreed Rewen. "They attack openly for a time, and it seems as though a renewed war with them is at hand, and now they disappear."

"I don't like it," grumbled Findlin. "You don't find it in a snake's nature to burn and loot at will, and then just grow tired of it and retire. I hawe newer known nature to be so perwerse as when it made those things, and I'we newer known of a time when a wolf would stop and turn about when it came to lambs and his supper!"

Ulen Scarlett, listening to the conversation silently, twisted the Rhion Stone on his finger, following the orders of the persistent, soothing voice in his head. The Archaelian had finished speaking, and Coglan had the attention of the others, making marks on the ships's chart spread out before him.

"There are two ways we may reach Eirn Bol from here." He indicated the routes with his finger. "Wind and tide favor this course, but it is the well-known way everyone goes. It might be more closely watched."

"Those flying devils could be waiting for us to knot up in a bunch, and fry us in a lot," suggested Stearborn, tugging at his beard. "One of the first rules of engagement is that you never show too broad a flank before you close with your enemy. Gives them too much chance to do you a mischief before you ever get in range!"

Coglan nodded. "That's where this little sack of wood chips comes in. With a little help from Rewen, we can have the fleet out of sight until we could come within striking distance of Eirn Bol."

"My friend has his misgiwings well placed," joined Lorimen. "I newer trust an enemy who doesn't behawe as he's supposed to! There's an old Archaelian tune that's sung about the man who's sworn to kill you, but only sends you gifts. That's wery disturbing, if you take my meaning."

Lofen and McKandles had come topside, and listened to the others for a moment. They watched Ulen, who never took his eyes off them.

"It don't make no sense what's been ahappenin' to him," whispered Lofen. "We ain't never been so thick as mates, and I ain't never thoughts I would be agin' my own, but I is astartin' to believe that there ring is aborin' into his head with thoughts that is plum agin' us and these here folks who is his friends."

"We is agoin' to have to snatch it back," agreed his companion. "We has already been adoin' that, but they went and give it back. I still ain't been able to unbridle that mulhash."

"I just don't get the point of this here dart and plunge! First we has him atalkin' to us, his own hostlers, like we was one of them Leech bandits, and then he is all honey and cake and amakin' up to us."

"Hush, you two," ordered Rewen, who had overheard them. "You were doing nicely as you were. We have need of your silence in this. Give me your promise you won't say anything more." Her beauty was marked by the sadness of her eyes, but the two Gortlanders lowered their heads, muttering their agreement.

"This route is used by Railan Dramm. We hawen't sighted any of his ships, so he may be in Hulingaad, but we can't count on it." It was Culin who spoke.

"Who is he, sir?" asked Stearborn.

"The worst sort. He came from a good family on the Delos Sound, had all the opportunities in life he could hawe wanted.

He came into his first wessel when he was not full grown, and had three ships of his own before his Marking Birthday. Then something happened that we hawe newer quite fathomed. The Black Hood raided all up and down that part of the world, and one of the raiders kidnapped his family, or so the story goes. Since then, he has preyed on the merchants who feed the war going on from the Delos Sound out into the South Roaring. Tales of him began to grow more bloodthirsty. Now he's known as the Red Scorpion, among other things.''

''We'we dealt with Railan Dramm a time or two,'' went on Findlin. ''Our bad luck was that we didn't send him to the bottom with all his scurwy crew.''

Jeremy sat at the rail oiling his scabbard and wiping down his sword and dagger. ''Would this pirate be a threat to so many ships? Surely he wouldn't dare to confront us all?''

''The threat he poses is not so much from him and his men, but who he has cast his lot with. Wherewer he is, you can count on a hunting pack behind him. If he sights us, we can count on the full fleet of the Wipre being down our throats in a flash.''

''No one would be the wiser if we had him hoisted on our brace-trees,'' growled Stearborn.

Findlin laughed. ''The fleets of all the settlements up and down this stretch of water hawe been trying to lengthen his neck for a long turn before this. It's almost as though he disappears right out from under our noses.''

Rewen spoke up again. ''He may have a leaf of one of the Golvane, from the same place the wood came that was used to construct the Thistle Cloud. It would allow him to disappear for a time. It's a trick easily learned, if you are friendly with someone who knows of it. It's possible he has learned how to use it, but so have we.''

''Then I hope your plan will work, my lady. It will be a long haul right down the Gullet to the Hulin Wipre and their cohorts! If this sawdust doesn't do its work, it will mean the end of many another seaman from Fionten, damn our eyes!''

''We shall hawe our chance to ewen those old scores with Railan Dramm, or I'll know the why of it,'' vowed Lorimen, clutching his sword so tightly his knuckles were white beneath his cloak. ''We're close enough now to do some damage to the Wipre, and all who follow them. I say we skate down that backway, and catch them looking for us elsewhere! Then we can see the mettle they're made of! By Rhorin's Jib Sheet, we'll find the place they're soft, and put our best steel next to their black hearts!''

The Archael's enthusiasm had fired up Stearborn, who now paced about excitedly, his sword drawn. Ulen Scarlett, still standing beside Deros, raised his voice to be heard over the roar of approval that greeted the sailor's speech. ''You'll find the way laid with snares, if you try that trick. Who is to say your ships will stay invisible long enough to reach close enough? You'll lose half your fleet trying to toy about with outwitting these foxes. Doesn't logic argue that the backway is exactly the route they would be watching? It's the way they think. They wouldn't dream of sailing straight for a mark, for all to see. If you just sail straight in, that's your best chance. Stealth and treachery, that's their flag, and it's flying plainly enough for all to read here!''

Deros looked at Rewen, searching her face. ''He does make a point of their tactics,'' she said thoughtfully.

''A valid point, and well taken,'' replied Rewen. ''It will be of no matter if the power of the Golvane stays strong enough. We have enough wood chips to do most of the ships here, but we might do more if we had some piece of the living trees. It's too bad we aren't close enough to harvest more of the leaves.''

''What is this Golvane you speak of, my lady?'' asked Jeremy, his handsome features puzzled.

''An Old One, good Steward. One of the ancient race of beings who has been here since these Lower Meadows have existed.'' Rewen moved a hand before her, and a shower of sparkling stars whirled into a shimmering picture that hung on the clear morning air, slowly coming to focus on a high cliff overlooking a tranquil blue sea. All along the edge of the land, great trees grew upward to heights that seemed to almost touch the very hem of heaven. As the companions watched, fascinated, they became aware of a low droning noise, almost a chant, that grew stronger as they listened, and caught the deep, sonorous rhythm of it. ''They would help us, if we could but reach them,'' said Rewen.

Ulen Scarlett's face grew contorted with rage, but he held himself in check, fighting for control of his voice. The hammering in his head was incessant now, and his temples felt as though hot lead was pounding behind his eyes. The ring burned into the flesh of his hand, but he could not remove it. His hand gripped Deros's arm until she cried out in pain, which brought Jeremy and Judge to her side.

The shimmering, floating vision of the tall cliffs and trees vanished instantly.

The horseman held a hand to his head, sneering into the faces of the two young Stewards. "I seem to have invoked the wrath of these two pups. Maybe they will oblige me in helping me remember what it is I have said to get their dander up so high?"

"We'll see what you remember when you taste a foot of good Steward steel," shot Jeremy, beside himself with rage. Deros had grabbed his sword arm, and he was trying to gently shove her aside when Stearborn waded into the middle of them, catching the two Steward troopers by the scruff of their necks, and carrying them out of harm's way. Ulen had concealed a short stabbing dagger in the folds of his cloak, and brandished it now behind the old commander's back. Coglan's blow was so swift no one saw him strike, and the knife went skittering across the deck and into the water below.

"There'll be none of that aboard the Thistle Cloud," growled Stearborn. "I don't know how they do it as seamen, but a Steward runs a war camp the same, whether he's on the back of his horse, or on one of these floating contraptions! Jeremy Thistlewood, I'm shocked to my gaiters to see you behave in such a manner. Chellin Duchin will hear of this if you ever give me cause to set you to rights again! And you, Judge Collander! Look at what you've let yourself into! You've been growing more lax the longer this voyage has gone on! I'll be badly surprised if you aren't worse than an ordinary citizen by the time we land and get back to a business we understand better than this!" Stearborn's voice hissed and creaked from his old throat wound, and his beard stood straight out before him. Deros had never seen him in such a state, except when he was gone full bore in battle. No one spoke for a moment, until McKandles, standing behind Coglan, announced to all that another party of boarders was alongside.

"Skittles and shiverdabs on all this tralahoo," burst in Lofen. "If we wasn't bundled up on this bucket, we would be ahoofin' it out through no tellin' what sorts of critters and varmits! If we has to be agoin' on to the Lady Deros's home corral, then I says we just starts aputtin' all them windsheets up and gets on with it. This here sittin' still ain't agoin' to get us nothing but more barn-sour, and fuller of rotten blood at everybody!''

Jeremy was trying to explain himself to Stearborn, but the old Steward would have none of it, and sent the two young troopers ashore to get them out of his sight. As they were rowed to the small beach, they watched in fascination as the spell Rewen had called up followed behind their skiff, spinning about them in rainbow colors until they grew dizzy with trying to follow the brilliant patterns that fell all about them, making the cool autumn sunlight dim and pale when at last it returned.

"I don't like the feel of this," said Jeremy, shaking his head. "There's something wrong in Ulen's head. He's gotten stranger every day."

"Do you think Stearborn will tell Chellin?" asked Judge, more worried about what his old commander would do.

"I don't think so. He's not that way. I don't know what his idea is about the Gortlander, but the problem has crossed his mind, I wager. Owen argued against him being along, and now what? We have Ulen, and Owen is lost!"

Judge looked away in the direction they had just sailed from. "I never would have dreamed it would come to this. Owen Helwin lost at sea, and you and I aboard the Lady Rewen's own Thistle Cloud. This shouldn't be the way it ends."

"It is not an end," reminded Jeremy. "All we know is that Owen is not here at the moment. I don't believe in my heart he's really lost. It wouldn't be right to have Ulen Scarlett left with us, and Owen gone."

A heavy silence fell over the two as they remembered the anguish and grief that was just below the surface. At that moment, Hamlin called to them to wait for him, and they watched with interest as he was rowed ashore to join them. He was too excited to remain seated, and started speaking before he reached them, shouting excitedly. "We're going on tomorrow! Coglan says we're to try to reach a coast where there are some trees that will help us!"

"We know that," answered Judge crossly. "We heard."

"But you didn't hear the end of it, Mr. Big Ears!"

"Then tell me."

"There are supposed to be the last of the Dreamers there. We may get to see the elven clans again."

"I think our meeting before was enough for me," replied Jeremy. "They weren't too fond of us, as I remember."

"But the times are changed, and they are said to leave the dream-dust there."

"That was only a story," reminded Judge. "You've gone on about that ever since you heard it."

"I want to see if what they say about it is true. We could make our fortunes with it, if it's there!"

"What? What nonsense are you spouting, my good fellow? A Steward is never rich nor poor, but serves his Elder."

"Who told you of the dream-dust again, Hamlin? Where have you been putting your nose that it doesn't belong now?"

"The horseman. He was telling the Lady Deros of it."

Jeremy's knuckles grew white from his clenched fists, and he glared across the water toward where the invisible boat lay.

"I wish Chellin were here," said Judge wistfully. "He might crack our heads, but I've always known him to be fair. And he knows something of the Dreamers."

"I would wish us all here, with the exception of Ulen," snapped Jeremy.

"I don't want to be the one to cast him away," argued Hamlin. "Where would we be if we left him, and it came time for him to pull his own weight and he weren't there? There's more to come of this yet. I can feel it in my bones."

"You and your bones," snorted Judge. "All they're good for is to tell us about a change in the weather. If we didn't have Scarlett thrown about our necks like a millstone, there would be less concern all around about what and where and what if!"

"What do your bones say about our supper, Hamlin? Is there anything in the wind there? Travel cake and ale for us tonight, or empty guts and rainwater? I think we should get back before they eat our share. The good Scarlett may be plotting to starve us all next." Jeremy's thoughts turned again to the brash Gortlander. A strange ripple of unease passed over him as lightly as a winter shadow, leaving him chilled and restless in the faint breeze that had picked up from the east. That had happened once before on the morning of the attack on Sweet Rock, and again as they fought the Olgnite at the entrance to the Ellerhorn Fen. It came again, more distinctly, and he wrapped his cloak tightly around him, and tried to think of the warm south, in the friendly settlements that used to line the rivers and coast of The Line.

Spies from Hulingaad

❋

By midmorning, the call had been sent out to all the ships of the gathered fleet of a great council to take place that night. The Lady Rewen and Coglan disappeared below on the Thistle Cloud, taking Deros with them, and were absent throughout most of the day. A faint band of stars had come out as the twilight darkened, and the sky above the ship was clear and bright, with a sharp easterly wind.

"This would be a good night for raiding," observed Findlin. "You can see from here to the Jugengate, and there's no hiding the fact that we're sitting here like birds to be plucked."

"Here now, you make me nervous, you old seafloat! I don't need to be made any more upset!"

"No one can see the Thistle Cloud, but that's no matter to the others," said Stearborn. "I think that's what they're doing below, making plans so that we can see to the other boats."

"You'd think they would trust their own comrades," grumbled Ulen.

"We shall know what they'we been up to soon enough, good horseman. Lorimen and I have found these secret meetings always mean a long pull on the oars, one way or another. You would be well adwised to have your sea kit ready, and stand by to mowe quickly, once they'we come up from their little gam."

Along the beach, scattered watchfires lit the sands, dotting the darkness with flickering red eyes. Behind them, the gathered ships rode to their anchors quietly, deeper shadows on the inky sea. A faint movement from farther away caught Findlin's eye, and he pointed it out to his friend.

"I can't make out anything there. Maybe it's another wessel come to join us."

"Too small to be one of the trading craft, or a corsair. Looked to be just a lugger."

"Are there locals hereabouts?" asked Stearborn. "Maybe someone here wanted to see what all the fuss was about."

"Hawen't been any locals in these parts since before the firesnakes," replied Lorimen. "Good fishing, and pleasant enough to hawe as shelter, but that always draws the raiders and the riffraff from everywhere. I can't recall a settlement through here since I'we been a tadwick."

"Not for a long time before that, either," added Lorimen.

"We might have a look," suggested Stearborn. "Probably nothing, but I like to know the lay of things about me before I put my head down to sleep." Jeremy and Hamlin were not far away, talking quietly near the stern. The old commander called to them. "You two make yourselves useful and get one of Findlin's men to row you around the boats here to look them over. Let me know if you find anything amiss."

"What will we look for?" asked Hamlin. "We don't know any of these clans. How would I know if someone belongs?"

"That's why I told you to take someone who does! Now mind you don't rile me, my boy. You know how much easier it is when you humor the old warhorse! Just do as I say." Stearborn's tone was light, but there was an underlying urgency that sent the two young Stewards hurrying to find a boatman, strapping on their weapons as they went.

"No sense in trying to talk to him when he's like this," conceded Jeremy. "I've seen mules who have a more lenient way of thinking."

"I wonder if the dream-dust would soften him up?" mused Hamlin aloud. "It's said to be powerful enough to affect anyone."

Jeremy laughed shortly. "Are you still on about that fire-tale? I thought you'd grown past that, Olenbroke! You surprise me."

"You wouldn't be so smug, if you thought twice about anything. It might mean a whole new way for the Stewards to operate."

"How do you mean?" asked Jeremy, lowering himself into the rowing skiff, which was held steady by a sailor off the Thistle Cloud.

"Think of it," went on Hamlin excitedly. "We have the dream-dust with us when we go back to The Line. All the enemies we have will come to our side, and there will be an end of fighting, and trying to keep our borders safe."

Jeremy nodded, holding out a hand to his friend. "Just like

that? No whys, or wherefores, just a wonderful time and a beautiful life awaiting us all?''

"You know I don't mean like that," argued Hamlin. "I know it will take some time, and I know nothing is ever as easy as you say. But after we have the upper hand there, it would be simple enough to invite all the other Elders from the borders to a council. We could give it to them then.''

"And if they didn't want this stuff?''

Hamlin's face took on a shocked look. "Why would anyone refuse it? Would you?''

The sailor rowing them handed his way down the side of the Thistle Cloud, and placed his oars in the locks. "Which way?'' he asked.

Jeremy pointed. "We'll start there.''

"Well!'' demanded Hamlin.

"I don't know. It would depend. I don't know why you're so fired up about this now. It doesn't seem like you.''

"If you mean why do I listen to the Gortlander, I'll tell you! His tale has a truth to it I recall from somewhere back along the way. It was when we met the elves with Chellin. There was talk then of this dream-dust.''

"I don't remember anything like that at all.''

"It was at fire afterward. Chellin himself spoke of it.''

Jeremy thought back to the time in question. "He always goes on so about everything. I might well have missed it. You know how he loves to ride us about history and lessons we've missed.''

"He spoke of the spells the elves could do, and this potion that they had to give to anyone who discovered them. It made everything change.''

Jeremy's face had taken on a sad look. "It doesn't seem to have brought them anything but grief. Do you recall any happy elves? Those we saw were not exactly overjoyed.''

"But when we were with them, the feeling was wonderful.''

"You mean you haven't felt good enough about all this? Hamlin Olenbroke, I'm surprised at you!''

"There wouldn't be anything wrong with having the change to look forward to,'' insisted Hamlin.

The skiff pulled from behind a vessel from the ruined fleet of Fionten, and the sailor who rowed them pulled alongside to talk with her crew, and introduced the two Stewards as heroes of Sweet Rock.

"Wery good to make your acquaintance. Good to hawe stout

hearts with us on this woyage. We may hawe lost Fionten, but we'll awenge her, and start anew on the bed of her ashes.''

"Hear, hear, me hearties! That's well enough spoken, but we hawe work enough to do between now and then. Giwe us a hand, and help us see if there's a wolf loose among these sheep here. We may hawe a spy come to see if we hawe tongues here to spill our secrets.''

There was a good deal of movement aboard the boat, which was called the Kattrel Nialin, and before long, two more skiffs full of the Archaelians had joined them in their search.

"I wouldn't mind these fellows so much, if they could only speak plainly," said Hamlin. "It drives me short of my wits trying to find out what they're saying.''

"I don't mind their talk as long as they can handle their weapons," replied Jeremy. "And they've proven they can do that well enough.''

The two companions were interrupted momentarily by a loud hiss of warning from one of the searchers who had just joined them.

"What is it?'' called Jeremy.

A moment passed as they neared a large skiff tied onto the stern of one of the later arrivals of the large fleet in the Straits. "Nothing. I thought this wessel might be a Wipre scow.''

"Vipre? Here?'' echoed Hamlin.

"Marks of one of the other settlements on her transom, though. I guess someone picked her up to replace one of their own skiffs.''

"Let's check around to make sure," said Jeremy. "Call up the watch aboard, and let's ask.''

After a few minutes wait, a sleepy young man emerged on deck of the craft, and was questioned about her skiffs.

"They are all tied off in the stern," the young man replied.

"Hawe you picked up strays? Any boats from captured wessels?''

"We have to keep ourselves shipshape as best we can since we were attacked by the fireworm. We have to take what we can get. If it's Hulin or Archael, it's no difference to us, if it floats.''

"There we hawe it," said the sailor, turning to the Stewards. "That's probably what your captain saw, one of the captured wessels mowing around on these roads.''

"Let's go back," said Jeremy tiredly. "I think we've rowed around out here quite enough. I don't like being too far from

Ulen now, either. He's got something up his cloak sleeve, and I want to be close by to see what.''

"The dream-dust," voiced Hamlin. "He says it's there, and if I know him, he'll try to have it all to himself, if we're not careful. He has that Hulin ring of his, and I see how he looks at us, like we were going to try to take it from him. He has plans to steal the dream-dust, as sure as my name is Olenbroke!"

"He has more in his head than just that, my friend. Never short shrift the redoubtable Scarlett. Owen said all along he would end up betraying us to the enemy. He has done so every time he found himself in harm's way."

Hamlin pointed to the low hills that rose up behind the gathered fleet. "Looks like another signal there."

"I wonder who they're trying to reach now? Can you see more ships?"

"Too dark to tell," replied the sailor. "It wouldn't be wise to try nawigating these roads without daylight."

"Let's go report to Stearborn. Maybe somebody knows what's going on."

Jeremy felt eyes peering at his back as they rowed toward the Thistle Cloud, but when he turned to look there was no one to be seen aboard the ship they had just hailed. The feeling persisted until they suddenly bumped against the unseen hull of their own vessel, and scrambled onto the deck.

After their report was given, Stearborn clasped his hands behind him, gazing out over the water at the gathered fleet. "With all these ships, it would be easy to slip in among us to do your spying and get away clean."

"But how would they tell anyone?" asked Hamlin. "We could easily stop anyone from leaving."

"They wouldn't hawe to be in a hurry," said Findlin. "When we leawe here, they could just bear off to wherewer they want."

"Have they come up from below? Do they have any ideas about it?" Jeremy was drinking a lukewarm cup of tea the cook had handed him, making faces at its bitterness.

Stearborn shook his head. "They haven't stirred since you've been gone. I'm beginning to think they're tangling with a problem that doesn't have a handle."

"The Gortlander," said Lorimen softly, nodding his head slowly.

"Do you think they're really trying to decide what to do

about him?'' persisted Jeremy. ''Why, it doesn't make sense! After all this time, and they're only now deciding he's dangerous?''

''We've known that all along,'' snorted Stearborn. ''You young bucks leap off to the strangest starts! He's been useful to us, if you haven't stopped to think. That ring of his is broadcasting our whereabouts to our enemies right now.''

Jeremy paled, and he began easing his small dagger out of his belt. ''Then I'll take him myself.''

''Fah! Look at you! You'd just as soon have a block of wood atop your shoulders for all the thinking you do!'' Stearborn took the knife from his young charge and laid it on the railing. ''A good thing to clean your fingernails, but not a good weapon for so dangerous an enemy. You must remember what you've been taught, youngster!''

Jeremy hadn't heard himself called that in such a long time, he was taken aback and stood still, looking at the old commander. ''Chellin called me that sometimes, when he wasn't too displeased with me.''

''We'we done this with our eyes open,'' explained Findlin. ''If the Black Hood has thought we were on our way to them, they weren't likely to try to attack while we were still so far away. If they think we're bound for their backyard, they'll be tempted to wait upon us.''

''Which giwes us time to prepare a surprise,'' continued Lorimen. ''They'll hawe tea ready for the small wessel Thistle Cloud, but they'll get the fleet of the Southern Seas!'' The Archael laughed a deep, contagious laugh, and doubled over in his high spirits. ''The fleet nobody sees!''

It was the note they went to their bunks on, and it was only much later that a warning whistle, low and barely audible, rippled the soft darkness, sounding like no more than a man's snoring. Jeremy had been unable to sleep, and had gone topside to take a turn of the deck. At first, he had detected nothing, merely hearing the surf in the inlet a few hundred yards away, and still being wound up in his own thoughts, he had almost missed it again. He could not say what had pricked his ears to the sound, but it seemed as deadly to him as the sound of an arrow slicing its way through the air toward his heart. Alert in every fiber of his being, he crouched behind the railing, and searched the dark shore beyond, now illuminated only here and there by the random watchfires of the shore parties. There was nothing to be seen there, but when he went to the seaward side of the Thistle Cloud, he found what had troubled him. There, not more than an arm's reach from him, was a small sailing skiff, its mast and boom lowered, attached to a rope that ran around the stern-post of the vessel anchored next to the Thistle Cloud.

Listening for any further noise, Jeremy slipped his dagger free and began to crawl soundlessly toward the boat, keeping to the shadows.

Another low whistle came, followed by whispers. He inched closer, trying to hear what was said.

Another Loss

The waves rippling against the sides of the boat seemed thunderous to Jeremy, trying to hear what the man in the skiff was saying. A faint outline of another figure lay close to the deck, holding the painter of the small skiff. The voices fluttered in the darkness like velvet, but he could not make out the words.

Creeping on his hands and knees, Jeremy moved closer to the two shadows, ears straining to pick up a clue as to why anyone aboard the vessels of the fleet would be using the darkness to cloak their meeting. Still unable to hear without the surf ringing in his ears, Jeremy lowered himself quietly over the side and, swimming underwater, reached the side of the boat where the men were at their secret business. Surfacing a scant foot away from the skiff, he instantly recognized one of the speakers as Ulen Scarlett, who was whispering at the moment.

"You can tell your captain that we have the route plan now. We shall be sailing tomorrow for Eirn Bol. The fleet will be going straight up the Gullet, whatever that means. Are you familiar with the term?"

"The Gullet is what seamen refer to when they talk of the easiest route to and from the Horinfal Straits," replied the man. Jeremy could not remember ever hearing his voice before, and at least not in a whisper.

"Then that's where they shall be. Can you get back to your ships in time?"

"I'll be back. Railan Dramm is somewhere about, too. We'll be ready."

"Good. You'd better leave now. I have to get back before they miss me."

"We'll be waiting," whispered the man. "It's been a long turning since the fleet has had so many ships to pluck!"

Ulen clenched his ring hand tightly against his side, feeling the sudden wave of hot energy that coursed through him. A movement in the water caught his attention, and he shushed the man, dropping the line to the skiff, and shoving the man away from the boat. Without another word, the man unshipped his sweep and moved silently out into the darkness behind the shadows of the other boats.

Jeremy moved slowly along the vessel until he was far enough from Ulen to swim back to the Thistle Cloud, but he didn't see the small punt glide quickly past him on the opposite side, and was taken by surprise by Ulen when he pulled himself aboard on the rope he had left trailing over the stern. He hardly had time to lift an arm to ward off the blow, and then suddenly he was in the water floating, wondering what it would be like to drown. He knew he must be bleeding, but his mind was far from that thought, thinking about Deros, and if she would miss him as much as she had Owen. It seemed strange to him to think that he and Hamlin and Judge had just been talking of Owen, and the dream-dust not long before.

An odd sensation crept over him then, and he began to grow faint. Colored lights circled above him in the black vault of heaven, but then he realized they were stars. He was trying to force himself to swim to the beach, when hands reached into the water and dragged him over the prow of a boat that had a carved head that he could have sworn was a swan. Nobody spoke, but he was aware of a face that smiled at him from beneath a bright yellow hood. There was a faint note of a reed pipe then, that grew stronger as he listened, and the music followed him into the warm darkness of his dream.

Aboard the Thistle Cloud, Stearborn had rousted out Judge and Hamlin and, together with Lorimen and Findlin, had scoured the ship from stem to stern, searching for their missing comrade.

"He can't just have upped and swam to Eirn Bol," grumbled the old Steward anxiously. "Scour this bucket until you find him!"

Hamlin and Judge, familiar with Stearborn from long hours spent in dangerous places, recognized the sense of urgency there, and hurried off to carry out his order.

Coglan had come on deck to see what the commotion was, just as the Archaels prepared to search the area surrounding the ship. "What's passed?" he asked. "Are we missing someone?"

"One of my men," answered Stearborn. "I'd rather have a dozen other things come to pass right now than to lose that lad. He's an aggravation of the worst sort, but I've come to like having him about to torment me."

"I hasn't seen no sign of Master Jeremy, but I was ahearin' some mumbly sort of gab a while back, and then there was a scrabblin' of some sorts on deck, then a keploosh right next to my ear, like. I thoughts maybe it was that lop-eared mule of a cook athrowin' out his slop, but there wasn't no thumpin' or bangin' around on them pots of his." McKandles stopped to pop his knuckles, which caused Lofen to put his hands over his ears.

"One of these days you is agoin' to do that, and old Lofen Tackman is agoin' to come slat-sides to the wind and tromple you plumb to nubbins!"

Before his friend could comment, Ulen Scarlett came from below, following Deros. "What's happened here?" he asked, pretending to be wiping sleep from his eyes.

Deros went to Stearborn. "What is it? Rewen said we've lost someone else."

"Jeremy is out of pocket. I'm sure he'll turn up. He may have gone ashore to stretch his legs."

"He's never without Hamlin or Judge. Where are they?"

"Looking for him."

The Archaels had lowered themselves over the rail of the Thistle Cloud, and were carefully probing the water near the vessel with their oars, moving slowly in a line toward where they knew the next ship was anchored. Ulen had watched through narrowed eyes as the pair searched, although he yawned again loudly, and made as though he were returning to his bunk.

"I think the good Thistlewood is quite capable of keeping his own hours. If we're to leave tomorrow for the coast where the Golvane are, I shall need my rest.'' He had felt Deros's eyes upon him, but he never returned her gaze. Rewen stood at the bow of the boat, looking at something away in the direction of the horizon.

The two young Stewards arrived just at that moment and reported no trace of Jeremy, although they had found a rope dangling over the stern of the Thistle Cloud, and discovered what appeared to be fresh blood there. Stearborn's brow darkened, and his eyes took on the cold, hard look Hamlin and Judge had seen so often in Chellin Duchin, when their losses had been heavy.

''Show me,'' he growled softly, and followed after the two. The rest of the ship's party brought up the rear, except for Ulen, who stood at the rail, still gazing out toward the faint silver-white lights on the beach. Deros had lingered a moment, studying him.

''Do you think it's the Dreamers?'' she asked suddenly.

''It hardly seems likely. They have no reason to show themselves. From all I've ever heard, they're secretive and ill-tempered.'' His face was calm, but she detected a tautness to his voice.

''I have never heard them described as ill-tempered.''

''It depends upon who you hear talk of them,'' he said shortly.

''It would be helpful to us, if they did come to aid us. We need everyone we can call to our cause. Even if they're ill-tempered.''

''I'm not so sure I'd want their clans as allies. There are stories about that say they vanish just when you need them most.''

A cry from the stern drew Deros away, and she soon joined the others there. Stearborn and Coglan were kneeling beside a bright patch of still damp blood.

''Someone's taken a blow here, no doubt of it,'' confirmed the old Steward. ''I wish Findlin would hurry his search. A man wounded badly might not be able to stay afloat long.''

''Do you think it might be Jeremy?'' Deros asked, gazing into the dark face of the water that lapped at the boat. First it had been Owen who had gone, and now Jeremy, she thought, struggling to hold back her tears.

''If it's the lad, he won't just roll over and drown,'' said

Stearborn firmly. "He's a Line Steward, and our code is not one that allows a man to give up without a fight of it!"

"Here's Lorimen," cried Enlid, waiting at the rail to throw a line to the two Archaels as they came alongside, so they could find the hidden ship. "What news?"

"There's no one in the water," replied Findlin. "You can rest easy on that score. If he's on one of the other wessels, then we'll hawe to call up a roll and check them one by one."

"You won't find him on one of the other ships of our fleet here," said Rewen, still watching the silver-white glow along the beach, which had grown fainter, as if moving away into the distance.

"You mean you think he's dead?" asked Ulen anxiously.

Rewen shook her head. "I mean, I think he's not with any of those gathered here. I'm not sure what has occurred, but the presence of the Dreamers has been felt strongly here. Deros knows of another such one who was helped by those clans in a time of grave danger."

"Are you speaking of Elita? They brought her back from death after she was burned with dragonfire."

Ulen's heart fell, and the voices in his inner ear began again more urgently. It was difficult now for him to discern the real from the voices he heard, and he had taken to holding his hands to his temples and pressing, hoping to squeeze the persistent drone away. The promises that the one soft voice made him kept him sane, and the past few days, he had been able to see the face of the one who spoke, a kindly looking old man with a long white beard. There was a warm hearth behind him, and Ulen felt the same safe feelings he had felt when he was a very young man, sitting in the small hut his father had used to tend to his herds on their winter grazing grounds.

"Are you all right?" asked Deros suddenly, right at his ear. "You look like you've seen a ghost."

"Maybe a little blood bothers him," said Judge cryptically, angry and frightened by the disappearance of his friend.

"We have enough to do to leave the baiting alone," growled Stearborn. "I won't rest until we've found the lad, or know what happened to him. You can put that shaft to your bow and get on with it! Right now I want a party formed up to go ashore and cover the beach from one end to the other." The gruff old commander paused, his voice wheezing and squeaking like a leaky valve when he breathed, as always happened when he was exhausted. "And one of you tell me what that infernal light is that's sashaying along yonder!"

Hamlin and Judge were the first in the boats with the shore party, while Lorimen and Findlin alerted the other crews of the vessels in the protected anchorage.

McKandles was shouting from the shore a moment later, calling out to those aboard the Thistle Cloud. "It's them elves, sure as rain! I hasn't ever seen no more plain sight than these here tracks, and I thinks they has got Master Jeremy!"

Ulen Scarlett's face was blank, and he seemed to gaze away at the dim shoreline without a thought, but Deros caught sight of the viselike grip that turned his fingers white on the rail. He turned and stalked below before she could speak.

Rewen went ashore with Coglan, and the torches and rushlamps aboard all the other vessels soon were making flickering reflections across the water, giving rise to a fear in Stearborn that maybe the lights and activity might be a beacon to the firesnakes, if any were near, and a danger to them all of being destroyed before they had ever struck a blow on Eirn Bol.

As he stood at the rail watching the progress of the shore party, Stearborn's keen ears picked up the faintest hint of an odd sound coming from the quarters where Ulen bunked, but by the time he turned his full attention to it, it had passed. His eyes wandered back to those ashore, now marching along at a rapid pace after the vanishing silver-white light, hovering at the edge of his vision like faint images of fireflies on a hot summer evening in the hills of his old home.

Ulria

Jeremy came to with a start.

There was a reed pipe playing softly, familiar old tunes that his mother used to hum to him when he was a small boy following her about her busy kitchen, cooking and cleaning. She always seemed to have a house full of Stewards, and from his earliest recollections, he was bounced on the knee of one or another of the gruff soldiers, or left to stay up past his bedtime, so he could hear their stories, sitting safely beside his father. He was allowed to hold their horses or weapons from time to time, and he remembered the day when his father came to him with the news that he was to be given to Ardin Wagen, the Master of Arms for the Third Oak Squadron, which his father commanded.

Those times faded, and Jeremy blinked in the subdued light. It was not daylight, nor lamplight, but it hung like a soft golden white halo around the bed where he lay. At the thought that he was in bed, he quickly raised himself on his elbows to try to find his boots and weapons, but there was nothing there beside the simple bunk but a table with a water urn, and a small ivory box that had gold and mithra arrows across its top.

His head spun then, and he had to lay back quickly, to keep from fainting. When he looked again, the table was a small tree, with willowy branches, and the objects that had been there were now floating upon the empty air. His eyes traveled upward to try to find the nature of a room that would be so large it would have a tree growing in it, and was mildly surprised to see a dark blue dome, with faintly gleaming stars.

"By Windameir's Beard," he heard himself utter, in almost the same tone as his old commander, Chellin Duchin. "Somebody's parked me outside!"

It was not cold, which was odd, for he half expected to need his winter cloak. As he thought of that, he tried to remember where it was.

"The Thistle Cloud!" he muttered, filled with a sense of discovery. "I am aboard the Thistle Cloud!"

But he knew there was no tree aboard the vessel, and he had to force himself to his elbows again for another look around.

A voice from the tree startled him for a moment, but it was a woman's voice, and reassuring. He grew nervous again at not having his weapons, for he remembered another time, when he and Hamlin had been captured in a snare by the two witches.

"You look much improved, my young friend. You have had a long sleep."

"Where am I, ma'am?" he asked, remembering his manners in spite of his discomfort and confusion.

"You are where few sons of Hamen have ever been. We are

resting now in the Winter Havens of Elanmora, on the coast of the Silent Sea.''

''Am I dead?'' asked Jeremy, suddenly wondering if this was what it was like to cross the Boundaries. He couldn't remember a battle, or any reason why he should have died, but the thought still nagged.

The soft voice rippled with a faint laugh, which made his heart jump, the way it did when he looked upon Rewen.

''No, you are very much alive.''

''Rewen?'' he called hopefully.

''My name is Ulria.''

''Why am I here? Where are the others?''

''Your friends are well. They are yet with Rewen and Coglan.''

''Can I go to them?''

''When you are better. You have been hurt.''

''I'm weak, all right, and dizzy. How was I hurt?''

''You'll know in good time. It would not help you to know that now.'' Ulria appeared at his bedside then, with a silver cup full of a glittering liquid. She was much older than her voice sounded, yet when he looked again, he saw her as no more than a young girl in the bloom of youth.

''What is this?''

''Something to heal you, Jeremy.''

He looked over the rim of the cup at her. She seemed older again, but her face constantly changed as he watched, unable to take his eyes away from her steady gaze.

He remembered where he had seen eyes like that then, with Chellin Duchin, when they had met the Elboreal on a long ago afternoon somewhere in his past.

''You are one of the Dreamers,'' he said gently. ''So I am here where Chellin always wanted to go.''

''Chellin? Is he a friend?''

''Yes. He always spoke of your race with a little envy. I never thought I could live to see any of you again. Atlanton is too harsh, now. They have said you and your race are all gone.''

Ulria took back the cup from him after he finished drinking. ''We are here, but you have forgotten how to see. Atlanton has changed in only that way. It was not always so.''

Jeremy suddenly recalled Hamlin's infatuation with the dream-dust of the elves.

"Did you give me something to make me forget how I was hurt?"

Ulria nodded slowly. "You must heal, and it would not help you now to know everything. It will all await you, no matter how long you linger or if you hurry."

"The dream-dust is real, then," he muttered.

"Where have you heard that," asked Ulria.

"My friend Hamlin. He has heard it from someone else. We have all heard it ever since we were small."

The beautiful elven woman looked away, her features saddened. "We have paid for our sins for all these turnings," she said softly. "There is never an end to the mistakes of being young and naive."

Jeremy held out a hand for the mithra cup. "Was it in the water? Is that how you gave it to me?"

She nodded.

"What did you mean about the mistakes you made?"

"I wasn't speaking of only me. I meant my people."

"What mistake do you speak of? I don't recall ever hearing anything evil of your kind."

"Oh, there are many stories of the Elboreal that are sad chapters in our history. The Dreamers are not above the same wishes and desires of everyone else here in the Lower Meadows. There were some who were tempted and were pulled away from the High Homes."

"How do you mean?"

"You said you had heard of the dream-dust! That has far outrun anything else you know of us, or our ways. We found the flowers when we first came into Atlanton, and discovered the healing power they had. It was to be used for the benefit of all races. We were all so naive then. We could not see the trouble that was brewing."

"What trouble? Were you here then?"

Ulria silenced the rest of his questions. "You must rest now. I'll tell you more when you awake. You were very nearly finished when they brought you to me."

"How was I hurt?" he persisted. "Was it in battle?"

"A battle? Not in the way you mean, but it was a battle. It is not finished yet. The others thought that perhaps we could mend our past error by this, so that we may return to the Boundaries in good conscience."

Ulria rechecked the bandage on his head and shoulder, and found he was asleep before she had finished.

An Old Proverb
✳

The small lamp in the cabin threw soft golden shadows on the bulkheads of the cabin where Deros lay tossing uneasily, unable to sleep. The Thistle Cloud had remained in the anchorage for three days running while they searched for any sign of Jeremy. Rewen and Coglan had been aboard each of the ships in the Horinfal Straits, and rubbed the bark and shavings of the Golvane on every one, until the growing fleet had disappeared into thin air.

A changing of the watch drew the nervous girl on deck, where she looked to the sky, trying to read how the weather would hold. It had been fair and warm again, almost an echo of late summer, but she could see that the trees and bushes on the islands around them were already well into losing their leaves, and turning the deep russet orange and gold of autumn.

"A fine night to be lifting our hook and slipping away," reported Findlin gloomily. "And with all this Golwane rubbing, we can't see another wessel out there in front of us! It would take the Darjarls Boot, if we stowe and sink each other before we struck a single blow with anyone who's a true sworn enemy to us all!"

"You fuss too much," scolded Deros, but as she looked out over what appeared to be an empty anchorage, she saw that the Archael had made a valid point.

"At least we know Railan Dramm isn't a weirdoch," confessed Lorimen, who stood beside his friend at the port rail. "Seeing how simple it was to treat the wessels with the bit of the Golwane the Lady Rewen has, I'm surprised that ewery ship plying the Silent Sea has anything left to see of it at all."

"They would hawe to be friendly with someone who knows the secret," reminded his companion.

"How does the Red Scorpion know of it? Has the Lady

Rewen betrayed the Sacred Thistle by telling that rogue of the secret workings?'' Ulen Scarlett had been on deck for some time unnoticed, listening to the others talk. His head hurt constantly now, with a dull, throbbing ache that seemed to make even the brightest day dimmer. The Rhion Stone had grown so tight about his finger he could not remove it, and had lost all desire to do so. McKandles and Lofen steered very carefully away from their old chieftain, and tried to take turns at night on watch, to see if they could catch him in some move that would possibly give away his intentions.

Rewen had shown her ring to Deros late in the last quarter of the midnight watch. ''Look! You will see something of who controls Ulen now.'' She held her hand quite still, and they watched as the blurry face of a kindly looking old man began to float in the great depths of the stone's center.

''We have used these stones to help us since Gingus Pashon fell under the spell of Astrain,'' said Rewen. The blurred image of the old man in the watery, pale crimson depths of the stone suddenly focused, and Deros could feel the eyes of the old one searching the cabin for her. A hand, dark and which filled her with dread, seemed to seek to grasp and crush her heart in her chest.

''He sees me,'' whispered Deros, backing away.

''He senses something here. This one cannot overpower my ring, for the stone is uncut, and still has more power than the one that Gingus Pashon stole.''

''Whoever it is, he wears the colors of Hulingaad.''

As the two women watched, another face appeared in the milky light of the ring, calling out a name, but it was mumbled, and they could not make it out.

''It's Ulen!'' gasped Deros.

Rewen silenced her friend, holding the ring steady. As they looked on, they heard the horseman's voice speaking in a dull monotone.

''He's told that man of all our plans! They even know you have used the Golvane on our fleet, and that they won't be seen!''

''Shhh, little sister. There is much to be said for letting someone know too much. Sometimes it is more effective than having too much secrecy.''

''Then Ulen has done well by us here! He has told them everything!''

Rewen spoke a soft chant over the Rhion Stone she wore, and the faces and voices faded. "Now I want you to look again, little sister. The news carried by the stones is not all of an ill nature."

When Deros looked again, she saw a line of pale stars in a pink dawn, pulsing softly like prayer flags blown about in a soft breeze. She had forgotten the ancient orders of monks who lived, and remembered that her father had once said they would have to be called upon to help when the final battle came. A silvery light that strengthened drew her attention back to the center of the stone, which became brighter still, until Deros could see the figures that were there, marching along in time to a small pipe, which played a tune she had not heard since they had returned home from the Fords of Silver.

"It's the Elboreal. They have called their clans, and shall be sailing to join us on Eirn Bol," explained Rewen. "But their help will also bring us news that there is one among us who is a traitor."

Deros's face hardened. "Ulen. I know it has to be Ulen."

"And it is something that we must overlook for the time being, for those who watch in Hulingaad need to think he is theirs. We will not inform everyone of my other fact just yet. I hate to subject them to so much hatred and repulsion, but those who spy through the ring read a great deal of how things really are by the feelings they pick up of those near Ulen."

"Then they will be much impressed by the wave of opinion that flows so hard against him."

"That is what we need, along with the idea that there is dissension among us. If we can convince the Black Hood that our fleet is small and divided, we may create a cloak of surprise to help us when the hour has come to strike at the armies of the Dark One."

Deros glanced down the deck toward where the young horseman from the Gortland Fair lay below sleeping.

Rewen smiled sadly. "Don't be too harsh a judge of him, Deros. It could as easily have been you who plays at this role. He has jumped into a game with stakes so high he could not imagine."

"An old proverb from my home is that you test the depth of the bucket before you try to carry the sea," said Deros. "The oldest Poet of Eirn Bol once made a story of the man who attempted to bring the sea to his garden fountain. He got bigger buckets, and hauled water all day with the help of a horse. His wife finally left, and his friends deserted him, except for one old comrade he passed every day in his toil.

" 'Come in for tea,' " invited his friend.

" 'I can't,' replied the man. 'I must move the sea to the fountain in my garden.'

" 'Come to tea.'

" 'No.'

" 'Then we shall build your fountain next to the sea. Then we shall have our tea and watch the waves rush to greet us, and to bid us good-bye. It is the nature of the sea to do that.' " Deros had reacted to the old tale exactly as her tutor recited it to her when she was but a small girl.

"We shall find our way, little sister. The Master who told that story waits for us on Eirn Bol. Whoever goes away shall return, and those we have bid good-bye to, we shall greet again with great joy."

Deros had fallen silent, feeling the empty sadness inside her. "I hope it is so, Rewen. It is too hard to live with so much remembrance of things lost to us."

"That is the sure call of home, little one. It rings in the heart like a signal horn, and we must obey. Look at the great white birds going south. They linger for a time in the warmth of the mild climate, but they always return to their true homes to have their young."

A silver-white light had become visible along the shore, and now one after another of the sentries on the other ships called out to alert the fleet. As the two women watched, an elven rainbow-colored rocket shot up into the early morning light, bursting into a shower of brilliant white stars above the fleet, then dissolved into the soft golden glow of the late autumn sun.

"There is our signal," went on Rewen. "Now is our time to sail for home." She raised a hand and motioned on the wind, and an answer to the sparkling rocket lit up the sky above the gathered fleet, and soon the ships were under way on the new morning, outbound for Eirn Bol.

A Voice on the Water

✳

Standing on the beach with a small knapsack upon his back, and his face wearing a puzzled frown, Jeremy Thistlewood peered out over what appeared to be an empty bay on the Straits of Horinfal. A voice from nowhere startled him badly, and he spun about on the beach, remembering with a sinking feeling he was unarmed.

"Stand still, mate, and we'll have someone ashore in a wink!"

The voice carried strongly over the water, and Jeremy dropped his knapsack at his feet to wait. A moment later, two men in a small tender appeared not more than a dozen yards away. "Hail, brother! How did you get left ashore?"

Jeremy waved, but did not answer immediately. He did not recognize either of the men.

"You're lucky we had that fouled hook, or we would've been gone, too!"

"I told them that anchor would foul! There's nothing but rocks along this bottom. If it don't foul the hook, it'll cut the rode, and then you've got your hands full!"

"Where's your ship?" asked Jeremy as he placed his knapsack into the tender. The two men held it steady while he got in, then pushed off back through the surf and rowed powerfully back toward open water.

The sailor introduced himself as Salts, laughing. "Takes a smart eye to see us. That's some of the crafty work the Lady gave us. Me and Pelro here have been at sea since we was shrimps, and I never put no mind to any of this oliphan works."

"Glad to make your acquaintance. Jeremy Thistlewood, of the Lost Elm Squadron, Line Stewards." He was shading his eyes to try to make out where a boat might be anchored.

Pelro stopped long enough to point out where the ship lay. It was a barely seen shadow floating in the clear blue waters of the shallow inlet.

"So Rewen has done her work on all the ships?" asked Jeremy, feeling anxious to be back aboard. His wound still troubled him if he moved suddenly, but Ulria's healing had saved him. "Has the Thistle Cloud sailed?"

The sailor called Salts nodded. "They're all gone, but us. We fouled our anchor. If you hadn't shown up when you did, you'd be marooned here on the Straits."

Jeremy shuddered, looking about. "Then I'd say I was in good time."

Another few strokes of the oars brought the tender to a bumping halt against the sides of the unseen ship. "Come up, lad," called an invisible voice. "We've got time to make, and not much tide to clear the chute on the outward passage!" A hand grabbed Jeremy's wrist and hauled him aboard, where he found himself looking about over the busy deck of a ship preparing to make way. "Captain Telig, my good man, master of The Crane."

"Jeremy Thistlewood, Line Steward, most recently off the Thistle Cloud. I hope you can get me back to my ship, sir."

Captain Telig laughed robustly. "It'll be a fine day the Crane could catch *her*, but we'll make a match of it, or I'll know what for! Come on, Pelro, Salts! Let's be off, lads!"

The sounds of anchor chain rattling up the windlass and sails being spread mingled with the shouted orders and replies of the ship's crew. Jeremy found his knapsack, and stood by it, watching.

"You look tired, lad. Come below, and I'll find you a bunk."

"Thank you, sir. I have dire news to deliver to the Lady Rewen. We must catch up."

"What nature of news is so important, lad?"

"A traitor is in our midst," said Jeremy, feeling his stomach turn again, as it had in that dim memory of the night he was attacked and thrown overboard to drown.

Captain Telig frowned, and his features took on a more serious nature. "And how have you come by this news? Walking about on the Straits of Horinfal all alone?"

"I was attacked because I overheard the spies at their plans. They threw me into the water to drown, but a friend pulled me out."

"You are a fortunate tadpole, then," answered the captain.

Jeremy didn't mention Ulria, for he was never quite sure how someone would react to talk of the Elboreal.

"We are the last ones out of the Grotto," went on the captain. "The Thistle Cloud was out first thing this morning, so she'll have an advantage on us. The Crane is no slug, but she can't claim to be as swift as the Lady Rewen's boat."

"Which course have they gone?" asked Jeremy.

"The one we all decided on, after the Lady Rewen brought the Golvane leaves to us. Straight up the Gullet, and on to Eirn Bol. With any luck at all, we should be fetching the island in a week's time."

Jeremy pounded a fist into his open palm. "Damn his eyes! They will know we're coming that way, and have an ambush ready!"

"It's all well and good to know something, but unless you can find a bug that's biting you, you can't squash it. The Hulin Vipre fleet may be strong, but they can't fight ships they can't find."

"Unless I can catch up to the Thistle Cloud, there's one aboard her who will call the Black Hood down on us all! He has to be stopped."

Captain Telig called out to his second in command to bend on more sail. "Who is this fox among us? And on the Lady Rewen's ship?"

"A horseman from a traveling fair. He's tricked all of them."

"But Lorimen and Findlin are aboard that ship! Surely they would have done something!"

"So are a few good Stewards! But no one knows how far he's gone! I heard him betray us with my own ears."

The ship rolled and pitched about as the helmsman altered his heading, and a lookout high on the main mast shouted out at the same time. "There's another of our ghost ships coming down into the Grotto! Off the starboard bow! Look alive, mates!"

Captain Telig cursed under his breath, and took the companionway steps two at a time. "Who in thunder would be coming about on us now?"

Jeremy had followed the captain, and stood beside him now, gazing away at the empty blue water, laced here and there near shore with the whitecaps of the waves washing in. Just a bare shadow of a shadow glided across the calmer water of the protected bay, coming directly for them. A cry from somewhere in front of them came over the water as the lookout of the other vessel spotted The Crane.

"Free your weapons," called Captain Telig, and the command was echoed up and down the deck of The Crane. A clatter of swords and shields was heard from the other unseen ship as well, and Jeremy, having left all his weapons aboard the Thistle Cloud, turned to his new captain for arms.

He had barely managed to secure a proper sword that suited his task when the first sounds of the two ships closing rang out over the deserted Straits. Boats had been lowered, and as they pulled away from the spell the Golvane leaves had worked over the ships, Jeremy saw the black-clad sailors pulling toward them, making ready to board.

A Welingtron Wind

"Look to it! All hands! Hulin Vipre!"

War horns brayed from the Hulin vessel, to be answered by the high, pure notes of the pipes on The Crane, and soon battle was joined in earnest. Jeremy remained beside Captain Telig, and turned briefly to speak.

"You see? It's already begun. He has betrayed us before we have been able to leave the Straits!"

He had no further time to talk, for they were hard-pressed in an attack that was launched from a boat that had grappled next to them. Jeremy's arm felt weak, and the sword grew heavy after only a few strokes. His near miss with death had used much of his strength, and even the Elboreal's tender care could not make him strong before his body had recovered. He remembered the dream-dust Ulria had given him, and suddenly was tugging at the small pouch of it beneath his tunic, and without wondering why, he had put his tongue into it, and tasted the lightness of it tickling his nose and making him want to sneeze.

A warm glow enveloped him then, and he felt a resurgence of strength wash over him, and his sword seemed to be no more than a feather in his hand.

Maybe Hamlin had been right after all, he thought fleetingly as he engaged a black-clad soldier across the gunwale of the boat, and struck the man a telling blow off the side of his shining black helmet. A great pandemonium dulled his hearing then, and it seemed they were beset on all sides by the growing number of enemy soldiers. Jeremy was vaguely aware of a ringing noise in his head, and he thought a blow must have caught him by surprise. He fought his way to the rail of The Crane, and tried to check himself for any fresh wounds.

In the next instant, he was face-to-face with the terrible features of a great eel, its mouth gaping wide, revealing the rows of razor-sharp teeth. He fell back, instinctively raising his hands.

"Be careful how you sling that weapon about," scolded an odd, high-pitched humming voice. "You will need your sword!"

Jeremy recovered himself somewhat and watched as the powerful body of the great eel shimmered upon the deck, as though it were armored in a pale silver light. Captain Telig's voice reached him next, calling faintly from the stern of The Crane.

"To me, lads! To your captain!"

The Welingtron's body turned into a mirror-smooth motion, and with flashing blows of its lethal tail, it surged toward the stricken ship's commander, flinging Hulin warriors left and right as it went. Jeremy followed close behind, being careful to stay clear of the deadly blows.

"Come on, lad! Sturdy fellow! Look to our guest, me hearties! See to your blades!"

A fierce battle was being waged on the small afterdeck near the companionway to the captain's cabin, and it was there that Jeremy set upon a middle-aged Hulin soldier, pulling his blade from his latest victim. They circled each other, oblivious to the shattering din going on around them, looking for an opening to strike.

A flurry of blows followed, which were blocked, and the enemy warrior pulled a long-bladed dagger from his waistband, never taking his eyes off Jeremy. At the next lunge, his feet went from under him as he stumbled over a fallen sailor, and the man was on him in a flash, ready to slit his throat. With all his remaining strength, Jeremy held the man's knife hand away from him, struggling to try to throw him off his chest, but the man was large and strong, and the blade inched closer to his face.

The small pouch that Ulria had given him was pulled from beneath his tunic in the fight, and as a last-gasp measure, he grabbed it and forced it open and blew some of the contents into the reddened face of the straining Hulin Vipre. At first, nothing happened, and Jeremy was cursing the cruel quirk of fate that would have him badly hurt by Ulen, saved by the Elboreal, and then slain by an enemy soldier almost as old as Chellin Duchin.

Thinking of his old commander brought a renewed rush of strength, and he kicked and struggled violently, just as the man's eyes went wide in surprise. The Hulin's grasp on his blade relaxed, and Jeremy was able to roll out from under his attacker, who sat as if stunned on the deck, looking about him as though he were watching a sunset. Not wasting his chance, Jeremy struck upward with the man's own dagger, putting the blade under the rib cage and straight into the heart. The surprised look never changed, and the man's eyes caught and held his own as he fell. There was such a look of blissful serenity that Jeremy wished for a moment that he had experienced the blow.

"The Dreamers make even death seem beautiful," said the Welingtron, suddenly beside him again. "They are a sad race. I hope one day they shall be free of this world, and can go home with the rest."

There was no time to ask anything of the great eel, for the battle still raged forward. When the fighting had at last ended, Jeremy looked over the dead that lay about the deck of The Crane, searching for Captain Telig and the two men who had brought him aboard. As he neared the helm, he found the commander talking to the Welingtron.

"Their boats must be here somewhere. We should board and sink them," the captain was saying as Jeremy neared.

"There are prisoners aboard the Hulin vessel. We shall have to take both boats."

"Both? I only had enough men to sail The Crane before these bloody louts attacked! Now I doubt I shall even manage my own boat very handily."

"I shall assist you," announced the Welingtron. "We have been dispatched to gather all those who yet still follow the Light. We must hurry, if we are to be in time."

"I thank you for your thoughts, sir," said Captain Telig. "But what can you do to replace a dozen lost able-bodied men?"

"You must open your mind, Captain. There are more ways to sail ships than to wait upon a wind."

"Then I shall be glad to learn of them, my friend. I'm an old sea dog who has been up and down these Straits and never yet found a way to go from one place to another without a breeze of wind in my sails. And how am I to find the men to watch the prisoners?"

"The prisoners aren't your enemies, Captain. These poor unfortunates were caught by the Black Hood and forced into slavery. We must take them to Eirn Bol." The great eel seemed to change colors again in the growing sunlight. "They may be able to help you with your ship, as well."

Captain Telig looked doubtful. "Allow them aboard The Crane?"

"You might be surprised. There are some passing fair sailors. Most are women, however."

"Then we shall make a grand caravan, sir! A ship short of a full contingent of sailormen, and two Black Hood vessels full of women!"

A lookout called from aloft the topmast, pointing away to the north. "Wakes, sir! Off the starboard bow! I think it's more of the ghost ships!"

"They are, Captain," agreed the Welingtron, who was called Eared. "We can steer clear of them, if we go now. Make ready to sail." It wasn't an order, but even Captain Telig wasn't foolish enough to argue with the great eel, whose shining golden green body slid gracefully over the side of The Crane. "Set out your lines off your bow! We'll give you the benefit of a Welingtron Wind!"

Jeremy barely had time to help the others roll the bodies of the slain overboard. The captain paused over each of his lost crew to say a few words of peace and farewell, and then the ship lurched forward, propelled by a force that made the timbers groan and creek, accompanied by an eerie humming sound that reminded him of the great winds that blew down the lost canyons of the South Channels, where he had served for a time with Chellin Duchin in the border wars that now seemed but pale skirmishes.

He knew they were on their way to Eirn Bol, a faraway place where Deros had come from, but which now loomed larger than any of the battles he had yet fought, or dared dream of.

The
Black Hood

The Long Bow

*

Salun Am waited at the very back table near the scullery of The Long Bow, his face covered closely by the billowing hood he had drawn about him. A husky henchman he employed to guard him whenever he came into the lower keep lounged beside him, huge fists wrapped around a flagon of mulled wine. The man's eyes were muddy with drink, but there was no mistaking his brute strength or the vacant way he stared about. He had killed before for Salun Am, and was well paid.

"Look lively, Nitches! He's coming."

"I see," muttered the brawny man. "He has been in the stables again."

Salun Am looked blankly at the man, who had the shadow of a smile playing around the edges of the cruel mouth. "Nitches knows his man."

Salun Am offered a stool for the new arrival, and turned to his bodyguard. "Make sure we're not disturbed, Nitches. You know who to keep a lookout for."

A cold smile cracked the face of the big man, who was sincerely in hopes that he could be called upon to crack a head or break a limb. He had enjoyed that sport since he was young, and he always seemed to place himself well with employers who understood his particularly savage talents.

"Sit down, Agrate, sit down! You look as though you could use a drink."

The man's eyes met his host's, then slid away to run over the other faces in the dimly lit ale-house.

"Did you have a profitable trip, my friend? How do we find the weather on the other shore?"

"Trouble," spat Agrate, downing a half tankard of ale that the serving maid had brought. "I was caught at the rendezvous! There was some young cur in the place when I got ready to leave. I tried to kill him, but he was too quick."

"Does he know of our plan?" asked Salun Am, going pale. His mind raced with thoughts of Jatal Ra getting wind of his own secret preparations for the taking of Eirn Bol. Mortus Blan had on more than one occasion let drop a casual remark that made him wonder if the crafty old counselor were on to him, but then nothing more came of it, so he went on.

When he had devised the scheme, he had intended to tell Jatal Ra, but after the calling up of the Lost Fire without his knowing, he put the plan into motion in secret, and planned to keep it from everyone. Agrate was good enough in his own way for the role of spy, and had had his own contacts and network of people below him, but he was too lustful to be trusted with the full knowledge of the entire operation. Nitches was the perfect silent partner, for he cared for nothing but drink and women, which Salun Am provided in abundance. Salun Am had always found a happy servant was not easily lured away from his master.

Still, Jatal Ra had his own eyes and ears everywhere, and so extreme care had to be taken. The Long Bow was one place where Salun Am knew he might meet and talk to his conspirators without much notice, for the place was always full of those who were involved with one hidden plot or other. Twice he had seen men known to work for his brother Collector, but they had passed from the ale-house before Agrate arrived.

The other man shook his head. "I don't know how much he heard. He was young. I couldn't place his brogue, but I don't think he was from Cairn Weal. He seemed a stranger." His face darkened and he glowered into his mug. "He was carrying a fancy sticker that I don't like the looks of. It had the mark of a weirdoch on it!"

Salun Am leaned over the table and clutched at the man's arm. "Marked? How so?"

"I thought to draw him into a snare and kill him easily. He was young, but turned out to not be so green. And the sword kept shooting out light, like that was some sort of your business put on it.''

The Collector of Quineth Rel scowled darkly and ran through all the possibilities in his head of which enemy he might be dealing with, and how best to deal with them, whoever they were. ''Did he say a name?''

''None that was familiar. It sounded like Onan, or Ohan.''

Racking his brain, Salun Am rose from his stool and paced, hands clasped tightly behind him. He couldn't approach Jatal Ra, and there was no way to use the Eye without the others knowing. He would have to risk sending Agrate back through the tunnels below the two islands sooner than he had planned. It would be of no consequence if they moved their attack forward, for the new Emperor had already placed the entire army on full alert warning, and was already preparing the Hulin Vipre fleet for the imminent invasion attempt.

''You shall take the advance party through sooner than we had originally thought,'' he said finally. ''We must contact the traitor on Eirn Bol so that we may move ahead.''

Agrate was not such a patriot that he wished to turn Salun Am in for a reward, and he thought of what his chances would be of coming back from the raid through the lava flows that formed the tunnels between the two warring islands.

''It will be difficult to reach Efile. The stranger knew about him. It will be risky, now.'' He knew he was treading on thin ice here, and that dealing with the powerful Collectors was a risk. There was a great struggle going on in Hulingaad over the crowning of Baryloran as the new Emperor, and the choosing of friends was dubious at best. He felt no love lost for the old ruler's youngest son, but he had always feared Tien Cal, Lacon Rie's pride and joy. Now here was Salun Am with a plan of his own, and a good chance of carrying it off.

Except that Jatal Ra had been the one who called the Lost Fire, and he was the only one at the moment who had any way to direct them, which was to his advantage over his rivals. Agrate didn't intend to reach the next part of his life without allies who were capable of the ultimate victory over Eirn Bol, and all the other places that yet defied the Black Hood.

He looked back across the littered table at Salun Am and smiled. ''When do we go?'' he asked.

''In two days' time. I will make the preparations here. In the meanwhile, you are to go with Nitches. I won't risk you getting drunk and telling anyone of our little outing.''

A flash of red covered Agrate's vision, and he had half risen, his hand to his dagger. At the motion, Nitches had covered the short space across the floor, and lifted the man up by his throat, leaving his booted feet kicking wildly in the air.

"Let him go," ordered his master. "See to it that he stays with you until I send the word.''

Agrate grasped his throat and gulped in air as he was let down. He was driven into a killing rage, but he knew he was no match for the brawny man beside him. The only way to kill that one was a knife in the dark from ambush. Instead, he choked out an apology to Salun Am. "I lost my head for a moment. Sorry. I'll do as you wish.''

"I know you will, my good fellow. Nitches will see to whatever you need, and bring you to the crypts when we are ready to proceed.'' Salun Am bowed and excused himself, walking quickly through the crowd in The Long Bow. No one had paid any attention to the altercation at the back table, except for a figure who sat alone at a table with a half-empty ale mug before him. He went unnoticed as he left, and fell into step behind the Collector, keeping careful strides and managing to hide in the shadows when the man looked back.

At the entry gate to the upper keep, where the Emperor and his court lived, the man fell back a pace and removed his heavy cloak and cowl. After Salun Am was safely gone, he went forward to be challenged by the guard, who drew a surprised breath and saluted.

The Tombs

❋

Agrate had chaffed at the bit while he was constrained by the presence of Nitches, but the moment that Salun Am had expressed his wishes to move ahead with the invasion of Cairn Weal through the old lava flows, he had been freed to go on with his planning. Men and arms were amassed daily in the underground maze of tunnels beneath Blor Alhal, and Salun Am laughed to himself to think of the great ruse that was going forward beneath the very feet of the new Emperor, and his own ally, Jatal Ra. The Lost Fire had been called back first by his rival, and Salun Am understood enough of the Book of Warl to know that whoever called the beasts back would be the only voice they would hear.

But if he could somehow manage to get to the Alberion Novas before his rival, then it would be another story, for it was rumored that the power to keep the Purge at bay was held in the heart of Cairn Weal, and other untold mysteries would be revealed to whoever held them. Alban Ram was a doddering old man, like Lacon Rie, and no longer had the will or courage to wield the untold mastery of the Sacred Scrolls.

He had sent for his spy, and welcomed him into his rooms in the high keep, next to Norith Tal.

"Yes, sire," said Agrate, bowing and sweeping his cap across his boots. "You have need of Agrate?"

"Need of your services, not of yourself," sneered Salun Am. "We can forgo the civility. You know the way to our contact on Eirn Bol, and have the plans given you here with the road you are to take to reach Cairn Weal. Your mission is to see to it the troops are guided through the shafts safely, and set at their work. We must go quickly and quietly, and no alarm given either here or on Eirn Bol." He placed his hands together and formed an arch with his palms together, studying his servant intently. "If you succeed at this, Agrate, you shall find I am a man who does not fall short on his rewards of loyal service. There will be a position of great favor for you once I am Steward of the Scrolls."

Agrate bowed low again, grinding his teeth in contempt, although he was terrified of the weirdoch, and knew well that he was not powerful enough, nor clever enough, to cross him. "Your wish is my command, my lord. I'll leave first thing in the morning."

"You'll leave now, this instant," corrected Salun Am, wagging a finger at him. "You will need these." He held up a leather pouch that contained several metal objects. "The keys to the kingdom." He smiled. "I have been at work these past few weeks, and here they are."

"The harps to keep the rats at bay," observed Agrate. "How many of them have you made?"

"Enough for the companies you will lead through the flows. Once you are safely on the enemy side, you won't have need of these any longer."

"Then the invasion is set? Why are there not more ships and men in the harbors? I've seen no recent signs that the Emperor is ready to order the full invasion."

"Yours is not to doubt what goes on among your superiors. All that's necessary for you to do is carry out your instructions."

"Will it coincide with the fleet landings?" persisted the spy.

"It will coincide with the master plan, sir. Now you will oblige me by taking your leave and carrying on with your errand." A wicked smile crossed Salun Am's face. "Nitches will be in your command to assist you in any way. He's a good man to trust."

A cold sliver of fear pierced Agrate's heart. "I have my own second officer," he began limply. "He is already planning our route."

"Nitches will go to back him up then," smiled Salun Am. "Now here are your keys to the backdoor. Go carefully, and mark me well, do not rouse suspicion elsewhere."

"Like alerting your friend across the hall?" asked Agrate, unable to resist the taunt.

A smoldering fire came into the old man's eyes, and his servant felt a fiery hand at his throat, slowly crushing his windpipe. His insides seemed to be scalded, and it felt as if his brain would explode from his skull, but he managed to utter a plea for mercy.

"There now, you see what it's like to irk me, Agrate. I know you will behave wisely and carry out your orders as they were given. The little taste of pleasurable sensations you just experienced can be dragged out for days, if need be. I find that a particularly helpful thought to leave you with."

Agrate stumbled out of the room into the hidden passage that led back to the stables behind The Long Bow, clutching his aching throat and gasping for breath as he went. As he emerged from the hidden door on the wall, he was aware of Nitches, nodding slowly and smiling.

"Come along!" snapped his commander. "We have work to do and not much time to do it. Round up the leaders of the groups waiting below. We have to pass these out." He handed Nitches the leather bag with the Dolrides that Salun Am had crafted.

"Pretty," muttered the big man. "Make music for Nitches."

"Not for here, idiot! We can't let anyone know we're leaving!"

Nitches glowered at Agrate, thinking of how much pleasure it would be to dangle him by his throat until he turned blue. "Nitches won't let anyone know nothing."

Agrate thought of the rendezvous on the other side and hoped the fool traitor there would hold to his side of the bargain. They had promised him gold and a seat of power at the head of the Bellream Readers, although it was known the man was dead as soon as his usefulness was finished. It amazed Agrate to think a man could be so stupid as to think his sworn enemies would show gratitude or reward him, for when the Black Hood was entrenched upon Eirn Bol, all the survivors would be used as slaves, or slain. That had always been the policy, from Gingus Pashon on down, and he knew it was not a good thing to change something that had always been. He rankled at his treatment by Salun Am, but continued on with his own plans. He feared the weirdochs and their powers, but he had seen enough in his time with the armies of the Black Hood to know that there were ways you could kill one of them, or destroy their power. Once he was on Eirn Bol, and they had found the Sacred Scrolls in Cairn Weal, he and his band would kill Nitches and his master, and take the prize for themselves. It was, after all, the quickest blade that plunged the deepest and took the spoils.

All the bindings and spells of the weirdochs and their kindred were not as deadly in the end as a shaft through the heart. He had seen dead weirdochs, and knew that to be true. Salun Am and Jatal Ra were dangerous, and dangerous to have as enemies, and Mortus Blan, the old advisor to Lacon Rie, was half crazy and unpredictable, but it was said he was over two hundred turnings, and was growing weaker every day. He had heard that the way to the old man was his fancy for young girls.

"No matter what they say or do," chuckled Agrate aloud, "they are still men, and a pretty wench will be their downfall every time." He had forgotten Nitches trailing along at his heels, and was surprised for a moment when the big man answered.

"What?"

"I said we'll meet our men back at The Tombs at midwatch.

You could be helpful if you rounded up the louts out of The Long Bow and brought them.''

"Nitches stays with Agrate."

"Then let's go together," he said in an exasperated tone. "We're late as it is."

"Nitches don't like The Tombs. Cold and clammy there. Can't breathe."

"We're using that shaft below the burial grounds because there's no one around. Nobody likes it there."

Nitches brightened. "Will I get to break heads tonight?" he asked, off the subject, his face full of childlike pleasure.

"As many as you like, Nitches! We're going to Eirn Bol."

A sly look passed over the man's simple face. "Is we going for keeps?"

Agrate looked around at the huge man. "This is it," he replied. "Make sure you take enough food to last until we take one of the settlements on the other side."

They had reached the courtyard beside the stables, and found the first group of their company formed up. Agrate had Nitches pass out the small mouth harps to the leaders, and they collected the rolls of men who would be going. After an hour or so of issuing their orders, and finding out what their missions would be, the invasion troops began the slow, methodical tramp down into the passageways that led to the old burial grounds for the keep. The ways were small, and the men could not march more than two abreast, so it was sometime after midwatch by the time the last of the troops were through the hidden door, and in place to move across beneath the sea onto the enemy isle.

Agrate placed himself at the head of the first squadron, so that he would be able to reach Efile quickly, and make his plans to be rid of his watchdog, Nitches. Once that was done, he had the rest of his plan laid out, and it would not be long before he had his revenge on the high-flown Salun Am. Even weirdochs had been known to plead for mercy, and he wanted to be among those who had heard them.

The invasion forces were almost to the middle of the channel between the islands when he caught snatches of the terrible sounds of the Aldora, ranging through their domain in search of intruders, and then there was another sound, like distant thunder, but it was rolling through the solid stone of the shafts, and set them reeling about as the first shock wave of the tremor hit.

Past and Present

❋

Baryloran went directly to the inn called The Long Bow, and stopping a moment to let his eyes adjust to the darkness, he lowered the hood of his cloak and stepped to the back of the room and took a table. No one seemed to notice his arrival, but it had been marked by all, and the pretty young bar maid hurried to take his order. When she leaned closer in the gloom of the room, she recognized him and let out a little startled gasp, but he grasped her arm firmly and spoke in a loud voice. "I'll have an ale, wench." Under his breath, he motioned a hand toward the back wall. "There is a way out there, is there not?"

The girl could only nod.

"Good. Point it out to me, but don't let anyone see. Here, lean down and act as though you're kissing me." He pulled the girl down to him, and turned her away from the room. "Now if you want to help me, you'll show me this passage."

The girl pointed again, whispering, "It's there, my lord. Beneath the lamp."

"Good. Now there is going to be some men who come in here soon. They will come to join me. There will be a fight, and they will act like they have slain me, and take my body out. But I will be in the passage, and you will show me the other way out."

The girl stared wildly at him, beginning to cry.

"Now hold on to your wits, girl," he hissed, the grip of his hand hardening. "If you want me to see tomorrow, you must get hold of yourself and help me. Help the Black Hood!"

As he finished speaking, a loud group of men entered, talking and calling for drink and food. Their group was followed in by another, less in number, but no less rowdy. Baryloran's eyes narrowed for a moment, then he released the girl. "When you bring my drink back, you must stay near me. It will happen fast, and there will be no time for a second chance."

111

She dried her tears and hurried away, just as her father called to her over the din in the crowded room. "Denale! Denale! Hurry, girl, help me!"

Various raucous voices echoed the order. "Hurry, Denale! Help me! Help me!" Rough hands reached to grab her, but she brushed by deftly, avoiding them all. Her mind raced with the image of the young Emperor sitting at the back table, his steady gray eyes imploring her. He had said he would die if she did not help him. She was filled with conflicting thoughts then, for she knew there were men who came to The Long Bow who wished him dead, and had spoken of it while she was bringing drink or food to their tables. They treated her as if she wasn't there, and went on with their talk, but she had heard. She had never known what to do with all she knew, for it was forbidden for anyone of the lower keep to go above the First Gate without being invited, so she had been left to her private fears and guilt, until today, when the very man she had wished to warn suddenly showed up seated at her father's inn.

His grasp had been as hard as the others on her arm, but there was a softness in his eyes, a kindness there that made her heart race beneath her apron. He was not as handsome as his brother had been, and she had come to know Tien Cal well, for he often came to The Long Bow, but he had been as cruel and hard as every other renegade and assassin who frequented the place, and she was frightened of him. He had threatened to send her to one of the troop camps along the new borders of the Black Hood's growing boundaries, but her mother had intervened and kept her from the young prince's list of conquests.

Now it was said he was dead, and she felt no sorrow. She was angry she could not have spit on his corpse, although she knew she would not have been able to, had they buried him in Hulingaad, for he was a hero to many, and the next in line for the Emperor's robe. She liked the thought of the lame prince sitting in the throne room now, and that Tien Cal was dead. Her mother had never spoken of what she had had to do to free her daughter, and Denale had never pressed her, but she could see the horror still fresh behind her mother's eyes. As she loaded her trays with the ale, she hoped in her deepest heart that Tien Cal had died screaming, a slow, horrible death that would have taken hours.

When she turned back to the room, there was a group of men already surrounding the Emperor's table, so she hurried back, her hands sweating on the tray. Denale looked to the lamp on the wall that controlled the passage behind it, and prayed that she would be able to find the lever on the first try.

A hand reached out and circled her waist, and she was dragged into the lap of a leering, red-faced man called Clandin. Her tray clattered onto the table, spilling some of the mugs. "Come alone, Denale. Help me, lass," he roared, and his rowdy companions cheered him on.

Denale looked over his shoulder and saw the knot of men drawn closer around the young Emperor. She kicked as hard as she could, and struggled free of the smelly man. "You pig! You leave me alone, or I'll have my father throw you out!"

"Your father, lass? Hah! You would have your father throw Clandin out of The Long Bow?" A roar of laughter swept around the table. "Here, I'll go and find him myself and give up." The drunken man wobbled from the table, and set off in the direction of the innkeep, who was watching from behind the bar. Just at that moment, a half-dozen new arrivals came in, elbowing their way through the crowded common room, toward the table at the back where Baryloran sat. Denale could not see him now, and ran to the wall to stand beneath the lamp that hid the lever that would open the passage into the lower tunnels, some of which served as sewers for the keep and which ran through all parts of the settlement. Just as she arrived, she saw the momentary glint of bare steel, and had just started to scream when the Emperor called her name.

The Dark Tunnel

The room was filled with struggling men, and Denale used her tray as a club to fight her way to the lever that would trip open the secret passage. She could not see the Emperor among the confusion, but heard him call out to her again. Just as she touched the wall bracket that held the lamp, an arm grabbed her waist from behind, and a knife was put to her throat.

"Touch that, wench, and you won't need any more trinkets

for this pretty neck of yours." The voice was familiar, but she could not turn around enough to see the face. Her assailant tightened his grip as Baryloran called out again. Denale ceased her struggling for a moment and felt the harsh hand about her waist relax the barest amount, then she kicked out with all her might, moving the lamp bracket, which set the mechanism for the trap door into motion. She heard a grunt from behind her and saw the knife come up beside her to open her throat, but it dropped suddenly, and the crushing pressure was gone. She sprang for the opening of the entrance to the secret passage, taking a quick glance over her shoulder to see Arman, a giant of a man who was a bodyguard for Salun Am, on his hands and knees, blood gushing from his head. Her father was behind him, holding up the chair he had used to stun the man long enough for his daughter to escape. She had time for a fleeting wave, then the wall rolled shut behind her, closing off the din in the common room of The Long Bow.

She barely had time to catch her breath before she heard urgent whispering in front of her, and hurried forward. It was Baryloran, calling out her name.

"You almost failed me," he said, his voice full of reproach.

"I was almost killed by Salun Am's man," she replied. "He tried to hold me from the lever."

"Salun Am!" shot the young Emperor. "I should have known he would have heard of our plan and tried to foil it."

"What plan, sire? Why are you doing this?" The girl was beginning to feel the dark hand of fear return, now that the excitement had died away behind her.

"You need only know that Salun Am and his friend Jatal Ra killed my father, and now they are trying to remove me. There is a bloody plot afoot to put them in power."

"But the people won't follow them, sire? Can't you have them taken for justice before your court?"

"Too much danger now, girl." Baryloran called her girl, but he saw that she was not much younger than himself.

"Danger for you, sire? Where are your guards? Why don't you arrest these mongrels?"

Baryloran laughed. "My old advisor has other plans for them. And the two of them, Jatal Ra and Salun Am, have opened the old books, and have called back the Purge."

Denale paled, looking ghostly white in the dim passage. "What can you do, sire?"

"We must get away from here first. Guide me away. They will be taking my 'body' back to the Council soon, and we must be ready to move when the traitors come forth to claim their prize."

"But what will you do, sire? Won't they bring the firesnakes to fight you?"

"Mortus Blan has the names from the books. The beasts will turn on those who called them from their mountain sooner or later, and there are bindings that will cause them to do that sooner. They planted the seed of their own destruction when they brought them back from their slumber."

A noise from behind made the girl start. "We must get away, sire. Someone else may come after us. Hurry, I know a way they can't find us, even if they follow."

The roar of voices reached them, and a brief brightening of the light in the tunnels signaled that someone else had come through the passage behind. Shouts and a cry came then, and a bolt from a crossbow snapped past Baryloran's ear. Denale grabbed his arm and darted to the left side of the passage, and after another few feet turned right again. Even in the poor illumination, he could tell they were in a different part of the tunnels, and could hear men in the other shaft yelling and cursing as they passed on by.

"You know these tunnels well," he whispered. "My brother was familiar with them, too."

"I knew Tien Cal's ways," the young woman replied. "And not only of the tunnels beneath the keep."

He waited for her to finish her thought, but she was silent, and simply pulled him along behind her. They went silently for what seemed a long time, stopping to listen every now and then, but the voices of their pursuers were gone.

"How far do these shafts go?" he whispered at last.

"I don't think anyone really knows," Denale replied. "Your brother was one who knew of most of them. I think Salun Am must know something. There is a man called Agrate who speaks to him all the time. I think he does something in these tunnels."

"Mortus Blan has shown me charts of the keep and the island. It seems that he said once there are shafts that connect Hulingaad to Cairn Weal."

"It may be, my lord. My father spoke once of the terrible

beasts that were turned loose in some of them, to keep someone from going through them to the other side.''

Baryloran's mind lit up with a sudden revelation. "Of course! It would make good sense. The two of them have fallen out, so now Salun Am has found his own road to reach the Alberion Novas. Now they will be fighting among themselves.'' He laughed softly. "Mortus Blan reads a man's soul like an open book. Jatal Ra has called back the Purge, and plans to murder Salun Am as soon as he can possibly do it safely, and his good friend has found a way to beat Jatal Ra to the prize, so that he can destroy Jatal Ra and the beasts. A perfect pair!''

A slight tremor rippled beneath their feet, sending them reeling off balance against the shaft wall.

"What was that?'' he cried, louder than he intended.

"My father says it is the Old Ones on Corum Mont moving in their dreams.''

The walls and floor of the tunnel rumbled and rolled giddily again, this time lasting long enough to knock them off their feet. The dank smell of ancient passages was overpowered by a fine mist of stone-dust, and another unmistakable tang of the sea.

"We have to get out of here,'' said Denale. "I have never felt it this way before.''

"Are we near the upper keep?''

"Just around the next bend of the passages we will find five shafts. The center one runs to the bottom of the First Gate.''

The pale, shimmering light came from inside the walls, casting eerie shadows that rippled and flowed as they went, making the small, glittering particles in the stone look like stars shining from the bottom of a deep pool. As the ground swayed and jumped beneath them again, one of the shaft walls began to crack with a heart-stopping groan, and then in a single breath, the tunnel roof came down in a great jagged heap in front of them.

"Hurry!'' Denale yelled. "Our only chance is to go on! Hurry.'' They stumbled forward then, on into the tunnels that led toward Eirn Bol. She choked from the dust and felt a blind horror begin to grip her heart, slowly squeezing it until she thought it would burst.

The
Muster

The Minstrel's Key

Fearing being detected, Lanril Tarben kept the Marin Galone close in to the coast on the first part of their passage toward the Horinfal Straits. As they sailed along the dragon-ravaged shore, a growing stream of refugees pleaded with them for food and arms, or safe passage out of the blighted lands. There was nothing they could spare in the way of supplies, and little else but hope to give the hollow-eyed survivors.

It was one such survivor who found them late one afternoon as they were searching for a place to anchor in a small cove not far from the homeport of the Archaels, Lorimen and Findlin. The man traveled with a single scrawny horse, and approached the ship only after a long wait, where he was hidden in the rocks.

"Any Fionten men aboard that ship?" he called out at last, but keeping himself hidden behind his cover.

"None from Fionten, but good seamen from the Delos Sound! We be friends of Fionten!" replied Lanril, encouraging the man to come out. "We are trying to gather all those left into a force to move against the Purge."

"You can count me out of that little fish fry," shot the man. "You think you and that tender-box full of fools is going to stem up them flying stovepipes? I ain't had a good laugh since they took my missus, but you barkies sure comes close with your talk about sticking one of them cinderaters!"

Emerald stood next to Lanril, and played a tune that seemed to affect the man strangely.

"Who be that?" he asked after the notes had died away.

"I am a minstrel who is well traveled, friend. I recognize your brogue as that of a fellow gypsy, if I'm not too far from my mark."

The man laughed easily, and spoke in a more refined tongue. "You are a welcome treat to me, my good fellow. I am called Begam Greeneyes by those who follow harpists."

Emerald had a sailor row him ashore then. The two of them sat back in the sand and exchanged news, and were lost in earnest conversations so long that the crewman rowed Lanril ashore at last, to find out what was of such interest.

"Another of my ancient, worthless trade," laughed the man, Begam. "Of all the luck that could have run contrary to me here, I draw on the Fates' good fortune to run straight into a man who has come from my own parts."

Lanril Tarben was polite, but very much more interested in the current news of the coast, and said so plainly.

"This coast! You ask about this coast? Why, look at it, my man! It's nothing but soot and ashes all the way to the Straits, and there's not much improvement once you're past there."

Lanril's eyebrows arched curiously. "How have you managed to do all this traveling without having your skull split? That's a question I'd like to have answered."

Begam laughed. "You sport about with a cold fish," said the man to Emerald. "Have you not told him of the Minstrel's Key?"

"He's a seaman. He has a practical head. I don't believe he thinks of anything but wind and water."

"And right well glad of it," shot Lanril. "You'd be thankful for it, too, if you had any sense. I daresay you'd notice an absence of it, if I were a jolly kite off here with you and your wife, thinking of some old tunes my mother had sung me when I was a tad."

"We were jesting at your expense, Captain. Forgive us," apologized Begam. "I've taken on the guise of a country minstrel for protection. My good colleague may not have mentioned the Minstrel's Key, but if not, it's merely an old unwritten law that we have free hand to pass anywhere without harm."

"Does that hold for even the Hulin Vipre and the firesnakes? And Railan Dramm?" asked Lanril skeptically.

"I have sung for the one who flies the red flag. He finds my tales amusing."

Lanril gasped, his hand edging to his dagger.

"Rest easy, my man," laughed Begam, standing and doing a handspring about the beach. "In my line of work, it is a handy thing to be known as a wastrel and scoundrel, or a minstrel. You come across the oddest pieces of information that way."

"What did you find out?" asked Emerald.

"I found out that making a journey to the east will not be easy. Most of the ships here are burned or sunk, or if they escaped, they are bound for somewhere away from the firesnakes. You are the first ship I've seen that's come close enough in that I might hail. And wouldn't you know it, when my luck changed, it changed with a bang! Not only do you have the foolish courage to bring your vessel inshore, but you have an old countryman of mine aboard as well!" Begam slapped his leg, and did a backward flip that left him standing on his feet. Lanril, beet-red and fuming, fought to control himself.

"You are trying the patience of a man who has a terrible anger. As a boon to Emerald, I have not stove in your timbers, but I can't hold off in the face of ridicule!"

With a double forward flip, Begam was at Lanril's side, and placed his hand on the captain's arm. The seaman started to jerk away, but noticed the look on the minstrel's face and hesitated. "I try you sorely, Captain, and I shall stop. When you live among danger for as long as I have, you learn to make light of everything. When you asked how I was able to travel so freely among enemies, and even to entertain the Red Pirate, that is how I've done it."

"He shall need to come with us, Lanril," said Emerald softly, looking into the eyes of the seaman. "From here on, we shall have need of something more than just knowledge of wind and tide and sea."

Lanril Tarben nodded, looking away to the east, where he knew Eirn Bol to be.

The Harpist's Tale

✳

A smell of pine trees and salt air filled the bright autumn afternoon, and the harp of Begam Greeneyes joined with Emerald's in songs so sad and gay at once that there was not a dry eye aboard the Marin Galone. Lanril Tarben had called his men to stand down, and after securing the ship and setting out his customary double anchors, he invited them to enjoy the company of the new minstrel.

"There's no telling when we may find our pleasure next, and Emerald says this fellow is one of the greatest living harpists yet below the Boundaries."

Elita listened to the two, her eyes guarded, but following the songs with interest. They had not much to make them laugh since they'd sailed from White Bird, and Elita could not fathom what her husband had found to make him so full of smiles. Emerald and Begam sat and played another round of tunes, and Elita had almost ceased listening when the first reference to the Dreamers crept into their songs. Without realizing it, she had begun to hum along as well. "That tune," she said, finding tears welling up in her eyes. "It is the greeting song the Dreamers use when they are traveling." Her voice trailed away. "It seemed as though they were here. I almost felt their presence."

Emerald reached out and touched her hand gently. "Begam has been with them not long ago. He has talked with them." Emerald bowed to the other minstrel, and sat down.

A freshening breeze had begun to come up as the ship lay snug to her anchors, and Lanril cast a concerned glance at the minstrel, waiting for what was to come next. Begam did a backflip, and landed gracefully next to the master, touching his hand to his cap in salute. "My good captain and hardy crew, and most beautiful lady." He bowed low to Elita. "My news is such that it hardly bears weight in the bright light of day, but since this is where we are, it is here I must divulge it." He reached into his tunic and brought out a small, silken cloth of some sort, and unfurled it with a snap of his wrist. There fluttering at the end of his hand was a pale blue pennant, with white stars and a smiling half-moon, and Begam held it aloft for all to see. Lanril Tarben felt himself moved strangely by the odd sight, and fought to hold back his tears, although he could not have said why he was crying. Elita rose and walked to the new minstrel and took the small flag gently from him.

"So you have been with them?" she said, hardly above a whisper. Her heart was hammering, an she felt at once faint, and beyond all elation. Her mind swam with the gentleness of her healers when she had been so gravely burned by the dragonfire in Trew, and she wondered what it was that had happened to this man that would have moved the mysterious clan to have taken him in. Even Emerald, trained as he was in the lore of many kinds upon Atlanton, had never been allowed to see more than a glimpse of the elusive folk. "Where have you come upon our friends?" she asked quietly.

"They are not far from us, my lady. They never are."

"How did you find them?"

"I didn't," he replied simply. "They found me. I was caught alone and without cover by one of the firesnakes," went on Begam. "The Minstrel's Key is nothing to them. I looked to be the only morsel on a long empty road, and the beast attacked."

Lanril Tarben interrupted brusquely, "You were attacked by one of the Purge and you sit here to tell us about it?"

"Had it not been for the Dreamers, I would have been no more than bones out here now. I doubt you would have chanced to hear my harping, either."

"The firesnake attacked! And then?" prompted Emerald.

"All I remember next was waking in a silver ship of some sort. It was shaped like a great swan," said Begam.

"I remember that," added Elita. "It was soft as down, and there was some sort of music that I had never heard before."

Begam picked up his harp again and began the refrain of a haunting melody. "Those are not the notes exactly as they play them, but I think only they can produce it in the way it is meant to be heard."

"They once dwelled across all Atlanton," said Elita absently. "They were true friends to all our race, until the betrayals began."

"Who are you speaking of?" asked Lanril. "Who are these people you speak of? What lands do they come from?"

"The Elboreal. You've heard of them, I'm sure, good captain. They are spoken of in all the tongues of man, in one way or another. Mostly now it is songs and stories of our childhood." Begam smiled. "And they are supposed to build superior vessels, those of them who took to the sea." The minstrel struck another chord on his harp, and sang quietly:

> "There was a red dawn
>   upon the sea,
> and a ship with
>   a golden sail,
> twin moons across
>   the face of night
>   mark the paths
>   of their havens trail,
> Beyond the Southern Oceans,
>   beyond the Fallen Tide,
>   and far beyond
>   the human kind
>   who once fought
>   by their side."

After a long silence, Lanril Tarben spoke. "Why did they stop liking our race?"

Begam laughed, but it had a melancholy sound, and Emerald saw the same look in the minstrel's eyes that he had often seen in his wife's, after her stay with the Dreamers. "There have always been those who would trade on trust and friendship for their own ends. There were small betrayals little by little, and then the Dreamers reached a time when they wanted to go back home, to be with their own kind."

"The Dreamers long for a home that is beyond what we called hearth and field," said Elita, rolling the material in her cloak back and forth between her fingers. Her eyes were a smoky gray, which Emerald remembered as their color the day he first saw her in Trew.

"I long for a hearth with the madam, but it is a pipe-flit to think of in times like these." Lanril had shaken himself out of the reverie he had fallen into as he sat listening to the two minstrels. "I'm more concerned now with a high tide and a fair wind." He was cut off in midsentence by an anchorage suddenly filled with whitecaps, and a strange motion that slowly began to ripple beneath the Marin Galone.

An Unknown Rendezvous

The master of the Marin Galone shouted out his orders on the run, and in moments men were at the anchors and masts, making ready to set sail. Elita stood with Emerald at the rail near the helm, watching as the strange sight drew toward them.

"Not a swell in sight out there, and now it looks like a storm surge, only there's no storm," muttered Lanril. He turned to shout over his shoulder to the men at the bow. "Leave the anchors set! If the two of them don't hold, we're done for! Look to the skiffs if we ground!" He had no more time to speak, for the sudden swell of the sea rapidly abated, lapping gently along the sides of the ship, and a great eel broke the surface near where Elita stood.

"Greetings, travelers. I am Rhule, sent to bring you to a council of friends."

"What is it?" asked Lanril, looking at the apparition before him, thunderstruck.

"Someone sent to fetch us, it seems. Let's see where he takes us." Begam pulled a small reed pipe from his tunic and played a short, merry jig. The eel moved in time to the music, curling and rolling across the water so gracefully some of the seamen began to clap and shout at the sight.

"We would love to follow you, sir, but the wind is having a holiday! When it pipes up again, we'll be most happy to oblige you."

Rhule stopped his graceful dance and glided closer to the captain of the Marin Galone. "I have brought you better than the wind, sir. Please take up your anchors and make ready for sea."

Lanril hesitated, but the eyes of the great eel seemed to transfix him, and he called out the orders to ready for sea.

"I have heard stories of those old sea clans," said Elita.

"While I was with them, the Dreamers told me of the ones who were upon Atlanton first. I think these are called the Welingesse Fal."

"You have called us by our proper name," exclaimed Rhule, spinning about on the water in a graceful arc. "There are not many left now who remember us." He fell silent, and sang out in a low humming voice, and as the ship's company watched in fascination, a large number of the huge green eels surfaced before the Marin Galone and took her into tow, moving her slowly out of the protected anchorage.

Lanril shook his head in disbelief. "I have sailed these waters from the time I was just a tad, but I never heard of or saw such things as this! My shipmates at home would never believe this tale."

"Your crew has seen it, too," reminded Begam. "And I'd lay my life to the fact that a lot of others have been seeing these things as well."

"No matter. It's easy enough for whole crews to be taken with sea madness. I have heard about that all my life. Sail in certain waters, and there are the evil things that will steal your mind."

"These are no evil things," said Emerald. "I would like to have more time to hear what they have to say of themselves, and where they have come from."

A song from the eels rolled back to those aboard the ship, and the two minstrels listened carefully, trying to piece it together so they could remember it.

"It's not a rhythm I've heard before," said Begam as they sat strumming their harps.

"Nor I," agreed Emerald. He paused, turning the subject to another matter. "Where did you find your horse back there?" He had recognized Deros's old friend Gitel immediately, even though he was in such a scrawny, ill-kempt form.

Begam smiled. "He was with the Dreamers when they found me. From what I gathered, he had been sent to scout. You had known him before, I take it?"

"We were in the South Channels and Trew. His brother, Seravan, was there, too. They have both been sorely missed."

Begam watched the great eels pulling them steadily along for a time without speaking. He sighed at last, taking out the small reed pipe he carried in a small pouch at his side. "I wonder what it's all turned to, now. We've got the old allies back again, just as they were spoken of in the songs we were taught."

"We're going to find out something soon, I'd wager! Look!" Emerald pointed to the coast ahead. The Welingesse Fal had been pulling them along at a good speed, sending spray back over the deck from time to time, and they were now nearing a rocky headland that jutted out for a long way into a deeper channel. The companies could just see a faint blue flame leaping up from the rugged shore, as though it were a signal fire to call them home.

Lanril had leapt forward, and called out over the bow to the great eels. "Stop! You'll have us beaten to death on the Gray Dagger Reef! Look to it! We're in too close already!" At any moment, he expected to hear the death cry of his ship striking the long finger of reef that extended out a great way underwater, but no dreadful sound of the ship's hull grinding against the cruel killer came, and as an answer, Rhule sang out over his shoulder in high spirits.

"We don't drag our friends to their death, Captain! We try to make a point of fetching anyone we are after all in a piece, and that goes for the ship they may be aboard. The Welingesse Fal have their orders in mind at all times, and I think we have borne our duties well."

Lanril Tarben was still anxious about his ship, and knelt in the bow of the boat trying to mark the depth of the water, and to see if his keel would carry over the reef without touching.

Storm Watch

The weather had taken a sudden turn for the worse, and Lanril Tarben kept a worried lookout at the helm of the Marin Galone. Low, gray clouds scudded along over the horizon, and the wind was building steadily.

"This is a bad time to be making this passage," he shouted to Emerald to make himself heard. "Too late in the season."

The minstrel, finding it difficult to hold himself steady at the rail, agreed. "We might just as well have cooled our heels at White Bird. Do you think the Welingesse Fal can continue on through this?"

Lanril laughed grimly. "They can, but this vessel can't."

It was hardly midday, but the darkness and wildness of the sea made it seem as though night had already begun to fall. After the ship had pounded into the rising seas for another hour, Emerald went below to find Elita. He discovered her wrapped in a robe, lying quietly in her bunk.

"The Welingtron are uneasy," she announced as he entered.

"They aren't the only ones. I am a musician, not a seaman, but I can see that we won't be able to continue on this way, no matter how badly we need to press on."

As if to confirm his statement, the Marin Galone rose high up on the face of a wave and skidded away down the other side, leaving him dangling in midair for a moment, before he crashed back down, holding to the cabin table for support. He heard the cries of the sailors as they worked the ship, and Lanril's voice came in ragged starts, as it was blown away at times by the howling wind.

The next wave carried the ship up, where she paused, trembling, then slid down again, her timbers groaning. Lanril's face appeared at the companionway, his hair plastered to his forehead, and he motioned for Emerald to come nearer.

"I've given Rhule the word to find us a safe hole, if he can. We'll have to weather this as best we're able."

"Where are we?" shouted Emerald.

"Not far enough along, but from all I can make of my charts, and the speed of Rhule and his friends, we could be close to one of the out islands of the Straits."

"A bad time to find hard ground. I hope the eels know we draw more water than they do."

"Not much choice here, Minstrel. It's a hard chance, no matter what way we look to it. We can be broken up here, or dragged over a reef, or turned turtle by the wind. If we hadn't already lost our foresails, I'd be for having the eels let us go, and just set her shoulder to it, but we can't even do that with bare poles. Right now, I think Rhule wants to run off and see if we can't come up in the lee of one of the small islands. That would serve our purpose better than being slowly pounded to splinters here."

A sailor's cry from the deck pulled the captain away.

"It's land, sir! Off the starboard bow! The eels are making straight for it!"

Another sound was heard then, above the roar of the wind and crash of the sea. The high, eerie song of the Welingcssc Fal seemed to electrify the listeners, and Emerald felt the hair at the back of his neck stand out.

Lanril shouted out a warning to someone on deck, then ducked his head into the companionway. "You two had best look to find something that floats and hang on to it. I'm not so sure we shall see another morning aboard the Marin Galone." His voice was even, but the look on his face betrayed his grief.

"Buck up, Lanril, the Welingesse Fal have not wrecked us yet. They may have something left in their bag of tricks. Rhule has probably seen this weather before."

"But not while towing a ship of mine."

Elita sat up, listening intently to the eels. "They've seen another ship. It's just in front of us."

Lanril cursed under his breath. "By Antlach's Anchor, that's all we need! Now we'll have to keep a close watch that we don't wreck from running each other down!"

Emerald went up the companionway steps, and shielded his eyes from the flying spray, trying to pierce the storm to find the other vessel the great eels had seen. "I can't make anything out. Can you see the other ship?"

Lanril shook his head. "When we come up on the next crest, we may be able to make her."

"Who else would be out?" called the minstrel. "Surely it is one of our own."

"Hard to say. I'll worry about who they are when we've run out of this. I haven't seen a nor'easter come up this quickly since I was sailing as my father's messboy."

As the captain of the Marin Galone finished speaking, the ship climbed a long roller and paused momentarily at the top.

"Ship ho!" sang the lookout, in time with a half-dozen others of the crew.

Standing off to their port side was a sleek vessel, trimmed for heavy weather, footing her way along in the same direction as the Marin Galone.

"Now there's a proper ship," called Lanril. "He's got her shoulder down, and she's working like she should be, not being dragged about like a piece of cork on a fishing line!" He had barely finished his sentence when he saw the distinctive scarlet pennant flying off the taffrail of the other ship, and recognized her to be the Dart, captained by none other than Railan Dramm himself.

The lookout aboard the ship had given the warning, and Emerald saw the men on deck bustling about as best as they were able, looking as though they were preparing to try to launch a boarding party.

"That looks like they plan to try to board us," observed Emerald, astounded that the notorious Red Pirate would attempt something so dangerous in the treacherous weather.

"That's why he has his reputation following him about," returned Lanril. "He's a gutsy blackheart, if he's nothing else! But he'll never get a boat over in this."

"And if he does, there are other secrets about his ship he hasn't realized yet."

At that moment, Rhule appeared on deck, his glistening dark green skin changing colors in the gray light. "It is your old friend from the Delos Sound, Captain. They are making good time, and I think they may have the same storm haven in mind. We shall beat them to it, though."

"You know this place?" asked Lanril.

"We pass this way often. It is good for any weather. Your ship will be quite snug."

"And you think Railan Dramm will be making for the same anchorage?"

"No doubt. But it will be after tomorrow's sunrise. He will have to stand off now. He couldn't risk a night passage through the reefs."

"He's bold enough to try to put off a boarding party on us in this storm, so I don't see a reason he wouldn't try to reach safety, if he knew of the place."

"He won't have our eyes, Captain. We have had some dealings with this man. He will wait until first light tomorrow."

"I'll never understand what gets into a man that makes him want to go to sea," said Emerald, looking a little green.

Lanril laughed. "A very perverse nature, Minstrel. Of the most stubborn sort."

"You can add mad to that as well, Captain. Only madmen would be dancing here with the elements tonight."

"Madmen and friends of the Welingesse Fal."

After making sure Elita was safely in her bunk and needed

nothing, they set out for the captain's cabin, where Begam had taken the spare bunk to store his gear and sleep.

Winter Squalls

At first light, the companions aboard the Marin Galone saw a thin sprit of land jutting out toward them, swallowed on both sides by high waves breaking over it. Jagged heads of exposed reefs dotted the area, and behind that they could see the main bulk of the island rising above the storm clouds and blowing mist. As Rhule brought the ship nearer, Lanril Tarben began to gesture wildly to try to stop the Welingtron.

The captain was gone before Begam or Emerald could stop him. A wavering note was struck then, which rose above the roaring of the sea, soothing and at once terrifying in its message.

"They know what they're doing," said Elita.

"Try to convince Lanril Tarben of that." Emerald pointed to the soaked figure of the ship's master, dancing about on the bow of his boat. At last, the shimmering form of Rhule appeared on deck out of the white frothing sea, and spoke to the agitated man.

"What do you think he's saying?" asked Begam.

"Probably trying to explain to a prudent seafaring man about his qualifications," laughed Emerald.

"He'd best have a word with Railan Dramm. No matter what else you've heard of the Red Scorpion, you'll have to give him credit for being one bold sailor to be out and about in this blow."

"I'd just as soon thank the Morranzi swordsmen for having made such fine steel to stick me with," growled Emerald. "Do you see his ship?"

"Not yet. Rhule is bringing us through a pass that someone without the Welingtron couldn't make."

"Not if you gauge reactions by Lanril Tarben."

The Marin Galone groaned and shook her masts under the

strain of the great eels pulling her along, but the dreaded moment of grounding had not come, and in another few moments, she was floating smoothly over a quiet stretch of water in the lee of a high outcropping of land covered with low, rough scrub brush.

"This is a lonely enough place," said Begam. "I wonder where we are?"

Before the friends could try to guess their location, Elita came to the rail and pointed over the stern rail. "It's them," she said simply.

It was not hard to see that the ship that had been following along behind them was built by the Elboreal, and it glided along toward them as though its hull did not touch the water. The Marodinel was plainly heard now over the crashing roar of the ocean against the land, and even Lanril Tarben, still lost in his great agitation over the safety of his ship, stopped and stood motionless on the bow of his ship, lost in the voice of the Dreamers.

Elita burst into tears, and stood hugging her husband.

"What is it?" asked Emerald, dumbstruck. "Are you ill?"

She shook her head, unable to speak, sobs racking her body. Begam was weeping too, and watched transfixed as the elven ship came next to the Marin Galone.

A white aurora of glowing light shone on the sails and the rigging, and the voice of the Marodinel was woven onto the morning and the sea, and through each heart that beat on the deck, and locked in time with the eerie songs of the great eels. Rhule's graceful body arced into the air and disappeared beneath the surface of the water without a ripple, coming up a few moments later with his entire following of Welingtron. They linked themselves together and formed a huge circle about the two ships, their bodies glowing a golden green as they swam, the music of their history blended into the bitter sweetness of the Elboreal's long memory.

A majestic figure appeared on the deck of the elven vessel, dressed in soft blue cloth, with a golden staff crooked in the bend of his elbow. A crown with five stars sat atop his golden head, and even before Emerald saw, he knew the eyes would be a deep, misty blue, such as the color Elita's eyes had been when she was brought back from the dead after her dreadful dragon wounds. A voice, or what could have been a voice, spoke, although it was hard to decide from whence it came;

it was the wind and sea, and the beating of their own hearts.

"Wind and sea greets you, wanderers. Drafe Arrowfine brings the tidings of the Havens, and the hopes of safe journeys there."

Lanril Tarben was struck speechless, but Elita stepped forward and bowed to the startlingly beautiful figure of the tall elf.

"Greetings, Drafe Arrowfine. Our hearts are yours, and the hopes of the Dreamers are the dreams we dream."

The elf smiled, his blue eyes full of deep joy and sorrow. "Little sister, you have spent your time well with the Elboreal. You are well?"

"Well, and happy, my lord," she replied. "This is my husband, the loremaster Emerald."

Emerald was recovering himself, and bowed. "Forgive me, sir, I will find my tongue in a moment."

"It would be good business for a minstrel to be able to use his voice," chided the elf.

"We weren't expecting so distinguished a visitor," protested Emerald.

"Nor were any of them." His beautiful features hardened, and he turned to look over the Marin Galone. "Good captain, I have caught you up to warn you of the scourge from Hulingaad. There is one of the nasty fellows about now, beyond the last island here."

"We've seen the flying snake," said Lanril Tarben, finding himself able to speak at last. His eyes were wide with astonishment at the sight of the elf on his ship's deck.

"There's another ship, as well. I think it may be dangerous to you."

"It's the Red Pirate. We almost collided with him in the dark last night."

"The beast is called by the ship. They try to lure you on to your doom."

"We're but a single ship," protested Lanril. "There must be other fish to fry out here."

"You have two who have been touched by the Marodinel aboard. The beasts detest all our race with a far-reaching hatred, for we are a grave danger to them."

"Is there a way we can avoid them?" asked Begam.

"That's why I am here, little brother. We shall escort you past the Straits, and guide you on to Eirn Bol. There are others we are taking there as well."

Emerald could not hold back. "Do you know of the fate of a lad called Owen Helwin? He was aboard a ship bound for Eirn Bol."

"There are rumors of him from time to time," answered the elf evasively.

"Only rumors?" persisted Emerald.

"Only rumors of all of us," replied the elf. "In these meadows, there is only our shadows here for a time. There is no substance to this illusion."

The minstrel remembered how Stearborn and Chellin Duchin always dreaded dealing with the Elboreal. It was difficult speaking of reality to them, for their own realities were of a far deeper nature, and they could not always discern the need for a plain and simple answer.

"But you have heard nothing of his death?" went on Emerald.

"I have heard of all our deaths," said the elven Elder. "They ring before us like a bell." He raised an arm and sounded a fine mithra bell, which peeled so sweetly upon the air, it drowned out the crash and roar of the storm-driven sea. "But that is not for us to think of now. There is still a scene or two left to play before we're through."

"I'm glad of that," confessed the master of the Marin Galone. "I can't say I'm fond of contemplating my departure."

That drew a laugh from Emerald. "Nor I, good captain. I fear we're not wise in the ways of the Elboreal, so we aren't familiar with their manner of expression."

Elita had taken the elven king aside, and spoke earnestly to him at the rail, out of earshot of the others. Her husband watched her beautiful features streaked with tears, and felt a pang of sorrow strike his heart as he saw the tall elf holding his wife's hand and drying her tears with a silk scarf he had removed from his neck. When she returned, he did not ask her what they had spoken of, but held her close to him, feeling the soft sobs against his shoulder.

"I'm glad I have not yet understood the Elboreal," he said at last. "I don't think I would be able to stand the pain."

Elita let out a half laugh, half sob. "It's not all pain," she said. "The other side of it is the joy of it all. They are the last of the old races left here to guide us. They can remember the other side of the Boundary, yet they still feel the beauty of Atlanton."

"Unless you're a lover of storms, there's not much of the

beauty today," said Lanril, eyeing the sky again. "This is going to get worse before it gets better." He shook his head, grasping the rail. "In my book, we should be back in our homeport, riding out the worst of the season and fitting out for the spring. All this has taken the sense out of everything, wandering around on the very edge of the Verges, and acting as though it was a sane and ordinary thing for a prudent tar to do. I don't like it, even if we do have the help of the Welingtron and the Dreamers. It's not natural!"

"Better than not having them around at all," argued Begam. "If we have to be out in it, I'm glad enough for their help."

"You know what I mean," snapped Lanril. "A simple sailor understands the sea and weather, and that's as far as it goes. When it goes beyond what's natural, then it begins to wear like salt on a raw wound."

"Which is what we'll have plenty of, if we don't remove ourselves from here." Emerald was looking away toward the east, and there, visible just above the sprit of land, were the topmasts of the Dart, sailed by the Red Pirate.

"The fool is going to try for a rounding!" cried Lanril. He ran forward, calling for all hands.

"The Welingtron are there," reminded Emerald. "And Drafe Arrowfine."

"We don't wish to discourage him from following," said the elf, his deep blue eyes shrouded with odd visions of old storms and older seas. "You mustn't let Rhule move you too fast. We want Railan Dramm to feel he has a chance to board you."

"Dangled like a carrot to a rabbit," snorted Lanril Tarben. "I never thought I'd see the day a Delos Sound man would be brought to the likes of this!" He gestured disgustedly and stalked back to the helm of his sleek ship.

The Decoy

Lanril Tarben had grumbled and complained the whole time, watching the Welingtron take up their places at the bow of the boat, and once more pull the Marin Galone back out into the open waters beyond the protected lee. Drafe Arrowfine had returned to his ship, and almost before their eyes had vanished from sight.

"That's what I hate about dealing with the likes of them," the captain snapped. "Nothing you can depend upon when it comes down to it."

"It wouldn't do if Railan Dramm saw his ship," replied Elita.

"Fine that he sees mine," he complained.

"Does he sail for the Black Hood?" asked Emerald. "I thought they killed all outsiders."

"The Red Scorpion uses the harbors of Hulingaad when he pleases, or so I'm told. He was a great gambling friend with Lacon Rie's son, Tien Cal."

"If there is a story behind that, I'm sure Drafe Arrowfine would know of it," said Elita.

"I don't want to ask him myself, even if he does prove to have a certain innocence," added Emerald, looking over his shoulder at the sight of the Dart, heeled into the wind, moving steadily forward through the waves.

"Whatever else, he has a fine vessel," admitted Lanril. "She's as pretty as a picture, working like that. You don't see many ships with such sweet lines, or that are as sea-kindly."

"We've made good time, at any rate," said Elita. "We were not expecting to have reached the Straits of Horinfal so soon, and already we're going on."

"That's according to Rhule. I still don't know how he keeps all his figures straight in his head, but that's what he's said. At this rate, we'll be fetching dangerous waters inside three days."

"Even this slowly?" asked Begam.

"Look at her, sir," said Lanril, pointing back to the driving figure of the Dart. "Even without the Welingtron, she's making fine time. If those were indeed the outside islands of the Straits of Horinfal, we'd fetch the waters of Eirn Bol without having to tack but twice, and be there for dinner not more than a few days from now."

A lookout cried out from the main mast at the moment, his voice thin and blown on the wind. "She's gaining! Ship gaining!" The man's hand directed their attention to the Dart, driving to windward now at an alarming speed.

Emerald peered more closely at the vessel. "If I didn't

know better, I'd say some of the Welingtron are pulling that boat, too!''

"You can make out the faces of the crew there," observed Lanril. "Look! You can make out Railan Dramm! He's the big red-beard urging the others on!" The master of the Marin Galone turned to his own crew, raising his hand above his head. "Look alive, me hearties! Stand by to repel the Red Scorpion himself!"

The seas were running as high as the railing of the two ships, and both vessels were struggling to stay upright. Rhule and the Welingtron had slowed their progress so that the sailors could trim the sails, easing the motion and making the boats ride more easily.

"Our friend has gotten his chance at us now," shouted Lanril. "If you two can handle a weapon, now's the time!"

Elita has lashed herself to the railing near her husband, and brushed aside the seaman who had come to help her below. "I'm staying here," she cried. Emerald went to stand beside her and handed her the small engraved dagger he had been given by Famhart after they had come home from the Fords of Silver. "You may need this if we fail to deter this fellow," he said lightly, although his hand grasped hers and held it very tightly.

"Rhule has not let this ship down. I hear many things from their speech, but they all talk of something else, and not this Red Pirate."

"Can you still feel the dragon?" asked Begam, looking about in the cold, gray light of the storm. White patches had formed on all the wave tops, and the wind increased in volume and speed.

"With any luck, the flying oven won't be the death of this ship, but if we get any more wind, we're going to be finding out how well we can swim." Lanril Tarben had straightened his tunic, and now stood looking out over the roaring sea toward where he thought Eirn Bol to be.

In the next instant, a squat lookout posted in the crow's nest of the main mast called out, pointing toward a leathery-winged beast lumbering along the wave tops, its blood-red eyes ablaze with a hatred that froze the ship's crew where they stood.

A Pentograph Recalled

❈

Emerald and Elita watched from the afterdeck as the great beast lumbered along over the wave tops, bearing straight down upon them. He reached out to touch her, but found her flesh hot to the touch, and a powerful current ran through her slim body, and her blue eyes were aflame with a strength that came from her old wounds and healing by the Elboreal. A lilting verse passed her lips, spoken in time to the beating of the heavy wings of the dragon as it approached.

> "Nine sacred names
>   of nine sacred trees
> split the shrines
>   of the darkness's eaves
>   and draw away the power
>   of those who grieve
> for the worlds before
>   the golden door,
>   where the souls of the Purge
>   will find rest once more."

"What was that you said?" asked Emerald, his sword already drawn and ready. The rest of the crew had taken up their battle positions, but there was no sign of the Welingtron as yet, although the minstrel could feel the presence of Rhule in the depths below the Marin Galone.

Elita's eyes cleared, and she blinked, as if coming to herself. "I don't quite remember. It was something the Dreamers repeated to me."

"It was a good poem. I hope you can remember to tell me when we have a chance. It would make the start of a good tale."

"A good tale to tell of all this," went on Begam. "That was

138

a Pentograph from a minstrel called Wylch.'' He smiled, although thinly. ''That is if we live to tell it.''

Lanril's archers had loosed a barrage of razor-sharp arrows in the direction of the dragon, but it flew on, out of range, wheeling awkwardly in long, lazy circles. It held itself aloft above the Dart, then flew farther away. The enemy ship had closed near enough to the Marin Galone so that they could see the forms of sailors aboard, and could make out plainly a flag that was flying at the top of the main mast. Lanril stood gazing at it in amazement for a moment, then held up an arm to stop his archers. ''Hold, lads! They're asking for a parley!''

''It's a trick, Lanril,'' growled a barrel-chested sailor beside his captain.

''Hold, Dorsin, I hear your thoughts. But look!'' Lanril pointed to a figure on the afterdeck of the Dart, standing close by the rail, waving another banner that signaled a desire to talk.

''What do you make of it?'' asked Emerald, turning to Begam.

''The dragon is easier to read,'' he replied. ''I'm surprised he hasn't attacked, but then it may be the Wylch song that's keeping him back. This bird''—he indicated the Dart—''I don't know about.''

''There haven't been many who have had a palaver with Railan Dramm and lived to repeat it,'' mused Lanril. ''I'm tempted to heave to, and find out what the bloody rascal is up to.''

''You surely can't mean to trade words with this black-hearted rogue!'' snapped Dorsin, loosening his sword in its scabbard.

''My mate is almost as bloodthirsty as the Red Scorpion,'' laughed Lanril. ''We shall see if you don't get your chance yet, Dorsin. For now, I think I shall run up my own white flag and see what disaster that brings.''

Elita pointed to the foaming wake behind the Marin Galone. ''It's the Welingtron. They have brought him up to us.'' A sleek green head sliced through the surface of the sea in front of the Dart, and the companions saw Rhule glide effortlessly up and over the side of the enemy's ship.

''I wondered how he was pinching up like that,'' whistled Lanril. ''The Marin Galone is as fleet as any on these waters when it comes to going in a blow, and they were pulling us like we were anchored.''

''I hope he swallows them whole,'' growled Dorsin. ''Then we'd be rid of one plague that's hunted these waters too long.''

''I don't think that's what the Welingtron have in mind.''

Begam was watching closely as the great eel appeared next to the dreaded figure of the Red Pirate, the Scorpion of the Silent Sea. Beyond, far out of bowshot, the leathery wings of the Purge raked the morning air with gaunt, hollow sounds, like giant bellows being pumped in an empty hall.

The sails aboard the Dart began coming down, and Rhule called out for the Marin Galone to heave to as well. Soon Lanril's men had all but a riding sail on the main secured, and waited as the Welingtron pulled the pirate's vessel close enough so that the two captains could speak to each other more easily, although the sound of the wind still made hearing difficult.

"What ship are you, and where from?" The man who spoke was powerfully built, with a full red beard and a flowing cloak of the same color. The battle shields that lined the side of the ship were a dull silver-gray, with a red scorpion emblazoned on the front poised to strike.

"I am Lanril Tarben, aboard the Marin Galone, out of the Delos Sound."

"Tell me, Lanril Tarben, have you seen my lapdog hovering here?" Railan pointed back toward the heavy shadow of the beast low down over the surface of the sea now, circling away behind.

"We have seen the flying cook stove, sir, and remark it. Was it the nature of those foul things you wished to discuss with us, or is there something further."

The burly man stiffened, and his nostrils flared out as he spoke. "You would be wise to consider keeping the peace with me, Captain. If I wished, I'd make fish food of you and your crew, and send that splinter you sail to blazes!"

Dorsin raised his voice from behind his commander. "You'd find that a most excellent chore, sir, and one that I think might skin your nose in the process!" A murmur of angry assent went around the deck of the Marin Galone, and was echoed on the other boat.

"We serve no good purpose here at odds," went on Begam. "You must know we have Welingtron escorting us, and that you would be powerless to defend yourself against them. There was a purpose to your offer to parley, and we waste our good time and yours trying to find out what manner of business you had that made you seek us out."

The red-bearded man pointed toward Elita. "She was the reason we asked for a parley. It is a standing order of mine that when we spot vessels with women aboard, I always speak to them first before an attack."

"Very mannerly of you, I'm sure," replied Emerald. "This is my wife, Elita."

"I can see that she is not the one I seek, now that she has her cape pulled back," returned the pirate gruffly, but there was something in his tone that caused Begam to speak up again.

"Why is it you are searching out vessels with women aboard, Captain? Is there a particular woman you are seeking?"

A subtle change played over the fierce face of Railan Dramm for a moment, but he quickly covered it with a harsh scowl. "My motives are my own. Not even the Black Hood dares interfere with the captain of the Dart."

"Is there one you have lost?" asked Elita suddenly, her voice gliding across the wind like a seabird's soft call. The unexpected kindness of it took Railan aback.

"Yes. My sister and mother were taken." He gripped the railing of the Dart so hard his knuckles showed white, and a terrible grief passed fleetingly through his gaze. "I have sworn on my father's name I will find them and avenge myself on their captors."

"You need not stop vessels from the Delos Sound, sir," shot back Lanril Tarben. "We are not in the business of piracy or slavery. You might draw that conclusion before you attack honest ships and crews, you thieving devil!"

"You won't draw me into a fight, Captain," replied Railan. "I have had reports that brighten my hopes. We have aboard a survivor who was sailing aboard a vessel with a cargo of women for their outpostings. His life was spared because he described one of the women to me who had a small mark, like the Daelmen use to color themselves. My sister and I had those when we were but shrimpen, at a fair that came to our port."

"And was it you who sank the ship, sir?"

"I have told you my methods of search."

The eels had begun another of their haunting, eerie songs, and Elita listened for a moment. "He wishes to sail with us," said Elita suddenly, her eyes gone a misty gray.

"Sail with us? Is that true, sir?" asked Lanril, his voice unable to conceal his surprise.

Railan had opened his mouth to speak, but his eyes met Elita's, and he bit off the words he was about to utter, and his face softened. Rhule was behind him then, and the eerie humming songs of the Welingtron grew louder, and the crew of the Dart stood transfixed at their battle positions, hands lowered.

The captain of the Marin Galone looked about in disbelief. "Well, shiver my timbers, but I don't believe I've come to this!"

"We shall have need of a vessel that's known to the Black Hood," said Begam, taking Elita's hand for a moment. "And there are more ways to take an enemy vessel than by destroying it."

Emerald looked at his wife more closely. "You show me new surprises every day, Elita. I'm not so sure I truly know the woman I've spoken my vows to."

She smiled at her husband coyly. "You know the most important part of me, husband. My heart is all too plain to read."

"Rhule says he will arrange for the Dart to be taken with us," said Begam. "We have not much farther to go."

Lanril snorted out a short bark of mirthless laughter. "That would be grand words to an old sailor in other times, but I don't relish this landfall, not by a long pull."

"At least the wait will be over," said Emerald. "And we might see less of the ugly fellow back there in our wake." He watched as the dragon lazily made a wider circle, drawing farther away from the two ships. "He seems to have some reservations about coming too near us."

"It is Hulingaad he stays clear of now." Begam raised his arm and pointed away to an invisible place on the horizon. "They have probably posted it out here as guard, and to warn them of anything moving toward the relief of Eirn Bol."

"Come along then, good captain," called Lanril. "If you want to hook up and sail with us, let us find out which ship is truly the quickest of the two. Shall I ask Rhule to let us have the run of our vessels, so we can settle the matter in a gentlemanly way?"

Railan resumed his former fierceness. "Take your whipdogs away from us, and let us run. I'll show you a thing or two about the Dart! Do you have the price of a wager?"

"Whatever you think fair," returned Lanril.

"First to port is victor, and they claim any spoils they want."

"They claim any spoils they may be able to take," corrected Lanril, a thread of hardness laced through his own tone.

The Red Scorpion broke away from the railing then, and shouted out orders to his crew, who leapt to set sail, and fell off to port, with the Dart setting her shoulder down, and driving powerfully into the churning sea. Lanril was only a split second behind, looking over his shoulder to see Rhule and his followers gliding swiftly along on the wake of the Marin Galone.

Autumn
Gales

A Terrible Beauty and Tears

Aboard The Crane, Jeremy grew stronger day by day, and felt a growing fondness for the wonderful sensations he would get from the small leather pouch he carried about beneath his tunic. Ulria had said nothing more of the white dream-dust, other than it had helped him recover from a wound that would have killed him otherwise.

His biggest fear now was running out of his supply. The pouch was noticeably thinner, and he began to fret about the eventual reality. There was no one aboard he could speak of it to, except the Welingesse Fal. Eared was sometimes aboard in the presence of Captain Telig, but something held the young Steward back from talking about the dream-dust. Hamlin must have come across some at one point or another, he knew, for he could now understand his friend's desire to find the Elboreal again. Chellin Duchin never mentioned anything pertaining to it, other than a short poem he always recited when he spoke of the elves, or their doings.

> From beyond the Golden Age
>   they fared,
> when the World was younger,
>   bringing a terrible beauty and tears
>   as their children.

Chellin would be too old to understand, and Jeremy presented the best argument of all, by convincing himself that the dream-dust was what had saved him, when nothing else would have.

They were four days into their voyage behind the powerful eels, when Captain Telig asked Jeremy to go aboard one of the captured Hulin Vipre vessels to question the former prisoners.

"You've got an easy way with you, lad. I'm afraid my tar would show, and I don't have another man to spare right now."

Jeremy nodded, although feeling short-tempered. The small pouch was lighter still, and he was finding himself opening it more and more often, in order to keep away the dreadful depression that hovered at the thought of having no more.

"Salts will row you over when the eels have their sundown rituals."

"It's the only time they stop all day," said the seaman standing at the rail watching the broad, powerful backs of the Welingesse Fal flowing through their liquid motions that pulled the small invisible fleet quickly along.

The winds had been easterly, which trailed the high, thin clouds into feathery lines across the pale blue sky. A faint blush of pink was present, down low on the horizon, and the captain studied it for a long while.

"We've had our share of luck, I'll grant! Every day I expect to see smoke and fire, but those devils from Hulingaad must have their firesnakes on a short leash at home."

"Who are these prisoners?" asked Jeremy, trying to take his mind off the pouch in his tunic.

"Local people captured by the Hulin Vipre. They're carried into slavery if they're able to work." He paused. "The women are used as well." He left the last thought unfinished.

"Then what can they tell us?"

"Perhaps how large a fleet there is. Who the commanders are, where they were bound, how they were eating. All small things, but you'd be surprised how much you can learn by developing an eye for detail." Captain Telig pointed away to the south toward a distant rocky headland that they were passing at the moment. "We were set on by the Black Hood there one fall, and had a smart time of it to escape with our lives. If the Vipre chieftain had been at his best, he would have seen how high we were carrying, and known our ships were lighter than his. We outran them into Fionten."

"I don't understand," said Jeremy, puzzled.

"If the dog had looked, he would have known to close with us when he had the chance, instead of letting us get sail on. He was so sure of the mighty Black Hood fleet, he forgot that a hare can sometimes outrun the hound. Especially if the hound is too well fed and slowed down by his dinner."

The Crane bore on through the dark blue water, leaving a foaming white wake behind, which Jeremy pointed out as Captain Telig came back to the quarterdeck after attending some duty with his first mate.

"Even the leaf from the Sacred Grove can't cover up tracks, my lad. Not while we're under way."

"Then a firesnake could see that and know where we are!"

"But you forget that they have some of their own ships under the leaf as well," reminded the captain. "A flying fireplace would have no way of knowing who it was attacking."

The vessel was beginning to slow, and Jeremy saw the heads of the great eels as they surfaced, floating at full length in the darkening shadows of the sea. The haunting, eerie call the eels made filled the air, and even the waves seemed to calm for a time, until the twilight songs of the Welingesse Fal were over, and the sun dropped down below the horizon in one last flaring explosion of red and gold.

"It'll be time for Salts to take you aboard to talk to the Hulin prisoners. I'll see you in the morning, lad. Find out everything you can for me."

Captain Telig moved on below, and the sailor who had brought him safely from the beach on the Horinfal Straits waved him over the side into the tender, and steered him straight toward a dark shadow across an empty stretch of water, where a rushlamp suddenly shone to guide their way.

A Former Prisoner

The Hulin ship smelled strongly of soap, and the former prisoners were occupied in scrubbing down the decks to try to clean the stench of blood and death from the wood. More rushlamps were lit and placed about the deck, and Jeremy could see pale faces in the flickering light, working to ready the lines for the Welingesse Fal to resume their journey. Salts came aboard, too, and secured the tender to the stern rail.

"Not a happy ship," he observed, keeping his voice low. "None of these Vipre vessels are ever built to my standards. I hope we'll last the night out aboard this bucket."

Jeremy's hand was toying with the pouch beneath his tunic as he struggled with the thought of using more of his precious supply of the Elboreal's dream-dust.

"Here's a likely tongue," said Salts, pointing to a barrel-chested man dressed in the tattered remains of a uniform. "How are you called, matey? My friend here and I would like to speak to you."

The man's eyes were dull and lifeless, and it was obvious that he had suffered much at the hands of his captors.

"Have you had your mess, mate? Didn't they feed you yet?"

The man remained expressionless, never stopping his scrubbing.

"He doesn't hear," said a girl's voice from behind. "They broke his ears."

"What?" shot Salts. "They did what?"

"He tried to escape, and they broke his ears."

"What's your name, miss?" asked Jeremy, trying to see the young face beneath the hood she wore.

"I am called Laeni. Where are you taking us?"

"Eirn Bol is where we're bound. You might find your way home from there. Where were you from before? The Straits?"

"No, sir. I am from the Delos Sound." The girl's voice broke, and she was near tears. "They took me and my mother."

"Why, you're still a child, girl," said Salts. "Look at you, now! Is your mother with you?"

The girl lapsed back into a monotone, her eyes gone lifeless again. "She was used in the men's houses until she died. I don't remember when I heard."

Jeremy's hand still toyed with the pouch, but he was moved by the young woman's pain and beauty. She had long auburn hair that showed on both sides of the cowl to her cloak, and her features, although worn with fatigue, were still young.

"Can you tell me anything about these men?" asked Jeremy. "Where you sailed from, or how many ships there were?"

"I have been with the captain of an outpost on the South Fetch. He had me for his wife until the others came." Her voice was flat and emotionless, and she spoke as though she talked of some stranger. "I don't know exactly how many ships there were. When they stopped, they spent a week at their cups. It seemed there were many of them."

"But why would they bring you, if you were a wife of one of their own."

"He lost me at cards. The master of this ship was to put me and all the rest of the women in a house he has at another settlement in the new territory the Black Hood has taken." The girl's tone was even, as though she were reciting something that had been told to her.

"They won't be taking anyone anywhere this trip," said Salts bluntly. "The lot of them are fish food now, and I pity the poor brutes their meal."

Laeni looked at the two of them, lowering her face. "Do you gentlemen wish to use me? It's your right, since you've slain the others."

Jeremy and the sailor looked at each other in confusion.

"Why, you're free, miss," explained Salts hesitatingly. "That life's all over. You don't have to do that now."

The girl stared at them, unblinking.

"Don't you remember anything about where you came from?" asked Jeremy. "Before you were stolen?"

"I remember my brother took me into the woods to look for birds, and we fished. He made my mother and father laugh."

"What's his name?" asked Jeremy. "Is he still alive?"

"They never caught him," went on the girl, smiling at some secret thought. "He was gone with one of my father's crews. He will come for me one day. He always promised he would find me, if I ever got lost. He found me in the woods, once."

"Then you've heard from him?"

"No. But I hear stories of him. A friend was in the men's house near where the big bay is before she came to us, and she told me of him and his men. He played at cards with Tien Cal, the prince of the Black Hood. He gave her money and sent her from the room when Tien Cal wanted to gamble for her."

"It sounds like a right fine lad, miss. I'd be proud to call him a mate of mine."

"Tien Cal is dead," declared Jeremy. "He died fighting the Line Stewards."

A strange smile crossed the girl's face. "Sobia said he was handsome."

"Tien Cal? I never saw him," replied Jeremy.

"Railan. Sobia wanted to marry him. I told her he was my brother."

"Railan? Did you say Railan, miss?" asked Salts, his eyebrows arched.

"A good name. My father's name was Railan, too."

"Did your father escape?" asked Jeremy. A sudden motion of the ship beneath their feet announced the great eels of the Welingtron were on their way once more. The hull creaked and they listened as the water began to flow by, making a soft splashing sound, and he turned to watch the white wakes begin again. He knew The Crane was there next to them, but he could see a low star, down near the horizon, right through where the mast and sails of the ship should have been.

"They killed him before he could get his boat unmoored. Poor father."

Salts took Jeremy aside and spoke into his ear to avoid being overheard. "This poor young thing is saying she had a brother called Railan. Now there's a certain devil loose on these oceans by the very same name, and I'm wondering if we've got the man's sister here?"

"Who? What's this poor girl got to do with some renegade loose on the sea? There are plenty of them about to go around."

"Railan Dramm. The Red Pirate. He's played both ends against the middle for a long time. At first, no one thought to bother with him, for he always seemed to go for the crooked merchants, or mercenary tradesmen who have been at it now ever since the border wars have opened up their markets for arms and loot again." Salts paused, scowling. "Then he got a little less picky about the vessels he boarded. He'd put the crews off on the Straits, or ashore somewhere along the coast, but he still got a lot of hackles up over his brashness."

"And you think this girl is his sister?" asked Jeremy, growing more concerned.

"We'll ask her what her brother looks like," suggested Salts.

"It's been a long time since she's seen him," reminded the young Steward.

"Miss, is your brother redheaded like yourself? Does he wear a beard?"

A hopeful look passed over the girl's exhausted features. "Do you know him? Has he come for me?"

"Is he called Railan Dramm?" went on Salts.

To his surprise, the young woman fell to her knees at Salts's feet. "Oh, bless you, sir, bless you for bringing his name to my ears again." She was choked with her tears and couldn't go on. She clutched at the seaman's hands, who looked to Jeremy for help.

"Here, miss, come up," he stammered. "We'll see you get some tea and biscuit, and you can go below to rest a bit."

"Your brother isn't here," said Jeremy. "But we'll try to get word to him. You must rest now."

Laeni had hidden her face in her cloak, and they watched her shoulders heave as she sobbed.

"Poor lass," said Salts. "I have a daughter about her age at home still. I don't like to feel what I feel in my heart now for those brutes who have done this to this poor slip of a girl." Salts's face was hard in the dark shadows, and Jeremy felt the cold rage that consumed the sailor slowly spill over into his own heart.

"And his Railan Dramm? Is he such a bad one?"

"I don't think the fellow was ever up to this sort of work, but he's sent a shipmate or two to dance with the sea gods."

"She makes a good argument for him."

"I would soften my judgment of the fellow by the goodness of this girl's tears. Anyone who has a lass crying over him like this can't be such a black-hearted devil as I might think."

"You're too soft, Salts," teased Jeremy gently, moved by the man's kindness. Another thought came to him then, and he undid the leather pouch from around his neck. The Elboreal used its powers to heal wounds of the body, and it had saved him from a traitor's murderous blow, and Jeremy thought to try it now on the terrible wound the beautiful young woman had suffered at the hands of her captors.

He took a small pinch of the dream-dust and held it out to the weeping girl.

Laeni

Salts stood at the rail of the captured Hulin ship, watching the wake trail behind him in a long, white line. The weather was cold and clear, but a dark bank of clouds lay ahead of them on the horizon, directly across their path. When Jeremy came up from taking the girl below to her bunk, he lifted a hand to point out a star, brilliant white-gold, burning clearly near the horizon.

"That's the Rhure Torch," he said. "Guide for all good seafaring men. Burns clear, and usually means fair passage, when you see it this late into the Verges."

"It has turned out to be a good passage for these poor folk," said Jeremy with a trace of bitterness in his voice. "She's trying to get some sleep now."

Salts nodded. "That powder you gave her, where'd you come by it, mate?"

"A friend," he replied evasively. "When I was wounded, she tended me, and left me this to help me heal."

"I've heard of such things, even being a common tar like I am. We had a lad once who was scorched by one of the firebats off the Southern Coast, and the healer in the port we put in to gave him such a powder to ease his pain."

"Was the healer a man?"

Salts nodded. "Good fellow, knew his stuff. Had the poor devil on his pins again in short enough time. He was scarred up, and looked a sight, but he's still under sail, even as we stand here gamming."

"A human healer, then."

"What else would he abeen, lad?" laughed Salts. "Hard to have truck with anshee's and such, who can't touch a hand to your flesh, or speak a word to your ear."

"I just meant it wasn't an Old One, or anyone like that."

The old sailor turned his head from studying the sea, his kindly face weathered with time and sun. "What would you know of such as that, lad?"

"I ride with Chellin Duchin, of the Line Stewards," he replied. "I got my lessons every day on all manner of things, from the proper handling of a sword and horse, to the historical mysteries of the Elboreal. He was a very demanding taskmaster."

"It does my old pump good to hear there's still some out there who try finishing off the raw lumps we are when we first slip our moorings," said Salts approvingly.

"You might not be so quick to agree if he were here to hound us."

"That might not be a bad notion, a little hounding. With the way things have been sinking, I wouldn't think a bit of salt to keep the dish tart would hurt.''

"Chellin Duchin would find a way to do that,'' assured Jeremy. "I hope wc shall meet up again as soon as we secure Eirn Bol.''

"That may take some doing. Will he come with his men?''

"He was in White Bird when I last heard. Our squadron is there.''

"He sounds like quite a soldier,'' said Salts.

Jeremy nodded, suddenly overcome by emotion at thinking of his old commander. "I used to think I couldn't wait to get away from him, but now I miss him. I never thought I'd find myself come to that.''

The old sailor smiled, looking away at the distant star. "Those things start to happen to you when you have a few turnings in your holds.''

Jeremy changed the subject suddenly. "Do you think her brother really is the same man you're talking about?''

"Railan Dramm? It seems likely.''

"But what will happen to her now? We can't just take her to some settlement and leave her. Or the rest of these people, either.''

"They have their freedom. They can do as they like.''

"But you heard her, Salts! They have used her like that for ten turnings! What would she do now?''

"The same as you would do recovering from any kind of wound, lad. Sometimes the sword or blow leaves a wound that's easier to heal than what she's taken.''

"I hope there's someplace we can leave her where they'll know how to help her.'' His thoughts turned to Ulria. "I wish my friend who helped me could be here now.'' He fingered the small pouch under his tunic.

"You mean the one who gave you that?''

"Yes. She could help her.''

Looking out over the dark water, Jeremy wondered where Ulria was, and if he would ever see her again. His heart was torn with many emotions, but the girl who had been held prisoner by the Hulin Vipre kept sliding back into his thoughts. Her eyes burned into him, and he had a difficult time thinking of other things.

A Childhood Lost

❋

As they proceeded on their passage, Laeni had begun to talk to him, of little things at first, then very slowly she began to speak to him of her childhood, and the life she had come from before she had been taken by the Black Hood.

"We had a double oven in our kitchen when I was little, and my mother taught me how to bake. I made my father and brother special cakes to take with them when they went out in the boat. They always said I made the best. My father was named Railan, too."

"I came up in a Line Steward camp," said Jeremy. "I never had a sister to bake for me, but I would have liked it."

"Would you? I can remember how to do it. Do they have an oven aboard?" Laeni seemed to remember she was on a Hulin Vipre vessel. "I don't know if I would want to do it here."

"The cook aboard The Crane has a fine oven he makes biscuits with," said Jeremy hurriedly. "You could do it there. I'll ask Captain Telig. I'm sure he won't mind such a pretty cook in his galley."

"My mother was much better at it than I am, but everyone always seemed pleased." She smiled softly to herself. "I pretended to be married, and to have a family." A cloud of sorrow filled her eyes, and she looked suddenly at her hands. "That's all changed now."

"Has it? Why would that change? You're still young, you have your whole life ahead of you."

"Not after what happened." She turned to him. "You're a friend, and I trust you, Jeremy. You're different. But I could never be a wife now. I wouldn't know how to act."

Jeremy laughed. "Why, you just told me you could bake so good it would break my heart, and then you say in the same breath you wouldn't know how to act. Now does that make any sense?"

"I know how to do that fine," the girl admitted. "But I

154

wouldn't know how to be with a..." Her voice trailed off. "You know what I mean." Her features had hardened again, and he felt her slipping away from him.

"What if you baked enough sweet tarts for a party?" Jeremy asked, changing the subject. "We haven't had a regular sit-down party since my old friend Emerald tried to get himself hitched to Elita."

"That would take some flour," she said. "Is there enough aboard your ship to do that?"

"More than plenty, my girl. I think I shall inform Captain Telig that it's high time his guests and crew had a day off!" Jeremy raised an outstretched arm to include the great eels who propelled the boats. "And we'll have the Welingtron, too. I don't know if they like cakes, but we'll ask, all the same."

A ghost of her old laugh crossed her lips. "That would be nice."

Salts was called for, and Jeremy outlined his plan. "A victory party for all these people," he explained. "It wouldn't take long, and it might help them realize they've been freed."

The old sailor studied the survivors of the Hulin Vipre toiling at the job of scrubbing the decks, then turned his attention to the sky. There were mare's tails streaming away in high curls from the east, but the wind was steady, and the sea lay out before them with white splashes of wave tops in ordered rows. "It might prove to be a needed thing, laddie. A few hours spent in that line of work might not be such a bad cargo. I'll speak to the captain."

"Thanks, Salts. You're a real stump!"

"You won't be thanking me when we have to double up to make back the lost time," he growled. "And that's what Captain Telig will demand in exchange. We still have the fleet to catch."

"The Welingtron are strong, they can keep up with their own."

"Aye, they can, lad, but you never really know what goes on with them. I have been here fifty turnings, with all but twelve of those at sea, and I never before now crossed wakes with these fellows. I always heard tales, and believed as a child would believe, but I tell you, it's shaken me down to my keel bolts to find myself towed about like a leaf on a pond."

"They would be good mulch for Chellin to chew on," agreed Jeremy. "I guess I must have grown up in a place where the lore of others was constantly being spoon-fed to me. The Line Stewards are protectors of many clans, so I always had plenty to keep me busy at my lessons. I think the Welingtron are close to the Elboreal. They have been allies since the Dark One has been active again.''

''We'll find out how well they savor their stomachs, then. If they won't eat cakes the lass bakes, then we'll know they dream of seaweed and deep holes in the ocean, full of the bones of old salts like me.'' Salts left to find the master of The Crane, and Jeremy went back to his job of helping the other former prisoners scrub down the decks of the Hulin ship. It was the same story on the other vessel, and it seemed there was more than blood the freed captives were trying to scour clean.

By midafternoon, Salts was back, saying the captain had given permission for a small celebration to take place at sundown the following day, which would allow Laeni, and any of the others who wanted to help, plenty of time to prepare a small feast to mark their release from their enemies.

Salts looked around at the former prisoners. ''It will take some time for this to sink in,'' he said. ''It must be as bad now as when they were first taken. Nasty business, what those curs do to their victims.''

Laeni's face darkened, which Jeremy saw. ''But the thing now is to get the supplies you'll need for your baking. You're to come over with us, so we can introduce you to the cook, and show you the galley. He says he has everything you'll need.'' Jeremy and the old sailor exchanged worried glances, but the girl was soon thinking of what she would need to cook for the crews.

''I think I shall try my brother's old favorite. He always liked it the best.''

''That's fine,'' said Salts. ''I just hope he doesn't smell your cooking and decide to come for a bite.''

''I wish he would,'' said the girl softly. ''It would help me to see something from my past. Anything would help, but seeing my brother would give me something to live for again.''

Jeremy felt something moving in the pit of his stomach, and he realized he was near tears. He forced himself to stay busy, and to think of other things, but the raw young girl had lost her toughness and distance, and spoke what was nearest her heart, which almost unnerved him. He felt again all the terrible darkness and confusion of that night struggling in the water near the Thistle Cloud, and his near escape from death, and Ulria, playing the soft notes of the reed pipe over him while the fever of his wound raged.

In the sky away to the east that night, the Torch of Rhure

seemed to burn ever brighter, and even Captain Telig's prediction of a storm failed to dampen their spirits. Jeremy watched carefully, looking on toward the island that Captain Telig said lay under the Torch, wishing with all his heart that he might catch up to the old Line Stewards, and be with them when the battle began in earnest.

It seemed to him then that they had been at sea for all of his adult life, and he wondered if his legs would remember how to walk on solid land.

The Island

An Old Warhorse

Stearborn stood on the deck of the Thistle Cloud watching the sun turn the slate-gray sky into a blazing inferno of clouds, and wondered if it was a dark omen of things to come as he watched it redden the sails of the graceful ship. Ulen Scarlett emerged from the companionway for a moment, then saw the old Steward and disappeared again. Coglan had been talking with a sailor forward, and now came to join the Line commander.

"This weather has slowed us down. Even the Thistle Cloud can't find her best pace when she's hard-pressed to keep her feet."

"It's been worsening all night," agreed Stearborn. "I used to lay in my tent and listen to the wind howl through the trees, but it was never as nerve-racking as this commotion. I'll never make you a good sailor."

"We might make one of you yet, my good fellow. At least you haven't come down with the lubber-bends." Coglan laughed, having to find a handhold in a sudden gust of wind that leaned the sleek vessel far over on her side.

"Not yet, but with this blow, I might find out how to feed my supper to the fishes."

Coglan grew more serious. "This storm is a good shield for us." He leaned closer to the old Steward. "Rewen thinks we shall raise Eirn Bol by midday tomorrow."

"By Windameir's Beard!" breathed Stearborn. "I was be-

161

ginning to think I would be lost aboard this bucket until I drew my last snort!''

"I'm not so sure getting to Eirn Bol is going to be such a relief," laughed Coglan. "And calling the Thistle Cloud a bucket might draw you more than you bargained for."

"I meant it only as the highest salute. I'm grateful to my bones for having her between me and the bottomless drop of water that's beneath us." He shivered, drawing his cloak more closely about him. The wind had a biting edge, and the spray peppered his face like tiny arrows.

"Our young underling of the Black Hood is readying his move," said Coglan, turning the subject in another direction. "Our only safe place to talk is here, where we can't be overheard."

"With that blasted ring, I'm not so sure," growled the old commander. "I feel like I've got a prying eye on me, no matter where I am."

"The Rhion Stones are not all powerful, but they can be a bother. Like now, although it has turned out to be a boon for us, as well."

"I hardly see it that way, but I'll take any edge I can get."

"Rewen has seen who has Ulen in his grasp. Deros has seen, too, and says it is Mortus Blan, the advisor to the old Emperor, and to his son, Baryloran."

"What have they got up their cloak sleeve?" snorted Stearborn. "More of this blatherskite business with fire and smoke? Why can't they make a clean breast of it, and come on us like men?"

"Weirdochs never do what is expected. And Deros says Mortus Blan is not the worst of the lot in Hulingaad. There are at least two others who have a hand to play out in all this."

"Is there nothing you and the Lady Rewen can do?"

"We have our plans, although it is sometimes a hard chance when it comes to this." He made a motion of his head at the stormy sea. "I would take my chances a hundred times over with this, rather than deal with the danger of a man struggling with the dark side of himself."

"What's our course, then?"

"Rewen has found that Ulen has been instructed to try to take Deros from us, and deliver her to Mortus Blan. He feels that Alban Ram would surrender the Sacred Scrolls to save his daughter."

"Would he?" asked Stearborn, glad that he was not in a position to betray his strict Steward Code.

Coglan's face grew sad and old beneath his handsome features. "I don't know. No one would be able to say, except Alban Ram himself. He has had the care of the Alberion Novas all this time, yet he has not had to face the threat of something so dear to him. It is easy to make sacrifices when it concerns something that does not cost you too dearly."

"That's what this Vipre weirdoch is hoping for, then? That the Keeper of these Sacred Scrolls will surrender up the rest of us to rescue his daughter?" Stearborn spat into the roiling sea below. "The Black Hood has a strange sense of honor, if you could call it that. Leaving dead and wounded, and trying to use a woman to threaten an elder! It grates on me like a Rogen bite, just keeps seeping and won't heal." He unloosed his sword in its scabbard for relief. "I have found it doubly hard in these times, for some of our enemies have learned to call upon the fine line our Code draws. Saying yield means we can't slay them, and they know that. And if we lop off their head, we have the devil to pay for stepping across what's not done."

"What are you going on so about now," teased the Lady Rewen. Stearborn had not heard her come on deck for the roar of the wind and sea, but he was surprised nonetheless when she suddenly appeared at his elbow, her long blond hair trailing behind her. She struggled to cover it with her hood, and finally managed to tie it beneath her chin.

"About how this is the only place it's safe to talk aboard the Thistle Cloud," he growled kindly. "Everyone else is below having mulled apple cider, warm and dry."

"They're below, but they're not having mulled apple cider," Rewen replied. "Lofen and McKandles are at it again, and the two Archaels haven't stopped arguing about what has been the roughest winter storm they've sailed through."

"And how about the good horseman? He poked his nose aboveboard for a wink, but saw me and dodged back."

Rewen looked away toward the lowering sky. "We have to watch our step now that we are so close to Eirn Bol."

"How is the Lady Deros? Is she ready for his move?"

"As ready as anyone can be. The poor beggar is tormented out of his mind with the ring, but there's nothing we can do until it's over."

"It would be dangerous to try to take the ring from him

again now," added Coglan. "I had thought of that when I began to see how it was affecting him, but the cure might kill the patient."

"I hope that's all the worst of it," mumbled the old Steward.

Findlin came up the companionway and stalked as best as he was able across the tossing deck. "He's stiff-jibbed again, and hard to make tack," said the Archael. "There's no reasoning with him, and I'm afraid he's going to bait Lofen and McKandles until they're driven to the point of harming him!"

Coglan nodded for Rewen to go below to try to separate the warring parties. "He may still respond to you, my lady. We still have need of our ruse for a bit longer."

"If it comes to it, we must hold him, although that will make our landing more dangerous. As long as they think Ulen is in command of this vessel, we will not be bothered about. In one more day's time, we shall be on Eirn Bol, and the Sacred Thistle can perhaps sever the hold they have on the poor horseman."

McKandles had burst out of the companionway shouting, pushed along by Lorimen. "Help me," cried the Archael. "He's threatening to cut Scarlett's throat!" The Gortlander was still waving a wicked-looking dagger about, his eyes bulging from his head.

"He's drove me plumb past my wits!" he shouted. "If I hears one more jibe at my family, it won't do no harm to loosen up his gills a bit to watch him drown in his own bad blood!"

Lofen appeared then, hanging onto Lorimen's cloak sleeve. "You ain't got no needs to throws him off this bucket! I'sel gets him smoothed down, just gives me a jug and a bit of jawin' time!"

"You ain't agoin' to talk me out of splittin' his gizzard, Tackman! I has heard it and heard it, and now I says it's him or me!" The hostler was bright crimson with rage, and waved his dagger about in front of his friend's face.

"Let him have at me," came a cold voice, spoken loud enough to be heard over the roar of wind and sea. "We can settle this now, while he thinks fit." Ulen Scarlett was standing in the companionway, his sword drawn, a pale flicker of red light glimmering in his sunken eyes. He had steadily grown more gaunt as the Rhion Stone of the Hulin Vipre prince had taken control of him, and now he looked as though he had been wandering in the Leech Wastes without food or water.

McKandles struggled free of his friends and, before anyone could move, had thrown himself against Ulen, his battle cry formed on his lips. His adversary stepped back to bring his weapon into play, and he never saw the butt of Stearborn's sword descending, and he slumped limply into the old warrior's arms.

"That won't be necessary now, lad," he reprimanded, and McKandles caught himself in midblow, and lowered his dagger sheepishly.

"He's abringin' it on hisself," he mumbled, calming down. "It's that infernal Hoolin ring that's done for him!"

Stearborn had laid the tormented young horseman on deck, and turned to Rewen. "What now, my lady?"

"I smell the land, good Steward. We shall be making our landing tomorrow. Leave him to me." She moved her hand across his brow, and there seemed to come a softening of his features, but he struggled about, as though he were having a bad dream, making mumbling noises that they could not understand.

"It's the ring. They are calling him now."

"Can they see what's happened to him?" asked Findlin.

"I think I can muddy their stone enough to confuse them," replied Rewen. "Maybe give them a message of our own."

"That's always the best stew to serve up," agreed Stearborn. "When you've got a bit of news for the enemy, it's always best to get it to them the fastest way you can." He laughed a rough laugh. "We used to like to volley off fire-arrows with a tender note attached to post someone we were laying siege to about our intentions. It works every time."

"They think they're getting Alban Ram's daughter by keeping Ulen under their binding. We can't let them down." Rewen called below, and Deros appeared, her hands held behind her as if tied, and she stumbled forward to kneel beside the unconscious Ulen. Rewen picked up the still hand with the ring on it, and held it out in such a way that it had full view of the form of the girl. Then there was a fleeting image of the storm-tossed boat, and a hazy line of gray covered everything, as though the gale had blown up so much spray that sea and sky was concealed among its wild fury.

In the Norith Tal, all Mortus Blan could make out in his fire was the wet, frightened figure of the daughter of Alban Ram, and a confused blurry scene of an enemy vessel being sailed by Hulin sailors, bringing home to Hulingaad the most important prize to have ever been won by the Order of the Black Hood.

A Twist of Fate

❋

Crale led the way cautiously past their now-silent stone prison, peering into the murky gloom ahead. "Where are the others? Who are they?" he asked the young bear, his tone not unkindly.

Lanidel, relieved to be off the spot for their near disaster, grunted. "More of the chubblets' kin, but I smell the scent of the Black Hood on these."

Owen's grip tightened on his sword, and he saw and felt the blade begin to hum its warning note, and the same deadly blue flames flickered and lit the dim tunnel. "There's danger there, right enough. How many were there, Lanidel?"

"Not many, but too many for me," replied the bear. "I was coming back for help when the wall reached out and swallowed me."

"It was a good thing I was along," scolded Owen softly, still shaken by his narrow escape. "But do you think we can deal with the Vipre?"

"We're bears," said Crale simply. "Unless there is an army of them, we have nothing to fear." His large brown eyes met Owen's steadily.

"I have the sword of Skye," answered Owen. "It can take the place of ten men." He replaced it in its sheath. "But I think for this chore, I shall take up your own weapons. They might prove to be of more worth in these tight quarters." He repeated his couplets and felt the odd, tingling sensation that always coursed through his veins as he took on the form of the bear. His hand holding the sword disappeared, to be replaced by a huge paw, with long, deadly claws.

"Now we shall see to business in the proper manner," said

Crale, turning to pad silently off toward the increasing noise of the voices ahead. He had not gone far before Owen called out in a hushed voice to stay still. The older animal froze, testing the air for danger, every sense alert. "What is it?"

"Shhh. I think I might be able to make out these voices, if I can just have it quiet!"

"Chubblets! Leave it to chubblets to be whispering in this shaft! Even if they are enemies, you'd think they would have the strength to at least talk loudly enough so they could be heard." Crale's hackles had risen, and Owen saw the terrible apparition the old bear presented. Owen plodded silently on in the direction of the noise, his ears pricked to pick up a vaguely familiar-sounding voice that had begun to speak more urgently.

"Can you understand them?" asked Lanidel.

"It's still too low for me to hear plainly," said Owen. "I shall try to get a bit closer. There's something familiar about this one voice I'm hearing."

"Since the gray horse has come, it seems he has brought all our old enemies back to us again!"

"Gray horse? Where did you see a gray horse, Crale? Is this now, you speak of, or part of your lorebooks?"

"Part of our lorebooks, but not many dawns have passed since we saw the gray horse. He found us in the mountains of the barren side of Gulen Bol, and brought us news of a new coming."

Owen's mind raced, for he knew he had information concerning his old friend Seravan. The desire to see him overpowered him for a moment, and he forgot he was in his bear form. Reaching out a powerful forepaw to touch Crale, his unfamiliar strength surprised the older bear and sent him tumbling along into a sprawling heap on the smooth cavern floor. Crale was up into his fighting stance immediately, his ears laid back tightly on his head, his fangs bared.

"I'm sorry, Crale," quickly apologized Owen. "I can't get used to how powerful my bear part is. Please forgive me, old one. My heart is troubled that I've hurt you."

"You haven't managed to dislodge my old bones from this worrisome path we're on. I know you are a chubblet, and I must accept a certain pattern of rude behavior. Bear manners require I correct what wrong has been done to me, and I beg your forgiveness for it. But it must be done, if we are still to have any hope of a continued life beyond this narrow shaft."

Owen studied the big animal a moment, comprehending soon enough he was intended to submit himself to punishment from the old leader.

"It was my fault, old one. If I must have punishment, then deliver it, and let's get on."

"It must be done," apologized Crale. "It is part of the Warl Code."

Crale moved suddenly, sending Owen flying backward from a short, powerful cuff that took his breath away for a moment, but left him unharmed otherwise. Rising gingerly, he checked himself to make sure he was all of a piece. "I'm glad you weren't angry, Crale, or I would have more to fear from you than our common enemies ahead of us."

"That blow I gave you wouldn't knock down a cub, chubblet. But we must keep to our ways, and I thank you for your courtesy."

A distant voice, raised in giving a command, drew Owen's attention back to the problem at hand. "I know that voice," he said. "It's the man the traitor was talking to in the Culdin Bier." He paused, straining to hear anything further from the voices in the old lava flows ahead of them.

A Blow from Behind

Agrate and his troop of raiders had been driven forward by the tremors that had triggered many cave-ins, and rising water in some of the lower shafts, and they now stood talking excitedly among themselves. Owen had heard the man he had fought in the Culdin Bier calling out to leaders of different assault forces, and listened to them going over their plans. Crale and Lanidel crept along behind him, halting in a broken cross-shaft.

"Where can they be going?" whispered Lanidel. "Surely they do not have the numbers to take Cairn Weal."

"They don't have the numbers, but they will hold a good

advantage in their surprise. They will come up in one of the Culdin Bier, where they won't be expected, and strike from behind.'' Owen's huge bear brow knit into a worried wrinkle. He had been aware for some time that something was not right, but he had put it off to the tense closeness of the journey through the shaft and his anxiety about Deros. Now he realized that it was something else, more subtle, and just at his finger-tips, but he had forgotten until this moment what it had been.

The Aldora were silent.

"There are no rats," Owen said simply. "The Aldora aren't here!"

It was Crale's turn to be puzzled. "Maybe they have been sealed off in the lower tunnels," he said slowly. "This little jiggle the mountain has given might have locked them below."

"If that's the way of it, then we have our own work cut out for us here, my friends. We aren't many, but we can't let this man and his troop get through to the other side. Cairn Weal hasn't been warned yet."

"They might be, if we can cause enough of a tumblebash here." The old bear paused. "I don't know if we can last long at it, but it may be the only way we have left to get word to the Elder in the White Cliffs."

"They're chubblets," reminded Lanidel, then looking quick-ly to Owen. "I'm sorry, I mean you no ill will," he added. "But we must see to our own first."

"They're chubblets, indeed, and many of them, but I am here with two stout fellows who are Warlings. If this pack of wolves wins through, then both our clans will be chased and hunted until they have killed us all. We stand together in this, and that stands for much with me. I have fought alongside many brave men and animals in my time, and if we are to perish in this hole, I am honored to have two such comrades to stand by me. I hope we shall meet again across the Boundaries, where I can properly thank you."

Crale grunted. "Let's don't bury ourselves yet. The Black Hood have always feared us, unless they're in great numbers. There are old parts of their lore that reminds them that the Warling will one day come back to have their revenge for their betrayals. We animals have always been too innocent and easy to deceive, but that time is over."

"Now is a time to call that to accounts," rumbled Lanidel, low in his throat. His eyes were wide with excitement, and he was shuffling his forepaws rapidly on the smooth stone wall in front of him.

Crale looked deeply into the younger bear's eyes. "You must say the words from the Warling Stone on war," he intoned. "If something should happen to you, it will get you home safely to the Caves." Lanidel nodded his head and shut his eyes tightly, trying to recall the words.

> "My heart is bear,
>   my soul is bear,
>   my mind is bear,
> and I come to my death as bear.
>   I come gladly home."

Owen looked over at the two animals. "May I say those words, too. It seems to be as good a prayer as a soldier might have."

"It speaks well for your courtesy, youngster. This is a powerful prayer, and one that must not be taken lightly. That is an old Warling vow, sworn to the highest Elder."

"All hail Borim Bruinthor, may his reign be long, and his honey sweet."

Lanidel let out a small chuckle, in spite of himself. "Is there nothing of our lore you don't know about," he asked, still keeping one eye to the corridor ahead. The voices had grown more agitated.

"I only know as much of your lore as you tell me, but I am a good student and a loyal friend." As he spoke, Owen was aware that he was almost waist deep in the frigid underground stream.

"These devils ahead will be dealing with the same mess we have here. If we play our hand right, we should be able to take advantage of their numbers. This small space will confuse them, and if we're lucky, they may help us out by slaughtering some of their own."

"A dark shaft and a swift blow can sometimes achieve that," said Crale grimly. "And they won't be expecting any of the Warlings here."

Owen was worried for a moment that Crale might launch a full frontal attack at that moment, and reached out a cinnamon-gray-colored paw to restrain him, should he try to bolt off to the attack.

As they stood in the cold, rising waters, another sound reached them, grating and unsettling in its fierceness. Owen recognized the stomach-numbing fear and the dry mouth as he listened. Mar'ador had taught him well how to use the advantages that were available to them, and had warned him of the moment when it would be time for him to give what was his to give, when no other creature could stand in his place to face the worst, or to surrender to that terrible darkness that was growing stronger every minute, as though the Dark One had already somehow found her way into every source of light on Atlanton Earth, and was amusing herself with the rising numbers of members from the older clans, trying to reach the patient spider in her broad web, spread out like a fine mist over the grass in the mornings.

"There are your guardians," said Crale quietly. "We may not have to act at all."

"Except to keep ourselves from being mistaken for an enemy." Owen had reached for the small necklace that held the Aldora Jaren had given him when he arrived on Eirn Bol, and it took another moment for him to remember he was in another form. "Forgive me, friends. I must return to my chubblet form if we are to reach safety." He spoke the words of transforming immediately. He already heard the notes from the Hulin Vipre commander, and he quickly put his own instrument to his mouth, hearing and feeling the soft, quiet line of music that rushed to soothe the jangled senses, and made him forget for a moment that they were in a confining tunnel, filled with rising water and enemy soldiers, and that there was nothing more he could do without calling on the odd power of the small harp he wore on the chain about his neck.

Owen knew it was also very dangerous to move now, for when he sounded the notes to signal the Aldora, the enemy would know they were not alone in the passages to Eirn Bol. He was readying himself to fight for his life when another voice was added to the confusion down the tunnel, and a shout of "the Emperor" echoed dully back to the waiting companions.

A Traitor Uncovered

※

Owen held back the two big animals, both now raised into their fighting stances. The dreadful sight of Crale with his red eyes and huge maw opened and his claws unsheathed made him glad he was not an unfortunate soldier of the Black Hood at the moment. He remembered the terrible vision of Coglan aboard the Thistle Cloud, and his thoughts darted swiftly to Deros, wondering where she was and if she was safe.

"The Emperor," repeated another voice in the shaft ahead. "And look! He has a pretty trollop with him!" Rough laughter echoed along the smooth stone walls and floor. "Who would have thought he had it in him to be out playing with such a pretty young thing."

Lanidel's ears raised, and he lowered himself to speak into Owen's ear. "Chubblets are so rude. Is that not their Elder? Even if they are Black Hood, why do they speak to him so?"

"I don't know. I want to get a better look. You two wait here, and don't move!"

"You can't get closer without being seen," growled Crale. "If we lose our one advantage, they will have our hides before we see daylight again, and your precious White Cliffs won't be any the wiser."

"I'll be careful," replied Owen. "Just don't swat me when you see me coming back!" He laughed, repeating the words that opened the way for him to go into the bottle worlds of Politar. Lanidel gave a little surprised woof, and jumped back in spite of himself, when Owen disappeared right before his eyes.

"There will be no good come to these weirdoch tricks," snarled Crale, making his voice gruffer to cover his own shock. He strained his eyes to try to see anything left of Owen, but there was nothing. His attention was drawn back then to the enemy troops, who had gone on taunting the new arrivals.

"Stand back, you fools. You recognize me well enough. I

order you to help me get back to Hulingaad! Every minute counts. If you have gotten this far, you must surely know a path back!"

"Nitches knows the pretty one. She is Denale! She never smiles at Nitches, but he always gives her gold."

"Shut up," snapped a voice, which was the leader.

"Nitches don't like Agrate to talk mad," said the hulking man. "Salun Am says I keep eye on you." He laughed a rough, threatening laugh. "Nitches might get to break your neck, too!"

"Shut him up," ordered Agrate, motioning to two troopers of the Black Hood next to him.

"Nitches ain't doing nothing, and he ain't about to start," went on a tough, bearded sergeant-at-arms. "Now we have a key to the palace as well, and a pretty bauble to help us bide our time."

Denale had not spoken, but stood behind Baryloran, holding to his arm.

"You know you've signed your own death warrant," said the crippled young man. "Mortus Blan is in the Norith Tal now, clearing out the traitors who murdered my father."

"Mortus Blan is a blind old fool who has seen his last days in Hulingaad. Salun Am is in charge there now."

"And Jatal Ra? What of him, Agrate? He has used the Warl Book and called the Lost Fire back. Now we shall have them to deal with once more. I don't know if you've been watching the night sky or not, but you can see them in the distance, looking for victims."

"They are our war dogs," protested Agrate, although his face clouded, but he passed the remark off. "Salun Am has struck the first blow to seize the Scrolls. With them, even the Lost Fire will be as but a torch in a windstorm. The Scrolls hold the real secret to power."

"You always have proven the fool," replied Baryloran. "My father said at the last that the cause would be lost by ambitious little men who would end at cross purposes." He held up the hand he wore the Emperor's ring on, and the blood-red Rhion Stone came slowly to life. "This is who you shall answer to."

The water standing on the floor of the shaft began to steam, and the low rumbling noise of the very stone walls grew louder. Over the noise of the rest, there was still a distinct roar, as of a sea crashing on a shore, which was the Aldora. The soldiers who had come with Agrate began to grow restless, and look to one another for reassurance.

A wavery vision appeared in the shaft then, of a stooped, old man cloaked in black, his gray beard trailing all the way down to his knees. His face at first seemed kindly, as if he was smiling, but when the figure came clearer, it was the look of a hunting beast, just before he pounced on his prey. Agrate, who was standing next to the young Emperor, suddenly leapt behind him, and held a razor-sharp dagger to his throat.

"One trick, one move, and I shall let the water out of him!" he shouted. "You make one play with those weirdoch ways of yours, and I'll open him up from his talk-apple all the way to his belly-pot!"

"He can't hear you," gasped Baryloran. "This is only the ring speaking." Denale, shaken with sobs, was held roughly by another soldier.

"So you say. I've dealt enough with the likes of these shysters to know they only kill you with stealth and trickery. Turn your back for an instant, and they'll have a swarm of bees, or a nest of scorpions loose on you quicker than you can blink an eye. You stay with me, and if there's any question about it, I'll gladly cut out your gizzard right here in front of your tart! You don't want to upset her like that, now do you? After all she's done?" Agrate turned a sinister smile on the young woman. "You see how the Emperor repays kindness and loyalty, my dear!" He laughed a cruel stab of laughter. "You should know who can protect you and who can't," he went on. "This will be a good start for you, wench. I'll make a believer of you yet."

The girl struggled, looking away, but another tremor rippled through the shafts, and for the moment all Agrate thought of was to get safely through to the other side. In an instant, he had the young Emperor and the girl bound tightly, and marched along ahead of them, making for the entrances to the lower cellars of one of the Culdin Bier on Eirn Bol.

Behind them, Owen noticed a slight incline in the stone floor, and could feel they were nearing the outer exits, for the air had become fresher, and there was less a smell of dust clinging to his nostrils. He turned from time to time to see the two shadowy figures of the bears following closely along behind.

Messages from a Bottle

✳

What always astounded Owen was the incredible neatness there was in the cool, green-lighted place that was the inside of the glass worlds Politar had given him when he embarked upon the barrens of the Gray Wastes. He always meant to explore how far back the woods would go, although he could not allow himself to believe that the insides of the bottles could extend for too much farther than those places he had seen when he first entered.

Yet there was another part of him that now thought there might be no end to the levels there, that it might run on forever, like putting mirrors in rows. One was simply an illusion, the other a shadowed reality, and on those upper levels, Colvages Domel told him, the reflections go on forever, much like the bittersweet harp music of the Elboreal.

And sometimes the illusions were useful, as now, when he was trying to find out all he could of the man they called Emperor. He was able to glide along quietly beside the man who escorted the young woman, who still sobbed softly to herself, although she kept pace with the others. There was something about her that reminded him of Deros. The man they called Agrate, who Owen recognized as the man he had heard talking to Efile before in the Culdin Bier, stalked along at the head of the raiding party, deep in conversation with one of his squadron leaders. Efile's name came up more than once, and Owen's heart grew full of a black rage that made him clench his teeth in frustration. He knew he might be able to kill this man now, although it meant the danger of exposing Crale and Lanidel, and he was still not satisfied that he knew what the wily Agrate had planned.

One thing he hoped for, and it crossed his mind numerous times as they trudged along, was that somehow or other the citizens of Eirn Bol had been successful at keeping the Lost

Fire at bay without the Bellream Readers, until they could come up with something more lasting than the heartbreaking solution of simply giving up their settlement, or their shelter, or the crops or animals they raised to try to keep their family together.

Agrate was speaking again at the moment, and his attention was brought to bear once more on the enemy leader.

"I can hear those infernal beasts again. Wait while I use this toy. We're almost through." He took the small locket from beneath his tunic and blew another note, which filled the tunnel with the same sound, although more harshly played by the Vipre chicftain. Owen had not heard the Aldora, but once the other noises of the voices stopped, he discerned what might have caused Agrate to sound the signal again.

Owen listened more closely now. There were sounds intermingled with the jingle and squeak of arms or equipment, and the noise men make walking on smooth stone with rough boots, but this was something else, distracting and curious. It seemed to come not from in front of them, where he knew the lower entrances to the Culdin Bier were, but somewhere off to the sides, and lower. He remembered the guardian of the Limanol Gate, and wondered if there were others, but put the idea aside, for Agrate had obviously gone back and forth between Hulingaad and Eirn Bol unharmed more than once.

Which struck Owen as extremely odd when he began to ponder on it more. There was another line of thought trying to gain foothold in his conscious mind, but it was too thin to grasp, and so improbable it began to make sense. Almost as an afterthought, he reached out and sharply jabbed the hulking man called Nitches, who turned and growled at the soldier beside him. This provided some distraction for Owen, so he would occasionally do it again as they made their way along, whenever the mood struck.

What if Deros's father knew of the enemy troops using the old lava flows, and he had not hampered them because of his own plans for springing a snare? What if Alban Ram knew of the traitor Efile, and the Bellream Readers all along, and was certainly laying out a plan to defeat them? The Alberion Novas he protected were supposed to be the source of great power, and the one who was their guardian would have knowledge of them, and be able to use them to ensure their safety. Deros had never spoken much of the Scrolls, other than to mention they were there, and Colvages Domel had spoken of them in passing when he was in the halls of the Dragon. Ephinias always alluded to them in his unending, pointless stories. Owen's head was full of buzzing bees, so he left off confusing his nattering mind, and tried to piece together the source of the new sounds that had triggered Agrate's alarm.

Crale and Lanidel still lingered along behind, hanging like shadows in the dim light, and when Owen turned to look once more, he was startled badly to see that there was a third figure there momentarily. When he blinked his eyes to confirm it, there was only the two bears.

But there had been another, he could swear, as plain as the animals, only larger. It was not a threatening figure, and it had not harmed his friends, but it spooked Owen, who was already full of apprehension about what lay in these endless shafts and tunnels beneath the sea between the two old warring islands.

He was turning to look again when Agrate barked out a short word of warning, and the raiding party suddenly was in action, moving toward a pale outline of light in the shaft ahead.

If he was to do anything at all, he would have to move quickly, and before they reached the outer hall, for he knew Efile would be there with more reinforcements.

At least in the dim light of the shafts, they would have surprise and confusion on their side, and they might just make an escape. He waited a moment longer, until Agrate was almost at the entrance to the outside, when he suddenly jabbed Nitches again and grabbed the Hulin Emperor. The big man whirled on the guard who held the girl, knocking him down, while Owen sprang back toward where his friends waited, dragging the shocked man and woman along with him. They were too stunned to resist, and Owen turned the corner to join the two bears just as the first shout of alarm was spread.

Agrate had bellowed out in rage, and leapt to follow the retreating forms, cursing as he ran and trying to draw his stabbing dagger in the confines of the close tunnel. Nitches, in his agitation, had reached out in the confusion and broken the neck of the poor unfortunate who had been next to him.

Daylight!

❉

The floor and walls of the old lava flow took a sudden bend and dip, causing Owen to trip and almost go down. He held the girl up, and Lanidel simply lugged the crippled Hulin Emperor along, running with an odd, three-legged gait that looked comical, but did not really slow the awkward bear down. Shouts and cries came from behind, led by Agrate, whose voice rang out above the rest. One of the faster of the enemy troops had the bad luck to catch up too closely, and was dispatched by a powerful swat from Crale, who never broke stride and lumbered along bringing up the rear. At the next twist of the shaft, Owen shouted out in relief.

"Daylight! We've made daylight!"

A tumble of great blocks and stones lay crumbled and fallen in their path, and the sudden light blinded them, but it meant safety if they could get free of Agrate and his troop. Owen thought of Jalen, and hoped the lad would be somewhere about.

Half stumbling, half crawling, he and the bears got Baryloran and the girl up the treacherous path that led outside. Crale's great war cry rang out as Owen's foot touched the grass that grew on the courtyard in the sunlight, and after a short skirmish, the old animal burst forth from the dark shaft entrance, his gray muzzle and front of his chest covered with his enemies' blood. His eyes were blazing, and he reared upon his haunches, swatting the air with terrible blows, until Lanidel was able to calm him.

"I've never seen him like that," he said to Owen, still holding the terrified Baryloran, who went limp, watching in horror as the huge animal was slowly coming back from his killing rage.

"I have seen it in others," replied Owen. "It is a frightening thing."

"I think he would have stayed in the tunnels to die, if we hadn't found this way out. The Warling Code is strict."

178

The old bear was slowly coming to himself, content to stand guard over the entrance. Two others of the Black Hood raiding party blocked the shaft opening with their bodies, and the rest beat a hasty retreat.

"It may seem that way, Lanidel, but there is kindness in it, too."

As the small group stood catching their breath for a moment, the young Hulin Vipre Emperor wriggled free of the bear's grasp and straightened his tunic. It was a shock to him to find that he was not to be killed by the beast. "You have me prisoner, soldier, and I also owe you a debt of gratitude for saving my life back in the tunnels. I am ashamed to say I have subjects like Agrate."

Denale had dried her tears, and stood clutching her arms to herself in a tight hug. "I'm sorry, my lord. I don't think we can get back through there."

"No question. My brother Tien Cal was never even this far, though, girl, and I, the crippled weakling, stand first on the soil of Eirn Bol! He could never make that claim." Owen's surprise showed for a moment, and the Emperor went on. "Not that it will do me much service, since we will both probably be killed before dark." The autumn sun was in the late afternoon quarter, and there would not be much light left. A cold, steady wind blew, and looking at the sky, Owen saw the tail end of a gale, which had left the high, pale blue dome swept clean of all but ragged white tatters of clouds.

"You won't die by our hands," replied Owen. "We don't kill women, and even the Warling Code does not allow for prisoners who have yielded to be murdered."

Crale, in a somewhat subdued mood now that the fight was in a lull, nodded his big head. "Warlings are not such cowards that they have to slay cubs or women."

Baryloran bristled, his face reddening. "I have not said I yield, and you would be wise to watch your tongue, beast or no! I am Baryloran, Fifth Collector of Hulingaad. You have me at an advantage, and I doubt my life would even be worth a ransom, but I still have the other option left!" His hand flashed to his tunic, and he had a short, deadly looking stabbing dagger in his hand before any of the companions could move. Denale was the one who stayed his move, holding to him frantically until Owen could wrest the knife away.

"Leave me be," hissed the distraught young Emperor. "Save me my honor!"

"This is the second time that word's come up," replied Owen, standing back with the blade safely in his grasp. "First we have it spoken of as the Warling Code, and now I hear it again from the Emperor of the Hulin Vipre, sworn enemies of all I love and hold dear. It seems honor is a very pliable piece of goods if it can be bent back and forth so easily from two separate sides."

"Who are you?" snarled Baryloran. "A common soldier? A guard in these shafts? How low must I be dragged before I am slain? How much shame will you heap on me?" Denale tried to comfort him, but he thrust her away. "And now this! A common barmaid is the last to soothe the doomed man. I wish I had my brother's strength for once, and I would make my life dear to you." Words failed him, and the young man sat down in a heap, weeping silently into his hands.

Owen, despite his suspicions, was moved by the sadness and despair he saw there. Tien Cal's brother sat before him a prisoner, and they were all in more immediate danger from both sides of the ancient struggle that had played itself out over the long turnings. Crale suddenly was on the alert, and woofed a soft warning.

"Someone's coming," he said, lowering himself and waddling away toward a low stone parapet. He crawled onto it, looking away toward the distant village Owen had first seen when he arrived on Eirn Bol. "More chubblets," he growled, turning to the others. Owen went to see what the huge bear had discovered.

There before him was a perfectly serene autumn afternoon, the pale golden sunlight shining off the roofs that were left unburned in the small settlement, the new whitewash on the buildings being rebuilt a starched white against the parched black earth and the dark blue lip of the sea. There were more ships riding at anchor than Owen remembered, and he also noticed the distant group of red-cloaked figures winding their way along the road from the settlement toward the place where they now stood watching. "So there was to be a rendezvous," he said half aloud. "The only surprise ingredient was you." He had turned and was addressing the young Hulin Emperor. "That was something Agrate had not planned for."

Baryloran had regained his composure somewhat, shaking his head. "This young woman was helping me. We were in the tunnels when the old mountain breathed again."

"They were trying to kill him," explained Denale, unsure if she should speak.

"Who? Who was trying to kill you? They were trying to kill their Emperor?" Owen sensed there were deep waters here, and he sized up his young adversary more carefully. He knew they were in a tight spot, with the Bellream Readers upon their way, and Agrate and his raiders searching for a proper place from which to launch their attacks.

"The men who murdered my father," answered Baryloran. "My brother was to be next in line for the Black Mace, but I hold it now, through default. They murdered my father, and then they planned to murder me."

"What sort of bashwaggle is all this?" asked Crale. "Don't you chubblets have a Code?" His great gray muzzle whiskers spread out angrily as he thought of the possibility.

Owen studied the Hulin Emperor for some time, unspeaking. "It seems we've both ended in a fine kettle, sir."

"You? How could that be? Your fortune will be made! They'll make you a hero. Tunnel guard captures the Black Mace himself! Promotions and good fortune will follow you now, you simple fool!"

In spite of himself, Owen laughed, slowly at first, then it grew to a huge release of tension that had built steadily inside him. "This is too good," he said, recovering somewhat. "I think even Ephinias might have indulged himself." The bears, both stolidly watching him with their big, earnest brown eyes, set him off again.

Baryloran snorted in disgust. "Not only am I driven from Blor Alhal by a nest of murderous traitors, but I suffer the last blow of being caught by not only a common tunnel guard, but one that is daft at that!"

This idea seemed to send Owen into almost hysteria. The girl suddenly dipped and picked up a fist-sized rock, and threw herself viciously on him. Lanidel easily stopped her, but she kicked and scratched at her captor, her teeth bared and eyes blazing in her head.

"You dim stonewit! You wart on a pig's belly! I'll mash your head and spit on it! Let me go!" Denale opened her mouth wider to scream, but the bear stiffled it.

"I'm sorry, she! You can't yell now. The others are too close."

Owen recovered himself and apologized quickly. "I know it

isn't what it seems, and I mean you no insult, Baryloran. We are enemies, you and I, through no fault of our own. We have no wrongs between us, except those done long before we came along. And now we shall have the protection of you to look to, as well. I don't know which side you are in the most danger from, the natives of Eirn Bol or those from your own court."

"At least here I have the luxury of seeing my enemies eye-to-eye. That is almost a relief."

"And you have one, at least, who is loyal to you." Owen bowed to the young woman. "I beg your pardon, my lady. I did not mean to anger you."

Denale looked confused and hung her head. "I don't understand you," she said. "You are enemies, yet you saved us. And these!" She indicated the two large animals. "What sort of weirdoch are you to travel with these companions?"

Baryloran's brow shot up. "Is that who you are? Not a tunnel guard, after all? Then I shall be vindicated somewhat, if I have been captured by a powerful spellmaster." He twisted the ring on his finger absently, then glanced down at it, another line of thought running through his head. "You might be curious as to this ring, if you are in that line of work. It came to me from my own advisor, Mortus Blan. You may be familiar with the name." He had removed the ring, and held it out to Owen as he spoke, a strange light flickering behind his eyes.

The Eye of Norith Tal

Without thinking, Owen reached out to touch the offered ring. It lay in the palm of the enemy Emperor's hand, glinting up in the late sunlight, a small globe of reddish gray, as if some wisp of fog was imprisoned in its fiery depths. Owen remembered the ring Ulen Scarlett wore, and this was an exact copy of it. The Lady Rewen wore one as well, along with Coglan, but theirs seemed to be different somehow in his memory. The stones were the same deep red, but the setting of the band was different. He tried to recall what he had heard of Gingus

Pashon, and the Rhion Stone he had stolen from the High Council to give to Astrain, long before.

That history all flashed through his mind at the same instant he reached out to touch the ring off the hand of the Black Mace, for that was how they described the high Elder. Denale stood watching sullenly as he held it up to the sun and studied the band more closely.

"Be careful of that," she warned softly. "It has powers."

Baryloran silenced her with a look. "Of course it has powers. My advisor taught my brother and I all about them. You could do wonders with such a ring." He lowered his voice. "Would it not be worth something to you? Perhaps my freedom, to simply go back into the tunnels? I would be willing to take my chances of eluding that cowardly traitor back there."

"Take me with you," pleaded Denale.

"Of course," Baryloran replied. "There aren't many left for me to trust. You have served me well, wench. The shake in the tunnel was not your fault."

She smiled and bowed to her Emperor.

Crale had lumbered closer, and stood staring at the glittering object in Owen's hand. "Was this what made all the commotion back in the earth combs?"

"Yes. Or rather who was behind it. The ring is nothing of itself. It must have the power of whoever is wearing it for its strength."

"Then you do know something of these," went on Baryloran.

"I know something of them," confessed Owen, debating about whether or not to tell the enemy Elder of the death of his brother. There seemed little more to gain by being anything less than truthful with the young man, but something of Ephinias's roundabout way kept him silent. That innocent relating of odd, off-subject stories and endless moral tales could be used to good advantage sometimes, as he was finding out. "It is sometimes used to communicate with allies," remarked Owen casually. "I remember reading something about them being given by the High Council, back in the Golden Age of Atlanton, when the High Council still held session openly in these Lower Meadows."

"Do you have a name, my good fellow?" asked the Emperor in an open way. "You have my name, and the name of the good Denale. Am I to be afforded the same courtesy?"

"This is Crale, and his companion Lanidel. They are honorable Warlings who have been hounded and hunted by your armies for endless turnings. They were once seated at the High Council as well.''

"That may well be,'' said the young Emperor, brushing the information aside. "And your name?''

"Owen Helwin. I come from The Line, far from here.''

Baryloran's face was blank. "I don't recall any name of that order. Why are you here on Eirn Bol? Have they hired you to come fight for them?''

"There are others who are on their way here, my good fellow. It seems your armies have been active in many places other than here on Eirn Bol. It was some of your soldiers who were partially responsible for the burning of my home in Sweet Rock, in The Line. For that, my good fellow, I could bear you a grudge.''

"My armies? My father's armies, you mean. Why would they be so far afield?''

"Trying to catch a young woman," replied Owen. "But she has outlived them all, it would seem. They did not succeed, and they all perished. Including your brother, I think.''

"Tien Cal?''

"Yes, that was his name. He is dead in the Grimpen Mire.''

"You know that for certain?''

"Yes.''

Baryloran's face collapsed for a moment, then he regained control. "He was my brother, no matter what else. I loved him as well as Mortus Blan, who raised me. Even if my father cared more for him, it never made me bitter about it. After all, I was malformed and had no strength. It was not fair the Black Mace fell at last to me.''

"It was not fair that a lot of good citizens have died, or that the Line Stewards are a fair number shorter of her finest soldiers since all this began. You have brought back the Purge, as well, Baryloran, and you will have to answer for that.''

The young Emperor shook his head. "I am not guilty of that, Owen Helwin. Even my father, Lacon Rie, fought with Jatal Ra over the recalling of the verses from the Book of Warl. The last time the beasts were at large, they killed and burned our settlements as well.''

"The Dark One controls them. They are always attractive to some fool or other who thinks he will use their great strength to reach his own ends.''

"We have a word for that kind. Rincher! Jatal Ra, and Agrate, and Salun Am, they are all Rinchers! The worst of it is that I'll never see them come to justice."

"You may, Baryloran. Something else has taken my fancy about our unlikely meeting. Here we stand, exposed on a signal hill in the outer walls of one of the Culdin Bier, on Eirn Bol. Do you know what a young fellow told me about them?"

"These keeps? What would he say about them?"

"That they are also the burial mounds, where they will make their last stand, on the last day, when the old Monks from Corum Mont awaken."

"Corum Mont," repeated Baryloran. "We have sayings of those times, too. We are not so unlike, you and I, even if you come from the wilderness that grows beyond the sea." He searched his memory for what he had heard of the place called Corum Mont. Denale answered his question.

"They were from the last of the old monasteries. The lines of power ran through their halls."

"The Dragon Lines, that's what they called those places. And they faded away sometime, but I can't remember why."

"Like we shall have to fade from here, it seems." Owen looked to Crale, who was making broad motions with his paw to come observe. The red-cloaked figures had grown in number, and were marching steadily on directly for the keep. They were still too far away to be able to make out any faces, but Owen felt quite sure that the leader of this group was Efile, coming to carry out his part of the conspiracy to land enemy troops by the back way on Eirn Bol.

Signals

❋

Owen watched the advancing party of the Bellream Readers, their bells tolling in time with their steps as they came along, their low, murmuring chant tossed about like dry leaves on the wind. Looking again toward the gate of the Culdin Bier, he saw nothing, but knew that Agrate would be emerging at any moment.

"How are you at tag?" he asked Crale.

The old bear grunted, looking evenly at him. "An odd time for games, chubblet."

"We have one chance, and that's to go out the back way and make straight for the settlement. Efile wouldn't dare bring Agrate with him, and we shall be in time to warn the others."

"What if they should move straight to the White Cliffs?" asked Lanidel. "If there were these weasels in the combs, there may be others coming behind."

"We'll have to take that chance. And Jalen and his settlement must surely have some signal to warn those in Cairn Weal of attacks."

"There are signals," confirmed Lanidel. "I've come and gone so much in secret, I've learned some of them." He gave a soft wuffling noise in his throat, and pawed the earth. "Sometimes I would lay and watch what the chubblets were doing. They never saw me, or knew that I was there."

"Do you know the warning signal, Lanidel? Could you do it?"

"I couldn't," confessed the bear. "I can't fly."

"What?"

"They use the windskates."

"The windskates! You mean birds?"

"Yes."

Owen racked his brain for the master words of earth and air, trying to remember everything at once, which made him forget. He had to slow himself down, taking deep breaths. He knew there wasn't much time, and already the procession of red-hooded men were at the bottom of the hill, slowly coming up the incline. Ephinias had told him many stories of the various bird clans, and had instructed him on their ways, but his head was so full of various tongues and codes, he could not recall a specific name. Crale was on the point of speaking when the young Steward suddenly stood.

> "Cloud and sky, wind behind,
> rise up now and heed my mind."

He repeated it again, trying to focus his thoughts on the form of a bird, and he took hold of the sword, clutching it tightly to his side.

"They are coming," said Baryloran smoothly. "I hope you

will at least give me my death quickly, and not turn me over to the rabble. You must know what they would do to the Black Mace.''

Owen had to grudgingly admit the crippled Elder had courage. Not of a flashy sort, or in the way that Ulen Scarlett might swagger about, but in a quiet, reserved way that told of a secret reservoir somewhere inside the young man whose twisted body betrayed his handsome face.

"If it comes to that, I won't let them take you," he promised.

"Nor me?" asked Denale. She had started to cry again, but did not let her tears show.

"I promise."

"Look! Look, coming from the coast!" Lanidel was on his hindpaws, gazing away in the direction of the settlement.

Sweeping up into the fading afternoon light, a hundred or more seabirds turned and spiraled ever upward, their white bodies turning from dusty rose to a reddish gold, then back to starched white again. Higher and higher they flew, until at last Owen lost count and just marveled at the unique sign the people of Jalen's small village had found as a way to warn their neighbors.

He peered away to the north, and Crale's sharp eyes confirmed what he saw. "More of them. They have set the warning into motion."

The Bellream Readers had stopped to watch the birds, pointing, but without breaking their monotonous chant. Their leader paused, then turned suddenly, striding quickly directly up the knoll toward the walled keep.

"Let's look to ourselves," whispered Owen. "Lanidel, can you carry our prisoner here?"

The younger bear gruffled a reply, and lowered himself onto all fours. "If he can hang on to my fur here at my neck, I can carry him easily."

"I'm very strong in my arms," said Baryloran stiffly. He pulled himself onto the stout animal and grabbed the loose fur at his neck firmly with both hands.

"If you strangle me, chubblet, I let the red hoods get you." Lanidel snuffled a short bark of bear laughter that was lost on the man, who immediately loosened his hold.

"Do you wish to ride, she?" asked Crale.

"I'll run on my own, thank you," she replied crisply. "At least as long as I'm able."

Owen did not wait for the bears to ask her again and set off at a brisk trot down the grass-covered alleyway between the two outer walls. There were shouts and the noise of hurrying men behind, but it was not nearby, so the small party went on, angling away from the fortified hill, toward the distant curve of the coast where it bent inward at the northern side of the island. The birds were wheeling and turning still, but had begun to slowly settle earthward again. Far ahead in the distance, Owen could just make out the birds there too, and Crale had seen something else.

"Smoke," he reported curtly.

And along the curving blue of the sea, there were more ships still, some flying the black flags of the Hulin Vipre. Baryloran let out a stiffled yelp at the sight, then contained himself.

"You will observe my fleet," he said smugly. "They were to concentrate on gaining a foothold today. We have been at stalemate so long, I think your friends in Cairn Weal have grown overly cautious. Too much prudence makes for a weak heart."

"There's one of the Purge there too," observed Crale. "I can smell it from here."

"We shall need to stay close to cover from now on," said Owen. "And if we see one of the beasts, you must all be near enough to touch me."

"If we see one of the beasts, we shall need more to protect us than you, chubblet," said Crale in midlope.

"We also have one of the Eyes," reminded Owen. "Our good friend Baryloran here might have the secret to keeping an errant dragon off our track. That ring there has the power to turn aside a good many things of foul content. Agrate may have done us an unlooked for good turn when he found our Emperor here." Owen laughed at the thought, and liked the irony of the fact that the schemes of the man who planned to strike a blow to the back of Eirn Bol had inadvertently delivered into his hands the very promising means of the salvation of Alban Ram.

The
White Cliffs

Windskates

Lorimen pointed out the birds to the others on the deck of the Thistle Cloud. Great flocks of them were rising up from places along the coastline of Eirn Bol, which they had first sighted during the last quarter of the night watch. Standing off until daylight, they had seen the various lamps and fires dotted across the dark shadow of the land, and on more than one occasion, they had seen the telltale dirty orange trail of one of the Freolyde Valg ranging about, low down on the horizon. The weather had turned clear and cold, and the storm that had tossed them about for the past few days had blown itself out into a steady north wind, leaving the sky a faint, pale blue with white mare's tails high up, and the clean, scrubbed smell of early morning air in their nostrils.

The last morning star, the Torch of Rhure, still twinkled dimly just at the line where the sea met the sky.

"A good omen, if ewer this Archael saw one," observed Findlin. "There hasn't been so many on this passage."

"Aye, you old salt block, not many. It's time we had something to hearten us." Stearborn, having risen from a short sleep, stood next to the Archael. "Now all we need do is find whether or not the island is still in friendly hands."

"The Lady Rewen is waking Deros now. She was too exhausted last night to stay awake any longer."

"Coming home can sometimes do that to you. I remember

191

more than once coming back off a long patrol, and breathing the high mountains in, and feeling the sun on my back in a place where I could leave my sword and shield in my kitchen without worrying about raids or skirmishes.''

Lorimen elbowed the old Steward into silence, for Ulen Scarlett had been brought up the companionway by Hamlin. He was in leg irons, and stumbled about like a drunken man. "The good weather is wasted on that poor devil. He's gotten worse ewer since we'we been in these waters."

"Coglan thinks the ring has broken his mind. I wonder." Stearborn put a hand to shade his eyes against the glare of sunlight off the water, watching the birds wheel and hover on the wind, rising higher and higher into the pale blue dome of morning. "I wonder about these, too. Something's afoot there, or I'll miss my stroke.''

The Archaels studied the birds in silence, looking up and down the coast. "There's a place or two here we could run in with the Thistle Cloud, ewen if we don't hawe the Welingtron. Any good Fionten man could nawigate in these waters."

Coglan appeared at the helm then, up from below. Deros was with him, and they were joined after another moment by Rewen. The old Line commander saw the tears glistening in Deros's eyes as she stood gazing away at her homeland.

"Did you ewer expect to hawe it take so long to get back to where you wanted to be, lass?" asked Findlin, patting her clumsily on her arm. She did not answer right away, but stood transfixed.

"Leawe her be, you floundering old walrus! Can't you see the lass is upset." Lorimen took off the brightly colored scarf at his neck and gave it to the girl to dry her eyes.

"Make ready for porting," called Coglan, taking over the helm from the sailor on watch. "We must hurry."

Rousing herself from her turbulent emotions, Deros ran to the port rail, pointing. "That's a signal!" she cried. "The settlements here are coming under attack!"

"Where do you see a signal?" asked Stearborn, squinting to see more clearly. "I see nothing!"

"The birds," replied the girl. "It is the signal they use. Look! See there! More of them."

"How far from this side of the island is it to Cairn Weal?" asked Coglan.

"It's not so far, but if we have to fight our way through, it may take us all day."

"What about dropping the hook in the harbor at Cairn Weal?" asked Findlin, his whiskers bristling. "By Rhordan's Jib-sheet, why don't we just hawe ourselwes a dandy-fine time of it, and slip ourselwes in right under their noses?"

Ulen Scarlett had stood passively at the rail, Hamlin's arm on his shoulder. His eyes were dull and listless as he looked out over the water, but somewhere deep inside, the voice of his master, Mortus Blan, spoke softly to him, his tone kindly, and his promises great. The Rhion Stone jolted him into consciousness of it with a surge of energy that ran up his arm in a thousand pinpricks, but he never gave any outer sign that he was not yet in the dull-eyed stupor he had fallen into while they were still at sea.

Rewen had said it was best not to remove the ring from him now, for until they had some way of knowing how to rid the young horseman of the one who held him with the powerful binding, it might be too much for him to bear. She and Deros had discovered it was Mortus Blan, the Emperor's advisor, who controlled Ulen now, but they had no way of freeing the young man from the weirdoch until they were safely ashore on Eirn Bol.

The Eye was active now, searching about. The ring took in the coast of Eirn Bol, and parts of the ship. At Rewen's urging, the young woman placed her hands behind her back again, and stood next to Ulen, where the stone could glimpse her. Hamlin removed his prisoner from the deck then, putting him back in the small cabin below that they had prepared for him.

Stearborn had Judge and Hamlin break out all their gear, and they spent the last time waiting in cleaning and oiling their weapons and readying their gear. Lofen and McKandles had brought up their own equipment and worked alongside the Stewards.

"I'd give my last meal for a decent horse for us," grumbled the old Steward. "I hate to think of my last battles carried on afoot."

"Aye," agreed Lofen sadly. "It ain't no good ahoofin' it. I ain't never thought no thought like this, but ain't it a bitter shame to ends up astompin' just like common blighters what never rode!"

"I says it's that blinkin' ring what's done it," said McKandles.

"It ain't been no good since that Hoolin prince got hisself drownded in them mires! If we was ahavin' our noggin's a little less damp from all this fish float, we mights have saved ourselfs a whole passel of grief."

"I think Ulen was the cause of our friend Jeremy's disappearance, and I don't doubt for a minute that it was the ring that turned a disagreeable braggart into something a lot worse. I know we've got to stick it a bit longer, but I, for one, will be glad when we can pull the shaft straight back and shoot straight to the heart of it all."

"It's wearing," agreed the old Steward. "You know me, lads, and my ways. Swords and shields, that's the way of it! Right in the thick of it, and no question of what's meant by it all." He slapped the blade of his sword across his open palm. "No questions ever asked about the nature of this."

Deros came and sat against the railing out of the wind. She reached her hand into her tunic, and pulled out the small knife Stearborn had given her when she had first come to The Line disguised as a young boy. "Do you remember this?" she asked, a small smile lighting up her face.

Stearborn's weathered features softened for a moment. "You were a spirited young colt. Old Stearborn has always prided himself on his good eyes, but I'll go to my final stand down and muster with that mistake staring me in the face. I thought I was giving a bit of encouragement to a lost young buck who had no one to help him."

"I loved you for it," she said quietly. "You were so gruff and frightening, I didn't know if I'd be able to fool you."

"Fool who?" asked Lofen. "Who was you atryin' to fool?"

"And why?" added McKandles. "Why was you atryin' to do that?"

The old Steward laughed. "You wouldn't have known her then," answered Stearborn. "She was gussied up just like a buck, and she had all of us fooled until we ended up at the Fords of Silver. Just like a butterfly coming out of a fuzzworm."

"Well, bake my cakes," breathed Lofen. "You mean you was atryin' to make folks think you wasn't a mare?"

"It was too dangerous to be traveling as a young woman. I left here to try to find help for my father, but it was difficult. Everywhere I went, the answer was always the same. They were under attack too, and could spare no one."

"And then she wound up in one of our war camps," said

Stearborn. "Dirty face and all. Wanted to learn the ways of sword and bow, so we just treated her like any other lad." He laughed. "Little did we know she'd turn out to be such a fiesty young pup." The old Steward reached out and took the small engraved knife from her and held it up to examine it in the sun. "It turns out she had backbone, and a Steward's heart. She would make many in my old squadron look like ladies at a tea social."

"And now here we are," said Deros. "I'm home after all this time, and I still don't know if my father is safe and alive." She took the small blade back.

"The signals must mean something," said Hamlin. "If they're still warning each other, then they must still be in control."

"It looks the same," admitted Deros. "I'll know as soon as we round the point there. If the White Dragon still flies above Cairn Weal, I'll know." She stood, looking away toward the headland they were drawing closer to. The birds had settled again on the White Cliffs above the sea, and now the Thistle Cloud was on a tack making straight for the point of land Deros had pointed out.

They all stood together on the deck, waiting silently as the Welingtron pulled the sleek vessel closer and closer to the ancient harbor of Eirn Bol, watched over by the white walls of Cairn Weal, where the Sacred Scrolls were kept. Deros had begun to cry again, and Stearborn put an arm around her and held her, his old eyes growing damp in spite of his efforts at maintaining his sternest look.

Homecomings always held a special place in his heart, and the feeling seemed to grow stronger in him as the gray tinged more of his hair and beard. Hamlin and Judge had witnessed the reaction of the gruff old Steward, but stared ahead resolutely, having their own share of strange sensations churning about in their hearts. Hamlin had brought up Jeremy's bow and quiver, and stood silently holding it, although his hand had begun to tremble, and both he and Judge seemed to have something in their eyes as well.

Now that they were actually in sight of their destination, exhaustion and elation took turns at their hearts, and all the companions on the deck of the Thistle Cloud that day could not help feeling the mixed joy and anxiety Deros was going through, watching her homeland and her fate inching slowly toward her.

They were close enough now to hear the thunderous wingbeats of the birds over the noise of the sea.

The Dart and the Marin Galone

When the heavier winds of the gale gave out, the more lightly constructed Dart began to gain way on the Marin Galone. Lanril Tarben's ship had been built for the Delos Sound, where the currents and wind were always strong, and she had been built to sail in a breeze. Anything less, and she ghosted along well enough, but the Dart, being a privateer, was a ship of speed and maneuverability, and she now began to shine.

Grudgingly, the skipper of the Marin Galone had to compliment the Dart, and the pretty turn of her stern, which she was showing to those behind.

"Maybe if we sang a tune to make our ship happier," suggested Emerald, trying to cheer up his captain.

"The Marin Galone is as happy as she'll ever be, Minstrel," he replied. "Look at the way she's set her shoulder, and how spritely she bounds off the waves! Gorend's Shoes, lad, she'd drive herself right under if she buried her nose now!"

"He gave his word to sail for Eirn Bol. If we don't settle this matter between us now, he wouldn't be able to keep his ship's reputation. If it got out a ship from the Delos Sound outran him, it would kill him."

Elita had been standing by her husband as the others stood talking, watching the sails on the boat ahead draw and fill, pulling the Dart slowly farther ahead. "There are a number of things on that boat that were touched by the Dreamers," she said. "I don't know if even the captain is aware of the full meaning of that."

"What do you mean?" asked Lanril.

"Anything that comes from the Elboreal has a hidden power that will slowly draw you to it. It's a terrible plight for the Red

Scorpion to be in, for I know he's being slowly drawn away from the Darkness. I don't know if he even knows any of that just yet."

"I'd have a hard time seeing that," grumbled Lanril. "From all I know of him, he's a devil through and through, rotten to the core! It would take more than some tug of goodness to lighten his black heart."

"Sometimes those who are most in darkness are the easiest to catch," smiled Elita. "There is an old saying to that effect. I grew up with it, even as a child, knowing nothing of what secrets there are in the human heart."

"I'd wager you, there are a few in the heart of that devil, if he has a heart at all." Lanril stalked back to stand by his helmsman, making an adjustment while looking up at the sails. The Dart was a bow shot ahead of the Marin Galone, her shoulder down and driving, very slowly pulling away.

"Do you think he'll actually show himself anywhere on the coast of Eirn Bol?" asked Emerald. "He must have many enemies in these waters."

"Railan Dramm? Every true tar on the South Roaring or the Silent Sea would sail through stone rain to catch him. But the blaggart leads a charmed life. He's disappeared from plain view, or outsailed anyone who might come close to landing that dainty ship of his. And the Vipre fleet has destroyed many of the fastest boats in these waters, so there's little to be done about him now."

Elita was watching the Dart, her eyes taking on the even deeper blue of the sea. "His danger does not come from an enemy he can see," she said softly.

"Then I'd like to know who that could be," snapped Lanril. "I'd like to clap my running lights on him."

"You have already met him."

"On this voyage? Now who would that be, my lady?"

"Himself. He is a troubled man."

Lanril laughed in spite of himself. "You have braced yourself there, my lady."

"Are you married, Captain?" asked Elita, turning her gaze on Lanril. He fidgeted, looking away.

"Profitably tied up with an outstanding woman of good family, with two small pups to help sail this ship when they've come up a bit."

"And do you love her?" went on Elita.

"I married the good woman," confessed Lanril uneasily.

"How long have your parents been dead?" she went on.

Lanril showed surprise. "Have I said my mother and father were dead?"

"No, not in words."

"They were lost at sea when I was thirteen," replied the captain, his face taking on the features of a young child.

"Did you believe they were dead?"

Emerald started to speak, but was checked by the look in his wife's eyes.

Lanril shook his head, looking away. "You know it's a strange thing," he went on, "sometimes when I'm in a new port, I find myself looking around to see if I might chance across them. I know it sounds silly, but not having seen them . . . dead," he paused. "It never seemed real that they were gone. My uncle raised me as his own, and took me to sea." He raised a hand to encompass the ship and sea and sky. "And here I stand."

"Do you think Railan Dramm might be looking for something like that as well? I feel much pain from the man."

"He's a murdering brigand!" spat Lanril, pounding his hand on the rail. "Whatever he's looking for, there's no excuse for lawlessness!"

"No excuse," persisted Elita. "But reason. There was something in his eyes that told me an old story. I make no defense of his actions, but when I feel pain like his, I wonder what drives him."

"If I could catch the Dart, I'd let you ask him yourself, my lady," said Lanril.

Emerald and Begam had moved forward, and were watching something with great interest. "Welingtron," explained Begam, pointing. "Up to something." They had recognized the sleek head of Rhule skimming along on the wave tops now, his powerful body glistening in the sunlight. "I think he's catching up to Railan."

"Firesnake!" sang out the sailor on watch in the foretop. "Off the port bow!" His voice carried on the wind, and the deck sprang to life with hands manning their duty stations and uncovering weapons. "Port bow, port bow!"

All eyes searched across the bright afternoon sky for the dreaded figure, flying low over the sea's surface making a straight line for the southern coastline of Eirn Bol.

"It looks like it has something in mind," said Emerald. "I hope it doesn't get interested in two ships out here at sea."

Lanril frowned, and he stood strapping on his sword. "One good weapon I've got is that the two of you could sing it to sleep if he gets too close! Never a bad idea, having a minstrel aboard. Double the worth if you've got two!"

"It doesn't look like it's lost," agreed Begam. "I don't know if Rhule is keeping it at bay, or if there's something there on shore that has drawn its attention."

"I see what's gotten its wind up," said Lanril. "Smoke!" He pointed to the thin, rising columns of smoke that now became visible, trailing away on the stiff breezes blowing off the water. "Where's the fire, there's always something to eat." He did not have to finish the thought.

"Are they signal fires, or do you think some settlement's been torched?" asked Begam.

"I can't tell. Smoke always looks the same, whether it's a burning watchfire, or a funeral bier. This might be either."

"Look! Railan is coming about! It looks like he's going to fall off and try for a rounding into Great Harbor." Lanril took off his oiled wool sea cap and ran his hand through his hair. "What has he gotten up his bonnet now?"

"I wonder if he's seen the dragon?" asked Emerald.

"How could you miss that flying stove?" growled Lanril. "No, he's seen it right enough. It's almost as though he were trying to rendezvous with the thing."

Emerald looked to Begam. "Could that be? Did he know this beast was to be here when he hailed us?"

"If this proves to be a trap Railan has set for us, I shall be sorely tempted to take it out roughly on someone." Began spoke in jest, but at the moment it looked as though the beast might be hovering just above the Dart, then flew on toward shore.

"Where's Rhule? We need the Welingtron now," said Lanril. "I hope he doesn't prove to be one of those louts who promise to sail on the tide, then slip their moorings and fade in the night."

"The Welingtron will be here when the time comes," promised Elita, a horrible fascination flickering in her eyes as she watched the lumbering beast beat slowly toward Eirn Bol, a dirty black trail of smoke billowing out behind across the clear afternoon sky.

As the Marin Galone drew nearer the coast, a small port settlement slowly came into view, with more than a dozen ships moored inside the stone breakwater that formed the harbor. There were roofs gone, and charred plaster, along with new whitewash and a knot of people on the quay, gathered to watch the two boats that ran in so perilously close beneath the dragon, who had flown on inland, the terrible menace of it growing worse with the seemingly endless wait for its attack.

Jalen's settlement had not seen the dragon until the very last, and when it was spotted, a wild, ragged skree of warning horns set off another alarm, calling the last of the inhabitants together to defend their homes as best they could. When the young man looked to sea again, he saw a sleek vessel coming into the breakwater under sail, followed by another not far behind.

It was another heartbeat before he recognized the banner of the Red Scorpion, dropping anchor in his own harbor. Between the pitching and rolling of the old fire mountain, and the appearance of one of the Purge, and now the brazen broad daylight attack of Railan Dramm, Jalen did not wonder that the arrival of the final hours would be marked in such a way not even someone so lowly as he could miss the mark.

And then he looked up to see the young outlander from the Culdin Bier, striding into the marketplace with two huge bears and leading what appeared to be two Hulin Vipre prisoners.

Ashore at Last

The Thistle Cloud ghosted into the harbor on the dying wind, and Coglan dropped the hook in a spot far enough away to avoid any vessels entering or leaving. No one spoke on deck, or if they did, it was in a whisper. The small rowing craft were put over the side with a slight rattle of wood against wood, but no one noticed, for the Lady Rewen had renewed the Golvane binding. Deros went over the railing first, and was taken ashore by Findlin and Lorimen, who made sad faces and exchanged glances now and then.

There were no bells ringing, no horns blowing, and no throngs lining the streets to greet her when she stepped foot out of the small tender onto the soil of her homeland for the first time in many months. The harbor was full of Eirn Bol's war fleet, and there were many of the sailors there she recognized from the old days, but they seemed somehow different, more weary. A pall of hopelessness hung over Cairn Weal, and even the whiteness of the walls and streets were colored a dirty tan. It was difficult for her to lift her feet to walk but she set her course for the court where her father dwelled, and willed her legs to carry her. She had not gone more than a few paces when she saw the familiar white beard and the kindly blue-gray eyes, supported by two household guards coming down the long rampway that led from the lower castle gardens onto the common quay.

"It's my father," said Deros quietly. "He hasn't seen me."

The weary old man slowly wound his way toward the sea wall, but gave no indication of recognition as the young woman stepped out of the rowing tender and stood waiting for him. One of the soldiers noticed her then, and called out.

"Who are you?" he asked, resting his free hand on his sword hilt.

"What is it, Marak?" asked the old man, staring blankly in front of him.

"A stranger, my lord," replied the man. "A young woman has just come up from a boat at the quay."

"A young woman? Have her come forward."

"You heard my lord," ordered the guard. "Come forward! Give us your name."

Deros fought back her tears, seeing her father in such grave health. She came slowly to the old man, her eyes misted over. "I have come back," she said at last, her voice wavering and unsteady.

A tremor passed through the old man, and he lifted a hand, holding it out in the direction of the voice. "Come, whoever you are, give us your name."

"You only have to hear me to know who I am," replied Deros. "You have only one daughter."

The old man's face worked painfully, and a tide of emotions played across the worn features. "Yes, I have but one daughter, but she is dead. Gone for a long time now. I have heard she was lost in the wilderness of the South Roaring." His voice trailed away, then resumed. "I come here every day to lay a flower on the sea in her memory."

Lorimen and Findlin had gotten out of the skiff now, and stood behind Deros. The guards saw them and advanced to stand between their charge and the new intruders. "My good Elder, my name is Lorimen, a seafaring man out of the late settlement of Fionten. This young woman has been with us now for a good deal of trawel ower the better part of most marked charts, but she wouldn't ease her sheets until she was back here on Eirn Bol. She has told us amazing stories of you and your deeds, and the sore need you hawe to find allies to help you contain the scourge out of Blor Alhal."

Bowing in the direction he had heard the voice from, Alban Ram asked for a riding chair to be brought, and suggested that they might all retire to a safer quarter of the settlement. "I must apologize to you, strangers, for sounding so cynical. You have found out that I carry a cruel bond of guilt about, and I know it is only just that I should be held accountable, but I never knowingly sought to bring harm to anyone."

"Father, you have no need to carry my death over your heart! You can see I have come back to you." Deros's voice broke, and she advanced to try to touch the broken old man. The guards blocked her way.

"Here, wench! What cruel jest is this! Can't you see his pain!"

"It's all right, Marak. I do not fear the lash of my conscience. If the young woman is sent by Windameir to punish me, then it is only fitting that I receive every blow."

"Belay that way of thinking, sir," interrupted Lorimen. "Here she stands right before you, waiting for a port-o'-call hug, man."

The old man's figure sagged, and the soldier called Marak slipped his hand under his elbow.

"My daughter convinced me some time ago that she should be the one who sought out the remaining allies left to defend Windameir's Light. Like a fool, I allowed myself to be convinced by her. You are strangers, so you wouldn't know how elaborate a plan we conceived to fool our enemies. I deceived myself into believing that the proof of her death would free her from pursuit, and that she would be safer away from Eirn Bol."

"Oh, Father," sobbed Deros, her small shoulders shaking. Alban Ram waved a hand loosely. "It's all right, my child. All my subjects are like children to me. We have seen some dark times come on us, and there is enough to cry about, I know." He turned sightless eyes on the young woman, a faint trace of a smile creasing his worn face. "But we shall perhaps see better times, yet."

A squad of household guards arrived with a noisy tramping sound, and Alban Ram raised a hand. "No need of this. We are going to the Shell Garden to find out the news of these strangers."

"There are signals, my lord," reported the officer of the guard. "Away to the south. We have come under attack."

"We are always under attack, Salan," replied Alban Ram.

"This one is broader, sir. And they have sent word one of the Purge has attacked Dalrhin."

The old man scowled. "Where are my Bellream Readers? Were they not in that vicinity?"

"Yes, my lord. We have no further word."

"We saw one of the brutes," confirmed Findlin. "Heavy and black as coal, and lighting up everything he could reach. He couldn't see our ship, so he flew on toward the coast."

"Find the Readers," ordered the old man. "Send them as quickly as you can."

"Shall we put the fleet out of the harbor, my lord? We don't want to have them trapped here. There are more reports coming in by the moment. This is the largest Vipre movement we've seen!"

"Yes, yes," muttered Alban Ram. "Do what you must, Salan. Leave my boat for me."

"Sir." Salan withdrew bowing. He had not been gone long before they heard the toll of alarm bells and the notes of signal horns. The waterfront was soon bustling with activity, with sailors boarding their ships to prepare to get under way. The upper streets of Cairn Weal were soon full of hurrying citizens, clamoring through the narrow ways, dragging weapons and supplies to their posts. Voices shouted back and forth the news, and soon everyone had heard of the impending attack, and the news of the dragon at one of their settlements on the south coast. In the melee, no one seemed to notice their Elder, or the beautiful young woman who walked slowly along behind him.

The small party had come to an arched entryway into a small enclave, edged in colorful shells of all sizes and designs. Deros wept ever harder when she stepped into the archway, for the lawn and flower beds that had once been well tended were nothing but gray dirt and straw now, awaiting the winter. "Oh, Father," she cried. "You have let the fountain go dry." She walked to a small niche in the stone wall and touched the opening of the fish's mouth, which normally would have filled the pool below with the cool water from beneath the keep.

"It ran dry not long after my daughter left us," replied the old man.

"But I am back now. Come, let me show you." She opened the collar of her tunic and withdrew a small mithra and gold chain. Dangling on it were the symbol of the Sacred Thistle and a small, delicately engraved key-half. "Let me see the chain beneath your robe, Father. The small key there."

A flicker of pain crossed the old man's eyes. "Who told you of that, child?"

"You told me of it, when we sat before the fireplace that's shaped like the lion's head in your study. Mother had not been gone from us long, and you told me of the duty that we must both perform."

The air escaped from Alban Ram's lungs with a groaning sigh, and he sat down heavily on the stone edge of the empty pool. Deros went on.

"You said that when we put the two halves together, it would open the Sacred Altar. We must do that now, Father. The time has come for that."

The two guards passed a look between themselves, growing confused. "What shall we do, my lord?" asked Marak. "Do you wish to return to your rooms?"

Alban Ram sat hunched over, his face hidden in the folds of his cloak. It sounded as though he were coughing, for his shoulders moved up and down rapidly, and then he sat up, his beard tangled, and his sightless eyes red from weeping. Lorimen and Findlin thought at first the old man had slipped into madness, that his mind would not linger among the sadness and wreckage of his life a moment longer. "Have you brought the locket?" he asked, barely above a whisper.

"Yes, Father."

"Leave us," he ordered, waving a hand to dismiss his guards. "Leave us alone a moment!"

The Archaels hesitated at leaving their companion with the wild-eyed old Elder, but the two guards brusquely escorted them to the archway, and posted themselves at the gate. By standing on tiptoe, Lorimen was able to peer over the shoulder of the guard named Marak, and he could see the pair in the garden standing awkwardly for a moment more, then Deros fell at the old man's feet, holding tightly to his knees. Alban Ram was running his hand through her hair, trying to get her to rise. There was too much noise from the street to make out what they were saying.

"What is it?" asked Findlin, trying to find a place to get a view.

"They're close hauled, and making for port," reported his friend. "The wessels are moored together."

"I was beginning to think we might hawe done all this sailing for nothing," laughed Findlin. "And now it's too late in the season to think much of taking any more cargo."

"And no place to take it to," added Lorimen. "We're here until we can find another harbor to drop our hooks in."

Marak, looking over his shoulder, turned his gaze back to the two Archaels. "How have you come here? Is your vessel behind one of the other ships? It might be smart of you to tend to her. We need the harbor cleared."

"We hawe seen to that, my good fellow. The Thistle Cloud is in no way of anyone."

"Is that your ship's name?"

"Aye, it is that," answered Lorimen, looking at the two figures in the garden. "What's happened to his running lights?"

Marak shook his head. "No one knows. His healer can find nothing wrong, and he had no wound." The guard lowered his voice, and he spoke confidentially. "Some say it was the caliphans in Blor Alhal that did it."

"He has no sight at all?" asked Findlin.

"He won't say. He didn't saying anything at first, but we soon found out he couldn't walk himself about without bumping into things."

"That's dewilish odd," commented Lorimen. "How long has he been this way?"

"Since the end of the last attack on Cairn Weal. He was in the lower keep, and someone said there were Vipre in the old lava channels under the cliff. He went with the squadron assigned to defend there. There was a fight, but they easily drove off the enemy, but when they turned to leave, Alban Ram fainted away and they carried him to his rooms. When he awakened, that's when it started."

"Marak! Come, man! Bring our guests!"

The guard turned in time to see Deros leading Alban Ram through the concealed door in the wall of the garden, straight into the Lanvin Hall of Cairn Weal. Marak started, then turned quickly to the two Archaels. "Come on with you! How did the wench know about the passage?" he asked, turning to his companion.

"She should know her own house," chided Lorimen. "And you two don't hawe much better eyesight than your master if you don't recognize the lass." He snorted in disgust. "I'm glad I don't depend on you to keep watch from my foretop!"

"His daughter was a plain little mouse," shot back Marak, stung by the accusations. "And the word that came back from the South Roaring was that she had died."

"You can see for yourself she hasn't gone ower. But I remember the stories they'we told on her, and how she fooled everyone by dressing as a boy."

"That would be hard to do now," said Findlin. "I think we'we seen the last of that disguise." He was ready to continue, but a dark shadow crossed the cobbled street, and a moan of despair rose up from the hurrying throngs. Even though the sun still shone, a chill colder than the impending winter pervaded the air, and the hair on the back of their necks stood out. Marak looked up and urged them on.

"Aye, me hearty, it's one of the flying stowes, curse its hide! I hope the Lady Rewen and Coglan hawe a card up their sleewe to play up for this."

Just as he finished speaking, he caught a fleeting glimpse of a familiar face in the throng of people passing by on the other side of the street. It took another moment to recognize it, and when he whirled to drag Findlin along with him, it was gone. "Ulen!" he muttered to answer his friend's questioning look. "It was Ulen!"

They darted through the crowd, with Marak and the other guard following closely, but the horseman had disappeared into thin air, and the Archaels were forced to call off their search and return with the household guards.

"Are you sure it was him? He was locked up below?" Findlin scratched his head as he walked.

"It was him. I got a glimpse of the ring. It was lit up on his hand like a flame."

"Then how did he get free?"

"I don't know. But I think we should put on sail and warn the others. One of us should go back to the Thistle Cloud."

"I'll go. You go on and find out what you can." Findlin reached out a hand to touch his friend's shoulder. "First the flying owen, and now the horseman. I don't like the shape of this blow, my friend. And we've been through some stiff ones."

"Go on with you. Hurry back with your news. Maybe one of these fellows can guide you?" Lorimen turned to Marak. "We have need to bring news of our ship to our Lady Deros. Can you send him with my friend to guide him back?"

"I'm Alban Ram's chamber guard," replied the man hotly. "I'm not an errand boy."

"Then can you find me someone," went on Lorimen. "I mean no offense, lad. Quickly, though! There's something afoot here that may spell mischief of the worst sort for all of us!"

Marak collared a young man running by with a large quiver of arrows and a longbow. "Here we go, citizen. This lad has strong legs." He turned to him and gave him his instructions. "And when they've done at the harbor, you're to bring them straight back to the Hall of Gialon. We'll be there."

Lorimen shouted his thanks over his shoulder and raced on toward their boats at the quay. They rowed quickly back in the direction of the Thistle Cloud, calling out, and finally were answered by one of the sailors aboard. The young guide with them opened his eyes wide in disbelief when the sound of solid wood touching together came from the dingy bumping against nothing but empty air.

A Fight at the Quay

❋

While the full settlement had been gathered to try to defend themselves from the sudden attack of the Purge, no one had time at first to notice the arrival of the two ships coming under full sail into the harbor. The dragon had appeared out of the south, flying low to the ground, and a single belch of flames had touched off a hay barn and a stable, then the horrible foul stench of the beast descended upon the settlement with a dark greenish cloud, darkening the sunlight. Jalen had been prepared to die then, and he remembered the stranger from The Line telling him of the dreadful mind of the dragon, and how it weakened its victims before it came. He struggled to fight the numbing fear and dark warnings that suddenly filled his thoughts, but felt himself being slowly overpowered. He knew in a moment of panic that he was unable to resist any further, and that he would be devoured whole in an instant, and stood trembling, his arms at his sides, when the beast's hold was broken, and faint horn was heard breezing along over the surface of the harbor. He became aware of the smell of smoke then, and saw the burning barn and stable, and at the same instant, he spotted the two ships under full sail reaching into the harbor, and the figures marching through the market of the settlement.

He knew the horn that seemed to call the dragon away came from one of the two ships in the harbor, and raised a hand to shield his eyes to try to make out the vessels. Then he turned to the one who called himself a Steward, named Helwin. The bears and prisoners he regarded with some interest, but the citizens had formed up into their bucket brigades, and busied themselves with dousing the fires the dragon had started. Even with the smell of the burning wood, the terrible stench of the dragon lingered on. It was said the place a dragon had fouled would smell of its destruction and rot for the entire time until the beast might be slain.

That was said to be the way they marked their territory, to keep it from being plundered by other beasts.

Once the fires were extinguished, the citizens formed up into groups, to stare at the newcomers. They were slowly coming out from under the deadly thrall of the dragon's mind, and seemed to be light-headed, some of them laughing wildly and dancing about, while others stood weeping among themselves, like mourners at a funeral. And then a slow chant from the very back ranks began to call for a public execution of the Hulin Vipre prisoners and the two big animals who sat quietly on their haunches at Owen's side. No one seemed to realize who Baryloran was, and he further angered them by his disdainful appearance.

"Kill the Black Hood cripple," shouted an old man who had shoved his way through the crowd. "His kind have killed my wife and family, and I call on my just rights to have his life in fair trade!"

Crale and Lanidel rose and stood behind Owen, their ears flat, and low, rumbling growls keeping anyone from coming too near them. Hands in the crowd reached for bows and quivers, but Owen crawled upon the older bear's back, standing to address them so all could see and hear.

"Hear me, people! Hold your hand until I can tell you what I know."

"We don't care what you know!" shot back another woman, brandishing a sharpened lance. "You are here with two of our enemies from that black scourge of a place over the channel, and two wild beasts who murder and plunder our livestock, and you shall die as readily for it!"

Owen raised his voice again. "Look to yourselves! The Black Hood fleet is nearing, and we have just escaped the lava flows ahead of a band of raiders come to infiltrate your rear! My friends and I have come to warn you. The Bellream Readers are traitors. Efile is gone over to the enemy!"

"Liar!" cried a woman who threw back the cowl from her cloak as she spoke. "Efile is as loyal as any of us, and the Readers have kept us safe from harm before this! You could have brought the dragon, stranger! Tell us of that!"

"Ships! Ships entering the harbor!" cried Jalen, finding an opening to turn the attention of the settlement away from his new friend and his traveling companions. He pointed away to a dozen Hulin Vipre ships that had entered the outer sea wall of the settlement, putting rowing boats over the side and looping back to sea as soon as their human cargoes were landed.

"The dragon is gone for now, madam! You have another enemy at your door now! Look to yourselves!" Owen freed the sword from Skye from its scabbard, holding it aloft. Crale raised himself into his fighting stance, and the two figures towered above the others, the brilliant blue-white light from the weapon in his hand blinding and terrible to behold. "Windameir, Light the breath of Skye!" he cried, holding the sword aloft, catching the pale autumn sun and sending it forth as sharp as the blade itself, reflecting off the sea and the dark red sails of the Vipre ships already making their way back to sea. A roar went up from the beach, and the soldiers and citizens of the settlement hurried back to their defenses.

A squadron of Black Hood soldiers was already in the lower streets nearest the quays, and a shower of black arrows sailed aloft and rained into the first groups who came to close with the enemy. The Hulin Emperor shouted out a word of encouragement, and broke free of his captors for a moment, and Denale had sprinted clear of the lines, but turned when she found her master not with her. Lanidel loped to her, waiting for Owen's orders.

"I am obliged to you, Helwin! You show great heart, for an enemy. If you get me back to my men, I will spare your life in return. This is no fight of yours. You can leave as you wish."

"And Alban Ram and the Lady Deros? And these good citizens?"

Baryloran's face flushed red with anger. "What do you know of what wrongs my people have suffered from these endless wars? Who told you the truth of the matter of the Alberion Novas? Gingus Pashon was the only man among the High Council who was fit to guard them, and the fools gave them away to the feeble Stewardship of Eirn Bol."

"Gingus Pashon would have given them to Astrain," replied Owen simply. "He was an able soldier and a wise man in many ways, I've heard, but he was clay in the hands of that woman. She did with him what she would, and look where it has led us. If she cannot attack with bloodshed, then she will come at you with a soft, perfumed promise of glory, or the sweet arms of a woman. She is at the bottom of this, as surely as we stand here."

They were forced to take cover then, for another volley of black arrows clattered off the roofs of the shelters nearby, and one of the shafts narrowly missed Crale. The big animal growled and frowned at Owen. "A strange time to argue this point," he complained. "Let's be gone, while we can."

"We have to take our prisoners with us," said Owen. "Can you carry him farther, Lanidel?"

"With ease. We should be on our way, before these kind citizens come back to take our hides."

The noise of the fighting swelled until the din of sword and shield filled the air with sharp jabs at the ear, and arrows grew up from the ground like some deadly crop waiting for harvest. The armies of the Black Hood surged slowly forward, then were thrown back, then regrouped and came again. A Hulin Vipre lieutenant at the head of a small knot of soldiers suddenly appeared from a narrow street behind Owen and his group, and threw himself to the attack.

"Here, Lieutenant! Your Emperor! Save the Black Mace!" Baryloran shouted at the top of his lungs, trying to break free to his troops. The soldier, a dark young man not much older than Owen, heard the voice and stopped to see who had called out to him. His eyes widened when he saw the two animals, one of which was holding the Hulin Emperor. He gave a hand signal, and Owen barely had time to set himself against the attack of two Black Hood troopers, who came at him through the doorway of one of the burned-out houses. Crale batted one down with a powerful, deadly flick of his paw, and Owen dispatched the other quickly with a stroke from the sword of Skye. The rest of the enemy then poured from the narrow street behind the young Black Hood officer, and Lanidel picked up the struggling Emperor and hauled him roughly away, followed by Crale and the girl, with Owen bringing up the rear. Heavy smoke from the torched buildings now hung so thickly over the settlement they couldn't see more than a few feet in front of them, and their eyes stung. It was a nightmare trying to find the end of the street that would lead to the outskirts of the settlement, and Hulin Vipre troops would appear out of the black, acrid smoke like howling ghosts.

It was an advantage then to have the two bears, for their shock value threw back many of the attackers, who fell on the small group viciously, only to be met out of the black shroud of smoke by huge animals, with fangs and claws that slashed right through a heavy shield as if it were parchment. Owen had tried to call out to Jalen, in hopes his former guide would be able to show them a way from the settlement, but had had no response. In a street strewn with basketware and pottery, Owen came across the young lad's mother, her head split open by a Hulin sword stroke. He thought of Lynn then, and wondered where she and his father were, and if they were alive. He knelt beside the slain woman, a heavy sadness weighing down his heart.

"It is useless to continue against my troops," said Baryloran. "You could avoid this slaughter if you would have your people lay down their arms."

"They aren't my people, but they won't stop fighting you," replied Owen grimly.

"It is sad," remarked the young Hulin Emperor. "When you have so little to live for, you would die for a wretched old fool who has held onto the Alberion Novas for all this time without using their power to help his cause or his people."

"And you, Baryloran, have an idea of how to use the Sacred Scrolls? To what purpose? And do you think the Dark One will let you keep them, once you have killed everyone who resists you, and burned their settlements to the ground?"

"Don't talk like a fool," chided his prisoner. "You make me think of you as the tunnel guard I mistook you for."

The swirling smoke cleared for a moment, and Owen could see the battle for the settlement still hung in the balance, and more Hulin Vipre troops had been landed from newly arrived boats. Denale had covered the dead woman's face with an apron, and she sat beside the body, weeping.

"Here, wench, what's wrong with you?" asked her master.

"Nothing, my lord," she replied, rising and wiping her eyes.

"Tears for an enemy? Has the Black Hood gone so soft that we weep for those who have stolen what was rightly ours, and who continue to keep us from our destiny?"

Crale uttered a terrifying growl and lumbered forward, striking down two Hulin soldiers who suddenly emerged out of the smoke. More buildings were put to the torch, and for a brief instant, Owen felt the probing thought of the Purge, but it passed. Then there was another mind, tickling the hiding place where the Olgnite spell had left a scar inside him. It wasn't as subtle as the dragon, but just as strong, and the sword throbbed heavily, pulsing in his hand until he looked quickly at the blade, where he saw a Black Hood ship under way. Whoever was at work was aboard that ship, and they were upon the road to Eirn Bol. His next thoughts were scrambled and disjointed, for the older bear was poised to strike down another enemy soldier, but held back momentarily, and the minstrel Emerald, followed by Elita, her beautiful face streaked with blood and soot, materialized like ghosts out of the dense smoke.

The Call of Corum Mont

Owen and Elita spoke at once, while Emerald went to one knee, supporting himself with his sword, and catching his breath in great gulps. Another man dressed as a minstrel, and showing the same exhausted face, stumbled into the small group. The bears kept an eye to their prisoners, and watched as Owen grabbed both the man and woman into a tight bear hug, tears of joy springing to his eyes. Even as the sounds of the battle raged all around them, they laughed and clapped each other on the back, and just when one would try to break away, they would all start to cry again, holding tightly to each other. A forward element of the Black Hood finally broke up their emotional reunion, and they had to give ground, falling back from the small square they were in, to a roofless building that still had three walls standing. Lanidel grasped the Hulin Emperor so tightly that Owen had to remind him to let his prisoner breathe, for Baryloran had begun to turn blue at the lips, and the girl was crying and tugging at the stout bear's forepaw. Horns were blowing everywhere at once now, and it seemed to Owen they were all Hulin war calls. Begam stood with his back against the broken wall, looking from the two huge animals and the prisoners they held, out at the steady advance of the Hulin Vipre troops.

"I hate to break up this lovely rendezvous, but it looks as though we may be forced to hold off on the hugging and do a little more sword handling."

"This is Begam," interjected Emerald, clasping Owen by the shoulders, and holding him out at arm's length so he could inspect him more closely. "We found the scoundrel on a bare island, riding a broken-down nag that turned out to be another friend of ours." The minstrel smiled, the black smudges on his face making him look like a court fool. "With the way things are pointed, I expect to see him next."

"Crale and Lanidel," introduced Owen, indicating the bears. "They are Warlings. Which friend do you spreak of?"

"Seravan."

A sudden thrill of excitement and hopefulness filled Owen. "Was he well?"

"He was on his way here," said Emerald, nodding toward the spot they stood on. He had pulled his cloak off, and found his shirt was blood-soaked beneath it. Elita wiped a small cut on her face with a piece she tore off her dress, and used the rest to bandage her husband's arm, where he had received a long slash from a lance.

"We came on the Marin Galone," went on Emerald. "We didn't expect to put into this nest of snakes. The Red Scorpion raced us here, and now it looks like Lanril Tarben will have to scuttle his ship to keep her out of the enemies' hands."

"Is he still aboard?" asked Owen. "If his vessel is still afloat, we could use a way to get to Cairn Weal."

Emerald looked about at the battle that had consumed most of the settlement. "I can't tell from here. Come on, maybe we can get a look from closer to the water."

"There is no hope from that quarter," said Baryloran. "You are doomed, now that you've landed."

"Who is this bird?" asked Begam.

"You wouldn't believe it," replied Owen. "We were coming through the old lava flows to warn Eirn Bol of a traitor, and came across Hulin troops in route to attack the rear."

"And he was with them?"

"No. He was with this woman, but the others are still there. This is Baryloran, the Fifth Collector of Hulingaad. He has somehow gotten himself tangled up in a civil war, and now everyone wants him dead. The woman is called Denale."

"He is the descendant of the Black Mace," snapped Denale. "It is an order from the blood. It has always been. There are wicked men in Blor Alhal who have murdered his father, and now try to kill him!"

"And we're supposed to bite at that smelly bait?" laughed Begam. "If this is really the Emperor, where is his proof? He could be a common soldier, trying to save his own wretched life by saying he was the king!"

"He is the Collector," insisted Denale. "He needs no proof."

"He's wearing one of the rings," said Owen. "He's who he

says he is, right enough." He reached over and raised the young Emperor's hand, displaying the Rhion Stone, its depths a reddish gray, with flashes of lightning far within.

"Would you like more proof?" asked Baryloran. "I could call the Lost Fire back to entertain you."

"And yourself, and your troops as well." Owen made a sweeping motion with his hand. "You know if you call one of those things back, they will destroy everything. They were used before, in the Dragon Wars. You must know how that ended."

"I know how my people were accused of something they were never guilty of. Gingus Pashon was betrayed by the High Council. He asked their forgiveness for his indiscretion with the woman, but they demanded their pound of flesh. When he refused, they destroyed him with the dragons."

Emerald saw the harbor through the smoke, and could see the Marin Galone yet afloat. The Dart was anchored next to her, and Railan Dramm stood on his quarterdeck, watching the fighting ashore. "We have two ships still afloat here," he reported. "But the captain of one of them might not be so willing to have guests aboard." Owen stepped beside him to look.

"Which is the fastest?" he asked.

"The Dart. But you'll have no luck with convincing Railan Dramm he should carry you into the very heart of the island where they have put a price on his head."

"He is very troubled," said Elita. "He is searching for someone dear to him. I felt a deep wound in the man. It is what makes him dangerous."

"I don't plan on convincing him. Could we take the ship by force?"

"With only us to do the fighting?" Emerald looked around at the small circle.

"I can get aboard without being seen," said Owen. "If you could get your captain to sail her for us, we might just be able to snatch the Dart for our own use."

"You tickle my sense of amusement, Helwin. I would like to see you attempt the Red Scorpion. He has won free passage upon our waters by the sheer force of his boldness. The Black Hood places much value in the weight of a man's nerve. He played at cards with my brother in the days before Tien Cal was lost. We leave him alone to come and go as he pleases."

"All the better to use his ship to ply our way through your fleet, your excellency. If they saw a familiar vessel, they wouldn't very likely be hostile to it."

Baryloran laughed. "I can only recommend your course of action, Helwin. Let's make all speed, shall we? I would like to rid myself of this beast that's crushing my ribs." Lanidel softened his grip on his prisoner ever so slightly, growling softly.

"Let's see if we can make the harbor. We shall need to reach the ship you came on, Emerald. Can you stop her captain from sinking her?"

"We can try. Come on, Begam. If you remember more of the Wylch poems, you might recite them as we go." He held his hand out to his wife. "I don't want to lose you in the smoke, my dear. Stay close."

"We'll be right behind," said Owen.

There was a lull in the fighting then, and the smoke had begun to be blown away by the wind. The settlement was still in flames, but the defenders had formed a square in the center of the village near the quays, and held the Black Hood invaders at bay.

"They must be waiting for reinforcements," said Begam, watching as the Hulin Vipre began to prepare for a siege. They had drawn back, and regrouped into units, and sent regular showers of black arrows into the fortified square, hoping to nibble away at the number of defenders.

"And they shall have them soon," said Baryloran.

"Then we need to move quickly, Emerald. Here, put these on. It may let you move onto the quay without being detected." Owen had knelt, and stripped away the black cloaks of three slain Hulin Vipre soldiers.

"I shall warn the troops," said Baryloran. "It is useless."

"You'll do nothing of the sort, chubblet. I may let the cub here see if he is still as strong as he used to be. It might be something to see to watch your eyes pop out of your head from a bear crush." Crale's great muzzle was close to the young Emperor's face as he spoke, the deep brown eyes turned a menacing black.

"Don't you touch him," cried Denale. "He won't try to warn the others. Please don't hurt him."

"Don't worry, she," went on Crale. "Lanidel isn't stern enough to really do it. But he must be quiet."

"Hush, wench! You shame me, pleading for me like this!" Baryloran's face was a deep red, and he turned his eyes to the ground.

"It is no bad thing to have someone plead for your life, good Emperor. It may be the most prized of all the possessions you may have in your treasure rooms." Emerald drew on the black cloak and drew the hood over his face. "Now we must go. Where will you keep the bears? They can't be disguised."

"I shall use the safest place." He stood between the bears and the prisoners, and touching all of them as he recited the words Politar had taught him, he entered the green sunlit world of the bottle with the food and arms. The animals wuffed and shuffled their paws, but soon settled down to their duties of watching the prisoners. Baryloran and Denale were dumb-struck, and sat down meekly on low, three-legged stools that ringed a wooden table laden with cheese and fruit.

"You'll be safe enough here. There is food and water, and a place to sleep." Owen turned to Crale and Lanidel. "The place is as large as your old tunnels, so don't let them out of your sight. If you have a need to find me, touch one of the walls here and call to me."

"How long will you be?" asked the older bear. "I don't hold much affection for this chore."

"Long enough to secure the boat. Once we're afloat, I'll bring you back."

"You can't just leave us," protested Denale. "What if something happens to you?" She was on the verge of tears again.

"In that case, you shall have a good but simple life, well fed, and amused by wandering through the whole of this place. I don't know how far it extends, or where it has an ending. If I am struck by one of your Emperor's henchmen, you can thank him for that as you like."

"Don't worry, wench. We won't be left." He had begun to recover himself, careful to conceal his hand under the table, feeling the reassuring weight of the Rhion Stone on his finger. What one weirdoch could spin, another could undo, and as long as he held the stone, he would be able to reach Mortus Blan, the oldest and most clever of all, and one who could be trusted.

"Thank you for your kindness. Good-bye for now." Owen gave the bear's sign for farewell to the two huge animals, and was gone.

The silence that fell in the world of the green bottle was deafening after the roar and clash of the battle they had just left. Crale and Lanidel sat on their haunches, listening to the music, their ears up, and their eyes a misty gray. It was the Old Ones playing, like they had heard many times in the depths of their mountains. If Politar had been there, he could have told the Warlings that the green bottle had come from the combs of the Monks of Corum Mont, and that the music now grew stronger as the bottle and its inner world returned closer to its home.

Outside, Owen and his friends reached the quay without incident, and rowed swiftly out to the Marin Galone, where they were met by Lanril Tarben, who hoisted them aboard himself.

A Reluctant Messenger

"I'm glad my men recognized you beneath that black hood, my lady," blurted Lanril, helping Elita aboard. "I thought it was time to scuttle the Marin Galone, and it was not a good feeling, I can tell you."

"Have you seen anything of Rhule, or any of the Welingtron?" asked Emerald. "I would have thought them a stauncher ally than this."

"They are here," said Elita. "I hear them. They are beneath the Dart."

"I wish they'd tow me out of this cockle-net. We have managed to put off a boarding party from one of the Black Hood ships already, but their numbers are growing. It looks like they're ferrying their troops to the assault. If we could get out now, we might have enough of a jump to outrun them."

"This is Owen Helwin, the lad I have told you about," said Emerald, pushing his friend over the rail from below. "He has a plan that will tickle your gills, Lanril. It might serve to save the Marin Galone, as well."

"Emerald and Elita have spoken of you often, lad. From their reports, I would have marked you down to having drowned in this good salt pond beneath us."

"I was washed off the Thistle Cloud in a storm and swallowed enough seawater to last me awhile. It was a near thing, I can tell you. I'll have to fill you in when we have time to sit at fire and give each other our news." Owen threw off the black cloak he had worn. "You might keep these, Captain. In case the next troops come before we're gone, they may think the ship is already captured. What we have need of now is a fast ship. Emerald tells me the Dart has a turn of speed."

Lanril passed out the cloaks the companions had brought, and went forward with Owen to look at Railan Dramm's cutter. "She's a fine ship, lad, but she carries the smell of death and destruction. It will be the end of her, one day."

"We might rewrite some of her debt by using her for good," replied Owen, and he recounted his plan to take her to Cairn Weal.

Lanril laughed. "Now that would be a touch," he admitted. "I like the boy, Emerald." He paused, lost in thought, watching the Black Hood troops re-form to attack the settlement square again. The defenders had repelled another assault, and there were many black-cloaked bodies now scattered about through the narrow streets and ways. "It would be easier to get Rhule to take us," he said at last. "The Welingtron can move the Marin Galone almost as fast as the Dart. Faster, if there's no wind."

"But the Black Hood know the Dart," continued Owen. "We would be better to not risk having to make a fight of it if the enemy caught on that we weren't part of the fleet."

Elita leaned on her husband's arm, her eyes turned a deeper gray, like the color of dreams of the Elboreal. "I feel Deros very strongly now. The Maridonel has grown louder."

The sword at Owen's side emitted a low, barely audible sound, as though it were a silver bell struck with a crystal. "I have been hearing this now since the battle started. I'd better check on our good Warlings and their prisoners." He motioned a hand toward his heart, and was gone from their sight for a moment, and when he reappeared, he stood beside two huge bears, who blinked warily about in surprise.

"These are my friends, Lanidel and Crale. They are Warlings."

"Where are the prisoners?" asked Begam.

"Asleep. I have heard this music before, when I met the Lady Rewen. They won't be going anywhere for a time. Then we will have a chance to think of what best to do with them."

"Is he really the Hulin Emperor?" asked Begam.

"Baryloran, the Fifth Collector," replied Owen. "It's odd to think that we were there when his brother was killed in the Ellerhorn Fen, and now he has fallen into our hands on Eirn Bol."

"What have you done with him?" asked Lanril Tarben, looking about to see the prisoner they spoke of.

"He's safely hidden, good captain. There's a woman with him, as well. We are by no means moored safely at our destination, and I don't want either of them to fall into the wrong hands before we reach Cairn Weal."

"What will you do with him then?" asked Emerald.

"We'll come to that bridge to cross, but not yet. I don't know. I hope to find the Lady Rewen and Alban Ram. They might have a plan."

Aboard the Dart, Railan Dramm saw the captain of the Marin Galone, and shouted out over the din. "Come on, Tarben! You've lost fair and square, and I demand my prize now. You've been a good sport of it, and you gave me a race. I'll give you an even chance of it. You and your men can go ashore now, and take your chances with the rest of these poor devils in this settlement!" He threw back his head and laughed, his red hair and beard catching the golden sunlight.

"He is a handsome dog," admitted Emerald. "Reminds me in a way of Ulen Scarlett."

"Don't speak his name," fumed Owen. "If he's not dead already, he will be the cause of grief to us yet."

Lanril looked to Owen. "Shall I invite him over to claim his booty? It might be a way to get aboard the Dart."

"Go on," said Owen. "I'll take my boarding party with me and scout the Dart. Go along with him as far as you can, and wait for my signal." He looked to his old friends. "Shall I take Elita with me? It will be safer." Emerald nodded, squeezing his wife's hand. Owen moved Elita to stand in a place next to the bears, and in another instant all four were gone from the deck of the Marin Galone.

"Now what?" asked Lanril.

"Call to him. Tell him to come on," suggested Emerald. "Let's see what note he'll strike."

Lanril cupped his hands and shouted back across the water. "You've won fair enough, Railan. I was going to scuttle the Marin Galone, but I'd rather see her stay afloat."

Railan had a tender put over the side of the Dart, and six of his crew rowed him over. When they drew alongside, he called up to Lanril Tarben for he and his crew to disembark. "I'm not so drunk with victory that I would walk in among this pack of wolves," he laughed. "Once you have your men off, you can show me my new vessel."

Amid many complaints and threats of mutiny, Lanril convinced his men to lower their tenders and wait for him ashore. "Steer clear of the Black Hood. There on the quay are the ruins of the customs house. Wait for me there." His mate refused to leave, until Lanril pointed out that he would be next in command if anything happened to him. "You must go on, my hotheaded friend. You've always done your duty. Now is no time to stop." The man reluctantly left with the shore party.

After some noisy protests and jeers, the crew of the Marin Galone was soon rowing for shore, and quickly drew up their boats and concealed themselves in the old customs warehouse, which was roofless, but with the walls still intact.

Railan sent one of his men up the rope ladder to be sure it was safe, and pulled himself quickly up when the all-clear was given. Standing on the deck of the Marin Galone, he saluted Lanril disdainfully with a flick of his wrist. "No welcoming speech, sir?" he asked, turing his back on them to look over the trim ship.

"You are an odd one to spout on about honor and keeping one's word," said Lanril, a cold rage edging his voice.

"I know more of honor and a true word than you might think, Captain. And I know well about those who have no honor and keep no word. That is what led me to this life. If you were to have sailed in my wake when I was younger, you would understand me better." Railan looked about again, turning to Emerald. "Where is your fair wife, sir? Was she not aboard?"

"She's gone ashore with the others," replied Emerald.

"You are too negligent, sir," chided Railan. "She is a beautiful woman. It could be dangerous to leave her with so many crude sailors."

"She's with my crew," shot back Lanril Tarben. "They have been brought up with some idea of civility."

Railan gave a mock bow, sweeping his hat off his head. "My pardon, sir. I forgot you are the paragon of virtue aboard this vessel. Maybe some of it will rub off on me and my crew," he laughed. "Now that we shall sail her."

Emerald could see that Lanril Tarben had been driven to his limits, and the thought of losing his vessel was too much for him to bear. "We had best look to giving the tour," he said, grasping the captain firmly by the arm. "It grows late, and we have a need to get on." He signaled with his eyes, and he breathed a sigh of relief when Lanril acknowledged he understood.

"Of course. Come along, sir. I'll brief you on her history, and show you her quarters and gear."

"Stand watch here," ordered Railan, posting a man at the boarding ladder. "If there's anything funny, sing out." He turned on his heel and followed Lanril below.

Emerald and Begam turned their eyes back to the Dart and watched to see any sign of something afoot. All was tranquil at the moment, with nothing but a few of the crew coiling lines near the bow. There was a small work party amidships, waiting to hoist the rowing tender back aboard, but otherwise, it looked peaceful enough, considering the battle being waged in the settlement ashore. They watched an attack carry forward toward the settlement square, falter, then fall back, and when they looked again at the deck of the Dart, not a single crewman remained to be seen. The sailor left on watch by Railan stepped up closer to the rail to peer over at the odd sight, for there was no noise of men hitting the water, or other sign of a struggle, yet the Dart was stripped clean of her deck crew.

As the man turned to call out to Railan, Begam caught him across the base of the skull with the heavy hilt of his sword, and Emerald caught him before he made a noise by hitting the deck. It was over in an instant, and for the first time in his life, Railan Dramm arrived back on deck as a prisoner in chains, and with his beautiful Dart commandeered.

The Marches
of Time

The Harp of Tirhan

✳

It was not a pretty sight to see.

Railan Dramm held his breath straining at his bonds, but the chains held fast, although he struggled with them until the metal bit into his skin, drawing blood. He bellowed and roared foul curses and swore vengeance on all aboard the Marin Galone, and watched helplessly as the ship's crew rowed back from the shore, taunting and catcalling the captive.

There were many calls to run him to the top of the yardarm in a noose, but Lanril Tarben soon put a halt to that talk.

"He will be kept alive. There is no man among you that would be willing to string this kite up to a yardarm in cold blood just to watch it fly. That would make you no better than he."

"No fancy excuses, Lanril," shouted an old seaman. "We both have friends that this blaggart sent to the deep trench! Fair is fair, I say! Let the sea sort them out!"

A roar of approval ran around the deck of the Marin Galone.

Lanril raised his hand to be heard. "Hear me out, you men. We will decide later what to do with this gent. First I need volunteers to help Owen sail the Dart to Cairn Weal. Do I have any takers?"

"Where's that pack of cutthroats that Railan sailed with? Are they taken?"

"Gone," was all Lanril Tarben answered, for he as yet did

225

not know what had happened to the crew. He stood looking over at the bare deck of the Red Scorpion's ship, and there was not a living soul aboard to be seen.

"How could that be?" asked one of the sailors. "They had a big crew on her."

"Gone," repeated Lanril Tarben. "We shall soon find out where." He called out for a boat and oarsman, and was joined by Emerald and Begam. "I hope Helwin has found some solution that will give him a quick exit from this harbor. If she doesn't move fast, the Dart will be taken by the Black Hood." Lanril had clambered up the boarding ladder, and stood looking at the neatly coiled lines and flaked sails, everything done shipshape and ready for use. The sight of the silent ship was enough to spook the captain of the Marin Galone. "I've seen strange things, but this one is new to me. Where do you put a boat's crew so they can't be seen in broad daylight?"

Owen appeared from below, a mischievous smile on his face. "Greetings, Captain. Welcome aboard the Dart, lately of the command of Railan Dramm, now in the service of the Lady Deros, and bound for Cairn Weal." The young man made a deep bow, and saluted Lanril with his sword.

"What have you done with the others?" asked Begam.

"They didn't have a natural inclination to be friendly with bears," replied the lad. "And some of them got a rude start, finding out that they will be spending the next bit of time in a root cellar in a country Politar brought me to." Seeing the growing puzzlement on his friends' faces, Owen quickly set them at ease. "They are gone. The crew is captured, and out of harm's way."

"But you never left the boat," protested Lanril.

"I never left the boat that you saw," corrected Owen. He moved his hand in a small circular motion over his heart, and there was nothing but an empty deck. In a few moments more, the young Steward was back, standing beside Crale and Lanidel. The bears both had visible wounds, although Owen had tended to them, and it was evident that the younger animal had just fought a fierce battle with someone who was armed with a boat hook, or fish lance. "My jailers! They are also handy lads to have about when the odds run against you."

"I think we should know a tune or two about these fellows," said Begam. "I seem to remember a whole Warling lore that was languishing away in the back of my father's library."

"There's a boat coming out from shore," warned Lanidel, letting out a low warning growl. "The Black Hood."

"You two will have to keep my small kitchen intact," said Owen. "I need you there for now." He stood near the animals, and within a few seconds, the two minstrels were alone on deck with Lanril Tarben.

"We'll have need of Rhule," said Lanril. "This mooring is getting too well populated." He signaled his ship to weigh anchor and put on sail. "Are you handy in the foretop?" he asked the minstrels.

"My back is good, but I don't have the bird's skills you need to dance to that tune," laughed Emerald. "I think we should call for Rhule."

As the Welingtron's name was spoken, a powerful surge lifted the Dart, and the great eel appeared at the ship's side. "We have our work cut to order," he said. "You should see to your vessel, Captain. My good companions will be ready to move in a moment." Rhule disappeared in a single, fluid motion, and at the same time, the Dart shuddered and gained way, heading for the seawall at the narrow mouth of the harbor. Owen was suddenly at Emerald's side. "Elita sent you this," he said, handing his friend a small cloth sack.

When the minstrel opened it, he let out a quiet laugh. "She's seen to my hunger," he said, holding up the small round of cheese and bread. "The woman is a marvel." The other cloth-wrapped object was undone, and he held it out to look at what it was. "Tirhan's harp," he said, examining it. "It is the very one Twig played when he called up the Elurin." He put the small instrument to his mouth and struck a note. A thin, pure sound filled the air, and for a moment, Emerald thought he saw the small, twisted body of Twig. "My wife foresees everything. I would rather have this with me than a baker's dozen of Leech shafts." He carefully rewrapped the small harp, and put it into his tunic. "What is Elita doing there?"

"She is tending to the wounds the Warlings got in the fight," went on Owen. "I was worried about the young one, but Elita says he will be all right."

Lanril waved, and was over the side and down the ladder quickly. His crewmen rowed swiftly for his ship, and the captain was pulled safely aboard. The Welingesse Fal had increased their speed, and now slowly outdistanced the Black Hood skiffs that followed behind.

The two friends turned their attention to the Dart, and went forward to see Rhule raising his great body above the waves, pulling the captured ship out into the open ocean, behind the Marin Galone. Lanril Tarben lifted a hand in passing as the two ships neared each other, and pointed to the barely visible White Cliffs that lay in the distance, which marked the entrance to Cairn Weal.

They could see the sails of other ships ranging out from the coast of the dark outline of Hulingaad, bringing more troops to the besieged island. Their dark sails turned blood-red in the dying afternoon sunlight, drawing a ragged scar across the horizon that raised a sense of dread in all who saw.

A Weirdoch's Arrival

The Long Bow was almost packed, and the noise of voices and clatter of ale mugs created a racket that was painful to the ear. Mortus Blan, invisible to them, prowled through the mob like a hunting beast, pinching and jabbing unsuspecting patrons, or turning their drinks over their heads. Fights broke out here and there, like sparks fallen into dry brush, but he went on, searching until he found his man, who sat with an ugly ex-palace guard, a plate of half-eaten food on the table in front of him. The old man drew out a chair across the table, and sprinkled the food with a bit a powder he had removed from the pouch at his waist. The two men reached a lull in their drinking, and both reached for the dish of meat, eating noisily. Mortus waited a few minutes longer, then began to speak after the other man drunkenly reeled away to relieve himself.

"Can you hear me, Almag?"

"What? Who's that?" shot the startled Almag.

"Mortus Blan. I have come for what you owe me."

The rough features of the man fell into a frightened scowl. "I have no way to pay you."

"Your boat is in the harbor, is it not?" went on the weirdoch.

"You know it is."

"Then we shall call it quits once you have taken me across to Eirn Bol."

Almag pounded a fist on the table, making the mugs and dish of meat jump. "You ask me something impossible! How can I get my ship out of the harbor without taking troops for the Battalions?" He scooted his chair back from the table, shaking his head. "I can't do it, I tell you!"

Mortus Blan laughed, an icy edge in his voice. "You will find a way to do it, or you shall not live past another noon watch. You have enjoyed your meat, I see."

"What? What are you saying? What have you done to the meat?"

"An old potion I use sometimes. Stays in the blood for a day or so, then eats its way out of the stomach. Rather painful way to die, Almag. I have seen it work once or twice. The victims screamed for a full morning, and finally died by drowning in their own bile."

Almag went pale beneath his unkempt beard. "You black-hearted lizzard! What will save me?"

"I'll give you the vial you need when you have set me ashore on Eirn Bol. You won't feel anything more than what you might if you'd eaten tainted meat." Mortus Blan laughed cruelly. "And I'll give you silver, as well."

"I'll have to round up a crew."

"I shall be at the guard tower on the quay at sundown."

"You want me to sail at night?" asked Almag. "The tide will be wrong. We'll be lucky to make Shadow Reef clear."

"You are experienced in night sailing, I believe," went on Mortus Blan. "I'm sure you can remember your charts, and where the dangers lie." The noise of his chair scraping on the floor was the only sign that he was gone. Almag sat, wide-eyed, trying to see if he could detect the poison acting in him. He knocked the plate of meat off the table, sending the tray clattering under the feet of two soldiers next to him.

When his companion returned, the unfortunate victim dragged the struggling man roughly by his beard from The Long Bow, calling out the names of his crew as he did. By the time they reached the harbor, he had managed to collect enough men to man his small cutter, and over their bitter protests had them all aboard, grumbling and cursing, and leveling threats of cutting his throat. It was two hours until sunset, and most of the others of the fleet had set sail, leaving only a few boats at anchor. Most of them would be back on the morning tide to ferry more troops, but for now, Almag had the quay almost to himself.

Just as the sun began to sink into the deep pearl-colored sea, he felt a hand tug at his cloak, announcing the arrival of the ancient weirdoch. "Come along, Almag. Secrecy and speed is what I must have, and if you value the small vial I have in my cloak, you'll see to it I am put by in one of your sturdy tenders off Cairn Weal."

"Sooner done, best riddance," growled Almag, although there was a waver to his threat. "I'll see to it you'll have what you want. Can I see the poison killer?"

"Certainly. No harm to that." Mortus Blan held out the small vial, which appeared to Almag a dull reddish green blur on the empty air. "Now you've seen it. Let's get under way."

Feeling the ravages of the deadly potion coursing through his blood, Almag railed and lashed out at the still-drunken crew, and they soon had sail on the cutter, and had cast off, falling away from the quay, and slowly gaining way for the harbor mouth. A coast guardsman commanding a rowing boat pulled alongside briefly, demanding his destination. "Eirn Bol."

"Where are you troops?" demanded the man.

Mortus Blan answered from behind Almag. "We're going to pick up the wounded. We have a healer aboard."

"Good speed, Captain. I have heard the reports all day. We shall soon be drinking wine out of the cellars of Cairn Weal, and pleasuring with their wenches!"

Even the thought of fine wine and new women did not reach Almag's heart, for he could not help himself from thinking of the vile poison that at the very moment pounded in the blood at his hammering temples.

"Very good, Almag. You shall have your reward for this." Mortus Blan released his binding, and suddenly appeared on the deck at the ship captain's side.

"I should throw you to the fish," growled the captain.

"You wouldn't live to enjoy your deed," promised Mortus Blan. "Now show me a cabin I can rest in."

He was shown to the best the rough vessel had to offer, and sat back on the bunk with his legs drawn up beneath him. He closed his eyes as soon as the sailor was gone, twisting the ring about on his finger, and searching out any news of Baryloran, or the other Eye, worn by the stranger. His mind was like a great black bat, hovering, watching, waiting to soundlessly descend upon its victim. As he searched, he caught a distant flicker, a dull glimmering of the Eye awakening to heed his call. At first he could not be sure of which it was, but the confused, tumbled thoughts of its owner soon told him it was the stranger.

He slowly quieted the mad ramblings of the ring-wearer, and soothed him into letting him peer through the Rhion Stone at where he was. Mortus Blan drew all his energy together and opened his mind to the Eye. He could see a cabin, with charts and a compass, but when he tried to go through the door, it wouldn't budge, and the ring-wearer became agitated. The old man calmed him again, and slowly concentrated on the stone, gaining control of the other man's mind.

He called out through his puppet's mouth, and a sailor's face appeared at the slightly open door. Mortus Blan watched as his surrogate's hand closed on the man's throat, and then he was free, running across the deck of a ship, and throwing himself into the sea.

Ahead, through a watery vision, he could make out the high white walls of his most hated enemies, and see the white banner with the golden dragon floating gently on the twilight breeze.

Lost and Found

The sound of the wind through the sails and the lap of the waves along the hull was even and soothing. The last stars before dawn were glimmering brightly low down on the horizon, and just at the moment the sun began to rise, a ray of light blazed a path over the dark water, dazzling the eye, and reflecting off the White Cliffs and walls of Cairn Weal. Jeremy stood at the rail of The Crane next to Captain Telig and Salts.

"Now the fun begins," growled the captain. "We've gotten this far without hurt, but even with the Welingtron and the Golvane leaf, we still have to sail this vessel into the harbor there, and it's full of the Hulin Vipre fleet, as likely as not, or soon will be."

"Or you can cut for cover, and keep The Crane safe. Let the lad and I take in one of the Black Hood ships. With all the comings and goings we've seen, one more among 'em won't raise any eyebrow."

"And once we're there, I can find out if the others have come yet," said Jeremy, a small shard of fear lurking deep in his heart. "And I can see to the traitor who tried to murder me, as well, if he's come through."

"First things first, lad. I wanted to have a sail by to see how the jib's set on all this business." Captain Telig raised his spyglass and looked shoreward for a long moment. "This is no small gullwash, Salts. I haven't ever seen this many Black Hood ships rafted up in one place before."

Salts pointed out a flickering, dull orange star that seemed to be moving toward them. "They've got their firebat out, too. Nasty brute. I hope he's not coming our way." The three followed the dragon's progress, flying on a line that took it toward the western coast of Eirn Bol. It was light enough now to see that there were tall columns of smoke coming from various points of land in both directions. "It's been at work here, blast its hide."

As the dawn grew lighter, the cost of the invasion became clearer. There were beached Hulin Vipre vessels along both sides of the harbor mouth of Cairn Weal, and pillars of dark smoke coming up from the very walls of the fortress inside.

"I think some of that must be the old fire mountain," observed Captain Telig. "I've seen this kind of thing happen before. I remember one year, it got so dark at noon, we thought it was midnight. Just one of the fire-cones going off. Took a month to get The Crane scoured clean of the soot."

Salts looked to his commander. "If we're going to take one of the Hood vessels in, we'd better look to it, sire. We'll have company soon enough."

Captain Telig scanned the sea with his glass. "You're right, Salts. If we're going to move, we have to do it now."

"Shall I pick the men, sir?"

"Take the first watch, and leave me the rest. You can leave the prisoners, too."

"Some of them will want to go," said Jeremy.

"Then take the ones who do. I'll take The Crane around behind the point there, and lay to the hook until you're in."

"We'll send the usual signal," replied his mate. "Red smoke will tell you we're safe." Salts took off his cap and wiped his brow. "Come on, lad. Let's go see who wants to take a closer look at the White Cliffs."

They were not long in boarding and readying the Hulin ship they chose to sail into Cairn Weal. It was decided that the other, smaller ship would be put under sail and set on a course that would beach her.

Jeremy helped the small crew hoist sails, and watched as the old mate lashed up the helm that set the boat on a course directly for shore. Salts muttered an old seaman's prayer over her as he stepped back over the rail onto the other ship. "I hope someone remembers to do as much for me," he said, turning to the young Steward.

"If I'm left standing, you can count on me, Salts. You've been a good comrade, and one I've been proud to serve with."

"Likewise, you lubber! If I'd had hold of you when you were but a shrimp, I might have made a decent sailor out of you."

"My mother wanted me to be a baker or weaver," confessed Jeremy. "I woke up with the night sweats, thinking about that fate."

"Weaving or baking wouldn't do you much good in these troubled times, lad." He smashed a fist into his open palm the way Stearborn and Chellin Duchin were prone to do when they were agitated about something. "My life's been spent wandering about without a hook on one pond or another, and I haven't seen any bakers or weavers that have cut these Black Hood devils down to size."

"Not likely, Salts! But I see you've been crafty enough to keep afloat."

The young woman who was the sister of the Red Scorpion found them then, and approached Salts timidly. "Captain Telig said that I should tell you I want to come ashore when you go."

"It's no place for you, Laeni. There's still a fight to come, and you'd be in great danger."

"I would rather be with you than out here worrying," the girl argued. Her looked melted Jeremy, and he looked hopelessly at Salts, hoping his friend would have a suitable argument.

"You're welcome to come with us, girl. You can make yourself useful in bringing up shafts and keeping our quivers full when we get into it."

Jeremy frowned. "At least stay below while you're doing it. We don't know yet what to expect. And the dragon is back.

"Now we'll get to find out if the old songs were true. The Lady Rewen knows ways to deal with them."

"Then let's hope your Lady Rewen is somewhere close aport when we have need of her. Now let's look to our course." The old mate prowled the deck from the stern to the stem-post, readying lines and studying the set of the sails. He called out his corrections, and the shorthanded crew leapt to trim sheets and lay out the deck to prepare for their arrival in the harbor. "Not the least of our worries is that someone there will think we *are* Black Hood, and hop on our backs before we can explain."

The day had dawned fair, with the white streaming clouds flying above the beleaguered Cairn Weal like tattered battle flags. Outer buildings near the harbor were burning, and there was even a thin plume of blackish cloud coming from an upper wing of the walled keep itself. As they neared the mouth of the inlet that led to the seawall and harbor, Jeremy's heart fell when he saw the wrecked ships inside and the bodies on the quays. An outguard of Hulin Vipre troops was working at driving off the defenders in the guard tower on the landings, but without success. When the enemy troops spotted the ship, they raised their helmets in excitement, motioning for the boat to land near them, thinking it was reinforcements. Salts let out a rough laugh.

"These toads will be hopping for better reason than they have now as soon as we drop our hook here. You better stand by to warn the tars there at the wall we're friendly."

"I'll do that," offered Laeni.

"It's too dangerous," protested Jeremy. "They might just put an arrow into you before you could call out."

They had a turn of speed on when they burst into the inner harbor, and the sound of alarm horns filled the air before they could get their anchor cleared and down. Jeremy was waiting at the railing, raising his hands and shouting out at the defenders.

"Long live the Lady Deros! Long live Alban Ram! We are friends! We captured a Black Hood vessel, and bring back many who were held as slaves!"

"What's your signboard?" asked a voice from behind a circular tower that looked over the entire quay, and which was filled with many slots where archers could hold control over the harbor in all directions.

"My name is Jeremy Thistlewood. I'm a Steward of the Line, and I ride with Chellin Duchin. My friend Salts here serves on board The Crane, under Captain Telig."

A stony silence greeted his speech, then someone inside called for Jeremy to step onto the wharf and advance. He did as he was told, every hair standing out on the back of his head. A trickle of sweat ran down his forehead into his eyes, even though the day was brisk. Before he reached the guard tower, more horns were heard, and he turned in time to see a sleek cutter making her entry into the harbor, although it was hard to tell what propelled her. A huge catapult was sprung then, and he watched a keg of burning pitch tumble high into the air, arching away toward the enemy ship.

"It's a ruse!" shouted a voice almost at his ear. "Burn them both!"

"Wait!" cried Jeremy. "That ship isn't with us. We've come aboard The Crane, and she's lying to her hook waiting until we can signal it's safe for Captain Telig to come in."

Two soldiers in full battle kit suddenly opened a small doorway at the bottom of the tower and escorted Jeremy roughly inside. They took his sword and dagger and placed him before an exhausted officer, who looked up from his rough desk, rubbing his eyes wearily.

"My friends are the Lady Deros and the Lady Rewen, on the Thistle Cloud. I am a Line Steward, and was on my way here at the Lady Deros's request."

"Now that is a clever ruse, I must own," said the officer, rising to stretch. He walked away to the tower wall and peered through one of the archery slits. "Fine lines on that ship. I think it must be the Dart, from the look of her." He took a spyglass from his drawer, and drew it out to full length. "It is the Dart. So you sail with the Red Scorpion, do you? I never would have put you down for that lot." He closed the glass and returned it to its place. "This will have you hung, you know. I personally would prefer to simply set you down in the lower keeps for the Aldora, but they've been on about setting a public example lately. A dreadful pity, but there you are."

Jeremy was at the wall, peering into the harbor almost before the man finished. "Her brother. If that's the one, it's her brother."

"What? What's that you're saying?" asked the weary officer.

"A prisoner we freed when we captured the Hulin ships said her brother is the Red Scorpion!"

"Your story won't hold weight. You may as well forget it. We'll pluck the others off your vessel, and string the lot of you up for the citizens to see." He was ready to go along with his thoughts, but a sudden commotion on the wharfs drew his attention away. He signaled for his guards to take Jeremy away.

"Where, sir?"

"The lock-hole. We'll get the others rounded up, then hang the lot of them."

"There's a weirdoch on the last ship in, sir," reported a guard, sticking his head in from the outside gate. "He's vanished out of the harbor tender we sent to fetch them in."

"If that had been the Red Scorpion, you would have had mincemeat made of your crews," reminded Jeremy. "If you'll give us a chance, we'll prove to you who we are."

"You said the sister of the Red Scorpion is aboard your ship. What would that tell us?"

"That the truth is what I told you. We rescued her from the Hulin Vipre and were on our way here."

There were more harbor guards coming and going, and one of the last ones ducked in to report that there was no sign of the Red Scorpion aboard the Dart.

Traces of the Old Days

❋

Looking through the slits used by the archers, Jeremy could see the ship riding to an anchor, the harbor tenders lined up at her side. The still-burning pitch barrel spread its black smoke, but had done no damage. The officer strode to the door, beckoning his troops to bring Jeremy along. They went back down the quay to where the Hulin ship lay against the landing, her crew still at the rail, now guarded by more troops. Laeni's face brightened when she saw Jeremy returning.

"Which of you claims kin to Railan Dramm? Is that you, wench?" asked the officer, leaning down to board the vessel.

Laeni nodded. "I haven't seen my brother since I was taken . . ." She could not finish.

Salts gave the girl a gruff hug. "She's had a rough time of it, sir," he explained. "We took this vessel and another from the Hood, and freed all the prisoners."

"That's what this fellow just told me," the officer replied. He walked slowly about the deck, examining the members of the crew and looking at the pile of weapons his men had taken from them. He took up a bow, pulling it to test its strength. "You could place a shaft well with this."

"The trees come from the Delos Sound, sir. We have good craftsmen who know wood. They build our ships, and give us our weapons." He nodded at the officer. "That bow belongs to a lad who could put a yard shaft into your gizzard from here to the harbor mouth."

More smoke had come up from behind them, higher up in the streets rising toward the outer walls of Cairn Weal. Another soldier came to the railing, calling for his commander. "There's been a landing around the point, sir! A large party of the Vipre are attacking the South Gate!"

"How goes it?" shot the officer. "How is Prolin holding?"

"Prolin is wounded, sir. His lieutenant is in charge. They said they would need more men."

"We're spread too thin now. Get word to them they'll have to hold with what they have."

"We could help," volunteered Jeremy. "I am a Line Steward. Give me weapons and I'll lend a hand."

"My crew is at your disposal," offered Salts.

There were more signal horns then, and a single red flag was run up a pole at the sentry tower that stood on the low point at the harbor mouth. "More Hood ships," said the officer, turning to his men. He glanced over the new arrivals and made a quick decision. "See to it the pitch is hot, and get the launchers ready! Stand by to repel attackers!" He leapt back onto the wharf, calling over his shoulder. "Come along, all of you. Guards, distribute their weapons! Hop to it! We won't have long to sit out here trying to make up our minds!"

"Thank you, sir," said Jeremy. "We can pull our weight.

The Lady Deros didn't want to drag us here to have a quilting party."

"This will be a party right enough, stranger. We have barely been holding out, since Alban Ram has been taken with the fever."

Jeremy remembered the small pouch at his neck. "I might have something to help your Elder," he offered.

"Don't push your luck," stranger," snapped the officer. "I've rearmed you against my better judgment because we're outnumbered. You will be given your instructions by my sergeant-at-arms. He'll show you where to go." The officer returned to the watchtower, speaking aside to a burly soldier in full battle kit. "Use them where you need them. You'd better watch your back, as well."

"Sir." The sergeant saluted, and turned on his new charges. "Well, hop it! We're going to take a little walk now, and take a peek at the beautiful South Gate of this fair keep. I want the men with the bows out front, and you others keep close alongside." When he noticed the girl, he drew her aside. "Where do you think you're going, missy? This is no place for you. Go on back to the captain. You can stay there with him."

Laeni drew away from the big hand that held her. "No. I'm staying with my friends."

The sergeant hesitated, then saw the smoke growing denser away in the direction of the garrison he was dispatched to help. "Come on, then. It's your own wash to hang." He marched along briskly beside the bedraggled group. Salts and his men were agile and quick aboard a ship, but they seemed awkward and clumsy ashore. Jeremy's legs were as bad, and he found himself continually making allowance for the roll and pitch of the motion of the boat. "I'm more used to horses," he said aloud. "I'm not used to fighting on my feet."

"That's a flea-bitten excuse if I ever heard one," came a gruff voice next to the sergeant. "You can't fool an old warhorse like Stearborn or Chellin Duchin with a lame reason like that. If there was a horse hereabouts, it would most likely step on your head."

The sergeant was peering about with a startled look on his well-worn features. "Who's the jester here? Come on, or I'll box your ears!"

"It's me, Sergeant," went on the voice. Jeremy's heart had stopped at the mention of the names of the old Steward commanders, and he had detected something familiar in the voice, although it was obviously being disguised by speaking in a lower register. "We have no business going off this direction, man. We have urgent news for Alban Ram. Turn us about, and be a good fellow."

Drawing his sword, the seasoned old warrior caught up the first man to his right. "Speak up, my buck! Who's doing the jawing!" The sailor's wide, frightened eyes did not lie, so he was pushed aside. "Who is it?"

In a brief moment, a young man dressed in Steward green stood beside the sergeant, a smile on his face. And just behind, a huge bear loomed up into sight, his eyes watching every move.

Before the sergeant could move, Jeremy had grabbed the figure that had appeared out of the thin air, and was waltzing him around in circles, laughing like a madman. "Helwin, you dog! You've come back from the fishes! You didn't swallow the sea, after all!"

Jostled and crushed by turns, and unable to get a word in edgewise, Owen motioned with his hand, and Lanidel reached out and picked Jeremy up by the scruff of his cloak. "I might have escaped those dangers, but I'm more worried about being crushed and spun to death at the hand of a comrade." He laughed, and took his friend down from the bear's stout grasp. "Now come! Where are the others? Is Deros here? I thought at first she might be." He looked at Laeni.

Lanidel took the sergeant, who was threatening to lop off a head if they didn't go on. "Hold him there a minute. We're friends, Sergeant, and have important news for your Elder. The life of Eirn Bol depends upon it." The old warrior ceased struggling, deciding to wait upon developments.

Jeremy searched for a way to start, stammering out a confused version of what had happened. "After you were washed overboard, I'll tell you it took the heart out of all of us. Nobody could believe it."

"I couldn't believe it either," laughed Owen. "And I was sorely angry at those infernal Archaels for having had me crawling around on the pitching end of a boat in a storm. I'll get my just desserts of them when I cross trails. Are they with you?"

"That's what I was saying," went on Jeremy. "You were gone, and then we came to the Horinfal Straits. The Lady

Rewen and Coglan didn't say much about your disappearance, and I was too shaken up to see that they must have known something. All of us couldn't think straight." He reached out a hand to touch Owen's arm, as if to confirm that he wasn't talking to a ghost. "There was a whole fleet gathered at the Straits. I was on deck trying to get to sleep when I overheard someone talking. When I found out who it was, and who they were talking to, I knew we had been justified in not wanting Scarlett along."

"What's that you say? What did he do? Is he here, too?"

"I guess I was in too big a hurry to report my news back to Stearborn. I got caught as I was coming back aboard the Thistle Cloud. He thought he had knocked me out, so he just threw me overboard to drown."

Owen's face reddened, and his hand closed tighter on the weapon at his side. "Go on," he said in a quiet voice.

"I've been gone off the Thistle Cloud since. I don't know where they've gotten to, or who is left aboard. I came to in a silk tent on shore." He paused dreamily. "The Elboreal had saved me." Jeremy undid his cloak, and pulled the small leather pouch out to show Owen. "It is the dream-dust," he said softly. "Hamlin was always speaking of it. This was what they used to heal me."

As he heard the news of his friends, Owen reached out to touch the pouch. "So Hamlin will finally get to see some."

"There's not much left," said Jeremy wistfully. "I gave some to Laeni, and told the sergeant here we could give Alban Ram some of it. He said he was ill."

Owen whirled on the man again. Is that true?"

"He hasn't been in command for a time now. We have done the best we could without him. He's gotten worse since his daughter left. It's like his spirit is gone." At a nod from Owen, Lanidel placed the old warrior back on the ground.

"So you were overboard, too. How did you get here?"

"The Crane. I was picked up by Salts here, and taken aboard The Crane while they were still on the Straits."

"Is your ship here?" asked Owen, speaking to the mate.

"The Crane is around the point. We sailed a Hood vessel into the harbor here. That's what's caused all the ruckus."

"I know. They certainly jumped when they saw the Dart."

Laeni spoke for the first time, in a hushed voice. "You have come on the boat they say belongs to my brother. Is he dead?"

"Railan Dramm? He's wound up as tight as a pheasant on Mulling Day. He's coming along with Lanril aboard the Marin Galone." He clapped Jeremy roughly on the back. "I've seen Emerald and the Lady Elita, too!"

Jeremy let out a stifled laugh that was almost a sob. "I could use a tune or two, that's for sure. I wonder what's become of the Thistle Cloud?"

"You can see Elita now, if you want. We should leave your friends here with her." He nodded toward Laeni.

"I'm staying with Jeremy," she announced flatly.

"You will be, lass. There's someone who needs your help."

She started to protest, but suddenly found herself in another place, with a pale golden light filtering through high windows. It was a kitchen, and she saw the other woman then. Jeremy had bowed and kissed Elita's hand. When Elita spoke, Laeni knew she would stay. "We'll be here when you return," she said, pushing an awkward Jeremy toward the girl. "Kiss her, and go on. We will all be together soon." The last look Jeremy had was of the girl beside Elita, raising a shy hand in farewell.

When they were back with the sergeant, Owen nodded to the startled old soldier. "Now let's get on with it."

The sergeant had been searching the empty road for a sign of what had happened to the strangers, and jumped suddenly when the two reunited comrades reappeared. He finally found his voice and gave his report. "There was word going around that Alban Ram met a stranger on the High Quay this morning, and sent everybody else away. Locked himself into the garden room with her. Marak said there were others, too. Seemed damned odd, what with them showing up out of nowhere. Just a tender, like they'd been sunk and had to row for it. Fionten men, I think Marak said."

Owen let the information sink in slowly. "That was this morning, you say?"

"Marak was put out that the guards let strangers so close to Alban Ram without question."

"It wasn't a stranger, if it's who I think. His daughter has come home, if I read this right."

"You mean she's here?" asked Jeremy. "Then the others will be here, too!"

"Stearborn!" cried Owen. "Lofen and McKandles!"

"Rewen and Coglan," added Jeremy.

"And our good Archaels, Lorimen and Findlin!"

Jeremy's face clouded. "And the one I want to see the most."

"We both have scores to settle with Ulen," said Owen. "But first we must look to the safety of the good Elder, and find Deros."

Salts had sat down heavily on the road, and removed his shoe. "All this hoofing is wearing my pins down from the bottom up. "You're going to have to find me a wagon, or get me back to my decks. I gave up life on land for this very simple reason."

"Oh, Salts, you haven't spent enough time ashore to get your feet acquainted with walking."

"I can set you at guard duty, Salts. All it would require would be to sit and make sure some birds don't fly the coop."

"That's my watch, then," agreed the sailor. "If I can get off my feet, I'll be good as new by the time we need to sail from here."

Owen placed a hand on Salts's shoulder and made a slight motion with his hand. He was only gone a moment, and when he returned, he was alone. "He's hit it off big with Lanidel. Laeni was going to make him a pan of cool water to soak his feet. I think they are beginning to have a good time there."

The sergeant finally worked up the nerve to ask a question. "Where do you keep disappearing to? I'd give a yard of boiled meat to be able to do that!"

"Come on then," replied the young Steward. "Stand here next to me." The sergeant did as he was told, and he was aware of a hand touching him, then a rush of lights spinning and whirling past his eyes, and a dizzying motion of having been whirled to and fro. When he blinked again, he was standing in a high-windowed room full of long tables laden with fruit and cheese and bread, with wine flagons standing nearby. There at the far end of the hall was the young girl who had just been with them, standing next to a beautiful woman who seemed to be speaking to a bear. Farther on, he could see a drop-gate lowered into position, and there were figures there as well.

Owen handed him an apple and touched him once more, and he stood blinking again in the weak afternoon sunlight, standing on the south road in Cairn Weal. He blinked his eyes, then rubbed them, then bit into the apple, finding it tart and filling.

"This isn't exactly the grand way I had imagined this,"

confessed Jeremy, addressing Owen as though he had just stepped around the corner. "I wish we were having a better time of it ourselves."

"Not much of a welcome, to my way of thinking." Owen turned to the sergeant. "What's the quickest way to reach Alban Ram."

The old warrior's creased face was filled with awe as he looked underneath his eyebrows at the two friends. "Only those who have the freedom to come and go in the High Court can tell you that. I'm a simple soldier in the Fourth Battalion, responsible for harbor and gates."

"Would your officer know?"

"Crimle? He'd know, but it wouldn't do you any good. He's by the law on everything. You wouldn't set foot inside the High Court for a month, if you had to depend on him."

"Then who could we depend on?" asked Owen. "If we wanted to give something to Alban Ram, and needed to talk to him, what would you do?"

Scratching his head and squatting on the cobbled path, he pointed down to the ground. "The combs."

"What?"

"The combs. Lava flows. Now there's another shake from the fire-cone, but from the harbor to the upper keep, I don't think there could be a faster way."

"Do you know how to reach them? I was in the tunnels until they were shut off with seawater and stone."

"It's an easy thing, for a man who knows his way around Cairn Weal. We'll have to get past Crimle, though. The entrance to the combs is in his tower floor. They were built that way in case Alban Ram ever had to escape the Vipre." The sergeant laughed gruffly. "Everyone knows the Elder would never leave Eirn Bol, so the shafts were always looked on as a clever jest."

"Then they will earn their reason for existence this day! Show us the way, my good fellow. If you've wanted to find some way to better serve your Elder, you've chanced upon it now."

"What will I do with Crimle?" asked the sergeant.

Owen smiled. "You saw my little world. I'll put him with the others there. All you have to do is show us the rest of the way to Alban Ram once we're in."

They followed the sergeant back to the wharf, and up to the

tower where the watch captain had his command post. Jeremy, walking alongside his friend, turned to ask him another question. "Do you think it's possible to fall in love with someone who has been used in the Hulin camps?"

"You mean Laeni? Railan's sister?"

Jeremy nodded. "I had thought once that maybe I would be in love with the Lady Rewen. This is an odd way to turn out."

Owen laughed, facing his friend. "You don't have any say in the matter, my friend. And I think you will find your heart speaks the truth in these things. She's seems a fine lass."

Jeremy wanted to go on, but at that same moment, the door in the tower opened to the call of the sergeant, and the officer who had questioned him appeared, looking more haggard and short-tempered than before.

In the short space of a breath, he was gone.

The Cauldron of Hate

Just as Crimle began to speak, he vanished from sight, leaving his underlings staring at the empty floor where he had stood but a moment before. The sergeant moved forward, probing the air with his hand. As he neared the place where the officer had been, he also disappeared. Jeremy was left with the others in the tower, who looked at each other in alarm. They had begun to move back toward the moored Hulin Vipre ship when Owen's voice reached them.

"I was beginning to think I had imagined all this," said Jeremy. "When you vanished, I was sure it had all been a bad dream."

"It is a bad dream, my friend. Come on. We don't have much time. We have our guide here ready to show us the way. Come on." A square floor stone was suddenly lifted near the back wall, showing a narrow, steep stair that wound down into the darkness below. Jeremy could barely make out the light of a flickering rushlamp somewhere in the shaft.

"I can't stand closed places anymore," he said, backing away, his face ashen.

"You'll have to stand it for a short while. Come on. We have no time to lose." Owen's voice had taken on an edge. "Come on, man!"

Sounds of the launchers began, with the odd whistling noise the burning pitch barrels made as they turned and tumbled out toward the enemy ships sailing into the harbor. War horns and the shouts and clamor of men joining battle became louder, and was drawing nearer to the tower. Jeremy bit his lower lip, and closed his eyes for a moment, then plunged down into the confining, stifling shaft.

"Good lad. Here we are." Owen appeared again, now beside the sergeant, who took a deep breath and started off toward a well-worn stone stairway carved from the rock that rose upward into the shadows of the cave. The closeness of the shaft gave way to a sense of space, and the rushlamps that lined the wall above them showed that the roof was high above them, and decorated with glimmering, glinting stones made to look like the stars in a night sky. Some of the pillars in the immense chamber had been displaced by the last tremor of the earth, and lay in broken pieces littered about the floor.

"I thought the place was coming down around us," said the sergeant, sidestepping some of the debris. "I've never seen them this bad before. Even the last of the big ones in the summer of the Black Fever was not equal to this."

"How far is it to the upper keep?" asked Owen, walking rapidly to keep up.

"We have to get through this next tunnel, and then we're there. These combs run all under the keep. It was a little farther on that the Elder was wounded. He and his guards encountered a Black Hood force, in these very tunnels. They weren't far from the Sacred Altar." The sergeant snorted in disbelief. "Can you believe a thing like that? Right in the heart of Cairn Weal."

"That's one of the things I was coming to warn Alban Ram about. There are traitors in the Bellream Readers. There is one among them called Efile."

"Efile. I have heard that name. Was he wearing a fancy scabbard and belt? A mark of a silver fish was on it."

Owen shook his head. "I don't know what his scabbard

looked like. I wonder what would make a man turn against his own like that?" asked Owen. "That's what baffles me."

"I knew it would come to me!" exclaimed the burly sergeant. "Efile! It was a long time back. Can't remember exactly when, but there was a big shuffle among the Fourth Battalion Guards. He was a young subaltern then. That's what it was."

"He was in the House Guards?"

"Well respected, too. Had a pretty wife, and that was the start of the trouble."

"How so?"

"They had a child, a boy, if I remember right. Used to play with the other whelps from the battalion. The woman started to resent the child, thought she was losing her beauty because of it. Scullery duties, washing clothes, oiling weapons. It was not a pretty life." They had reached a slight bend in the stairway, and now the steps rose visibly up toward a pale golden bowl of light somewhere above. The sergeant went on. "You know the end of the tale. She was a pretty thing, and soon was meeting her husband's commander in the passages that run beneath the keep. Everyone knew of it but him, or if he knew, would not believe."

"A subject for a minstrel's song," said Jeremy. "It will be good to hear Emerald's rendition of it." His breath was still coming in short gasps, and he spoke to try to take his mind off where he was.

"So the commander stole the wife from him?"

"He isn't a man who has those kinds of desires. He used her while it was convenient," explained the sergeant, bending to examine a mark on the wall. "There. We're getting close to the proper door now." Owen and Jeremy looked at where the man pointed, but saw only a small faint red shield painted on the stone.

"So the commander left her ruined?" asked Owen.

"In the kitchen of the battalion mess, we have a spring. It rises through solid stone, and makes the keep impossible to destroy by siege. But it is protected only by a low curb, and the baby was left with a friend. She looked away, and the child was gone. The mother was eaten with guilt, and being threatened with exposure, so she drowned herself, too. The husband never got over his loss. He swore revenge on the man who had done it to him. The name escaped me for a moment, but it was Efile."

"And what happened to the commander?"

"He was promoted. You have met him already."

"Your captain?"

"Crimle. Officer of merit, and ambitious enough to let no one get in his way."

"That may color my decision as to what to do with the good captain," said Owen. "But I suppose the worst thing to do to him would be to leave him to his own snares." He shook his head sadly. "The loss of a child is a grievous thing. It will do strange things to people. Poor Efile."

The old warrior pulled up short. "You said the Lady Deros is on her way here. Were you speaking the truth?"

"She sought us out in The Line to bring us to help her father."

"I have seen a strong man crumble before my eyes. Alban Ram has led us through the worst of times, and always was there to encourage us, even when it looked the blackest. I'm not saying a man can't be old and tired, but it seems his spirit has been taken away from him."

"I don't know how much help we may prove to be, but at least he will have whatever news of the Lady Deros I can give him. That might be worth more than my bringing a dozen squadrons of Stewards."

Jeremy was walking faster now, and was in front of them both. He was sweating profusely, and his eyes had begun to take on a glazed look. "I don't know how much longer I can stand it," he muttered. "It's getting hard to get my breath."

"Buck up, lad. We're there!" The sergeant touched a slight dent in the stone, and they all stood back and watched while a concealed door in the solid wall slid smoothly open, revealing a broad, comfortable room, elegantly furnished with thick rugs and tapestries, and heavy chairs and table that stood before a great fireplace higher than a man's head. A cheery blaze crackled cozily on the andirons, sending small sparks sizzling out onto the stone hearth. There were two tall chairs placed there, and at the noise of their entry, a white-haired old man peered out at them, blinking in surprise.

The Sacred Altar

❋

"What is it?" creaked the tired old voice. "Who's there? Is that you, my dear?"

"Sir, it's Sergeant Balre of the Fourth Battalion. I've brought two men who say they have news of the Lady Deros." The old soldier saluted, even though Alban Ram didn't see.

"Well, you've come too late, Sergeant. She's brought the news herself!"

"What?" cried Owen, not waiting to be introduced. "She's here?"

"Was, a moment ago," replied the old Elder. "She let out a little cry, and has disappeared out into the garden just now."

Owen's sword was out instantly, and he leapt for the long row of glassed doors that led onto a closed garden. The sergeant thought the stranger was attacking Alban Ram, and he had his own weapon out, followed by Jeremy, who was trying to protect his friend. All three arrived at once on the veranda, eyes wide, and were greeted by a low, whinnying laugh, and the bell-clear voice of Deros.

"It's about time!" She stood next to the gray horse, who lowered his head and put his nose against Owen's shoulder.

"Well met, little brother. We were wondering how long it would take you to get your wits about you and find us."

Owen's eyes filled with tears, and he had to cough twice to get his voice under control. Jeremy was pumping Deros's hand, bowing as he did so.

"You've had us worried about you both, since you pulled those foolish stunts to get attention. I think at the very least, you owe us all a detailed explanation of where you've been, and what you've been up to."

The two companions both started at once, stumbling over their words. Seravan pawed the stone veranda, laying his ears back. "You two take the prize for someone who is well adept with words. The next thing you know, you'll be trying to take away some minstrel's job!"

"Emerald wouldn't mind," shot Owen, throwing an arm around his old friend's neck. "He's with us now. So is Elita. They will be coming on the Marin Galone soon. I found this lout down on the wharfs, being marched off to help fight the Black Hood."

The old soldier had stood back, his features working beneath his neatly trimmed beard. At last he fell on one knee, bowing to Deros. "Forgive me, my lady. I hardly know what to think or do. I never thought we would see you again."

Deros put a hand on the man's shoulder, bidding him to rise. "Come up, Sergeant. We have enough to do to try to get my father's spirits up. I can't believe how he's aged."

"It has been since you were gone, my lady. And then he got tangled up with a batch of the Vipre in the combs. That seemed to have done him in."

"Were there any casualties?" asked Owen. "Did you take any captives?"

"From that fight? I don't think so. Why?"

"I have heard enough in those combs to know that the Black Hood aren't of a single will in their fight against Eirn Bol." Owen looked at Deros. "Your father might be interested to know that I have the Hulin Vipre Emperor captive. I rescued him from some of his own men in the lava flows."

"What?" Deros was taken aback. "You have who?" Jeremy stood beside her, wide-eyed.

"That's news," he managed at last.

"I didn't have time to catch you up. This isn't exactly a time to be sitting about jawing."

"But where is he? Do you have him aboard the ship you came on?"

"The Dart? No. We have the Red Scorpion, as well."

"Who do you mean when you say 'we'?" asked Deros.

"Friends. Warlings. They were so good as to try leading me to your father."

"The bears?" asked the girl. "What do you mean?"

"Don't you know about the Warlings?" asked Owen. "They are clans on Eirn Bol, and have served Windameir well."

Deros shook her head. "I don't recall ever hearing anything more about bears other than they lived in the wilder parts of the island."

"No wonder I had such a time convincing them of my intentions," said Owen. "I can see why, now."

"I had a visit with them earlier," confessed Seravan. "They have had a long road, here."

A dozen fire-arrows lofted over the high stone outer wall of the garden, landing on the roof of the small shelter that stood before a pond. Hulin Vipre horns blew from just on the other side of the closed gate, and a sudden smashing noise jolted the companions into action. Balre leapt to the gate and shot the bolt home, shouting orders to the guards who were supposed to be on the other side. "Sound off, lads! This is your sergeant! How do you stand?" The only reply was another flight of flaming arrows, some of which shattered a row of the glass panes and landed inside, setting fire to the edge of one of the carpets. It caught instantly, and only Jeremy saved the room from being engulfed by taking off his cloak and beating out the flames.

"Back to the combs," cried Balre. "It's our only chance. If they've come this far, then they've done the best of the House Guard! Hurry!"

"Father! Father! Where are you?" Deros raced back into the smoke-filled room, searching for the old man, who was stumbling along toward them, coughing deeply.

"We must get to the Sacred Altar," she said, leading him onto the veranda where he stood drawing in great gulps of fresh air. When he was able to speak, he argued against it.

"If we go there too soon, the wrong ones may take the Scrolls! We must wait until the last, my dear."

Balre spoke up then. "Sir, the House Guard is down, and the Hood are at your very gate. We can hold them from coming on us in the combs, but we are fish to be fried here!"

"That's what we want them to think," replied Alban Ram, a stronger note to his voice.

"Do you have the other half of the key, Father?" asked Deros.

"Yes, my dear, it's here. But we can't remove the Scrolls until we have drawn our prey to the bait."

Owen turned to Jeremy. "Do you think you'll be able to stand the undersides again? It looks like we may have some waiting to do."

His friend shook his head. "I was barely able to stand it for a few minutes. I don't know if I could stay there any longer."

"Then you must come with me to guard my bottle."

"What?"

"I'll bring Crale here to help me, and I'll put you in charge of someplace that won't give you the cramps." He stood next to Jeremy, and before anyone could move, the two were gone. Owen returned a moment later in the presence of a large bear, which had a bandage made of a dress torn into bits tied round his forepaw. "Sir, Lady Deros! I'd like to present to you a Warling who has served you both well, in better times than these, and without ever shirking a duty or forgetting a friend."

"Who is it, my dear?" asked Alban Ram.

"A bear, Father. A Warling."

"Warlings? Here? In Cairn Weal?"

"Yes, Father."

"There hasn't been a Warling set foot in this keep since Astrain took control of Gingus Pashon. What a surprise and wonder!"

"This is Crale, sir," introduced Owen.

"I'm Crale," said the older bear. "We have both knelt at the same streams for water in days long gone by, chubblet. I have seen you, and followed along behind your trains, listening to you talk and play your harp at night. Do you still play the instrument?"

Alban Ram's face broke into a rare smile. "You have a wondrous wicked way about you, sir. If I wanted to look for a fellow who would give me the most sass, I'd volunteer you, and put you in charge of my armies. And I'd rebuild the places where man has taken everything of the Warling away."

Crale bowed clumsily, and sat on the warm rug that lay before the hearth. "Thank you for your kind speech, sir. It would be best if we planned our attack as soon as possible. The longer we leave the Black Hood to themselves, the more aggressive they become."

"Where have you taken the lad Jeremy?" asked the old man.

"He's perfectly safe, sir," replied Owen. "Politar gave me the key to two small green bottles when we met, and I went along thinking they were but small green bottles." He laughed. "They are astounding, for all that."

Seravan had nudged his way into the room, having to lower his head to squeeze through the wide doorway. "They are breaking down the gate. This is no place to make a fight. You go on with Alban Ram, Owen. I am going to find Stearborn and Emerald. They are all here in the harbor."

"Will you be all right?" asked Owen. "Is Gitel here, too?"

"Gitel is with Ephinias. They will be along, I think, if we need them."

A loud roar of a Hulin Vipre war chant drowned out the rest of the conversation. With a single step, the gray horse was gone. Alban Ram turned and tugged his daughter's hand, pulling her toward the vast fireplace. Sergeant Balre called out that they were going the wrong way. "It's here, sir! You've missed the door!"

"I don't need my eyes to find my way about my own warren, Sergeant. We're not going back the way you came. Come along, quickly. We have work to do." The old elder touched a blue-veined hand to a place up in the hearth, and a slight whooshing noise was heard as the fire was fed with a new gust of cold air from somewhere behind the wall. Owen could make out an immense dark room behind, lit only with a few candles and rushlamps, all flickering in the draft from the opened entry. He barely had time to recognize the soft glint of light reflected from the tall statue near the back of the room, and was on the verge of speaking, when a black-tipped arrow zipped past him, snapping against the stone. Crale gave a bloodcurdling war cry, and there was the strangled explosion of a man's shout as his head was crushed by the bear, and then they were all inside the short hallway, listening as the door slid home once more, locking out the enemy.

"Where are we?" managed Owen, looking around at the soft glow of light off polished metal, which as his eyes adjusted he recognized to be gold and mithra, all worked exquisitely. He saw the hand of the Elboreal, and the older clans, the Dwarlich, and the soft mystery of the Order of the Sacred Thistle. As Deros led her father to a simple wooden chair at the foot of the icon, a faint music began, nibbling at his ears like the promise of a spring dawn.

The
Rainbow Bridge

The Quays of Cairn Weal
✳

Mortus Blan had come under cover of darkness, slipping over the side of the ship in the small tender Almag had provided. The man had begged and whined for the potion that would save him from the poison, but the weirdoch had rowed away, leaving the hapless victim screaming his curses on deck. It was a small pleasure to the old man, holding the power of life and death, and over the years it had become a welcome distraction for him, as his own flesh began to wither away. He reached the quays at Cairn Weal without incident, and performed his binding that would enable him to travel without being seen. His destination was the third watchtower from the gate, for that was where the passage was that would lead to the private garden of Alban Ram. There would be a shock for the fearless leader of Eirn Bol soon, when it was discovered that the wisest of men from Hulingaad had found a way to defeat him.

It was cold and clear, and droplets of spray clung to his face as he stood studying the harbor of Cairn Weal. He had not been here before, except in visions, and he relished the feeling of being so close to his lifelong dream. He trembled a little from the chill, but it only added extra relish to the moment. A guard, huddled against the wind, walked briskly by him, passing so close he could feel the man's warmth. Out of pure joy, he followed the man to the end of his perimeter, and shoved him into the cold sea below. A startled yelp, and a moment of frantic thrashing was all that came, for the man's battle kit weighed him down, and the stone wharf was high and slippery.

Sighing with satisfaction, Mortus Blan held up his hand and began to bring the Rhion Stone to life, his mind searching out the one who wore the other ring. It was not long before he found what he was seeking, and set his plans into motion.

On board the Thistle Cloud, Stearborn had Hamlin and Judge in their own battle gear, going over it all one last time.

"I tell you I have everything," protested Hamlin, strapping down his quiver. "If we wait here any longer, it's all going to be over."

"You must pat it down, lad. Stearborn doesn't want any lad beside him who suddenly finds nothing to shoot with, or no sword for his hand." The old Steward walked calmly between them, examining every piece of equipment. "It's been a while since we've had stand down, and I know we've gotten rusty."

"We may have, but this gear has been rubbed until there's nothing left of it, I doubt! Any more cleaning, and we'll break a blade on a twig, it'll be so thin."

"You go on being funny, Judge Collander, and I'll put that on your headstone. Here lies a man who was funny to his captain! He died."

"Here we is!" shouted McKandles down the companionway. "I's got no use for all this rattlin' mail shirt, but me and Lofen is as ready as we is ever agoin' to be!" He held out a sword and stabbing dagger, and carried his horse whip coiled over his shoulder. "I's a mite more handy with a bit and bridle, but I don't guess a man likes the whip any better than a renegade critter!"

Lofen looked peaked beneath his cap, and stood uncomfortably in his new battle dress. "If you was askin' me, we woulds all be better off to be awaitin' here a bit, so's we could sees what we was agettin' into!"

"Ulen got off, and the Lady Rewen says we have to follow him." Hamlin climbed to the deck, rearranging his kit as he went. "I knew we should have finished with him long ago. Owen said he would be trouble."

Stearborn cinched up a quiver strap on Hamlin's back until it cut into the flesh. "If the Lady Rewen says it, then we'll follow orders. He can't be far, we know."

"Soldiers aren't the ones who are after Ulen. Rewen says it is one who wears one of the rings, which means he's more powerful."

"That Hoolin ring has been the bits and scraps of us ever since he picked up the fool thing," complained Lofen. "If I was to have it to do all over, I's would throw it back in that bog alongside the man what was awearin' it!"

"We don't know the end of this story yet, Lofen." Stearborn threw up a heavy sack of newly made shafts for his Leech bow. "Someone give me a hand with that. I like the idea of being able to reach out a bit to get the edge on some of these blighters. Nothing like an arrow through your gizzard while you still think you're safe and snug."

"Maybe you could save us all the trouble of getting off this bucket then," suggested Judge. "We'll just sit back and hand the shafts to you, and you can whittle them down one by one from here."

The gruff old commander reached to grab his old comrade, but the lad was too quick, and soon was out of reach aboard the boat waiting to take them to shore. "We'll see you on the quay," he called after him. "See what you can do to keep our landing free of those louts!"

"I may puncture you a bit while I'm at it," growled Stearborn, although his attention was elsewhere, for he had noticed a slight motion on the quay. He couldn't be sure of his eyes, but it looked as though it was a tall gray horse, standing just at the beginning of the path that led down from the upper landings of Cairn Weal. He called out to Hamlin. "Take a gander there at that spot next to the tower with the blue roof! Do you see anything?"

"Plain as peas," answered McKandles, coming to stand next to the Steward. "Horse. What I wouldn't be agivin' for him if we is agoin' to be in some dust-up ashore!"

"A horse," replied Hamlin. "Kandles is right."

"Just a horse, or is this one of our old friends?" went on the old commander. The animal tossed its mane and began to paw the ground.

"Anxious to see somebody," added Lofen.

The Archaels, Lorimen and Findlin, came on deck then, dragging a sea chest between them. "It pains me to think of being off this wessel, but I know this is the end of the line. Sailors are supposed to do their battles on board a good ship, not mulling around in the dirt like a common beast." Findlin began to hand the chest down to his friend waiting in the skiff, which was ferrying everyone ashore.

"Speaking of beasts, the flying stowe is back," observed Lorimen. "I wonder how long he'll be kept in reserwe?"

"Probably have him to clean up the mess we'll make of the Black Hood," shot back Judge. "Like having dogs to lick the bones."

"Whose bones, that's what I want to know," put in Findlin. "I'we grown owerly fond of mine!"

"There'll be plenty to go around before it's all said and done," said Stearborn. He had lowered himself into the tender and turned his gaze upward, watching along the shadowy underside of the lowering sky. A faint trace of a dragon lingered there, then was gone. "I guess what I hate most about those things is their smell," he went on. "It never seems to leave your nostrils, once you've known it." When he looked again, there was the horse still at the lower landings, and now there was another there with him. At first he could not make out more than it was a man standing beside the animal, but as the boat drew nearer to the landing, he suddenly recognized the face of his old friend, the minstrel Emerald.

And the tall gray animal was none other than Seravan.

Into the Breach

The sword in Owen's hand was aflame with a brilliant white light in the Sacred Altar. It hummed and pulsed through his arm like he had never felt before, and his mind was full of exploding visions and sights that reeled past his eyes like a great whirlwind of fire. He saw Alban Ram, but much younger, astride a white horse that was rearing and pawing the air, and beside him was a huge bear, dressed in battle gear, holding aloft a spear with the banner of the white dragon.

When he came to himself again, Crale was standing next to the old man, looking up at the gold and mithra likeness of a bear, which stood next to the ancient chest that held the Sacred Scrolls. Alban Ram was speaking.

"Astrain had brought Gingus Pashon to ruin, and he was but

a puppet in her hands. After his fall from grace, no one knew whether his brother was to be trusted or not. The Dark One struck a brilliant victory there, the warping of the human soul. It was some time before we found the solution, and it came in the simplest of answers. We were on common grounds then, your clan and mine, and we simply left the chest to the Warlings to hold."

Crale nodded. "Our Book does not say more than that we took to keep a precious thing of the High King."

"That is why, my friend," smiled the old man. "It did not occur to you to pry as to what you held. Colvages Domel and Iochan and I were the only ones who knew for certain where it had been hidden. I despaired for a time that the Council might all end up in factions, and the Scrolls would be lost. It was a disheartening time."

"I mean no disrespect, sir, but I think I hear Vipre war horns right at our door," urged Owen.

Alban Ram laughed. "This is just a battle, my boy. There is no doubt as to the conclusion." His smile faded. "Quineth Rel began to plant the seed that the Warling had stolen the Scrolls, and were nothing but common thieves and murderers."

"That word spread," agreed Crale. "If you could see what we are left of our old world now, it would make you weep."

A slight shudder passed through the floor beneath them, tingling and light. "The Old Ones from Corum Mont are awakening," said Alban Ram. "They feel our presence here at the Sacred Altar."

More calls and shouts were heard outside, and the war horns of the enemy seemed to fill the air beyond the door. "Did you know I have the Hulin Vipre Emperor captive, sir? Has Deros told you?" asked Owen.

The old man shook his head. "Is he on Eirn Bol?"

"He's here," answered Owen. "I have Railan Dramm, as well. He's a prisoner aboard the Marin Galone." For a moment, Owen thought he saw the old man smile.

"Now there's a piece of meat to put before the dogs," he said, letting go a short chuckle. "How have you managed all that in such a short space of time, my boy?"

"The Emperor fell into my hands trying to get away from Hulingaad."

"How is Lacon Rie? I have not seen him in person since we went our separate ways when the Warling took the Scrolls."

Owen shook his head. "It is not Lacon Rie, sir. It is a son, Baryloran. The girl with him said they murdered his father."

A look of genuine concern filled the old Elder's face. "I am sorry to hear that," he said softly. "Truly sorry. I guess I was hoping to have time to mend our fences." He looked at the icon on the Altar, and touched a hand to the base of it.

Deros held her father in a tight hug. He patted her in a kindly fashion, holding her away. "Don't despair, child. We have played out our parts as best we could. Your mother would be very proud of you. Just look what you've done!" He motioned for Owen to come closer to him. "Here's this fine young man who unwittingly came to help you, and now look. The sword of Skye is at the Sacred Altar, and all the players are assembled."

"Not quite all," reminded Owen.

"Oh, but you don't see with your senses they way I can," corrected Alban Ram. "Our last tardy ones are upon their way now."

"Who do you speak of, sir?"

"Stop and feel the wind, lad. Try the air. It reeks of danger," replied the old man, his voice strong. Crale, who was still beside him, lowered his ears and rose into his full fighting stance, his nose testing in all directions. Sergeant Balre slipped along the wall to protect Deros.

"Should I bring Baryloran here?" asked Owen suddenly. "I think he is one you might reach. He seemed an odd choice for the leader of the Black Hood."

"They are bent on our destruction," reminded Deros. Owen was taken aback by the hardness in her voice, and the hatred he saw in her eyes. Her father reached out a hand to draw her closer to him.

He clucked his tongue at her. "Is that all I've managed to teach my beloved little sparrow?"

An odd look crossed Owen's face, and he disappeared for a moment. When he returned, he stood beside a lame young man, not much older than himself. "This is Baryloran, the Fifth Collector of Hulingaad. The Lady Deros, and her father, Alban Ram."

The young Hulin Vipre Emperor looked startled at first, as though he had been dragged along unwillingly. Alban Ram soon put him at his ease, offering him a chair, and pouring him out a cool drink from a mithra and silver pitcher that stood on the table before him.

"I would be a fool to touch your wine," remonstrated Baryloran. "I know it would be in your best interests to destroy me, but I have seen far worse going on this day than you could have inflicted upon me in a hundred campaigns.''

"I am sorry to hear of your father's death," said Alban Ram. "He and I knew each other before there was bloodshed between us. I would like to think there would be some honor left among us to share the grief of a fallen warrior."

Baryloran was genuinely shocked again, for he had come prepared to die. Deros looked in disbelief at her father. "His family was almost the death of me, Father. His brother, Tien Cal, would have brought me back in slavery to taunt you with, so you would trade away the Sacred Scrolls! You speak of mercy and compassion? Then let's kill him quickly, like he would not have done me!''

"His own family is dead because of it, my dear," said the old Elder. "His father and brother are both dead. You are left to me, my dear, and it is my greatest comfort to know that I will not have to go through the grief of burying my beloved little sparrow. My ship has steered many courses this time, but I will be spared that one."

"Not I," spoke up Baryloran. "I have already seen my father murdered, and my brother lost in the wilderness. Now the very ones who have blood on their hands have attempted my life. It strikes me to the quick to know that this outsider has earned my life."

"We came across him in the lava flows," said Owen. "One of his commanders was going to dispose of him there."

"But we waste our time gnawing over old bones here. Jatal Ra and Salun Am will do their worst now. It has come to the end."

"Don't forget Mortus Blan," reminded Alban Ram. "He has served your father for a long time, and has his own ideas of how the order of things should be."

"So you know Mortus Blan, as well?"

"I have met him once or twice. It does not take long to tell who is burned with the desire to consume it all. A terrible appetite, power. It drives even levelheaded men to great disaster."

"Then this has all been for nothing," said Deros bitterly. "We have the Hulin Vipre Emperor at our mercy, and we will do nothing."

"He is but the head of the dragon," replied her father, a great sadness in his eyes. "We could cut it off, but the body would crush us when it fell."

"I hope you don't debate my death in front of me," said the

young Hulin Emperor. "That would be very bad manners, talking before a guest."

"You won't be slain in this place, sir," replied Alban Ram. "It is not in my heart to do your family more harm. You are come to enough grief in your short life as it is."

Deros had drawn the knife Stearborn had given her, and held it in her palm, moving closer to Baryloran. Owen saw what she had done, and stepped between her and the enemy Emperor, placing a firm hand over her own. The pressure of his hand caused the blade to bite her palm, and she gave a little cry, turning such eyes of anger on him, he released her.

"What is it, my dear?" asked her father.

"Nothing, Father." She looked directly at Owen, her face a mask of cold anger.

Another war horn blew, directly beyond their hiding place, and another, finer and more subtle, reached their ears. "It is the Dolride," said Alban Ram. "Someone has come along through the flows."

The small instrument beyond sounded again, and the noise of battle reached them, at the very doorway into the Sacred Altar. Deros had taken the chain and small key from her neck, and handed it to her father. "We had better remove the Scrolls while we are able, Father. We can't let ourselves be trapped here with them."

Alban Ram removed a silken scarf, and undid a clasp that held a small, finely wrought chain. "Here is my half of the key, my sparrow," he said. "You know where they fit." Deros took the small object and hurried toward the icon of the bear. She knelt behind and worked rapidly. A tremor rippled beneath their feet, and a louder, more insistent noise of the Dolride began. Crale began to shake his head from side to side in rhythm to the notes, and Owen could feel the sword from Skye growing hot against his side.

Baryloran stood silent, watching. Owen thought of taking him back to the safety of Politar's bottle, then decided that it might be best if he were to bring the girl out. He had been surprised at the depth of the hatred he saw in Deros when she spoke of killing the Hulin Emperor, and he hoped that by bringing Denale, she might soften Deros's heart. He spoke the words, and found himself in the warmth of the great kitchen in the soft light of the bottle, where Lanidel sat on his haunches beside a table, helping himself to another dollop of the thick, golden honey.

"Where are the others?" Owen asked, looking around.

"They have gone exploring. They told me to stay here in case you came." The huge bear's paws dripped with the honey, and he smacked loudly in enjoyment as he ate. "How is Crale?"

"Not as full as you," replied Owen, laughing. "Did they say which way they were going?"

"The Lady Elita said she was searching for dressings for the wounded."

A distant shout reached Owen's ears then. "Listen! What was that?"

Lanidel stood and turned his great head in the direction of the cry. "It was a chubblet."

"Come on." Owen raced past the stocks of weapons, going on farther. He had not ever been so far into the interior of the mysterious place, and he had to stop and check his directions. He called out. "Elita! Laeni! Jeremy!" His voice rang hollowly back. A muffled cry answered him. "Here! We're here!"

Lanidel lumbered up beside him then.

"What's wrong, chubblet?"

"They must have wandered too far. I think they may have gotten lost."

"No understanding of shafts," commented the big animal. "They went down this way." Lanidel led off, loping along at a good pace.

"I hope you're keeping track of where we are," huffed Owen.

The big animal only grunted in reply. "There's another scent here besides chubblet," he added.

"What is it?"

"I can't tell. I don't recall ever coming across it. It's tart, like winter berries."

The voice of Elita reached him plainly then. "We're here!"

"Someone turned off the lights," shouted Salts. "We can hear you now, though. Who is it?"

"Owen. I hear you. Where are you?"

The hallway they had come down opened into another vast room, with wall hangings and rugs spread on the tile floors. A long wooden table filled one end of the room before the hearth, and a line of benches ran down both sides. A five-pointed candelabra cast of gold and mithra sat in the middle of the table, with five tall candles burning brightly. The bear stopped and raised himself onto his haunches.

"This is where the scent is," he said, looking about, a wrinkle creasing his great brow.

"We're here," called Jeremy. "Where are you?"

"Here! We can't see you. Elita, can you hear me?" asked Owen. He grumbled under his breath that Politar had not given him more instructions about the complex worlds inside the two bottles.

"Yes. We were looking for something we might use for wounds. We left Lanidal to tell you."

"He's here."

"We found a room full of bandages and potions, and decided to bring them back. I don't know what happened then. When we began to return, the lights went, and we got lost."

"Do you still have the things you took?"

"Yes."

"Put them down and walk away from them. See what happens. This place is still a mystery to me, too." Owen waited for a reply, but there was only silence then. "Elita!"

Silence. Then a voice, shrunken by distance, followed the turns and twists of the elaborate system of hallways. "Here! Owen! Call out to us!"

"I'm here. Can you find your way back now?"

"We are in the same room. We're leaving the potions. The light is back. Jeremy says he marked the way."

"Good. Hurry! I need to take Denale with me."

"The scent is stronger now," said Lanidel. "I think there's someone here." He had laid his ears back flat against his great head, but did not rumble a warning.

"You must return to Alban Ram," came a voice then, one that Owen was familiar with.

"Colvages Domel?"

"Yes. Iochan is with the Freolyde Valg on Eirn Bol. It is time for the sword from Skye to strike!"

As the voice faded, Jeremy, followed by Elita and the others, came through an arched door beneath a red and gold coat of arms embossed on a great shield with crossed spears behind. "Helwin, bless your eyes! You brought me here because I can't stand closed places, and leave me in the dark!"

"The Sacred Altar is under attack," said Owen, brushing his friend's comment aside. "We must go back now."

"All of us?"

"You, Denale, and Jeremy, if your sword hand is ready."

"It's ready. Just don't take me back to a snake's den!"

"Count me in," said Salts. "Even if it ain't to be fought on boats."

"Come on, then."

"The prisoners won't escape," said Laeni. "I will see to that."

Owen thought a moment. "There is really no place they can go here. All right."

"I want to go with Emerald," said Elita.

"Seravan went to find him. When we are together, I'll come back for you."

She held out a hand to him, her eyes glistening. "Find him."

Owen nodded, and stood next to his companions. He motioned on the air, and the brilliant light began, and a whirling blackness filled with stars and a crescent moon rose up, then faded, and they were once more in the room where the bear icon stood. Alban Ram leaned against it, his hand to heart. An inner door to the Sacred Door was open, and shouts and sounds of a pitched battle rang in their ears, as the old Elder motioned for Owen to come to him. Sergeant Balre lay dead at the entryway, four black arrows in his chest. Crale reappeared limping from the hallway, covered in blood.

"I've lost her," he reported. "There were too many of them."

"Find her, my boy! Find her! She's taken the Scrolls!"

"Are you all right, Crale?"

The bear nodded, sitting next to the weary old man.

"Catch your breath, then. We'll find Deros." Owen leapt for the door, the sword of Skye drawn and raised above his head, blazing in a brilliant blue-white light. Lanidel let out a terrible rumbling war cry, and Jeremy followed, a Steward war-horn at his lips.

As they fought their way clear of the doorway, Owen could see the back of Baryloran's head amid a knot of Black Hood troops, chasing someone into the corridor that led back into the great outer halls that formed the first landing of Cairn Weal.

Colvages Domel

✳

The sharp snap of an arrow sizzled past Owen's ear, then a half-dozen more. Salts groaned behind him, and stumbled to his knees, hit in the shoulder.

"Go on!" he cried, I'll be all right! I just have to pull this sticker! Go on!" Jeremy had knelt beside him, looking grim. The gregarious sailor who had plucked him from the barren spit on the Straits of Horinfal was already going into shock. A sick feeling passed through the young Steward, and he knew no healer could save his friend, for the Hulin Vipre arrow had been poisoned. He jerked the small pouch from beneath his tunic, and put a small amount of the powder Ulria had given him on Salts's lips.

"Rest here, Salts. We'll be back for you," soothed Jeremy, but the sailor knew the truth. The powerful dream-dust of the Elboreal stole away the pain, and his face softened for a moment.

"Safe passage, lad," he managed, the darkness already overtaking him. He was having difficulty breathing, and his head lolled back in Jeremy's arms. "We'll meet again across the Boundaries someday." His chest heaved, as though he couldn't get his breath, then he was gone, his sightless eyes staring up at his new friend. A wild rage touched Jeremy then, and he put off the grief with a terrible war cry, and he was tearing along after the others, a killing fire so great burning inside him, he ran past Owen before he knew where he was. There were two Black Hood archers notching arrows to shoot again, but the young Stewards reached them before they were able to loose the shafts. The sword from Skye split one Hulin Vipre from his head to his shoulders, and Jeremy drove home the point of his sword into the other's chest with all his might, pinning his victim against the stone wall for a bare moment, before he slid slowly to the floor, watching in awed fascination as his own life poured out his tunic in a bright red river.

Jeremy's sword stuck against the man's rib cage for a moment, until he put his foot on the man's chest and heaved the blade free. "The Line!" he shouted, setting off again at full tilt, forcing Owen to call after him.

"Wait for us, Jeremy! They have turned up ahead!"

The enemy troops were like water stopped by a dam, redirected by the appearance of the House Guard blocking one arm of the passageway, and they turned down a long corridor that held many doors, each one beneath white marble arches. Urns and chairs were turned over as the chase proceeded at full speed, and just as Owen turned another corner, he heard Baryloran shout a name.

"Mortus Blan! Here, man! The wench has the Scrolls!"

The clamor of running feet and the clanging of swords and shields drowned out the next words, but Owen had gone faster, shouting encouragement to those behind. He and Jeremy had outdistanced even the Warling. They paused for a moment in a door that was left half ajar, and as they caught their breath and waited for Lanidel, Owen happened to glance into the room. There, slumped into a chair before a fireless hearth, was Ulen Scarlett, blood trickling onto the floor from his arm, which was thrown carelessly out beside him, and a wild, half-crazed look in his eyes.

"Scarlett," uttered Jeremy, and burst into the room before Owen could stop him. His sword was raised to strike, but the empty stare the horseman turned on him stopped him cold in his tracks.

Owen pointed to Ulen's hand. "The ring," he said, "It's gone."

The hand that Owen pointed to was missing the ring finger, and the blood spurted out in a bright red pool on the floor beside the young rider of the Gortland Fair.

"We have to tie it up, or he'll bleed to death," said Owen, reaching to tear off a strip from Ulen's shirt. The horseman started then, and lunged for Jeremy's throat.

"You!" he cried in a terrible voice. "You've taken the ring! You'll die for it, you thieving blaggard!" His hands had closed around the young Steward's throat, but he broke free easily, for Ulen fainted again, hitting his head hard against the leg of the chair.

Jeremy backed away, trembling with rage. "Leave him," he urged. "He's no lookout of ours."

"We'll come back to settle with him," said Owen, who had tied up the maimed hand. "We have real trouble now, because someone has that ring!"

A pair of Hulin Vipre soldiers ducked into the room then,

thinking it was empty. They didn't see Owen and Jeremy until it was too late, and they were dispatched quickly. More of the Black Hood troops were in the hallway, all running toward the upper levels of Cairn Weal.

Another jolt was felt through the stone floor, and the companions were almost knocked off their feet. "I hope this stops. It doesn't feel like a safe place to be."

The next instant, the tremor rippled beneath their feet again, and at the same time, they heard the Steward rally cry blown. It was answered from two directions, and Jeremy threw back his cloak and pulled his own signal horn from his belt and blew a short reply.

"That was not far off," said Owen. "Seravan must have found Stearborn and Emerald!"

Below them, on the battlements of the west wing, the old Steward commander and the minstrel led a charge against a wall of Black Hood invaders, clamoring to enter the high-arched gate. The gray horse reared and slashed with his feet, using his great strength to bowl over the enemy troops, allowing the companions to enter. Callic led the way then, showing them to the inner grounds, and the entrances to the private quarters of the High Elder. Emerald heard the Steward signal, and urged their guide on.

"It's one of ours! Hear it?"

"Stearborn's ears aren't so worn they can't hear a Steward rally call," he growled during a momentary lull in the fighting. "It's come from inside!"

"Alban Ram and the girl went back inside after the first attack here, in good time. The others must have gone toward the Sacred Altar."

"How do we get in?" asked Emerald. He looked about at the strewn bodies of enemy and defender alike.

"This way. I have never really been in to the altar, but I know the way. No one but Alban Ram and the Lady Deros were allowed there."

The front of the fortress there was of white stone, with thin blue veins, and the walls rose up to a towering height above, smooth and impenetrable. A long, covered veranda ran the entire length of the wall, and a thick gate stood halfway down. The grounds in front of it held a row of hedges and flower beds that had once been well manicured, but were now left to seed. Callic took a careful route to check for hidden enemy archers. "This is the entry. I don't know if they've locked it from the other side." He stood up, and gave a tug on the big golden rings, but the gate would not budge.

"Let me help," said Emerald, and together they put their weight against the door, but it still held. Even with Stearborn's burly strength, they could not force the gate to yield.

"Is there another way in?" asked Emerald, catching his breath.

"Yes, but it's on the level below. If they went in from Alban Ram's private quarters, they would have come in from that way."

"How far is it?" asked Stearborn. He had expected the Archaels and the rest of their party to catch them up by now, and grew worried that they might have come under attack before they left the quay.

"Not far, but it may be blocked by the Vipre!"

Seravan stepped up to the gate then, whinnying to himself. He pawed the ground in front of it, and tested it with his nose, then stepped back, and with a soft grinding noise, the gate slowly rolled open. There were many bodies inside, and the noise of a pitched battle greeted them then, and the horn called again. "Forward, lads! To the horn!" Stearborn left the big horse to guide the others when they came, and put Callic out in front. The young soldier bolted to the top of the steps, where he looked out over the vast, awesome changes that had been wrought by the struggle with the enemies of Eirn Bol.

A portion of the high-domed roof near the middle of the room had been crushed with a single blow, and stone and mortar lay in heaps on the polished tile floor, which was littered with bodies and washed in blood. The foul stench of the dragonfire was so strong Callic was forced to cover his face with his cloak. Stearborn, close on his heels, arrived a moment later, his face grim as a hatchet.

"The Freolyde Valg," he spat, looking up at the gaping hole in the destroyed roof. A great shadow flitted across the opening for a moment, and they all backed away to cover, but the head and powerful forearm of the dragon that appeared did not belch fire, or attempt to snap up any of the men there. Stearborn took his bow and notched one of his Leech shafts, preparing to try to hit the eye of the beast, when the very air around him became still, and his arm grew too weary to hold up his weapon. A voice, warm and familiar, filled his head with the sensation of a cool forest glen, such as he had known in his old home high in the mountains.

"Hold, good Steward. I am the one you seek. I am Colvages Domel, and my brother and I have come for our rebellious kindred. You must hurry on to find your companions. Get to your ships. The end is coming for these islands.''

Stearborn stepped forward, looking up at the soft light that glittered along the golden scales of the dragon's body. Colvages Domel's eyes met his own, and he saw many things in a brief flash of fiery wind, of the islands in flames, and sinking beneath the sea, and many sails, silhouetted against a brilliant, cloudless sky, moving away to the west.

The old Steward opened his mouth to speak again, but the great being was gone, leaving the gaping hole in the roof empty of his presence. The horn sounded again, from farther in, and an ominous trembling began, a distant rumble of the mountain's ancient heart coming to life once more.

On the Landings

While Owen and Jeremy pursued the Hulin Vipre Emperor farther into the inner halls of Cairn Weal, Captain Telig aboard The Crane had finally hoisted sail and brought his ship into the besieged harbor on a following wind. There was another vessel entering the harbor as well, and when they were close enough to hail, Captain Telig met Lanril Tarben, aboard the Marin Galone, who had followed Owen up from a coastal settlement during the night.

"If we're lucky, we'll be able to reach the keep," shouted the master of The Crane. "I've already put half my lads ashore."

"We'll throw our lots together. We need to keep a watch aboard, but the rest of us can search for Alban Ram and his daughter."

There was an attack on the keep by the Purge, which suddenly appeared out of nowhere, bent upon destruction. They were defenseless as they lay to their anchors, but the beast seemed maddened and intent upon something inside the walls of Cairn Weal, and then it was gone just as quickly as it had appeared. A gust of cool wind had swept through the harbor, and the stench of the dragon seemed to be blown away, although the ruins of the broken walls above still smoldered from the scorching flames, and a thin wisp of black smoke trailed away, drawing a dark line up into the eaves of the blue sky.

Once ashore, Lanril Tarben left a small party to guard the ship and its prisoner, and with Begam and the captain of The Crane set off toward the upper part of Cairn Weal, where most of the fighting seemed to be taking place.

Railan Dramm had listened to the departing boats pull away from the side of the Marin Galone, and began his plan to free himself, reaching for the hidden knife he had sewn into the folds of his cloak. He had remained docile long enough to catch them off their guard, and now he knew it was time to make his move, while there were only a small company aboard the ship. He quietly slipped over the side into the cold water, and swam steadily away from his prison ship, determined to have his vessel back. After assuring himself all was well with the Dart, he swam on to shore, and armed himself with the weapons of a fallen soldier, and set off toward the upper landings of Cairn Weal.

Moving quickly, he hid from squadrons of Black Hood rushing to reach another part of the settlement, and defenders of Eirn Bol moving ever toward the higher towers of the keep. He had heard enough from his captors to know of the Sacred Scrolls, and that the daughter of Alban Ram was on her way back to her homeland. A vague plan had formed in his angry mind, and he laughed to himself to think what a bold stroke it would be if he were to steal the Scrolls, and the girl as well.

A fitting revenge for the Red Scorpion, and it would remake his reputation after his humiliating capture by his enemies.

Ahead of him on the quay, a large party of defenders were hurrying along the way toward the upper gate, led by two men he recognized as Archaels, and he hurried along, falling into the rear of their ranks as though he were a late arrival. He had drawn his cloak up close about his throat, and tucked his beard into it, and now had the helmet of the dead soldier pulled close over his head, so he was not recognized by his looks.

When they did encounter a squadron of the enemy, Railan accounted himself well for the Archaels, and by the time their group had reached the upper part of Cairn Weal, he was close enough now behind the leaders to hear them speak.

"I don't like leawing the Thistle Cloud so lightly guarded," one was saying, stalking along quickly. He sword was bloody to the hilt, and he carried a bow in his other hand.

"They can't see her, and if they did, the Welingtron are there. You forget our eels."

"I'll be glad when we're done with this, and can just go back to tending our nets and deliwering our cargo in peace. I'we had my fill of all this excitement."

"Look out," called the other. "Wipre! Hop it, lads! Swords and shields!"

A dozen Hulin Vipre troops rounded a corner, coming out of a side path in the inner settlement. There was a noisy skirmish, and what was left of the Black Hood soldiers ran back toward the higher gates, searching for reinforcements. One of the Archaels clapped Railan on his back, complimenting him on his prowess with his sword.

"Good lad. Well done. Did you see that, Lorimen? Three of the dewils jumped him, and they're all fish bait!"

"Handy work, lad," added the other. He was looking hard at the face beneath the cloak and helmet, but was distracted when the sound of another horn came again, this time from not far in front of them.

"It sounds like they're hard-pressed, lads! Faster! Mowe, mowe!" Findlin set off at a rapid pace that was surprising for such a short man. They had not gone far when they felt the air rushing past their heads, and they looked up to see the grotesque form of one of the Freolyde Valg swooping down on them, great bloody talons extended, and snout belching a stream of dirty orange fire. On its first attack, the beast carried off two of their party, and Railan could hear the doomed men's screams as they were slowly gutted and devoured. Turning with amazing quickness, the dragon whirled and swooped back, a low, gargling noise coming from its throat, and it spit up the skeletons of the men, leaving the bones clattering around among the remaining squadron.

Then the blackness of the beast's mind began to take hold of its victims below, calling for them to surrender to it. Lorimen raised his horn and blew a series of notes that rang out loud and pure, echoing back to him from the high, white walls of Cairn Weal, and it was answered by another horn, coming from away to the Archaels' right. In another a few moments, Lanril and Begam, accompanied by Captain Telig, appeared, showing signs of a fiercely fought battle.

"Greetings, friends! Well met, if we last the day!" Lanril held out a hand to Findlin. "This is the minstrel Begam, who claims to know of ways to keep those things off our backs."

"Findlin is what they tagged me with, and this is Lorimen, my sailing partner. We came of the old settlement of Fionten, which is no more."

Lanril Tarben shook the man's hand. "Lanril Tarben, master of the Marin Galone, now anchored in the fair harbor there. This is Captain Telig, off The Crane."

"Ware, all ware! The dragon's come back for another try at us!"

Begam pulled out the small harp that he carried about his neck, and began to blow random notes on it.

"Is that our funeral dirge?" asked Lorimen.

"It ain't agonna make no faltrahoot no way," snapped another man, dressed in simple riding clothes, and keeping an eye peeled for sign of the beast. "We is agonna be roasted if we's stuck out here of the open."

"Come on, Lofen," chided another man, dressed in the identical way. "You has been drownded and kicked, and I ain't got no doubt but that you will ends your days allollygaggin' in your turnip patch somewheres! Besides, this here fellow has somethin' that's gonna help us," said McKandles, pointing to Begam. The minstrel had gone on playing odd notes on his harp, and paused, calling out a series of words that the horsemen could not make sense of. Begam drew the shape of a crescent moon on the stones of the quay with a charred stick, and made crude symbols in a line below it. A horrible screeching noise tore the air, and every ear that heard the dreadful noise rang and pounded, and a dark wind howled in every head.

"You've stung it, sir," cried Lorimen, dancing around. "He was coming straight down on the harbor, and he dropped that long boat he had, and all the men! You've done it, lad! Good work!"

"Now how in Bobbin's Cork was you adoin' that?" asked Lofen, much relieved to see the terrifying beast beating a hasty retreat from the area.

"A Wylich song that was taught to me long ago," answered Begam, continuing to draw more symbols on the stones.

The stench of the beast was still heavy in the air, but another, lighter scent crept along on the slight breeze then, fresh from the sea. Another wave of Hulin Vipre troops were being ferried ashore from ships that sailed into the harbor, and hove to, disembarking the soldiers sent to reinforce the invaders. Lanril formed up his group, and chose a way to go, pointing upward toward the higher ground, where the white banner with the golden dragon flew.

"We'll rendezvous at the flag, men! Make for the banner!"

"I'll take the opposite way, and converge with you there," said Captain Telig. "May Rhorim's Wind carry us on to glory! Good speed, lads! Strike true!" His men lifted their swords and beat a tattoo against their scabbards, and moved away at a quick trot toward the left side gate at the second level of Cairn Weal. It rose in tiers from the quays on upward a plane at a time, until it reached the heights where the white banner flew, which was the very top of the fifth warren of the settlement and keep. That was where the Window of Sight was, and where Deros was trying to reach.

The Window of Sight

Deros's side was splitting and her legs ached from the constant climb, but she dared not stop to rest. A poisoned arrow had narrowly missed her only moments before, burying itself in the small wooden chest she carried. She had gained a landing on them when four of the House Guard had suddenly appeared from down a hallway that led on to the quarters for the higher officers, but they had to fall back again, for there was the frightening old man with the long beard who was beside the crippled young leader. His eyes burned into her own, and his voice called for her to stop and surrender. She had seen the face and eyes in the Rhion Stone Ulen had worn, and Rewen had said it was he who was controlling the horseman. Turning another corner, the dark gray steps loomed ever higher, and her aching legs threatened to betray her.

"Let us carry you, my lady," offered one of the guards, a young man not much older than herself.

"You need your arms to fight," she replied, although she secretly wished she could be taken up for a time.

"Ware, Vipre!" called another guard behind them. "Arrows!"

The whang of the bow strings reverberated, followed by the snapping whoosh of the shafts punching through the air.

"Down!" yelled another of the guards, and they all threw themselves forward onto the floor, listening as the arrows whistled harmlessly over their heads.

Judging from where she was, Deros quickly calculated it was still four more landings until she reached the Window of Sight. It was there she was prepared to die, if need be. She wished in vain that her father had had the strength to be there with her, but she would have to do this job alone. Not even the Lady Rewen or Coglan would be able to do what she must do. She would not let the Scrolls fall into Hulin Virpe hands, and was prepared to step through the Window, if she must, even though it would mean her own end.

A faintly recognizable sound began to reach her ears then, although it took her a few minutes to recognize it. Somewhere below her racing thoughts, she remembered the notes the horn blew, but her exhaustion dulled her senses. It came again, and she finally responded, her eyes clearing.

"I hear friends," she said to the guard closest to her.

"It is none too soon, my lady," replied the young soldier. "They have overrun the barracks below, and drawn off all of Marak's men. I don't think we will be able to mount more than half our troop here now."

"Then find whoever you can. If I can make the Window, all will be well."

"The Window, my lady?" asked the young guard, concern in his voice.

"Yes." Deros began to feel a strange tug at her consciousness as she answered the soldier, and a fleeting image of the old weirdoch touched her thoughts, as cold as a dagger against her skin. She hurried on, trying to remember what Ephinias would have her do.

There were three more landings until she was safely at the top, and for the first time, Deros began to believe she would make it.

Farther back in the great hallway, Baryloran went as fast as his crippled body would allow, hopping along at a rapid gait. Mortus Blan had removed the ring from the outlander, tearing away the finger from his hand and leaving him to bleed to death of his wound. He carefully listened to everything that came through the fiery red stone that had belonged to Tien Cal, the

Fourth Collector. His mind was locked onto the thoughts of the daughter of Alban Ram, and he knew when she made the decision to go through the Window of Sight. If he did not act quickly, the girl and the Sacred Scrolls would be gone forever.

A faint, rippling motion rolled beneath his feet for a moment, leaving a troubled afterthought of small shocks that made the stone floor dance to an odd, disjointed rhythm. He urged Baryloran on, and tried to concentrate on slowing the girl's thoughts, but she was stronger than he suspected, and resisted him fiercely.

Near the second landing from the tower of the Window of Sight, both sides were brought to a halt by the presence of the Lost Fire. Perched on the rubble of the wall it had shattered, the dragon sat immobile, with only its eyes showing any sign that it was alive. A dark shroud of fear cloaked everything, and Deros found herself caught between the mind of the Hulin Vipre weirdoch, and that of the Purge, its great, evil eyes riveted to her very soul. The hope of escape was destroyed, and all paths led straight into the gaping jaws of the beast, beginning to purr like a gigantic cat.

Seeing the dragon, Mortus Blan knew Jatal Ra would not be far behind, and he turned his attention to the worst of his adversaries. Seizing her chance, Deros and her small band darted into a chamber off the hallway, slamming the door behind them. Stout though it was, she knew it would be useless to keep out the dragon, but it might give them time to find another way past. She raced to the tall windows that lined the room, barely noticing that the chamber was the very one where her mother had died. The furnishings had been kept the same, and Alban Ram had taken his daughter there every night when she was very young, to sit among her mother's things, while her father told her stories of his wife.

But now, with the Purge and the Hulin Vipre at the door, her thoughts were not the bittersweet memories of long ago, but of survival, and protecting the Sacred Scrolls. As her small troop of guards barricaded the door and tried to plot their defense, Deros noticed for the first time that the hole where the Hulin arrow had struck the chest was gone, closed upon itself. And the sounds of the familiar horn were back again, cutting through even the thick knot of fear the beast put into every heart.

"There is someone signaling," cried her young guard.

"I hear. It is a Steward horn. I recognize it, now." She had at last remembered the different calls, and thought of Stearborn.

Deros turned, looking at the guard, trying to remember if she had seen him before she had left Eirn Bol. "Do I know you?" she asked. He was taken by surprise at her question, and took a moment to answer.

"I am Ruan, the son of Toland. I have been with your father since I came to my Standing."

"Are you afraid, Ruan?"

"My lady?"

"Are you afraid of the Purge?"

"More than the Black Hood," he replied. "At least I know skills to fight them."

"My friend Rewen and Coglan will help us. The Order of the Sacred Thistle knows a thing or two of these beasts."

"That doesn't settle my heart, my lady," returned Ruan, stacking another table against the door. A small gold and mithra icon fell to the floor as he did, and Deros knelt to pick up the object. Tears came to her eyes then as she looked around.

"This was my mother's room," she said quietly. "This was hers." She held up the intricately shaped object in her hand, and Ruan could see that it was a small otter, raised up into a standing position.

"She was a great lady," said the young guard quietly. "I was only a baby when she died."

"She was young, too. My father always thought he would be the one to go first. I think that was the hardest thing he ever had to deal with. For a time, I think he lost the Light, he was so saddened and bitter."

Another faint rumble rolled beneath the floor, shaking the walls. The beast outside let out a roaring hiss of flames, and the stench of its breath filled the room.

"It sounds like they have backed down the hall," reported Ruan.

Deros put her ear to the heavy wooden door, straining to listen, but it was ominously silent.

"Do you think they really control that thing?"

"That's what the Warl Books explained. When Lacon Rie asked for help from the Council, he realized the Purge knew no master but the Dark One. If the beast is not attacking them now, it is only because it smells this." She held out the chest that contained the Scrolls.

Another hissing blast of flames came from the dragon, and the sound of fire consuming wood was plainly heard. The stench became almost unbearable, and the blackness of the dragon's mind descended upon them. Deros closed her eyes tightly and concentrated on the image of Rewen's face, trying to hold the vision in focus against the insistent, crushing presence of the Purge. Barely aware of herself, she heard the sound of the horn once more, closer still, and suddenly the beast's mind was engaged elsewhere, and a dreadful flapping was heard as the dragon took to the air.

"It's going, my lady," cried Ruan. "Something has scared it away!"

"Let's see if we can go on. If the hallway is clear, we must make the high tower."

Ruan was hesitant about removing the fortifications. "The beast may be gone, but the Hood are still out there," he cautioned.

"Even if they are, we must risk it, Ruan. I have to reach the Window. My father has weakened in his old age, and he talked of leaving the Scrolls for the Vipre!" Her voice cracked, and she immediately felt guilty at having spoken of her father's weakness before one of his soldiers. The young guard stared at her incredulously.

"He hasn't been himself since he was wounded in the flows," he offered. "He wouldn't give up that way."

"I know he didn't mean it," went on Deros. "But we were attacked in the Sacred Altar, and I thought he might weaken." Her memory of Ulen banging against the door and begging to be let in was still fresh in her mind. Owen and Jeremy had disappeared somewhere, and Sergeant Balre had finally relented and opened the door to the desperate cries. He was killed instantly, and Deros had barely had time to grab up the chest and fly for her life. "Go on, open it! We have to reach the Window."

Ruan dragged aside the last table and cautiously cracked open the door to peer into the large hallway. Save for the few bodies of both the Hood and the defenders, there was nothing but the stench of the dragon, and the noise of the crackling fire, which still smoldered on the door. "It's clear, my lady."

"Hurry. They'll be back. We must use this time." She clutched the chest tightly to her, and stood at the door, getting her nerve up to plunge on. Ruan held her back. "Me first, my lady. We'll see if they're still here. You come next, then my men will bring up the rear." He stole one last look, and darted out, keeping close to the wall. When he was safely to the next doorway, he motioned for Deros to follow.

She took a deep breath and, saying a quick word of prayer, ducked her head and ran out, barely feeling her feet hit the ground. They were almost to the last landing when the next tremor came, a sudden sharp jolt so powerful it threw them all to the ground, and sent the chest flying out of her arms. When she moved forward to retrieve it, she saw the feet of the man first, standing behind the chest, and slowly lifted her gaze until she met the eyes of the weirdoch she had seen in her visions, the dreadful old man with the long, wild beard.

The new Hulin Vipre Emperor was close behind his adviser, a satisfied smile creasing his handsome face.

Three Weirdochs

"No!" screamed Deros, rising to her feet and grabbing the chest. She bared the knife in her hand, holding it out toward Baryloran's throat. He laughed, wagging his finger at her.

"You will get your chance to kill me now. Your father isn't here to stop you."

"Get the chest," ordered Mortus Blan in an icy voice, his hands folded into his cloak. "The others will be here soon enough! Get the chest." His eyes were bloodshot, and his gaunt features wild. He felt Jatal Ra and Salun Am very near, and was trying to ready himself for the confrontation.

And the girl was firing his blood with desire for her, which caused him great stabbing pains that racked his body.

The young Emperor advanced toward Deros, pointing out his limp to her. "I am only a cripple. You have no need to fear me."

"Get back," she shouted, retreating toward Ruan, who had just regained his feet and now advanced. She turned to warn him of the weirdoch, but too late. A single flick of the hand sent a blazing bolt of orange flames whizzing past her ear, singeing her cloak, and striking the young guard, who fell at her feet screaming and clutching at what was left of his ruined face. When the other soldiers tried to advance to help their leader, the old man's hand moved quickly from his sleeve, and they too were soon writhing screaming on the floor. Deros backed away, trying to reach a doorway behind her. There was nothing to be done for the guards, and she was still too far away from the tower that held the Window of Sight.

"Come along, my fine little bird! There is no place left for you to go. Give me the chest, and you shall be spared."

"Spared for what? Your slave camps?" Deros kept control of her voice, even though her heart was beating like a hammer.

"That would not be so bad, if you had the right master," cooed Mortus Blan. He had advanced toward her now, holding out a hand. "You could go right on ruling your ill-fated island." He smiled a malicious smile. "Only now as my bride."

Deros felt the wall behind her, and clutched her knife behind the chest, vowing at least to make her death as costly as she could. There seemed to be no way to save the Scrolls from falling into the hands of her mortal enemies. She was preparing herself to strike, when she looked over the shoulder of the wild old weirdoch, who was almost on her. Owen Helwin, followed by Lanidel, stepped out of the shadows behind the two, and called to Baryloran.

"So you've rushed to your doom," he said, moving forward. "You know how much she thinks of you. I'm surprised you're standing so close."

Mortus Blan whirled around, his hand flashing from his cloak. Deros screamed a warning, but the sword of Skye was already raised, deflecting the whirling ball of flame that the old man had flung at him. It careened off the blade, and spun harmlessly into the wall, searing its way through the solid stone. "You have made a fatal mistake showing your face here," snarled the old man. "You have the cursed sword, but you can't stop me from killing the girl!" His teeth were bared, and he moved his hand as though to strike Deros, but he was stopped in midaction by another voice ringing out down the hallway.

"Mortus Blan! You have struck your last. The girl and the chest are mine!" Jatal Ra floated over the stone floor on a carpet of flames, advancing toward where they stood frozen.

"Not quite," shot back the old weirdoch. "You have brought back the Lost Fire, but now they have gone berserk and attack our own troops as well! They know the name of who spoke the words from the Warl Books. They will be coming for you soon, my dear old colleague.''

Baryloran spoke up then. ''You murdered my father, and you have tried your best to kill me, but you won't leave here alive.'' The young Emperor's voice choked with rage then, and he couldn't go on.

Jatal Ra's lips parted in a thin smile, and he pointed to the girl. ''Give me the chest, wench. There is nothing left for you to do.''

Deros shook her head, feeling her way along the wall, her eyes turned to Owen and the bears. Lanidel had reared up into his fighting stance, his ears laid flat back on his head, his eyes blood-red, and his terrible fangs glistening.

But Owen was silent, watching. Quick as a spider closing on its prey, Mortus Blan darted forward and grasped the girl from behind, holding a hand to her head. ''Come any closer, and I will send her and the chest to where you can never have either! Get back, good colleague! Any of your tricks, and you'll lose the chest!''

Jatal Ra felt into the pouch at his belt and fondled the small bit of charcoal called the Nod lovingly, but he spoke smoothly, consolingly. ''Let's not be hasty, Mortus Blan. Giving the chest away would serve no one. It is not a thing of petty interest. We must find a way to common ground among ourselves.''

''The only common ground you seek is that which is stood on by none but Jatal Ra. We can speak openly now.''

''Yes, we can at that. We have the chance to take what we want, and no one stands in our way. This crippled freak is but a bug to be squashed and done with. His father led the Black Hood into ruin with his blundering ways and lack of courage. His brother, who was the born leader, is lost. Salun Am was plotting behind both our backs to have him murdered, and I see that the good fellow was as clumsy at it as he was at everything else, because here is Baryloran, alive and well.''

The young Emperor lunged for the weirdoch, but was stopped cold by an unseen hand that clutched him by the throat in an iron-hard grip, slowly strangling him. After his eyes had bulged, and his lips turned blue, Mortus Blan finally acted. ''Release him! I'll destroy the chest!''

Baryloran dropped into a heap at Jatal Ra's feet, unconscious. ''He is a bug to be squashed. Now is the time to do it, while we are at the dawn of the new order! You and I can wield the Black Mace together, Mortus Blan! There is no one to stop us!''

"Salun Am," said the old man. "He could stop us."

"How? He's not here, and he wouldn't stand a chance against the both of us."

A gray wavering cloud of smoke began to take shape upon the stone floor, and as they watched, the features of Salun Am materialized slowly. "So you would cut out your colleague, and divide the power among yourselves! Is that a proper way to treat a friend?"

"Not a friend, Salun Am. Where are you?"

"Where you can't harm me, Jatal Ra. I know you carry the Nod with you. I'm not so foolish as to let myself be caught out that way."

Mortus Blan looked over the girl's shoulder. "You've kept back one of the Nod?" he asked grimly. "You do play with dangerous toys, Jatal Ra. It will be your undoing."

"I have it here in my pouch," confirmed Jatal Ra. "It is but a trifle to call it to life."

"It would take all of us," warned the old weirdoch. "That was why the Warl Books said they were put away and made taboo."

"The faint of heart never dare dream the dreams that Jatal Ra dreams! We have wasted our powers and remained fettered and shackled over all these turnings. Don't you think of the Nod, Mortus Blan? Don't you think of the great power it would give you?" He held out the small black piece of charcoal. "See! It is so sweet, so loving. It rides in your pocket, and can stay there forever, if need be. But give it its head, and speak the words, and it will destroy every enemy, every threat that could possibly challenge you!"

Owen had never heard mention of what the two enemy weirdochs talked of, but the sword had become white-hot, and pulsed in his hand. A faint vision of Ephinias reached him, as though his old mentor was trying to speak. He clutched the sword tighter, and tried to center his thoughts on the light. There were hushed words, and flickering images of Ephinias, but all he could make out were the garbled words, "give up the chest."

Which was what Alban Ram had said, as well.

"Give him the chest," said Owen. Deros turned a look on him that made him cringe.

"Never!"

"Listen to the lad," cooed Jatal Ra. "He may be able to stay alive to work at rebuilding this keep. My pets seem to have made a mess of it.''

''Colvages Domel and Iochan are here for your lapdogs,'' replied Owen. ''If the Purge don't turn on you first, they will take you.''

''That's what I said all along,'' hissed Salun Am. His form wavered indistinctly, then firmed up again. Jatal Ra and Mortus Blan were seeking his hiding place, and Owen could feel their two minds struggling, searching out the real form of Salun Am. They were so occupied with their efforts, they failed to see the dark shadow come slithering down the hall and in another instant had reached out and landed on Mortus Blan's back, its hands locked together on the old man's throat. A horrible shriek passed the weirdoch's lips, but it was met with another, an inhuman utterance of pain and rage that sent chills down Owen's spine. He had heard similar cries from the Olgnite, and the despair and torment cut through his heart like a knife.

All in the same instant, Deros broke free of the grasp of Mortus Blan, but dropped the chest onto the floor, where it broke open, spilling out the contents onto the stones. She scrambled to retrieve it, but Jatal Ra swooped upon it, gathering it up into the folds of his cloak with a triumphant cackle.

The Sword of Skye

''Ulen!'' cried Owen, recognizing the crazed horseman trying to strangle Mortus Blan. He saw the old man's arm move beneath his cloak, and in a single motion, Owen had brought the sword down in a vicious side stroke, severing the hand at the wrist. The weirdoch screamed in agony, and fell heavily to his knees, still trying to throw his attacker off his back. When Owen turned to Jatal Ra, he saw a brief flash of orange light, and the man was gone, but there on the floor before him was the small lump of black charcoal called the Nod, smoldering and beginning to grow. Salun Am's image was gone as well.

''Come on,'' shouted Owen, motioning for Jeremy and Lanidel

to follow. He grabbed Deros's hand and dragged her past the Nod, on upward toward the last landing. "Where's Barylloran?"

The crippled young Emperor was gone. They searched briefly, but it was to no avail. He had vanished along with Jatal Ra.

"Is this the way to the top?" asked Owen, turning back to their escape.

Deros could not speak, but nodded, her eyes wild with fear and shame.

"Your father said to leave the chest. I heard Ephinias say the same! You did what you could."

She shook her head. "I lost the chest. I lost it, Owen. Don't you understand what that means?"

"Come on." He pulled her quickly up the broad stairway, higher still, Jeremy and the Warling close behind. The walls and ceilings were now blue and gold, with clouds so real it seemed as though he could reach out and touch them. He could still hear the old weirdoch screaming below, and the guttural, savage sounds of the crazed horseman.

And then there was the strange hissing noise, growing louder and louder, as though a tea kettle were brought to boil. A cold wind began to blow in the hallway, and Owen's vision clouded, as though he were looking at a white plain through heavy snow. In another few steps, they were at the tall wooden door that stood in the highest reaches of Cairn Weal, with its knocker of gold and mithra, and the elaborate carvings on each panel, depicting scenes from the very beginnings of the island. As they swung the door open to enter, another faint rumbling noise was heard far below, and the very foundations of the keep trembled gently, almost as though it were a sleeper, turning uneasily in a dream.

They entered the room stumbling, and Owen helped Deros to stand. At one end of the circular room there was a window that ran from floor to roof, covered with a royal blue drape, which was closed. The girl struggled free of him, and ran to the closed curtain. "I have betrayed Eirn Bol," she cried. "I can't face living any longer!" She pulled open the heavy cloth, revealing a window behind that was very much like what Owen had seen in the lair of Colvages Domel, deep in the mountain of Roshagel. It looked out over the harbor of Cairn Weal now, its sight closed but to the gathering dusk. Deros fell to her knees before it, sobbing.

Owen went to her, trying to console the weeping girl.

Lanidel lumbered up to the window, his hackles raised, and a low whine coming from deep in his throat.

"What is it?" asked Jeremy.

"This is one of the cracks where you can see your own death," replied the bear. "Mar'ador told us of them when we were cubs. I never thought I would see one."

"Don't look," urged Jeremy. His wounds began to ache, and he felt compelled to look through the window, although there was nothing to be seen at the moment but the landings and quays of Cairn Weal.

Or so he thought. When he looked closer, he realized it was not the dusk that was outside, but a vision of something more. "What is this?" asked Owen, frowning at the disconcerting vision.

"It is the way things will be," said Deros, weeping softly into her hands.

Owen's heart began to sink, but he could not turn his head away. Deros was there at his feet, but he did not see her in the window.

"I don't think I will ever get used to these things," he said quietly. "I don't want to know about anything until it happens."

There were more rumblings from deep inside the mountain, and the panes of the window began to flutter, rattling in their frames. "We have to leave," urged Jeremy.

"I know a way to one of the combs from here. It will lead us straight down to the harbor," offered Lanidel, although the big animal could not remove his eyes from the scene that drifted into focus next. Deros stood unsteadily, and with one motion tried to leap through the window. Jeremy and Owen and Lanidel all reached out at the same time, pulling her back from amid the shower of broken glass that began to crash into the room. A cut appeared on the girl's arm, and Owen tied a piece of his cloak around it, holding her to him tightly.

"You won't get away from me so easily," he said. "Not after all we've gone through."

"There is nothing for any of us now," replied Deros bitterly. "The Scrolls are gone! Don't you realize what that means!"

"We have yet to see what that means," countered Owen. "Your father and Ephinias both instructed you to let the Scrolls go!"

"Look! See now," said Jeremy. "It's just a window now!" Below, a battle still raged, but the Black Hood numbers were smaller. "It's Stearborn!" cried Jeremy. "Look there! They're coming!"

When Owen brought Deros to the window again, the scene was still dusk, but there below in all his gruffness was the old Steward commander, leading a charge on a Black Hood skirmish line right below them. Jeremy leaned out the window and blew a long, exulting call, a celebration of being alive, and Stearborn looked up, searching for who had blown the familiar notes.

"It's the Archaels," shouted Jeremy. "Look at them come along!"

Owen leaned out the window, and there in the center of a pitched battle, the two squat sailors toiled and fought their way through a solid line of much greater Black Hood troops. Seravan bowled into another knot of invaders, which allowed the House Guard to retake the gatehouse and barracks. As the sun sank lower, there were torches lit at sea, and the dark waters reflected back thousands of flickering lights, and in another few minutes, Stearborn's voice boomed up through the keep.

"Helwin! Thistlewood! Lady Deros! To your captain!" He blew a short, jubilant note on his horn.

Deros was wracked with sobs. "I can't face him! I can't face anyone. Let me go!" she pleaded. She tried again to jump through the Window of Sight, but they held her back. Even the broken shards of glass moved and danced beneath their feet, and when Jeremy picked one of the broken pieces up and held it before his face, he could see everything as it had been when the window was whole, only it was now smaller, as though viewed under water, or from a great distance.

There was a movement at the door just then, and they all turned to see Ulen dragging the limp body of Mortus Blan along behind him like a sack of grain. Jeremy unloosened his sword, and before anyone could deter him had stepped out into the hallway to confront the horseman, who stared at him without comprehension. Sheer willpower alone was keeping the man on his feet, and he put a booted foot on the unconscious weirdoch, calling out wildly, "Where have you put it, Helwin! I know they gave it to you!"

"You're wounded, Ulen. Come in so we can tend to you," replied Owen.

"I'll come in, but I want the ring back! It's mine! You have no right to it!"

"I don't have the ring, Scarlett. Mortus Blan must have taken it."

"It's not here," wailed Ulen, his voice rising. "I've looked."

"It's like the Olgnite curse, Ulen. It's going to take some time to recover from it. You haven't been yourself."

"I've been myself, right enough. But I've been among thieves and traitors all along. You wanted the ring for yourself. I saw it. I know you've taken it, and I want it back!" He stepped over Mortus Blan, and lurched into the room. As he did so, a flutter of sudden movement behind him caused Owen to look away for a split second, and Ulen plunged the blade of a short stabbing dagger into the Steward's arm.

Lanidel's motion was fluid and swift, and he batted the knife away and sent the horseman skidding across the floor on his back. What Owen had seen was the arrival of another person in the hallway outside, and before he could reach to stop the flow of blood from his wound, Railan Dramm stepped into the room, sword and dagger drawn.

"Your friends led me straight to you," he said, eyeing the huge bear warily. "Will you keep your friends out of it? A fair fight between the two of us?"

Deros had torn a piece of her cloak, and was helping Owen stem the bleeding from the deep cut.

"Let me fight him," said Jeremy, who had undone his tunic once more, and given Owen a small pinch of the dream-dust to ease the pain of the knife wound.

"You wouldn't be much of a fight, boy," laughed the Red Scorpion, cutting the air with a swinging arc of his blade. "Dealing with a young whelp like you would be nothing to tease and tempt me."

"He's wounded," argued Jeremy. "It wouldn't be a fair fight."

"He has that sword of his to protect him! Is he going to fight me fair, and not use those weirdoch tricks, or will he dishonor himself even more?"

"You're a fine one to talk," snapped Jeremy. "If you were a horseman instead of a sailor, the Line Stewards would have made hash of you long ago!"

"You'll swallow that along with your tongue," growled Railan. "I hate to be baited!" He began circling Jeremy, searching for an opening. The young Steward, handy with his weapons, was content to fence with the dreaded pirate.

Owen, seeing his chance, was gone in a flash, and when he

returned, led Laeni by the hand, pointing to the two combatants. "There! There's your brother. See if you can make him
stop his foolishness." Deros had been touching him when he
entered Politar's bottle world, and ran away from him when he
had called Laeni and been ready to return. He thought of the
vision the Window had shown, and wondered if that was the
reason Deros had not appeared in the glass.

Railan had not taken his eyes off Jeremy, yet when he heard
Owen speak to the girl, he turned. He had cast aside the cloak
and helmet that had covered his flaming red hair and beard, and
Laeni leapt into his arms, leaving him no choice but to cross
his weapons behind her, looking confused and ill at ease.

"Stand off, Jeremy. Let the two of them enjoy this." Owen
noticed his companion was still crouched into a position of
defense, yet his eyes lit up at the appearance of the girl. She
held her head into her brother's shoulder tightly, her sobs
racking her thin body.

"Laeni? Is that you?" The bloody reputation of the Red
Pirate suffered greatly in the close grasp his sister kept on him,
and if Jeremy had wished, he could have easily killed the man.

"You can see for yourself we mean you no harm," went on
Owen. "Jeremy and his captain saved her from the Black Hood
and brought her here."

The sarcastic smile disappeared from the face of Railan
Dramm, and he lowered his weapons. "I am obliged to you,
then," he said. "I cannot fight you now." He put his arm
around the girl, holding her out so he could see her face. "We
have to leave, girl. Are you with me?"

Jeremy was on the point of protesting, but could not think of
the right thing to say and turned helplessly to Owen for support.

"Where will we go?" she asked.

"To the Dart. My ship is in the harbor." He looked to
Owen. "Unless you mean to keep her?"

"There are many here who would think nothing of stretching
your neck from a yardarm, Dramm. You can take your chances
on your own, I'll not interfere."

"Will you come, lass?" he asked again.

"Will we stay together? Like the old times?"

"Always, lass."

"Then I'll come." Railan hugged his long-lost sister, and
smiled over her at Owen.

"You'll go far, if you keep up this pace, Helwin! I am grateful you and I do not have to find out who is best with the weapons."

"Can you raise a crew to get the Dart out of the harbor?" asked Owen.

"I'll find someone."

"Your old mob is locked in the drop-house ashore. I turned them out, and they're not sure how the wind blows for them. If you go now, you might be able to set them free and leave Cairn Weal."

Jeremy was looking at Owen grief-stricken. His affection for the sister of Railan Dramm was readily apparent.

"Where will you go?" asked Owen.

"These waters aren't going to be safe for me now. And I don't want to drag Laeni into the life I've been leading. Perhaps the Dart will find new seas. It would be difficult, but the Dart might return to a legitimate trade."

"The South Roaring is a good place," suggested Jeremy, in spite of himself, looking sheepishly at the girl.

Laeni handed Railan back his cloak and helmet to put on again. "They'll see your beard," she explained.

Owen looked out the window, and saw there was a lull in the fighting, and that the Archaels and Stearborn were almost to the last level. "You'd best go on. I don't want to have to make excuses to Lorimen or Findlin about turning you loose."

"Fair havens," said Railan, taking his sister's hand. She turned once, waving shyly to Jeremy, who stood numbed by an overpowering sense of loss.

"Be careful on the lower landings. There's something there one of the weirdochs left that may be dangerous."

"Anything left by a weirdoch is dangerous," shot back Railan. "You're a fine one to speak of it." His voice had an edge, but his eyes were twinkling. As the man and his sister reached the door, a long, rumbling tremor made the chamber jump, and chairs and tables overturned, and a large chandelier suspended from the ceiling came crashing down right at Jeremy's feet. The noise increased to a roaring thunder, and the rolling floor leapt and bucked. Cracks appeared in the walls, and a fine stone dust collected in the air until it was difficult to breathe.

When at last the sickening motion finally reeled to a stop, everyone was off their feet, sitting stunned on the floor. Owen raced to the shattered window, looking out over the twilight scene of Cairn Weal. The sword from Skye had burst into a brilliant white light that fired the darkness into a silvery shadowed world, and all the faces below turned upward, watching as the flames of Windameir flared and shone, a faint beacon flickering in the winds of change.

The Rainbow Bridge

Cries and shouts filled their ears, and every alarm horn on the island went off as one. Far down the outline of the curve of the coast, Owen could see flames and reddish lumps of molten rock boiling and jumping in open lakes of fire. Owen replaced the sword back in its scabbard, but the light lingered on in his eyes. Jeremy was at his side instantly. "Is it the Purge?"

"Worse than the Lost Fire. They are taken by Colvages Domel and Iochan. This is the mountain!"

A thundering voice tried to make itself heard over the uproar, and finally Owen recognized that his own name was being called. "Helwin! Where are you, lad! Sing out!" It was Stearborn, booming out his name, as he had often done, with that strange rattle and hiss he had, from the old wounds to his throat.

Owen stuck his head out the window and shouted back, blowing a short note on his horn. "Here! We're coming!"

"We'll see you on the quay, lad! Hurry! The water in the harbor is beginning to boil, and the Welingtron are calling!" Stearborn turned and led his party back down through the tumbling throngs, Black Hood and defenders alike. The Hulin Vipre troops were rowing for their own ships that were left, and were consumed by the rampaging great eels. The water was turned to blood in many places, and battles broke out along the harbor front as the enemy troops tried to escape the slaughter.

Owen saw the Dart tugging at her anchor next to The Crane and Marin Galone. He could not see the Thistle Cloud at first, then as he watched, he saw the vessel of the Sacred Thistle slowly come into view, with the same golden white lights in her rigging as he had seen aboard vessels of the Elboreal. A plain vision of a great red bear waved to him, and he had the clear impression of having been spoken to. "Get Scarlett," he said. "He was in the Window. We have to take him."

The horseman was still unconscious from the swat Lanidel had given him when he attacked Owen. A low, whining growl was coming from the big animal, and he paced nervously about, his ears flattened on his head. "This was from the Warl Books," he said. "I did not think that I would live long enough to see it."

"You have to get your clans together," said Owen, remembering the bears. "We'll find a way to get you off, even if we have to stack you on deck like cordwood."

Lanidel shook his head stubbornly. "The Warlings are not meant to be anywhere but these islands. That was always written. Don't fret, chubblet, your heart is right. I thank you for your tears."

"We can't just leave you," argued Owen. Jeremy agreed with a head shake.

"You can come aboard with us. We'll find enough boats."

Lanidel had lifted the limp body of Ulen Scarlett and carried him tucked closely to his side, and lumbered away. "The Warling have their own Bridge to take off these islands. None of us will live to see it if we don't hurry. There is another shake coming!" He was gone down the hallway before either Owen or Jeremy could protest. They ran along behind, trying to keep up with the fleet bear, but even carrying an awkward burden, the big animal still outdistanced them, calling encouragement over his shoulder as he ran. Fallen beams and ceiling stones were littered everywhere, and whole walls teetered precariously above them. Great sections of the hall roof were on the floor, and in more than one place, they had to detour around an open crack that had widened into a bottomless abyss, with the fiery lava bubbling in its depths. Turning a corner on the last landing, the two comrades had to skirt a narrow fissure, and Owen almost stumbled over something left lying on the floor right at its edge. Looking down quickly, and shielding his eyes against the fiery blast coming up from below, he picked up a staff that carried an odd icon on the top, of a dragon clutching the sun. He instantly remembered where he had seen it before.

"This belonged to Jatal Ra," he said, looking from it to the fiery pit, which flared up, and the earth began trembling beneath them again.

Jeremy looked quickly over the edge of the abyss. "I can't

think of a more just reward," he said. "And we're going to share it, if we don't go on."

"Look and see if you see the scrolls," ordered Owen, searching quickly around the area where the staff had been.

"Nothing," reported his friend, after a quick search. "The Scrolls are gone."

"Are they?" said Owen, looking about once more at the ruins of the elaborate fortress that had been Cairn Weal. "I wonder. They may be safer now, for no one shall have them, and they are where no one can get at them."

"The fire?" asked his friend.

"Our hearts," replied Owen. "The hope we have of them. You cannot destroy what you can't find."

A fountain of molten rock and sparks exploded from the pit not far from where they stood, sending them running for the main gate beyond the courtyard. As they cleared the tall archway, the doors came loose from their hinges and crashed forward with a deafening roar. Looking back toward where they had just come from, Owen saw the tower where the Window of Sight looked out over Eirn Bol, and watched as the white banner with the golden dragon slowly caught fire, then burned brightly, turning and billowing through the darkness as though an invisible wind had carried it away. When he last saw it, it had become one with the starry heaven behind it, blazing steadily in the vast blue dome of Atlanton Earth.

Stearborn's horn called again, and there was pandemonium all about, as survivors of the battle sought ships to carry them away from the rapidly crumbling island. The Welingesse Fal had begun circling in the harbor, their eerie voices raised in a long, droning chant. In the distance, the companions saw the same fiery light and spectacular explosions, as Hulingaad was racked by the same agonies of the fire mountain below.

"Here, lads! Come on! To the ships!"

McKandles was suddenly running at his side, taking a moment to stick out a rough hand to shake his own. "You and Master Jeremy was always a pair of skittish colts, but I is plenty glad to has you back. Me and Lofen was awonderin' what had come of you."

"I'm glad to see you, Kandles. I don't think any of these louts would have made it without you keeping a spur to their hides."

"Has you seen Ulen?" he asked, without breaking stride. "Some has said he was chopped by one of them weirdochs!"

"Did you just see a bear go by here?"

"Not only seed it, but come plumb near abein' run down flat by it!"

"That was Ulen. A friend is bringing him to the ship." Owen's heart grew sad at the thought that the new companions he had found among the Warlings would not be leaving the islands with them.

"Watch out for the horse," cried a voice, and Owen saw Seravan moving through the crowd on the street leading down to the harbor. His coat was bloody, but he seemed in good spirits. The minstrel Emerald was on his back, an arm tucked into his cloak.

"I've had to carry this lout from the field again," said the horse. "He makes a habit of relying on my good graces to keep plucking him from harm's way."

"Hold on, my friend," said Owen, and he motioned on the air, and soon had Elita back with him from the other world of Politar's bottle. He had seen no sign of Deros, but called out after her anyway. The minstrel's wife suggested leaving her to herself for a time.

Emerald dismounted, patting the huge horse gingerly. "We have taken a few blows this day," he said, wincing. Lorimen and Findlin rolled down the wharf together, leading a party that included Hamlin and Judge, who broke into shouts of joy when they saw their old comrade standing beside Owen.

"I knew it," lamented Hamlin, rushing up. "I told them we couldn't get shed of you so easy. I knew you'd come back and rake our hides for letting your weapons go!"

Jeremy gave his friends stout bear hugs, laughing. Just below the surface, he knew there was the loss and sadness waiting for him. His thoughts touched on Salts, and he had to bite the tears back, which made the reunion of the old brothers-at-arms all the more poignant.

Lorimen and Findlin were rounding up parties for the tenders, and Owen searched through the confusion of faces for anyone familiar.

"Do you see Lanril Tarben?" asked Captain Telig, who had appeared suddenly out of a knot of defenders. He had been cut off from his party, and wandered around on the wharfs, looking for members of his crew.

"The Marin Galone is making ready to sail," shouted Lorimen. "We should be, too! The eels are waiting!"

"What's happened to Rewen and Coglan? Has anyone seen them ashore?" Owen could plainly see the Thistle Cloud now, riding to her anchor in the agitated waters of the harbor. Great plumes of steam were rising from the sea's surface now, and the quay beneath their feet began to roll and buckle, jumping like a ship in a storm. What was left of the Black Hood armies was broken units wandering about, looking for a way home. In the distance, it was plain Hulingaad was in flames, too, and great fiery explosions went off in rapid succession, lighting the sky with brilliant flames and rivers of flowing molten rock.

"Is there no way to take the Warling clans with us?" asked Owen, turning to Seravan.

"There are many ways off these islands, Owen. Not all of them are by boat."

"What do you mean?"

"Look to the east. What do you see?"

Owen was helping load a tender at the quay's edge, talking as he worked. Jeremy and Hamlin and Judge had rejoined Stearborn, and the Stewards were busy making sure everyone had a way to the boats at anchor. When he looked at the darker sky beyond the harbor, he saw what appeared to be wavering clouds of different colors, forming an image there.

"I see the colors there. But how will that help Crale and Mar'ador, and Lanidel?"

"It's the Bridge," answered the tall animal. "It appears at all times for those who are ready to cross. Even when you don't think it's there, it is always waiting."

Owen shook his head. "Where does it go?"

"To the Crossing."

He reached out and touched the horse. "Deros is inside Politar's bottle. She lost the chest, and felt like she had betrayed us all."

"It was as it was written. You see the fire mountain come alive, and are watching these islands disappear beneath the sea. The Scrolls have set it off, and that's what has triggered this. The Monks of Corum Mont are awakened."

"I didn't know for sure Jatal Ra went into the pit, but I guess he must have."

"He is gone. They are all gone."

"Baryloran?"

The big animal whuffled and shook his mane. "The end of the line of the Emperors of the Hulin Vipre."

"There was a girl with him. Her name is Denale. What shall we do with her?"

"She's gone."

"How could that be? I didn't bring her outside," replied Owen.

"She's taken another way out. She's dead. She did not want to live after Baryloran crossed over."

Owen shook his head sadly. "I am sad to hear this news."

"There was nothing you could have done to have prevented it."

"And Alban Ram," Owen asked, primarily to hear the impact of his voice.

"With Colvages Domel." As the animal spoke, Owen saw the golden glint of the dragon reflecting back the fires that had spread across the island.

"I hope my friend Jalen made it." He was in the boat now, and being rowed away from the quay. "Where are you bound? Is Gitel coming?"

"Keep your eyes to the east. That's where you'll see us next."

"What shall I do about Deros?"

"Leave her to heal in Politar's little back kitchen. She will come out of this with time."

"I guess we'll plot a course back for the South Roaring. There doesn't seem to be a reason for staying in these parts." The tender had drawn away from the shore, and Seravan had to raise his voice above the roar of the mountain, and the hiss of the steam rising from the harbor. Owen watched as the gray horse grew smaller and smaller, still standing at the wharf, watching. When he looked back toward the ships, he was surprised to see that the Thistle Cloud was gone, and the crew was pulling for the Marin Galone.

He noticed with a sense of satisfaction that the Dart was nowhere to be seen.

Jeremy and Hamlin were talking earnestly on deck, and the old Steward commander reached down to give him a hand aboard. Judge stowed his gear in a locker, and turned to clap him on the back.

"They've been talking of nothing but the dream-dust since we reconnected," said Judge. 'I don't think I'll be able to stand it if this voyage lasts more than a day."

"It's going to last long enough to get us back to our home waters," growled Stearborn. "Lanril Tarben has promised me safe passage back." He frowned, tugging his beard. "We still have those louts out of the Wastes of Leech to deal with. They'll be strong again by now.''

Judge laughed, shaking his head. ''Won't we ever get a breather?''

''You're a Steward,'' snorted Stearborn. ''You've had your break when you were a wee bairn.''

Owen began to feel that that was the truth, and a flood of memories began to wash over him. He sat heavily on deck, listening as the sailors put on sail and took the Marin Galone back out of the doomed harbor of Cairn Weal. It was not like he had thought it would be at all. It almost never was that way, when he stopped to think of it. The winds created by the explosions of fire blew hotly over the deck, and the great eels drove the ship swiftly away from the breakwater, and in another space of time, he stood at the rail, watching as the island broke apart in fiery explosions.

From the very heart of Cairn Weal, a blazing mountain of white flames shot up toward the night sky, and there was Colvages Domel, outlined in blazing golden light, winging away toward the east, scattering stars as he went. Behind him, etched with stars, was the Thistle Cloud, now a ship of air, gone on with the rest of the Elboreal.

He had lost sight of Emerald and Elita in the confusion on the wharf, but he now heard the minstrel's voice, lifted in a soft song, drifting across the water from The Crane. The winds were still warm and fair from the fires, almost like a summer evening, and the sails filled eagerly. The Welingtron songs had changed to a powerful voyaging tune, and Owen watched as the steering stars appeared one by one. He listened as Lanril Tarben called out to the sailors, and heard him ask Rhule what course they would be setting. They planned to rendezvous at the straits with the other survivors of the long war, and try to start from the beginning once more, giving what they each had to give, and carrying with them all the heartbreak and joy that had been since the journey started in Sweet Rock, on the River Line.

When Owen thought of that, he remembered the deer ford near the hidden grotto where they had first met Rewen and Coglan. His mind was adrift in a thousand other thoughts, and he wondered about Famhart and Linne, and where they were, or if they were yet alive. He had enough questions to last him through a hundred sea voyages, yet in the end, he found himself rolled into his cloak, asleep on the deck of the Marin Galone, a weary warrior from the long day.

In his dreams, the dragon came to him, and one by one he saw the faces he had known so long, appearing in a room that he began to recognize as the one he had been in when he was in the High Halls. There was Ephinias, laughing and speaking to him, and turning into a small red terrier before his eyes and next to him was Gillerman and Wallach, riding cloaks dusted with a fine layer of white, as though they had just come through a snow. Iochan and Beran sat playing at whittles near the fire, with Politar looking on. Sitting in a distant corner looking out the window was the Lady Rewen, and beside her the huge form of a red bear read from a book bound in gold and mithra.

Owen blinked, and he was at the hearth, feeling the warmth of the flames, and looking into the clear blue eyes of his father. He sat beside Linne, and the two of them touched him gently, such great love shining through them that he had no time for sorrow, and through his tears, he saw the Light of Windameir burning brightly across the lands, and knew that the first order of business would be to build a comfortable shelter, and try to remember how it was to live when you were not at war.

Dreams of Light and Air

❊

The fall gales came in force two days after the twin islands were destroyed by the eruptions of the fire mountain below. The "verges" of Lorimen and Findlin lived up to their name, and the fleet of survivors sailing back to the South Roaring was forced to ride out the worst of the weather for three days near the very spot where Jeremy Thistlewood was left to drown, and picked up by the Elboreal and tended by Ulria. Ulen Scarlett, still in a state of delirium, hurled himself into the sea there. Two sailors pulled him ashore out of the surf, and when they had him safely back aboard, the dark cloud that had held him prisoner for so long was gone. He looked around the faces circling him on the deck, and felt as though he had just awakened from a long sleep, filled with dreadful dreams. Jeremy was unconvinced, and confronted the Gortlander, who sat unbelieving. Elita held the damaged hand up, and asked Ulen if he remembered how he got the injury. A fleet-passing darkness overwhelmed him, then was gone, and he said he seemed to remember something of a ring, but he could not recall exactly what. Stearborn had a lengthy talk with his old comrade, and in the end, Jeremy agreed to try to clear the air and go on, which he did, but with the general assumption that once they were back home in The Line, the Gortlander would be gone.

Forgiveness, he said, was one thing; to forget was another.

He need not have worried, for the day the ships made landfall off White Bird, on the South Roaring, Ulen Scarlett left ship, declaring he was going back to the Plain of Reeds. His followers McKandles and Lofen Tackman agreed to go with him, to get, as Lofen said, "as far away from this big fish barrel as I can be agettin'!"

They promised to return with a new Gortland Fair the following summer.

The Archaels set about the task of building a new ship to take them back to the ruins of Fionten, where they were to install Enlid as the new Elder. It had been a long interruption for them, and they had never suspected that their routine trip to the Grimpen Mire all that time before would have led them so far afield.

"Wessels are meant to be built from the liwing tree, just like an elder has to be caught as a sapling! If we don't get this fellow back to our own waters soon, he'll be ready to drop his leawes."

No amount of arguments could change their minds, and after the ship was built and launched, the old friends left after a tearful farewell feast in late spring of the following year.

They had named their vessel New Hope, and promised to return often.

Stearborn never loved a quiet time overly much, and once they had landed, he set about re-forming a squadron and setting up a field command to see to the first job at hand, which was to reconnoiter in all directions, to see how the situation stood, and where their enemies might be. Chellin Duchin had not been idle while his friends were away, and arrived a week later with news of the surrounding areas, and a detailed report on the movements of bandits from the outlands. The meeting of the two old warhorses was a thing to behold, and those who did not know them were convinced the two were bent on each other's destruction. Horses were rounded up again, and on more than one occasion it was rumored that Seravan and Gitel were in the far reaches of the country, bringing mounts to them.

Twig and a great bear were also seen in the eave of a wood one late evening during a snowfall, and they left their trail in the powdery white blanket for all to follow. It ended in a stand of majestic firs, on a ridge that overlooked the river valley, where one could view the silver thread of frozen water all the way down to the coast beyond. There was always a tune played by the wind through the ancient trees that sounded exactly like Twig's pipe, and it was said that if you sat very still there at sunset, you might see the small figure of the cripple dancing with the bear in the shadows of the evening wind.

Of Jeremy Thistlewood, it was sung in the old songs later that the young Steward followed the ships back to the River Line, and there found a piece of ground to build a shelter and stables for his mounts. It was also said that he left early every spring, and was gone until the first snows, wandering about like a minstrel, seeking news of the rogue known as the Red Scorpion. He grew to be an old man, gray-bearded and bent, but never married. When someone once asked if that had not been a lonely life, he laughed and hobbled away, saying his heart had always been full of a great love for the one woman he had found to marry, but she was the traveling kind and never had a fancy to settle down.

Hamlin Olenbroke and Judge Collander were among his constant companions over the many turnings, until their deaths in the Leech Wars a long time afterward. They had replaced Stearborn and Chellin Duchin in the ranks of the leaders of the Line Stewards, and had brought much renown to their squadrons. When Hamlin was fatally wounded during a fierce winter campaign on the Leech, Jeremy undid the small pouch he had carried all those years, and gave Hamlin the last of the dream-dust as he lay on his deathbed. His squadron carried him home, to bury him on a rise that overlooked the very deer ford where Jeremy had built his shelter.

Judge was killed the next year defending a small settlement from the raiders, and was buried next to his lifelong friend.

Not a fortnight passed that one or another of the remaining old comrades would visit the place, bringing flowers or some small memento, or sitting and giving them all the latest news. Emerald's voice could be heard there from time to time, as he sat composing a new song, or simply playing over an old melody.

The new Elder spent many months engaged in the vast business of setting out the boundaries of Sweet Rock, building again over the burned ruins of the old streets. There were endless small tasks to attend to, and no end of disagreements and arguments among the citizens, and there was the unending task of overseeing the daily life of the settlement. His courtship of Deros ran a rugged course, sometimes smoothly, sometimes rough, but she had come out of the deep black depression she had remained in for a time after their return to Sweet Rock. It was a memorable day when she awaited Owen in the soft light of Politar's kitchen, and agreed to return outside with him.

More and more survivors of the great plague of war that had run rampant began to make their way there, and it soon became apparent that the new village that rose from the ashes of the old would be far greater in size and number.

And new arrivals came every day, coming from every direction of the compass.

Below, the river washed into a small eddy near the bank, and a deer stood drinking, ears alert, looking at the faint pale spring morning reflected in the water. High, tattered clouds floated across the sky like ragged banners on an empty field, making shapes and forms as they changed in size and color in the wind. Owen and Deros lay back in the tall golden flowers, watching. A small child, barely walking, waddled onto his stomach, laughing and holding onto his father's finger.

It was all as a dream, and the Dreamer was the heart's own memory waiting in perfect stillness to welcome all the lost travelers Home, when the Light and the Darkness are One.

It was a moment perfectly formed in time, neither forward nor back, and every single living soul in the Heart of Windameir danced to the Song of Creation as it played, then paused, then played again.